The Good House

Center Point
Large Print

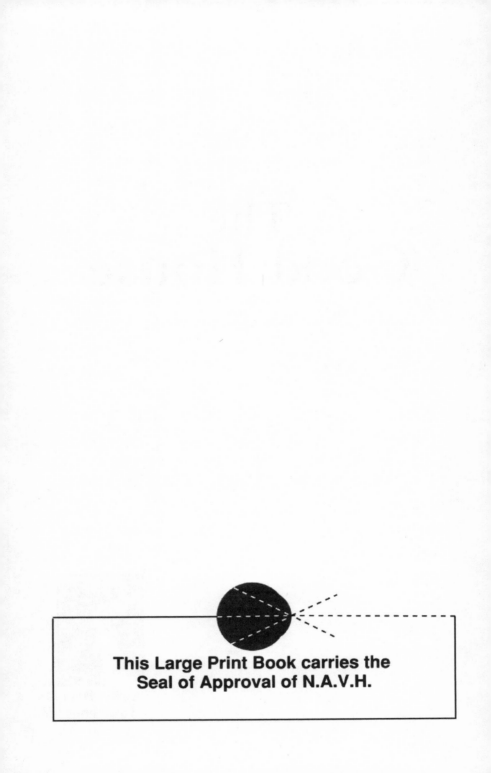

**This Large Print Book carries the
Seal of Approval of N.A.V.H.**

The
Good House

ANN LEARY

CENTER POINT LARGE PRINT
THORNDIKE, MAINE

This Center Point Large Print edition is published in the year 2013 by arrangement with St. Martin's Press.

"I Knew a Woman," copyright © 1954 by Theodore Roethke, from *Collected Poems of Theodore Roethke* by Theodore Roethke. Used by permission of Doubleday, a division of Random House, Inc.

This is a work of fiction. All of the characters, organizations, and events portrayed in this novel are either products of the author's imagination or are used fictitiously.

The text of this Large Print edition is unabridged. In other aspects, this book may vary from the original edition. Printed in the United States of America on permanent paper. Set in 16-point Times New Roman type.

ISBN: 978-1-61173-703-5

Library of Congress Cataloging-in-Publication Data

Leary, Ann.
  The good house / Ann Leary.
     pages ; cm.
  ISBN 978-1-61173-703-5 (library binding : alk. paper)
  1. Women alcoholics—Fiction. 2. Older people—Fiction.
     3. Boston Region (Mass.)—Fiction. 4. Large type books. I. Title.
PS3612.E238G66 2013b
813′.6—dc23
                                                      2012048485

For Denis

The
Good House

One

I can walk through a house once and know more about its occupants than a psychiatrist could after a year of sessions. I remember joking about this one evening with Peter Newbold, the shrink who rents the office upstairs from mine.

"The next time you get a new patient," I offered, "I'll sneak to their house for a walk-through. While you jot down notes about their history, dreams, whatever, I'll shine a flashlight into the attic, open a few cupboards, and have a peek at the bedrooms. Later, when we compare notes, I'll have the clearer picture of the person's mental health, guaranteed." I was teasing the doctor, of course, but I've been selling houses since he was in primary school, and I stand by my theory.

I like a house that looks lived in. General wear and tear is a healthy sign; a house that's too antiseptic speaks as much to me of domestic discord as a house in complete disarray. Alcoholics, hoarders, binge eaters, addicts, sexual deviants, philanderers, depressives—you name it, I can see it all in the worn edges of their nests. You catch the smoky reek of stale scotch and cigarettes despite the desperate abundance of vanilla-scented candles. The animal stench oozes up between the floorboards, even though the cat lady and her minions were removed months before. The marital bedroom that's become *his,* the cluttered guest room that's now clearly *hers* —well, you get the idea.

I don't have to go inside the house to make a diagnosis; the curbside analysis is usually enough. The McAllister house is a perfect example. In fact, I'd love to compare my original observations regarding Rebecca McAllister with Peter. She was depressed, for one. I drove past the McAllisters' one morning in late May, not long after they'd moved in, and there she was, out in the early-morning haze, planting annuals all along the garden path. It wasn't even seven a.m., but it was clear that she had been at it for hours. She was in a rather sheer white nightshirt, which was damp with sweat and covered with soil. People were starting to drive by, but Rebecca had become so absorbed in her gardening that it apparently hadn't occurred to her to put on some proper clothes.

I stopped and said hello from my car window. We chatted for a few minutes about the weather, about how the kids were adjusting to their new school, but as we talked, I sensed a sadness in the way Rebecca planted—a mournfulness, as if she were placing each seedling in a tiny plot, a tiny little grave. And they were bright red impatiens that she was planting. There's always something frantic about that kind of bold color choice for the front of a house. I said good-bye, and when I glanced back at Rebecca through my rearview mirror, it looked, from that distance, like there was a thin trail of blood leading all the way from the house to the spot where she knelt.

"I told her I would do the planting, but she likes to do it herself," Linda Barlow, the McAllisters' landscaper, told me later that day at the post office. "I think she's lonely up there. I almost never see the husband."

Linda knew I had sold them the house, and she seemed to imply that I had been derelict, somehow, in assuring the healthy acclimation of one of Wendover's newest treasures—the McAllisters. The "wonderful McAllisters," as Wendy Heatherton liked to call them. Wendy Heatherton and I had actually cobrokered the sale. I had the listing; Wendy, from Sotheby's, had the wonderful McAllisters.

"It takes time," I said to Linda.

"I guess," she replied.

"Wendy Heatherton's having a party for them next weekend. They'll meet some nice people there."

"Oh yeah, all the nice, fancy people." Linda laughed. "You going?"

"I have to," I said. I was flipping through my mail. It was mostly bills. Bills and junk.

"Is it hard going to parties for you? I mean . . . now?" Linda touched my wrist gently

11

and softened her voice when she said this.

"What do you mean, 'now'?" I shot back.

"Oh, nothing . . . Hildy," she stammered.

"Well, good night, Linda," I said, and turned so that she wouldn't see how red my face had become. Imagine Linda Barlow worrying about whether it's hard for *me* to go to parties. I hadn't seen poor Linda at a party since we were in high school.

And the way she pitied Rebecca McAllister. Rebecca was married to one of the wealthiest men in New England, had two lovely children, and lived on an estate that had once belonged to Judge Raymond Barlow—Linda's own grandfather. Linda had grown up playing at that big old house, with those gorgeous views of the harbor and the islands, but, you know, the family money had run out, the property had exchanged hands a few times, and now Linda lived in an apartment above the pharmacy in Wendover Crossing. Rebecca paid Linda to tend to some of the very same heirloom perennials—the luscious peonies, the fragrant tea rose, lilac, and honeysuckle bushes, and all the bright beds of lilies, daffodils, and irises—that her own grandmother had planted there over half a century ago.

So while it was laughable, really, that she might worry about me, it was positively absurd that she pitied Rebecca. I show homes to a lot of important people—politicians, doctors, lawyers, even the occasional celebrity—but the first time I saw Rebecca, the day I showed her the Barlow place, I have to admit, I was a little at a loss for words. A line from a poem that I had helped one of my daughters memorize for school, many years before, came to mind.

I knew a woman, lovely in her bones.

Rebecca was probably thirty or thirty-one at the time. I had Googled Brian McAllister before the showing and had expected to meet an older woman. *People must think he's her father* is what I thought then, except for the fact that there was something very wise and understanding about her face, a sort of serenity in her expression that women don't usually acquire until their kids are grown. Rebecca's hair is dark, almost black, and that morning it had been pulled up into a messy ponytail with a colorful little scarf around it, but it was easy to see that when she let it down, it was quite long and wavy. She shook my hand and smiled at me. She's one of those women who smiles mostly with her eyes, and her eyes appeared to be gray one minute, green the next. I guess it had to do with the light.

She was a little thin then, but her whole frame is tiny, and she wasn't as gaunt as she later seemed. She was petite. She was beautiful. *She moved in circles, and those circles moved,* same poem, although I still don't recall the name of the poet, but she was one of those effortlessly graceful women who make you feel like an ogress if you stand too close. I'm not fat, but I could lose a few. Wendy Heatherton is slim, but she's had all sorts of liposuctioning and flesh tucking. I don't know who the hell she thought she was kidding when she was carrying on about that gallbladder operation a few years back.

It's a well-known fact that the McAllisters had sunk a fortune into the yearlong renovation of the old Barlow place. Brian McAllister, for those who don't know, is one of the founders of R. E. Kerwin, one of the world's largest hedge funds. He grew up in the bottom of a three-decker in South Boston, with four brothers and a sister, and had become a billionaire before he turned fifty. Had he married somebody else, he probably would have been living in a mansion in Wellesley or Weston with a full staff, but he had married Rebecca, who, having grown up with a staff, and distant parents, liked to do things herself.

How do I know so much about the McAllisters? It's not just from their house. I know pretty much everything that happens in this town. One way or another, it gets back to me. I'm an old townie; the eighth-great-granddaughter of Sarah Good, one of the accused witches tried and hanged in Salem. My clients love it when I drop that into a conversation. That I descend from the witch called, so delightfully and ironically, Goodwife Good. (*Yes,* I always laugh with them, as if it had never occurred to me until they said it, *Good ol' Goody Good, ha-ha.*) That and the fact that my family has been in Salem and here in nearby Wendover, Massachusetts, since the 1600s.

My husband, Scott, used to tell me that I'd have been hanged as a witch myself had I lived in another time. He meant it as a sort of compliment, believe it or not, and it's true, I do rather fit the profile, especially now that I'm on the darker side of middle age. My first name is Hilda, which my children have always told me sounds like a witch's name, but I'm called Hildy. I live alone; my daughters are grown and my husband is no longer my husband. I talk to animals. I guess that would have been a red flag. And some people think I have powers of intuition, psychic powers, which I don't. I just know a few tricks. I have a certain type of knowledge when it comes to people and, like I said, I tend to know everybody's business.

Well, I make it my business to know everybody's business. I'm the top real-estate agent in a town whose main industries are antiques and real estate. It used to be shipbuilding and clams, but the last boatyard in Wendover closed down more than thirty years ago. Now, those of us who aren't living off brand-new hedge-fund money are selling inflated waterfront properties to those who are. You can still clam here—the tidal marsh down by Getchell's Cove is a good spot—but you can't make your living off clams anymore. Even the clams at Clem's Famous Fried Clams are poured into those dark vats of grease from freezer bags shipped down from Nova Scotia. No, the best way to make money up here now is through real estate: the selling, managing, improving, and maintain-ing of these priceless waterfront acres that used to be marshland and farms but that were recently described in *Boston* magazine as "the North Shore's New Gold Coast."

Brian McAllister happens to own *Boston* magazine. The day we met, after I showed him his future house, he pointed to a copy of it folded up on the seat next to me in the car and said, "Hey, that's my magazine you got there, Hildy."

"Really? Oh well, take it. My copy must be around here someplace."

"No." Brian laughed. "I own it. *Boston* mag. I'm the publisher. Bought it last year with a friend."

You're a wicked big deal, a real hotshot is what I thought. I hate rich people. Well, I'm doing all right myself these days, but I hate all the other rich people.

"It's one of my favorite magazines," I said.

I was showing him a two-million-dollar house, after all, a house that I knew his wife had already gutted and restored in her mind; had mentally painted and furnished and plumbed and wired and dramatically lit during the few short days since I had shown it to her.

"I bet we can give you a special advertising rate in the real-estate section, if you want," Brian said.

"That would be great, Brian, thanks," I said.

And I hated him a little bit less.

Two

Wendy Heatherton always likes to throw a party for her wonderful clients. It's her way of thanking them for their business and also a way of introducing them to other people Wendy thinks are wonderful. Her son Alex and his boyfriend, Daniel, always do all the preparations. Daniel is an interior decorator. Alex collects antiques. For the McAllister party, they decided that dinner would be in the garden. Alex and Daniel set a series of long banquet tables under a blooming magnolia tree. They hung paper lanterns in the tree's branches. Then they covered the tables with some of Wendy's antique white linen tablecloths, and used her best silver and china and crystal, which was rather unexpected and delightful at an outdoor dinner. They had bunches of fragrant lilacs flouncing over the sides of tall silver vases. Citronella torches lined the path from house to table and were also planted in the ground around the table, to keep the bugs away. It was "magical," everybody told Wendy and Alex and Daniel. And it really was.

The party began at seven, but I didn't arrive until close to eight, because I don't drink cocktails anymore. I'm in "recovery." I don't go to a lot of parties, but when I do, I try to arrive just before dinner is served and I leave right after dessert. The night of the McAllister party, I arrived at the same time as Peter and Elise Newbold. Peter, Elise, and their son, Sam, live in Cambridge during the week because Peter is a psychiatrist at McLean Hospital in nearby Belmont. He has a small private practice in Cambridge as well as here in Wendover, but he sees patients in Wendover only on Fridays and the occasional Saturday.

As we walked up the Heathertons' front steps, Peter clapped my shoulder and said, "Well, at least we'll know one person at this party." Then he said to his wife, "Elise, you know Hildy Good, right?"

Elise offered a sarcastic "No, Peter, I've never heard of Hildy Good."

Peter had been renting an office from me, upstairs from my offices at Good Realty, for years, but I've really only met Elise a few times. She teaches writing workshops in Cambridge, but I can't quite recall what kind of writing she actually does herself. Poetry maybe. Since Sam had become a teenager, he hadn't liked leaving his friends to come to Wendover for the week-ends, and I'd always had the sense that Elise never liked coming here at all, so in recent years, Peter had spent many weekends up here alone. He told me it was actually good for him, as he was writing a new book—*The Psychology of Communities*, I believe it was.

When we entered the house, a young woman ushered us through the living room and out onto the back patio, where cocktails were being served. She asked us what we'd like to drink and Peter asked for a beer. Elise asked what kind of white wine they were serving and, after wrinkling her nose at the two options, finally settled on the Pinot Grigio.

I ordered a club soda with a slice of lime.

My daughters, Tess and Emily, had surprised me with my very own "intervention" almost two years prior, the little dears. Emily lives in New York, but Tess lives in Marblehead, which is only about twenty minutes from here. One cold November evening, Tess and Michael, my son-in-law, invited me over for dinner. Their son Grady was just an infant at the time, and I was thrilled to go over for a visit. Tess had been distant since the baby had been born. Distant toward me, that is; she had Michael's mother, Nancy, over all the time.

"I'd love to watch Grady, anytime," I used to say to Tess. "You and Michael should go out to dinner and a movie some night. Leave Grady with me."

"Nancy lives right here in Marblehead. I'd hate for you to have to come all that way," Tess would say. I told her I didn't mind in the least, but then, she never did ask, so I guessed she really didn't want to bother me.

So that night I had driven to Marblehead and was surprised to see two cars in Tess and Michael's driveway, in addition to their own cars.

"Hello?" I called cheerfully as I opened the door. I was feeling quite good. I had had a closing that afternoon and had celebrated with my clients at the Warwick Tavern afterward. I only had one or two drinks. Maybe three, tops. I wandered into Tess's living room and was shocked to see that Emily was there, too, and she had brought her boyfriend, Adam, all the way from New York with her. And Sue Peterson was there. My secretary Sue. There was another woman, a stout woman with short, brassy hair. (Truthfully, the woman's hair was orange.) Everybody had been sitting, but when I entered the living room, they all stood up. They were all smiling sympathetically at me, and my first thought was that something had happened to Grady. My legs actually became weak. It was hard to stand.

"Mom," Tess said, blinking back tears. "Come sit down."

I let her lead me over to the sofa, and there I sat, with Tess on one side of me, Emily on the other. I was still in a panic about the baby. That's something about me that Tess and Emily have never been able to appreciate. That everything I have ever done is for them. That my first concern is always for *their* well-being. Theirs and now little Grady's.

I think everybody knows what happens at these things. The girls took turns reading aloud the excruciatingly elaborate details of my alleged sodden crimes. The day I drank too much at Emily's graduation party. The night I "passed out" (their words, not mine—I was napping) before Thanksgiving dinner. The times I had "staggered" out to my car and how worried they always were when I insisted on driving myself home. Then, of course, the DUI. I had been pulled over the summer before, on my way home from Mamie Lang's. Mamie is my oldest friend— we've known each other since third grade—and one night we had a little too much to drink, and as I drove home, I watched the moon out of my passenger window. I was driving past the salt marshes and that bright orange moon seemed to tumble along the tips of the wispy sea grass, right alongside me, chasing me, like a playful balloon. I was on Atlantic Avenue, and when I came to the stop sign at Route 122, I saw the car. I was stopping. But I misjudged the distance, I guess, and rear-ended it. I barely tapped it. I put a tiny dent in the fender, that's all, but, just my luck, it was a state trooper. Trooper Sprenger.

Had to be Sprenger. Our other local trooper used to date Emily, and our only town cop, Sleepy Haskell, is my brother Judd's best friend. I had never even met Sprenger before that night. He had no idea who I was.

So at my inquisition—oh, excuse me, intervention—I listened to the girls declare my various shameful lapses like tearful little magistrates. They had somehow convinced Sue to join forces with them, and she stammered something about how the clients were starting to notice. All the other brokers knew. She wept, too, and, like my daughters, she finished her statement by lunging at me so that she could encircle my shoulders with her arms and sob into my neck. I'm not a big hugger, but I placed my arms around each of them and tried to come up with the appropriate responses.

"Oh," I think I whispered. "That's an interesting point of view."

Really, what are you supposed to say?

I knew there was no use in arguing. No point in stating my case. I had read the Betty Ford autobiography. You can't prove you're not an alcoholic once everybody has announced your affliction and tearfully told you how your "disease" has affected them. The more you protest—"deny," as they say—the more they stoke the flames of shame that have been dancing around you since the inquest began.

But there was hope. Jenny, of the orange hair, was from Hazelden. She offered a solution: a twenty-eight-day program in Minnesota.

"I can't," I said. "I have a business to run."

"I've taken care of everything," chirped Sue. "It's so slow right now, I'll just have Wendy"— Wendy Heatherton was then my associate broker—"take over your clients. It's just a month. We'll say you're in Florida."

Sue did take care of everything, and I took care of Sue just a few weeks after I returned from Minnesota. I fired her.

At Wendy's party, I stood with Peter and Elise, scanning the crowd to see whom else I might know, and almost immediately Wendy was upon us. Wendy, in addition to being slim and bubbly, is one of those women who must always clasp everybody's hands. She won't just shake your hand; she traps it between both of hers and cocks her head so that she can smile at you from what she seems to believe is a captivating display of her profile.

"Peter! Elise! Hildy!" she exclaimed, taking turns sandwiching each of our hands and tilting her head this way and then that. "I'm so glad you made it. You're just in time. We're about to sit down to dinner, but first, come. Come meet our wonderful guests of honor, the McAllisters. Well, Hildy, of course you know Brian and Rebecca."

Wendy was leading us over to the far side of

the crowded patio. She was still holding on to Peter's hand, and he had reached around and grabbed Elise's, and as I followed them, I had a passing thought that I should grab Elise about her slim waist to form a snaking conga line.

I hadn't been able to admit it to Linda Barlow, but I really do hate parties now.

We finally reached a corner of the patio where a group had formed around Brian McAllister, who was talking about the Boston Bruins. Many people in the area know that Brian is a silent co-owner of the Bruins, along with Jeremy Jacobs and some others, and, well, this is Massachusetts. Most people are hockey nuts. Everybody had questions about the new recruits and where the hockey team was headed. Mamie's husband, Boatie, a slightly annoying Republican from an old Brahmin family, interrupted several times to bluster on about Phil Esposito and Bobby Orr and the good old Bruins of yore.

"Wait until this season," Brian promised him, swigging his beer and smiling. "I think we're gonna have a great season."

I saw Rebecca standing a little off to the side, and I walked over to say hello. The Newbolds followed me and I introduced them. They all shook hands and then Rebecca sort of peered up at Peter in that way she has, the way of the petite, and she said, "Haven't we met before? You seem so familiar. . . ."

"I'm not sure," Peter said. He was looking at her carefully then. "I don't think so. I have one of those faces. I'm always reminding people of somebody else."

Rebecca was smiling up at him, still not convinced, when Peter said, "I'm sure your husband gets sick of people wanting to talk hockey all the time."

"No, not really. He sort of gets off on it, actually," she replied.

I saw Peter glance back at Brian and then smile at Rebecca, amused.

"What do you do?" Elise asked Rebecca.

"Um, well, nothing really," Rebecca said, laughing nervously.

She seemed, suddenly, self-conscious, and I was aware of an impulse, which I of course resisted, but an impulse to pull Rebecca close to my side, the way a mother might shield a shy child from a stranger. Elise was asking Rebecca what she did so that Rebecca would, in turn, ask her what she did, and then Elise could carry on about her annoying writing.

"You're so pretty," Elise persisted. "Didn't I read someplace that you model or something?" She said this in an almost accusatory tone, and there was a moment of awkward silence before Rebecca, clearly flustered, stammered, "No, I, well, I used to do some acting, but now I just, you know, take care of my kids."

"Oh," said Elise. "But before that?"

"Well, I paint," Rebecca said. "I used to ride horses pretty competitively. Now I decorate our houses and . . . nothing really."

In fact, Rebecca had been short-listed for the U.S. Equestrian Team when she was only nineteen. In fact, she was the daughter of Col. Wesley Potter, the former Carter administration cabinet member, who had once been a CIA agent, and whose appointments had enabled Rebecca to live in Germany and Africa during her youth. In fact, she was the great-great-granddaughter of J. P. Morgan on her mother's side. You learn these things about a client. Her lawyer talked to mine. My lawyer talked to me. And, of course, we brokers all Google these days.

"How are the kids liking Wendover?" I asked Rebecca.

"Well, they love the beach and the new house. . . ."

"How old are they?" Elise asked.

I could sense Rebecca's unease. Why wouldn't Elise stop interrogating her?

"They're five and seven. Excuse me," Rebecca said, "I need to go inside . . . and wash my hands. I was in the garden all afternoon," she said, and then she turned and made her way through all the wonderful guests to the dark house. A few minutes later, Wendy rang a little silver bell and announced that dinner was being served, and so we all followed the torch-lit path to the dinner table.

Brian was seated across from me. On my right was Peter Newbold and on my left was my friend Mamie. Now Mamie gets all self-conscious about how much she drinks around me. We're still friendly when we see each other, but I haven't been to her house in ages, nor she to mine. It probably goes without saying that in a town like this, when you disappear for twenty-eight days, everybody knows where you've been. While I was at Hazelden, I imagined the gossip. *Yes, she did like her drinks. Remember the O'Donnells' Fourth of July party? Remember the Langs' Christmas party? Didn't she get a DUI?* There are plenty of people in this community who drink more than I ever drank, but I'm the one who is branded an alcoholic. If I had allowed the server to fill my glass with wine, there at Wendy's party, I imagine that everybody would have gasped in unison and then there would have been a spontaneous and unanimous attempt to wrestle the glass from my grip.

Rebecca sat toward the far end of the table, several seats away from Brian, and to Brian's right was Sharon Rice. Sharon is a lean woman in her mid-fifties who has allowed her hair to whiten naturally. She wears it cut in a bob. Sharon is the head of the Wendover Land Trust, which preserves all the beautiful woods and wetlands

27

and salt marshes that run in and around our town. She is also on the zoning board and the school committee, is president of an arts program for underprivileged children in Lynn, organizes weekly activities at the Wendover Senior Center, and, every Election Day, drives the elderly and disabled to the polls. Her husband, Lou, is in insurance.

After quickly introducing himself to those seated around him, Brian stabbed at his salad with his fork. Instead of placing his napkin on his lap, he gripped it like a little cloth bouquet in his left fist, which he rested on the edge of the table.

After a few moments, Sharon cleared her throat and said, "Brian . . . Rebecca . . . I'm so happy to finally meet you after hearing such lovely things about you from Wendy."

"Yeah? Well, nice to meet you, too," said Brian, barely looking up from his plate.

"What brought you and Rebecca to this area?"

"Well," Brian replied, rubbing his mouth with his napkin and glancing up at Sharon, "Rebecca went to boarding school here. . . ."

"Oh, Rebecca, you went to Wendover?" Sharon said, calling down the table to Rebecca.

Rebecca looked up at Sharon and was about to say something, when Brian said, "Yup. She loved it. Loved this area, and ever since we got married, she talked about moving up here. We lived in Boston until the kids were born, and while they were small, but Rebecca had horses that she was boarding up here, and, well, she grew up in the country, and that's how she wants the kids to grow up, too."

"How do you like it here?" Boatie asked. "Didn't you grow up in Southie?"

"Yeah, I'm a city kid. My dad was a Boston fireman for forty years. Most of my relatives still live there. But we love it here. I don't even mind the commute as much as I thought. Sometimes I stay in town a few nights during the week and then work from the house on Fridays and Mondays."

"Well, I'd love to talk to you sometime about the Wendover Land Trust. Your name came up at a recent board meeting," said Sharon.

"Sure, remind me to give you my card before we leave. I love all the work you preservationists do up here. It's what keeps the area so nice. We'd be happy to get involved."

This sent Sharon Rice into a sort of rapturous frenzy of praise, stammering about how fabulous that would be. How wonderful.

Those wonderful McAllisters!

Then Brian admired my watch. I had splurged the previous year, after a big commercial property sale, and bought myself a beautiful Cartier watch. I had never owned any fine jewelry and never a nice watch of any kind. But I had noticed this watch in a magazine and decided I had never seen anything so exquisite in my life. So I bought it. It was my little reward to myself. For my success. For my sobriety. I don't wear it every day, so I was thrilled that somebody noticed it.

"Nice watch ya got there, Hildy," Brian said. "I bought a Cartier for Rebecca, years ago, but she destroyed it. She's one of those people who can't wear watches. Something in her body chemistry, some static electricity or magnetic pull or something, makes all watches stop when she wears them."

"I've heard of that," Mamie said.

"Yeah," Brian said, "well, don't let my wife try on your watch, that's all I have to say. She interferes with car electronics, too. She's destroyed every goddamn stereo and GPS in every car she drives. Isn't that right, Becky?"

Rebecca had been talking to Lou Rice, who was seated next to her, and she turned to Brian with a quizzical expression. She couldn't hear him, apparently.

"I won't let her sit in my car," said Brian.

"I think I have that." I chuckled. "Things are always breaking on me."

"This is different," Brian said. "We're on our second TV in the den, and how long have we lived in that house, Becky? Three months? Now she doesn't go near the thing. Oh, and we've never had a refrigerator that will make ice. In our house in Aspen, the apartment in Boston. Here. No matter how expensive the Sub-Zero or whatever, the ice maker dies once Rebecca tries to use it."

Peter Newbold was laughing, too. "You don't really think these things could possibly have anything to do with Rebecca's body chemistry?"

Brian took a long swig from his beer and said to Rebecca, "BECKY . . . BABY . . . tell him about the time the cord on the brand-new toaster started smoking when you plugged it in. The thing was *brand new*. Hey, Becky?"

Rebecca had been about to take a bite of her salad, but she turned back to face Brian, and it was clear she didn't find this as amusing as he did. There was an awkward moment before she laughed and said, "It's because I'm a witch, apparently."

We all laughed, but truthfully, it was a little awkward. Then Mamie made it more so by hollering across the table, "IS IT TRUE YOU DESTROY THINGS WITH YOUR MIND?"

Rebecca said, "With my mind . . . no. But I do stop watches." Then she turned to those seated around her, and I could see her pointing to her wrist and shrugging some kind of explanation.

Peter was amused. "I hate to tell you this," he said to Brian, "but your wife's just had bad luck with watches and electronics."

"Peter's a doctor," I explained.

"Yeah? What kind?"

"I'm a psychiatrist," replied Peter. "I just think

31

we might have touched on this type of thing in medical school if it existed."

"I'm telling you, I've heard of this," said Mamie. "I know I have. I'm gonna Google this when I get home."

Peter just chuckled and shook his head. Then I saw him look down and across the table at Rebecca. She was playing with one of the rings on her slender finger, and when she looked up and saw his eyes on her, she looked away. After a moment, she looked back at Peter, who was still gazing at her.

"Sorry," Peter said, smiling and blushing a little. "My wife is always criticizing me for staring. It's what I do for work. I'm supposed to study the people I'm working with, so I end up studying everybody, everywhere we go."

"It's okay," said Rebecca.

"I bet she can make you stop. WITH HER MIND," shouted drunken Mamie.

"Maybe," said Rebecca, and then she smiled at Peter, and this time, after a moment, he looked away.

"Speaking of doing things with your mind, Hildy's a psychic!" Mamie exclaimed.

"Yeah?" Brian asked. "You a mind reader, Hildy?"

"No," I said.

"She is so," said Mamie. "It runs in her family. Her cousin, aunt, they all have psychic gifts."

"Is that really true, Hildy?" Sharon asked. "I never knew that about you."

"No, it's not true. Sometimes I can make people think I'm reading their thoughts. It's just sort of a parlor trick, that's all."

My father's sister Peg was a "psychic" who once made her living off of the occult-hungry tourists down in Salem. She also did readings in her home. My cousin Jane and I grew up watching her, so we picked up a few tricks, which made us wildly popular on the slumber party circuit. I'll still stage a reading for fun sometimes, just for skeptics, but I have to be in the right mood.

"Hildy, come on. Do Brian," Mamie said.

"Yeah, Hildy, let's see what you got," said Brian, and soon everybody around us, even Peter, was cajoling me.

"Oh, okay," I said. I wouldn't have agreed if Brian hadn't already proved himself to be a rather easy read. I paused for a moment, then said, "Okay, Brian, I'd like you to think about something that happened to you in the past. A memory. I'm going to present a few questions. Just try not to nod or give anything away with your eyes. It should be easy, here, by candlelight. Easier for you not to give me any signals."

"All right," said Brian.

"You'll have to give me your hand," I said.

Brian extended his hand as if for a handshake and I took it in mine and then turned it so that it was palm-up and resting on the table. His fingers curled in slightly toward his palm, and I smoothed them gently with mine so that they were lying flat on the table. I kept my hand resting lightly on his open hand, each of our fingers barely touching the other's wrist.

"Just look at me. By keeping your gaze passive, you'll avoid giving me cues. Sometimes people give cues, by kind of blinking or nodding. Try not to do that. Now think about this memory. Think about it. . . . Oh, it's a happy memory," I began.

I knew he was going to be easy, but not this easy.

"It's from your childhood—no, don't nod," I said.

"I didn't nod." Brian laughed.

"I didn't see him nod," said Sharon.

"He gave a little nod," said Mamie.

"Shush," I said. Then: "It wasn't a regular day. It was a special day. I'm not sure if it was Christmas. . . . No, it wasn't Christmas. Was it . . . Yes, it was your birthday."

Brian grinned. "You're good."

"Stop helping me," I said. Then I said, "It was when you were still a child, not very young, not very old. Were you . . . nine—no, wait, ten. I believe you were ten."

Brian was trying on his poker face now. Too late.

"It was something you were given. A present.

Think about where you were when you first saw it. You weren't in the house. . . . No, you were outside."

Brian was trying not to smile.

"Outside. You were led outside and you saw it and you were very happy. Was it . . ."

Now I paused. I always find this a good place to pause and look intensely at the other person, look intensely into their eyes and cock my head a little, as if I'm trying to hear something. And if I'm in a group, as I was that night, you can hear a pin drop. You want people to think you're still probing the other's mind. You don't want it to look too easy.

"Yes, I know," I said. "Your memory is of your tenth birthday, when your parents gave you a bike."

"Holy SHIT!" exclaimed Brian. "THAT WAS IT! That's amazing."

"EVERY TIME," Mamie said.

"You've seen her do this before?" asked Sharon. "Is it always a birthday that a person thinks of? Is that the trick?"

"No, it's always something different. She always nails it," said Mamie.

"Not always," Boatie said.

"I'm not always right," I agreed.

"You're almost always right, Hil," conceded Boatie.

"That's fucking freaky," said Brian.

I released Brian's hand and took a sip of my

nonalcoholic beverage. I won't lie; I was pleased with myself. I've struck out before, but this was easy. I'm so much better at this now that I'm not half-tanked when I do it.

"Why do you say you're not psychic, Hildy?" Sharon asked. "I never would have been able to do that."

"It's really not mind reading, I promise you," I said.

"It's not even a major memory for me. It's not something I've thought about in years, that bike," said Brian. "I don't know why I thought of it now."

"Did you tell him to think of a birthday?" Boatie asked.

"No," Mamie said. "Weren't you listening? It could have been anything."

Peter said, "It could have been anything, but I believe that Hildy did tell him to think of a birthday. Am I right, Hildy?"

"Perhaps." I smiled.

"Do you mind if I try to deconstruct what you just did?" Peter asked.

"No. Go ahead. I'm the first to admit that it's just a trick. Tell me what I did. This'll be fun."

"Well, first, I noticed that you said a few things that were suggestions. Like you said you were going to 'present' some questions, and then you said, several times, 'Try not to give anything away,' so maybe the word *present* along with *give*

36

and *away* formed a suggestion—that he think of a memory about a present or a gift."

"No, I don't think she said those things," said Brian. "I was listening to see if she was saying anything leading."

"She said them," Peter said.

"Did I? Hmmm." I smiled. This *was* fun.

"So that sort of narrowed it down to Christmas or a birthday. I think you said something like 'by candlelight.' Right? Something like that. Candles. Candlelight."

Mamie couldn't help herself. She jumped right in. "Yes, Peter. You're right. Who wouldn't think of a birthday? Candles? Candlelight?"

"More than once," Peter continued, "Hildy ran two words together. 'By candlelight' became 'bycandlelight.' Say it fast—'BYCANDLELIGHT.' It sounds like 'bike and delight.' The *bike* word came through a couple times. I think she said 'by kind of.' Again, 'bike-kindof.' These words weren't apparent to the others on a conscious level, but you had sort of anchored him with your touch and were able to access his subconscious a little, and so it's possible you made the suggestion."

I just laughed. "I suppose anything's possible."

"After that, it was a classic cold reading," Peter said to Brian. "She was asking you questions and reading your responses in the way your eyes moved. She had her fingers on your pulse. She knows a little NLP, some neurolinguistic programming techniques. . . . Do you know what that is, Hildy?"

I had never heard of it until then, so I shook my head.

"They're techniques to decipher signals people give subconsciously with their eye movements and other subtle body language."

"Oh, is that what it's called?" I laughed. Imagine! There was actually a scientific term for something my cousin and I just figured out on our own.

"Yes, and you're very good at it." Then to Brian, Peter said, "She was basically asking you yes or no questions and you answered her with subtle signals."

"I didn't move my eyes, I know that. She told me not to move them," said Brian.

"Which made it almost impossible for you *not* to move them," Peter said. "Then, once you had told her that it was not an indoor present, it was quite easy. What present would a ten-year-old have to go outside to see?"

"That's the part I don't get. It could have been a pony," said Mamie. "Anything."

"In Southie?" scoffed Boatie.

"It's all true," I said.

Mamie said, "There's more to it. I've seen her do this too many times; it's always different."

"Don't get me wrong. I'm impressed, Hildy," said Peter.

"Why, thank you, Peter," I replied.

I really was flattered. Peter is another reader, after all. That's what psychiatry is based upon, I presume. I wondered, then, how easy it would be to read him. I had never read another good reader.

I excused myself right after dessert, as usual, and was pleased to be heading out to my car dead sober. This is one of the things I'm truly grateful for the girls' intervention. I used to float through the town in my Range Rover, quite drunk. I can admit that now. I thought I was being safe, that I actually drove better when I was drunk. I'd cruise along, tree by tree. House by house. Slowly. Slowly. Blinking and smiling. All aglow. Of course, it was like a bad dream the next day as I tried, in a mild panic, to recall the journey. But in truth, there were times I didn't remember driving home at all, and now I was grateful that that craziness was all behind me. No more drunk driving. No regrets the next morning.

It wasn't even eleven when I arrived home. The girls were thrilled to see me. I have two dogs, both bitches—Babs and Molly—both mutts. Babs is part terrier and she can be nasty. You wouldn't want to approach her with an outstretched hand if you didn't know her. Best to let her approach you, which she will, usually with fangs bared. Molly is a Border collie mix, which puts her IQ level just a few notches above my own, and that's trying at times. She's also one of those dogs who smiles when she greets you—she pulls her lips back to reveal her teeth and narrows her eyes in a show of ridiculous supplication, which I find equally trying, especially when she throws in some whining, as she did that night.

I opened the front door and the girls flew from the house and raced over to the garage ahead of me. Our garage is an old boathouse. I say *ours,* though it's only the dogs and me who live here now. I'm right on the saltwater Anawam River, which feeds into the Atlantic just about a hundred yards downstream. I have my ex-husband Scott's old MG out there in the boathouse. He left it behind. For the longest time, I kept badgering him to take it. At one point, Emily said he had given it to her, but she lives in New York, so I'm stuck with it in my garage. It hasn't been driven in years. Mice have nested under its hood and bits of their nests can be seen on the front seat.

The dogs whined and pawed at the old wooden boathouse door until I raised it, and then they shot inside and sniffed excitedly around the corners of the leaning structure with their tails erect. I fumbled in my purse for my keys. Babs once killed a rat in the boathouse, and the girls have never quite gotten past that thrill. They're always in hunt mode when we're in there. Me, too, actually. My heart starts racing when I unlock the trunk, the "boot," of the old MG. There I keep my wine. That's all I drink now. Wine. No more of the hard stuff. I order wine online from a vineyard in California. I've developed quite a taste for California wine. I don't know why I so rarely drank it before. I felt wine gave me a worse hangover than vodka. But now I try not to overdo it. I try, but in all honesty, sometimes I don't remember going to bed at night. So what? I'd like to go back to Hazelden and bring that up in "group" one day. It might make for an interesting discussion. Is a blackout really a blackout if nobody is there to see it? Not even yourself? I say no. It's like the tree falling in the woods. Who cares?

But most nights, I just have a few glasses. I've come to love my nightly party of one. I've no need to go out with others—all the bothersome others—with their judgments and their quick looks between them. Stolen pleasures are always more thrilling than those come by honestly. It's what I imagine makes adulterous love affairs so exciting, having a wickedness concealed beneath one's everyday mantle of goodness. Anyway, I'm not completely alone with my wine, since the girls are always there, too, and sometimes, if it's a warm night and there's a moon, I undress on the patio and walk down to the river, where the dogs and I go for a swim. The night of Wendy's party was one of those nights, though there wasn't much of a moon. It was just an unseasonably warm May night. Wendy had been ranting all evening about how she always "conjures" the best weather for her parties. Now I sat on the patio with my wine and my dogs, and after my second or third glass, I was, finally, blissfully, at home.

At Hazelden, all these AA speakers used to come to the meetings at night to tell us their stories, and some of them were quite funny, while others were heartbreaking, of course. One night, a guy started his speech by saying, "I was born three drinks short of comfortable . . . ," and that's when I actually wondered if my daughters might have been right about my drinking. Up until then, I was confident that I didn't belong there. I knew I wasn't an alcoholic. If my daughters wanted to see a *real* alcoholic, they should have met my mother. She wouldn't drink for weeks at a time, but then she'd go on a binge and would be drunk for days. My dad would go out searching for her in local bars. Sometimes we'd find her passed out on the kitchen floor after school. I never drank before five. Never drank alone (before rehab). But I knew what that guy meant about the way he was born three drinks short. It made me think about the first beer I ever drank, down at North Beach with a bunch of kids one summer night. It made me think about that first exquisite relief. It made me think about my ex-husband, Scott, who always said I should stop after the third drink. "That's when you get out of control," he'd say. I had no idea what he was talking about. After a couple drinks is when I start to feel *in* control.

But everybody's different. Why must we all be the same? I'd like to ask my daughters that. The way they carried on that night about all the damage I had done. *Damage.* Tess smoked pot all through high school and managed to get into Wesleyan and graduate magna cum laude. Emily, well, Emily's a sculptor. She has a lifestyle in New York that she could never afford without my support. But do I get any thanks? Of course not. I know I sound bitter, but in truth, it's fine. It's better this way. No more worrying that the hosts will stop serving drinks before I've had enough. No more regrets the next day.

Now I stay at home in the evenings and slip serenely into myself. They'd think it was sad, my daughters, but those are some of the happiest moments of my life, when I can change comfortably back into myself. Not every night anymore. Not every night, no. But that night, after Wendy's party, there was a rather cordial atmosphere in the lovely darkness on my terrace, and by the time I had poured the last of the bottle into my glass, I was fully transformed. I was myself. I was myself again.

I dropped my skirt and stepped out of my underpants. I pulled off my blouse and unhooked my frayed old bra. I'm sixty. My belly is flabby, my tits sag, and my legs are skinny. I haven't worn a bathing suit in years, but I do like to swim. I love the water, always have, and I like the feeling of the night against my skin.

Like I said, there wasn't much of a moon, but I know the trail by heart, and padding along the sandy, pine needle–strewn path with my dogs at my side, I felt like some kind of primitive huntress, like an Anawam squaw, perhaps. When I reached the river's edge, I sipped my wine and felt the soft silt of the riverbed easing around my feet, then climbing up my ankles like a pair of ghostly silken stockings. I took a last sip, then dropped my empty glass onto the soft sand and poured myself into the icy river, which made me laugh and gasp and my dogs bark with the utter exhilaration of it all. How thoroughly delicious was that wine. And I had a case of it. There would be enough. There would always be enough for me.

Three

Sometimes I wake up too early. It's a problem. I read in a magazine that it comes with being middle-aged. Apparently, it's a hormonal thing. I have no trouble falling asleep, especially after concluding an evening with a little wine, but I tend to awaken with a start at exactly three a.m. filled with dread and self-loathing. It's my nocturnal sojourn to my own little hell, where I'm visited by the cast of demons who delight in reminding me of my daily wretchedness, my lifelong wickedness. An inventory of the previous day's missteps is reviewed, followed by the unscrolling of a decades-long catalog of my own sins, spites, regrets, and grudges. Sometimes I turn on the TV and watch an old movie and fall back to sleep. I always feel better after dawn.

In the three a.m. blackness after the McAllister party, though, I just lay there and, instead of turning on the TV, thought about Rebecca, and this managed to keep the night monsters at bay. I was a little fascinated by Rebecca. I had been ever since the day I first showed her their future home. There had been a calamity during that showing and Rebecca had performed a bit of magic. (Magic almost always guarantees a sale; any broker will tell you this.) I had been rather captivated by Rebecca ever since.

The calamity had involved one of the Leighton ponies. Though a lot of us still call it the old Barlow place, the McAllisters didn't buy the property from the Barlow family; they bought it from a rich Boston family named Leighton. Elsa Leighton had decided to raise Welsh ponies there. Very fancy Welsh ponies. The daughters were part of the horse-show set. The Leightons came up only on the weekends and they had hired Frank Getchell to run the farm for them. Wendover still has a number of horse farms. We're only a short drive from the Westfield Hunt Club in South Hamilton, and Frank grew up working on a few farms. So the Leightons were the sellers when Wendy called me to say that she had these wonderful McAllisters looking for a house. She said that she had shown them all the best properties and they hadn't seen anything they liked. So, she figured, why not show them the old Barlow place?

Most of the brokers in the area had just about given up on the Barlow place at that point. Some believed the Leightons were asking too much—it was listed at $2.2 million. Yes, it had almost twenty acres and was up on scenic Wendover Rise, with views of the tidal marshes and the Atlantic Ocean and the tiny Cape Ann islands beyond, but the house had been built in the early 1700s, and like all true Colonial homes, it was small, dark, and stood right on the road. Everybody who wants an estate in Wendover wants to have a quaint antique set far back from the road, with plenty of privacy. There's really no such thing. Colonists needed to have their houses right on the road. They liked their neighbors to be able to see them. Buyers find this concept hard to grasp, for some reason, no matter how much you try to explain about the original owners' fear of the Indians and wild animals that were wandering about when the house was built. I had sold the home to the Leightons, and now that they had listed it back with me, I told them to sit tight with their price. I always felt they had overpaid, and I didn't want them to take too big a loss on the place.

But, well, the Leightons needed to sell. Their star had been rising when I had sold them the house—Tom Leighton had just made partner at Bear Stearns. Now it was falling. Bear Stearns had dissolved. The Leightons were divorcing. One of the young riders was in a drug-rehab place. That's life. That's how I make my living, anyway.

The McAllister showing was early on a spring morning, and when I pulled up, Wendy and Rebecca were already walking toward the front door and Rebecca's two young sons were chasing each other around the yard. I wandered over to them and introduced myself, but I noticed Rebecca looking skeptically out at the road. Bubbly Wendy apparently noticed it, too, because she placed one hand on my wrist and one on Rebecca's, forming a sort of human chain, with Wendy as its effervescent central link. "Hildy," she gushed, "I was just telling Rebecca that the house *is* close to the road, but it's such a quiet country lane. . . ."

Wendy's been in the business long enough to know better than to offer up that little enchantment, and sure enough, no sooner were the words out of her mouth than a rattling diesel-engine pickup roared past the house, followed by a motorcycle and then, after a few beats, a rickety school bus.

"Liam," Rebecca called to her elder son, "take Ben's hand, honey. Don't let him go near the road." Liam was around six years old, and Ben around four. They were clearly adopted children, as I knew from Googling Brian that he wasn't South American. The boys appeared to be South American or Mexican. "Hispanic," my daughters would have corrected me. They were well-behaved boys, but I'm never overjoyed when people bring their kids to a showing. They just distract everybody.

"They're so adorable," I said to Rebecca, then, motioning toward the front door, added, "Let's go inside, shall we?"

I knew the other places that Wendy had shown Rebecca. Basically, everything at the top of the market. The Leightons had made the Barlow house charming enough—exposing beams, refinishing the woodwork around the huge walk-in fireplace —but it was a weekend house. The kitchen was tiny, as were the bedrooms, and, the kiss of death, no master bath. But I showed her around anyway, and as we gazed out one of the upstairs windows, Rebecca said, "Are those ponies part of this farm?"

"Oh, yes, I forgot to tell you, Rebecca's a horse person," Wendy chirped.

"Well. Let's go look at the barns and the paddocks, shall we?" I said.

Honestly, how could Wendy not have mentioned that? The best thing about the property was all the expensive horse fencing the Leightons had put in, and the massive barn they had restored. Wendy's sales figures are surprisingly good. I don't know how she sells a thing.

Rebecca's boys were chasing each other from room to room when Rebecca called, "Boys. Come on, we're going to go see some ponies." They ran downstairs and out the back door with us.

We were all wandering up the drive toward the barn just as Frank Getchell, the caretaker, pulled up in his pickup.

Frank is an old hippie. He's short and somewhat stocky. He wears his gray hair in a ponytail, but his tanned, weathered scalp is taking over. Soon there'll be nothing for the ponytail to cling to. He always wears beat-up jeans and old cowboy boots. A flannel shirt covers his paunch.

"Hi, Frankie," I said.

"Hey, Hil," Frank replied. He stole a glance at Rebecca and the kids, then stared straight ahead. Frankie Getchell can be a little awkward around people he doesn't know.

"Frank, you know Wendy, and this is Rebecca McAllister, and her boys. She wanted to see the barn."

"Ride up with me, if you want," Frank muttered,

still looking ahead. "We got two overdue mares and I got a feeling one of 'em might've dropped her foal last night."

Even Wendy, who's never sat on a horse in her life, let out a little squeal of delight at the prospect of glimpsing a newborn foal.

"Can we ride in the back of the truck, Mommy?" asked Liam.

"No, that's not safe, sweetie," said Wendy, but Rebecca said, "I always rode in the back of the pickup at my grandfather's farm when I was a kid. Is it okay with you, Frank?"

"They gotta ride in the back—there's hardly enough room for us four up here," Frankie replied, frowning. I could tell he already regretted his offer; he should have just let us walk. The boys squealed with delight as Rebecca lowered the tailgate. They climbed up into the bed of the truck and scrambled over the ropes and scraps of lumber and settled in next to an old lobster trap. Rebecca, Wendy, and I all squeezed into the filthy cab of Frank's truck, and then we were driving past the barn and up to the field at the top of the property. That field really has one of the best views in Wendover. I had forgotten that, hadn't actually been up there since I was a little girl.

Rebecca had been quiet during her walk through the house, but now that we could see the ponies, she became quite cheerful and tried to engage poor Frank in a conversation.

"Are they Welsh ponies?"

"Yup, most of 'em," Frank muttered. He glanced into his rearview and then hollered out the window, "You boys sit down on the floor back there. No hanging over the sides like that."

"My grandfather bred Thoroughbreds in Virginia," Rebecca said. She waited for a response from Frankie, a response I knew would never come, so after a moment I said, "Is that right?"

"Do the mares live out, even during foaling season?" Rebecca asked.

"Yup," Frank grunted. We hit a few ruts in the road and he slowed, checking on the boys in his rearview again.

"My grandfather always thought that allowing the mares to foal in a field was healthiest. It was considered risky by other breeders. These were racehorses, you know, so some of the foals were worth quite a bit of money. . . . Oh, what a lovely little herd," she said as we pulled up to the large grassy field.

Frank parked next to a gate, and as soon as we got out of the truck, Rebecca cried, "There it is." She was pointing to a little black foal that lay in a corner of the meadow, its nose resting in the grass. A gray mare stood over it protectively. The boys had jumped off the back of the truck, and Rebecca instinctively stepped in front of them. "Don't go in the field with the ponies," she said sternly. "Do you hear?"

"What the fuck?" Frank said, which made Wendy gasp and look anxiously at the boys. Then Frank mumbled a series of just the most unspeakable profanities. I know Frank pretty well, and I'd never heard him go off like this. I, too, glanced at Rebecca and the boys, and I saw a look of astonished glee in the boys' eyes. Rebecca was biting her lip, trying not to smile. Frank threw open the gate and stomped into the field. Rebecca told the boys, again, to stay outside the fence with Wendy. Then, after a moment's hesitation, she and I entered the field, Rebecca closing the gate carefully behind us. The grass was wet with dew. She wore a pair of dainty flats, but she didn't seem to mind.

"So . . . what's wrong, Frankie?" I asked.

"What's wrong is that foal don't belong to that mare. They didn't breed that mare this year."

Frank looked out over the herd of a dozen ponies and then he groaned, and we all saw it. A small black mare, covered in lather, was trotting frantically toward the gray and the foal, but when she got within about a dozen feet, the gray pinned her ears and charged the black mare, who had blood on her neck and her flanks, where she had been bitten over and over again.

Frank climbed over the fence and grabbed a couple of halters and some rope from the back of his truck.

"That gray is the boss mare. She's had a few

foals, but they decided not to breed her this year because of her temperament. She's wicked mean and she was turning out witchy foals. One of them kicked me in the gut a few months ago," Frank said. He stood for a moment. He was trying to think.

"You mean that pony stole the other pony's colt?" Wendy called from outside the fence. "That's just . . . awful. Well, you better get that baby back to her real mother, Frank," she shrilled, and I saw Frank shoot her a look. The poor black mare was now standing with her sides heaving. Milk was dripping from her udders. Frank started toward the gray, but when she saw him approaching, she nudged the weak foal to its feet, then herded it to the far corner of the pasture.

Rebecca said, "Do you have any grain in that truck?"

"No, but I was thinkin' the same thing. I can run down and get some from the barn," he replied.

"Leave me one of those halters and I'll catch the broodmare," Rebecca said. "We really shouldn't let her keep going after the foal. She looks exhausted."

"Thanks," said Frank. He handed her a halter and lead and then jumped into his truck and sped off toward the barn. The boys and Wendy were sitting on a couple of large boulders, just outside the fence.

Rebecca kept the halter and rope concealed

behind her back and she approached the black mare, nudging aside the other ponies that were crowding her.

"Whoa, Mama," Rebecca said in a quiet singsong tone. She was heading for the mare but not looking directly at her. She made a few kissing sounds while swatting the other ponies away. "Shhhhh, Mommy, shhhhh."

When she was almost alongside the exhausted mare, she tossed the lead rope over her neck. The mare obligingly lowered her head so that Rebecca could put on her halter.

"Be careful, Rebecca, your shoes! Oh, the poor thing," said Wendy. "I had no idea horses could be so . . . mean."

Rebecca stroked the mare's neck and ran her hands over her back, touching around her bite marks tenderly. The mare's head drooped almost to the ground. She still had some filthy afterbirth membrane hanging from between her hind legs.

"There, Mommy," said Rebecca. "There."

Frank came back and managed to lure the boss mare away from the foal with a bucket of grain. He caught her, but by this time, the black—the actual mother—had lain down. The trauma of the birth and then the fight with the alpha mare had been too much for her. Her head was on the ground. Her eyes were glazing over.

"Frank," Rebecca cried. She had been trying to encourage the mare to stand up by clucking and nudging at her haunches with the toe of her little shoe.

"Shit. Hildy, can you hold her?" Frank asked, nodding at the gray, who was now haltered and, amazingly, nibbling at the grass as if nothing unusual was going on. "She might lose it when we bring the foal to its mom. If she does, give her a good whack with the lead. I mean it."

I took the lead from Frank's hand and watched him run over to the mare, who was lying only about ten feet from her foal.

Frank poked at the mare's side with his boot. "HUP, HUP," he said. "Get up, you stupid cow."

"Wait," Rebecca said, and she strode over to the foal, who was also lying down, exhausted, just a few feet away. Rebecca ran her small hands all over the foal. She moved her palms under his tail and between his legs, where he was still damp, over his limp testicles and along the bloody umbilicus that lay next to him on the grass like a pale, wet snake. Then she strode back to the mare and held her hands in front of her muzzle for just an instant—I swear it was that quick—and the spell took effect.

Life, baby, blood, baby, lust, baby, the mare sucked it all in through her nostrils in one great wafting breath and then another. Then her eyes were open. She remembered something. Rebecca touched her muzzle again with her hands and then the mare's eyes were wide and alert.

Baby.

Within seconds, she was on her feet. Frank led her over to the foal and then it all looked like a Disney movie. The mare nudged the weak foal, and he rose, once again, straightening those spindly front legs first and then those crazy crooked kickers behind, and soon he was rooting about for his mama's udder, which Rebecca helped him find by guiding his velvety muzzle beneath the mare's belly.

"Where's their water?" Rebecca asked Frank.

Frank grunted and took the bucket that had been filled with grain and carried it to a long trough at the edge of the field. He dunked the bucket in the trough and then carried it to the nursing mare, who drank from it in long, sucking gulps. Frank had been right. The gray mare did start to struggle with me when she saw the baby with his dam, but I barked at her and waved the lead toward her flank and she settled.

We left the mare and her foal resting in the grass under a shady tree. Frank led the rogue mare to the barn and we wandered down with him, the boys running ahead of us. The mare balked once, when we were out of sight of her herd and her stolen baby, but Frank had had it with her and whipped her rump hard with the lead rope. "Move yer butt, Betty," he growled, and the mare hustled through the gate.

"She's called Betty?" I asked, amused.

"That's what I call her. They call her some other damned thing," Frank said. Now that we were on the other side of the fence, the mare had calmed herself somewhat. The night's mischief had done a number on her, too, and we all entered the barn, with Betty walking placidly alongside us. Suddenly, the mare stopped, whipped her head around, and let out a long whinny. She was answered with silence.

"Poor Betty," Rebecca said. I looked over and saw her wiping tears from her eyes. She laughed self-consciously when she saw me notice.

"I feel worse for her victim," I laughed. "The poor mare whose baby she stole."

Frank had led the mare into a stall far down the barn aisle, and Rebecca whispered to me angrily, "It was cruel not to breed her and then leave her in with the foaling mares. It was evil."

So, the McAllisters ended up buying the Barlow place. They paid the asking price. And the Leightons sold off their ponies, all except Betty. Rebecca should have just asked them to throw her into the deal, but I think she paid for that nasty mare, over and above the price of the property.

You used to see Rebecca riding the mare bareback down into the trails behind the salt marshes on warm spring afternoons, even before the house was finished. Rebecca was so petite, and the mare became quite plump. They made a nice pair, Betty and Rebecca. Rebecca would ride her with just a halter and a lead, and often she was barefoot, in a T-shirt and an old pair of cutoff shorts.

I thought about Rebecca, in the predawn after the McAllister party, and it soothed me.

I closed my eyes and no wickedness came.

Four

If you saw Patch and Cassie Dwight around town, you'd think them a happy, well-adjusted couple, especially given their circumstances. But I had been trying to sell their house for over a year, and I didn't know if I could sell it with them living in it, quite frankly. You didn't need to be a broker or a shrink to see how altered and unbalanced its occupants were, all three of them. Outside, around town, Cassie appeared cheerful and capable, most of the time, but I had known her since she was a little girl and I was beginning to see a change in her, a hardening around her pretty edges. I saw it one afternoon when I stopped at North Beach to take a walk before attending an open house at a property nearby.

There's a playground at North Beach with swings and a jungle gym and usually a cool breeze off the Atlantic. I frequently walk on the beach and I know many of the young mothers who take their kids there in the afternoons, and sometimes

I'll stop for a chat. That day of the open house was the first time I saw Rebecca at the beach. She was standing, looking down at the water's edge, with her younger son, Ben, playing near her feet. Cassie was seated on a beach blanket nearby, surrounded by a group of her friends.

As with a herd of mares or a pack of she-wolves, there's usually an alpha personality in any cluster of females, and in this group at North Beach most days, it was Cassie Dwight. Gregarious, outgoing, a lifelong Wendoverite, Cassie was the one everybody called to see if they should go to North Beach or to the school playground each day. She usually made the decision based on the weather and how her special-needs son, Jake, was coping on that particular day. Cassie remembered the birthdays of most of the other mothers and would often bring cupcakes for all, which thrilled the children and made the mothers exclaim at her generosity and goodness. With all she had on her plate! Her husband was the top plumbing contractor in the area, so Cassie had all the latest on who was doing what to their homes. What was being built and where. Who was using cheap materials, squandering money on imported marble, or trying to plant a rose garden too close to sea spray or road salt.

It was a hot day, for June, and most of the moms were wearing what looked like last year's slightly frayed, stretched-out bathing suits, which they were determined would see them through another season. The women who gather at the North Beach playground tend to be local women who grew up on the North Shore, in and around Wendover, and they hate spending money on new clothes when the old things will do. Most women who are newer to the area, whose husbands have bought up all the old estates or built new ones, spend their afternoons at the private Anawam Beach Club, or the few with deep-rooted connections to the local gentry join the Westfield Hunt Club, where they can golf, ride, or play tennis while the children frolic in the pool. Wendy Heatherton had urged Rebecca and Brian to join the Anawam Beach Club—had even offered to sponsor them—but, although I'd heard that Brian was quite interested, Rebecca never followed through.

I waved to Cassie and her gang and wandered over to where Rebecca stood.

"So nice to see you, Rebecca," I said.

She shielded her eyes with her hand so that she could see me in the midday glare, and then she smiled.

"Hey, Hildy."

"Do you come to this beach often?" I asked.

"Yeah, usually in the mornings. Ben loves the rockiness of this beach and Liam likes to skimboard."

I followed Rebecca's gaze down to the water and saw Liam leap aboard a wafer-thin board and ride it across a thin lick of surf. His arms flew up in graceful arcs above his head and his knees were bent as he skimmed across the wake.

"He's quite good," I marveled.

"He could do this all day," she said.

Cassie and her group were seated a few feet away, and Cassie got up when she noticed me and wandered over.

"Hi, Hildy," she said, smiling, but she was looking at Rebecca.

"Hello, Cassie dear," I said. "Do you know Rebecca McAllister?"

"We haven't met, but I'm Patch's wife—he did all the plumbing up at your place," Cassie said.

"Oh, of course," Rebecca said, smiling warmly. She reached out and shook Cassie's hand. "Patch is great; we love all the work he did."

"Thanks," said Cassie. "I've seen you here before, but I felt weird about just coming up and introducing myself. We come here every afternoon around this time so the kids can play. You should join us."

"Oh, okay. Thanks," said Rebecca.

I was quite pleased that Rebecca was meeting Cassie. She needed to connect with other mothers in the area.

Nine-year-old Jake had followed his mother over to us, and as Cassie asked Rebecca questions about how she liked Wendover, I saw that Rebecca was watching Jake out of the corner of her eye. He was sort of hovering over Ben, fascinated with the small boy's truck.

"We have lemonade," Cassie said. "Would you like some?"

"Sure," I said.

"Oh, no thanks, I'm fine," said Rebecca. She glanced down at her son in the surf and then back at Ben. Jake was walking in small circles around him, but Ben, squatting and pushing his truck through the pebbles, was oblivious. Cassie strode back to her friends and their cooler for my lemonade.

It was clear that Rebecca thought it odd that such a big boy was so keenly attuned to the much younger Ben.

"Hi, Jake," I said, but he ignored me, so I just smiled and said, "You've gotten to be such a big boy."

Just then, Jake lunged at Ben and tried to snatch the toy truck from the boy's hand. At first, Ben clung to the truck. None of the mothers, except for Rebecca and me, saw this.

"Jake," I said, "no, no . . . Jake."

"This is my truck," Ben said earnestly, looking right into Jake's eyes, but Jake just looked down at the truck for a moment. Then he jerked it from Ben's grasp.

"HEY," Rebecca cried out, positioning herself between the two boys. "Why don't we take turns?" she said.

Jake ignored her and just squatted there in the sand, spinning the wheels of the truck with his hand and watching them turn. Ben was trying not to cry.

"Hey, c'mon," Rebecca said again, gently touching the older boy's shoulder. The instant her fingers made contact with his shirt, Jake began a high-pitched wailing. He leaped to his feet and began springing up and down on his toes, flapping his hands in front of him. He flung the truck to the ground and turned in small circles, flapping, flapping and repeating the same high-pitched squeals.

"Oh," Rebecca said, seeing her mistake. "Oh, sorry . . ."

"WHAT . . . IS . . . WRONG . . . WITH . . . YOU?" Cassie was instantly standing in front of Rebecca, shouting the words into her face. Rebecca looked over to see that the other women, who just a moment before had been engaged in lighthearted chatter, were now glaring at her.

"I'm sorry, he's so much bigger than Ben, I thought I should step in. I didn't know . . ."

"Know what?" Cassie hissed. Her face was scarlet with rage. Then she turned to try to calm her child. "Jake," she said, "Jake . . ."

I had no idea what to say, so I just smiled at Rebecca sympathetically.

"Oh, I'm so sorry," Rebecca said.

"No," Cassie said, taking a deep breath and

leaving Jake to his twirling and flapping. "I'm sorry, too. I guess you didn't know. Jake has a severe developmental disorder."

"No, I didn't know. I feel awful. I'm so sorry."

"He can't bear to be touched. Would it be okay if I give him the truck to play with and see if it calms him down?"

"Sure," Rebecca said, glancing at Ben, who was still crying. As Cassie tried to get Jake's attention with the truck, Rebecca squatted next to Ben and gave him a little hug. "Honey, I brought other toys. . . ."

"It's MY truck. I want it BACK."

"I know, but it's not as easy for Jake to share as it is for you."

"Why?" Ben sniffed. "He's a big boy."

I saw Cassie shoot a wary gaze at her.

"Well," Rebecca said, "I know, but he's . . . disabled. . . ."

"OH MY GOD," Cassie said, glancing over at her friends, who were smiling sympathetically at her, and then leveling her gaze back on Rebecca. "Where have you been living? In a cave? Try educating yourself."

Rebecca's cheeks reddened and she stared up at Cassie. "What did you say?"

"Jake is a child with a disability, not a disabled child."

"Oh, I thought that's what I said."

"No, what you said was dehumanizing."

" 'Dehumanizing'? I don't know what you're talking about, and you know what? I wasn't even talking to you; I was talking to my son." Rebecca stood then and, grabbing Ben by the hand, called out to her other son in a shrill, reedy cry.

"LIAM. LIAM, it's time to go. Time to go BACK TO OUR CAVE."

Liam jumped off his skimboard. "What?" he called back.

"NOW," Rebecca shouted, and she started toward the parking lot. Liam scrambled up the beach after her, dragging his skimboard behind him.

"Mom . . ." he whined.

"My truck," wailed Ben.

"We'll. Get. You. A. New. One," Rebecca said as she dragged her sobbing child to the car. She jerked the skimboard from Liam and he ducked into the car next to his brother.

"Cassie," I said.

"*What,* Hildy? What?"

"Nothing."

We watched Jake spinning the wheels on the truck.

"She didn't need to treat him like some kind of monster. He's never hurt anybody. It was just the truck . . ."

"I know," I said. "I know."

Rebecca's silver Land Cruiser cut a sharp reverse in the sandy lot and then she sped off, leaving a wake of hot sand and dust behind her.

• • •

I remember Jake as an infant. Cassie brought him by the office a few times when she was driving through town. He was cuter than your average baby; all plump, with those big blue eyes. Just gorgeous. I guess it was when he was about a year old that Cassie started to notice he wasn't developing like the other babies his age. Her sister had a daughter four months younger who was more advanced—at everything. I have two daughters, but I remember telling Cassie that I'd always heard that boys are just slower. "He'll catch up," I said. That's what we all said to her. But Jake didn't catch up. When he was about a year and a half old, he started having seizures, and that's when they detected the chromosomal abnormality. There's a genetic problem of some sort—I don't recall the specific name—but by the time he turned two, anyone could see that there was something wrong. He never spoke, he laughed at nothing, and he twirled in circles until he was so dizzy that he fell over, or he spent hours spinning the wheels of a truck and staring at them. These were things he did during his good moments.

The day I first went to look at the Dwight house after they told me they wanted to list it, I got a little glimpse of their life. It was a Saturday morning, and when I rang the bell, I had to wait quite a while. Nobody answered, but I heard a high-pitched, repetitive screaming coming from inside. I waited and then rang again. Realizing they were unlikely to hear the bell over the screaming, I tried to open the door. It was locked. I walked around to the kitchen door and knocked again. Cassie saw me through the window. Jake was seated on the floor, with his back against the wall, banging his head against it and wailing. Cassie was trying to pull him away from the wall, but he repeatedly wriggled from her grasp and moved back to the wall, where he rocked back and forth in a rhythmic precision, like a human metronome, whacking his head against the plaster on every upbeat. Cassie left him for a moment, flew to the door and unlocked it for me, then returned to Jake.

"LOCK THE DOOR BEHIND YOU," she shouted. It took me a moment to find the lock, which was at shoulder level.

"PATCH," Cassie shouted over Jake's high-pitched screams. I have to admit, I was overwhelmed by what was going on. I'd really had no idea, until then. After a moment, Patch came out of the back hall, wearing old sweats and a T-shirt, his hair wet.

"I've been calling and calling you. He's having a total fucking meltdown, and Hildy's here to see the house," Cassie hissed.

"I was in the shower," Patch said in a tone of barely controlled rage. "Hi, Hildy," he said without looking at me. He was looking at Jake, his head moving back and forth in time with the boy's head banging.

"Hi, Patch," I said.

"C'mon, Jake," Patch said, grabbing the boy by his wrists. "Let's watch *Sesame Street*. Let's watch Elmo."

Jake said, "Sneakahs, Sneakahs," and continued his wailing as Patch hauled him away from the wall and lifted him up in his arms like a baby. Jake's fists swung at Patch's face.

"We'll find Sneakers," said Patch. "No hitting, Jake."

Cassie stood for a moment to catch her breath, and then gave me a little smile. "He's getting too big for me to handle."

"Yes, I see, he's getting to be so . . . big," I replied.

Really, what do you say?

Cassie gave me a tour of the house. It was, to put it mildly, a wreck. Holes had been punched through the plaster. What looked like a large dried turd lay on a closet floor. Blood had been smeared on the bathroom walls and adult-size diapers were stacked everywhere—in the bathroom, the bedrooms, the kitchen. Meds, charts, soiled clothing, doctors' bills, and magazine clippings littered the house. Cassie didn't really say much. There was no need. Like I've said, the house tells the story.

In the den (they had once thought it would be the room of a second child) were photos of little Jake in a bunny costume, his eyes fixed on something in the distance, unsmiling. Also displayed were wedding photos of Cassie and Patch, both looking twenty years younger. They hadn't been married a decade.

I asked Cassie what was under the stained carpets in the living room. She just looked at me vacantly and said, "The ground? Who knows." Patch thought his dad had put hardwood floors there. He would pull up a piece of carpet to check later, he promised. Jake was standing in front of the television, rocking back and forth to a counting song on *Sesame Street*.

The Dwights wanted to move to Newton, where they would be in close proximity to the best school for Jake in the Boston area. But they had to sell their house first. Cassie and I sat at the kitchen table, working out some numbers. From the next room, the TV volume was rising and Jake could be heard stomping about and singing. His voice was like nothing I had ever heard before. It was clear and tonal, and though there were no words, there was a distinct melody. It sounded like an Indian meditative chant, like something a Native American might beat drums to, a deep, guttural incantation, but, like I said, with no words.

We had to go back into the living room to get

some paperwork. Jake was sitting on the floor, facing away from the TV, rocking back and forth with his eyes closed. A large orange cat had draped itself across the child's lap. It was one of the fattest cats I'd ever seen, but you know the type, a real fancy-pants, with a handsome, regal head, a long, thick coat, and a beautifully feathered tail that twitched every few seconds, just at the very end, like the rattle on a snake's tail. He rolled onto his back and his massive white double paws kneaded the air, then he swayed back onto the soft blob of his belly and plucked gently at Jake's pajamas with his claws, purring away, his green eyes opening wide at times, and then narrowing back into little crescents that curved up at the corners. Jake's singing had become a sort of purring hum, and the cat lolled this way and that, his head moving back and forth merrily, pressing up into the child's open palm with first one bewhiskered cheek and then the other. Jake was smiling. He was rocking back and forth, eyes closed, stroking the cat's chin and belly, and the purring cat gazed at us across its great paunch with an expression of smug superiority.

"Nice cat," I said, and I meant it, though I'm not usually a cat person.

"That's Sneakers, and yes, he's a great cat. They love each other." Cassie was beaming now, watching her son cuddling his pet. "Feeling better, Jakey?" she asked, smiling at him, but he seemed to have no idea we were there. "He loves the sensation of the cat's fur, and his occupational therapist says there's something about the purring that he also finds soothing."

"So sweet," I said.

"We never planned on getting a pet. We didn't think Jake would cope with one very well, but this guy showed up one night last year, a stray. Just hung around on our porch for a few days, and we started feeding him. Whenever Jake and I went outside, the cat followed us around. Jake always understood that he needed to be gentle with the cat. We never had to teach him that."

Jake was moving his cheek against the fur on the cat's back, and the cat casually licked the bottom of one of his front paws and then the other.

"We had to move the locks up a few months ago," Patch explained as he let me out the kitchen door. "Jake let himself out last year. . . . It took us two hours to find him. I've never prayed so hard in my life. He doesn't know anything about traffic or dogs or strangers. I thought Cassie was gonna lose her mind. They did a whole Amber Alert and everything. Finally found him behind Stop & Shop, barefoot, walking through a bunch of glass behind the recycling bins. For weeks, it haunted me. I kept thinking, ya know, what if? What if . . ."

"You can't think like that," I said. "You'd drive yourself insane."

I listed the house at just under $500,000. I think I showed it three times that winter, but the Dwights hadn't been able to do much to improve the place. If anything, each time I went in, it looked worse. It's on a quiet road that leads down to the Crossing, and when I drive past, I often think about something Cassie said to me that first day I came to talk to her about the listing, and she explained abut the school in Newton.

"It's a day school. But someday, we're gonna be old, and I don't know who'll take care of Jake," she said. "I lose my temper with him twenty times a day, and I'm his mom. What would somebody do to him who didn't love him the way Patch and I do? What if somebody was taking care of him who didn't give a shit about him? Ya know, there was an article a few years back about an elderly man who shot and killed his thirty-year-old brain-damaged son, and then himself. I understand why, Hildy, seriously, I do," Cassie said. "I want Jake to learn enough skills to be without us some-day. He's happy enough to be away from us, but I worry about the people who will be responsible for him. At this school, he can learn some social skills that can enhance his life so much. . . ."

I'm not the touchy-feeliest, but I put my hand on Cassie's arm when she said that. I guess Cassie's not touchy-feely, either, because she pulled her arm away and we turned our attention back to the bank statements.

Five

My dad served on the Wendover Board of Selectmen during most of the 1950s and 1960s. For twenty-five years, he worked behind the butcher's counter at Stead's Market down in the Crossing, and when old Barkie Stead died, my dad bought the market from his family. When Dad retired, many years later, he sold it to Luke Farman, who eventually sold it to Stop & Shop. Stop & Shop had to agree to construct a sign and maintain a facade that fit within the zoning bylaws, which my dad always thought too restrictive. Dad was an old-fashioned New England Yankee who believed that people should be able to do whatever they damned well pleased with property they owned. I actually need the zoning laws, not because I think supermarket chain stores should be forced to look like Nathaniel Hawthorne once shopped there, but because my clients want things to look that way. They appreciate the history of our town, and the value of almost everything in our town appreciates as a result. Not everybody gains, of course. Some people who grew up in Wendover can no longer afford to live here, due to the increase in housing prices and property taxes, but some manage to stay on. Linda and Henry Barlow, for example.

Linda and Henry's grandfather, Judge Barlow, ran a sort of hobby farm up there on what is now the McAllister place on Wendover Rise, raising a rare breed of cattle. The judge once owned a great many things. He had the farm here, and the brownstone on Commonwealth Avenue in Boston, and the family had a place in Palm Beach—once. Now Linda and Henry Barlow still live here in Wendover, but the family money is long gone. Linda, as I've mentioned, rents an apartment down in the Crossing. Her brother, Henry, spends his days and evenings at AA meetings, and nobody is sure how he manages to feed his sober self, but he does—feeds himself and drinks lofty mugs of coffee at the Coffee Bean, the overpriced coffee shop in the Crossing, where he shouts hearty hellos at everybody he knows.

I've avoided the Coffee Bean ever since it first opened and I walked in and, in all my innocence, ordered a "regular." The dirty, blond, dread-locked girl behind the counter just blinked at me.

"Um, a regular what?" she asked.

"A regular coffee," I snapped. "This is a coffee shop, isn't it?"

In Massachusetts, a "regulah" means a coffee with cream and two sugars. It wasn't until I was in college that I learned that this is a Massachusetts thing. I thought that's how everybody ordered coffee. If you wanted a coffee with just cream, it was "a regulah, no sugah." Now I'm learning that it's a generational thing as well. Younger people order coffees that are "grande," or "dry," or "Americano," or some other craziness, and they don't mind spending three or even four dollars on a coffee. I left my coffee sitting on the counter that first day when the girl told me the price, and now I stay away from the Coffee Bean unless I have a client who really wants a latte or whatever, and then I'm forced to resign myself to Henry Barlow's overly enthusiastic "Hildy! How ah ya?"

"Fine, thanks, Henry. And you?" I'd say.

"I'm good, Hildy. Wicked good. Haven't seen ya around."

"No?" is usually my response.

"Whatcha been up to?" he brays.

"Working," I say with a forced smile. "Some of us have to work for a living."

"Well, nice to see ya, Hildy. Take it easy," he always says, and then he starts to give me that solemn smile, but I usually dodge it by turning my attention elsewhere. Why not shout, "One day at a time"? Or "It's the first drink that gets you drunk"?

The AA slogans. The cult's incantations.

I would say, "You take it easy, too, Henry," but that's all Henry does. Take it easy. It was no wonder he lived in that old shack near the boatyard, while the McAllisters built playrooms and sunrooms and tended the gardens on his old family homestead.

I had clients coming from Boston one cool morning in early October and we had planned to meet at the Coffee Bean. The wife told me that she would need a coffee after the drive, and we made plans to meet there at nine. When I entered the shop at 8:50, the clients, a young couple named Sanderson, were there, and I saw that Henry had already engaged them in conversation.

"Yup, lived here all my life. Never seen any reason to live anywhere else. . . . Oh, there she is. Hildy, how ah ya?"

"I'm fine, thank you, Henry," I replied.

"These are yer customers, the . . . What'd you tell me yer names ah?"

I reached out my hand to Hillary Sanderson, whom I had talked to on the phone. "Hi, Hillary, I'm Hildy Good. And you must be Rob."

I saw that they already had their coffees, so I suggested they follow me to my office, where they could park their car and then ride around town with me. As I followed them through the door, Henry bellowed after me, "See ya, Hildy. Take it easy."

"You take it easy, too, Henry," I called back. "And stop working so hard." I could hear his booming laughter as I followed the Sandersons out to the street.

Whenever I have out-of-town clients, I always give them a little tour of the town of Wendover. We start at my office building, which was originally a house but is the only building on Wendover Green that's commercially zoned. My offices—the offices of Good Realty—are on the first floor. On the second floor are the offices of Dr. Peter Newbold, psychiatrist, and Katrina Frankel, LCSW.

Our building, like all the other houses on Wendover Green, is an honest rectangular clapboard structure, erected in the late 1700s. It was once the parsonage for the Congregational church next door. The white-steepled Congregational church no longer needs a parsonage, as the number of congregants has dwindled over the years, not only here in Wendover but also in nearby Essex, and now both churches are served by one minister, Jim Caldwell. The Reverend Caldwell and his family live in Essex, where he conducts a nine a.m. service every Sunday, and then he drives here to do an eleven a.m. one in Wendover.

You enter the offices of Good Realty through the front door on the porch. Years ago, my husband, Scott, set a couple of antique rocking chairs and an old painted table out on the porch to give our building a hint of domesticity, and they have remained there ever since, though I don't recall anyone ever sitting on the chairs. I always keep a planter of seasonal flowers on the table and hang baskets of colorful fuchsia plants —my mother always called them "bleeding hearts—from the porch overhang. An ivory-colored hand-painted wooden sign on our front door modestly announces our business. A smaller sign on the side of the building shows the clients of Paul and Katrina the way to enter through a side door, where they climb a set of steep stairs to the therapy offices.

The Sandersons were living in a condo in Swampscott and were looking for a starter home. I invited them into my office and handed them some printouts of listings in their price range, and then we walked out to where my Range Rover was parked. It was the kind of fall New England day that every broker dreams of. The air was crisp and slightly cool, but it was clear and sunny. Somebody was burning leaves. A breeze whirled across the green, whipping bright yellow leaves from the towering maples on its perimeter, and we all stood for a moment and gazed at what appeared to be flecks of gold floating in the air all around us.

We climbed into the car and drove around the green and down winding Pig Rock Lane to River Road, where I live. I bought my house on the river when Emily was a senior in high school. It was the first year my business really took off. I had the record number of sales in Essex County that year (*and* the two previous years). It's a great house, a historic landmark, once owned by Elliot Kimball, a famous shipbuilder, who built the house in the mid-1800s. It's supposed to be haunted, and though I love to play up that intrigue, I've never seen or heard any signs of ghosts. My daughters, however, refuse to stay in the house overnight without me because they insist they hear and see ghosts in the house.

In the past, I've had clients offer me figures for my house that are triple what I paid for it, but until recently I couldn't imagine ever selling it. Now I had started pointing it out as my own house to a few of my clients with deep pockets. I wasn't going to list it, but if they wanted to make me an offer, I would listen. I had bought the house in 2004—the height of the market out here—and had mortgaged it heavily. It had been such a good year that I did something I would advise my clients against—I bought a house that I would *someday* be able to afford, not one that I could actually afford at the time. Yes, I should have known better, but I guess it's the whole "cobbler's children have no shoes" scenario. My dad had owned the only grocery store in town, but there was never food in our fridge when I was growing up. Now I, the top broker in the region (well, perhaps not the top anymore, but certainly right up there), stood a chance of losing my house to the bank.

Well, it wasn't really a huge risk. I just needed a good year.

From River Road, I drove the Sandersons to

Beach Street, which leads to the Hart Preserve. The Hart Preserve is the former home of Robert Hart, an early-twentieth-century industrialist who built a small castle on a beautiful eleven-hundred-acre estate with hills rolling down to one of the sandiest and most pristine beaches in Massachusetts. Most of the beaches here on the North Shore are rocky, but not Hart's Beach. The Hart estate is now a state wildlife preserve. The castle is rented out for weddings and other functions. We admired the castle and the grounds and drove a little farther north to North Beach—the public beach with all the playground equipment.

I showed the Sandersons three or four properties, but to be honest, there wasn't much on the market in their price range. We drove down to the Crossing, and as we did, we passed the Dwights' house, with the Good Realty sign planted on its lawn.

"That looks like a cute place," said Hillary Sanderson.

"Oh, yes," I said. "That's a great house, and it's in your price range, too. I can't get us in there today, but the next time you come up, give me a little notice and we'll have a look."

We drove back along River Road, past all the protected estuary land, and then we turned up Wendover Rise. Wendover Rise is the name of the road that the McAllisters live on, but everybody calls the whole hilltop "the rise," though there are many small roads that run across it. I always drive my clients along the rise, though there is rarely anything for sale up there. It's just to show them the view. You can see the salt marshes and estuaries and, in the distance, the ocean. That day with the Sandersons was so mild that the ocean was dotted with the white sails and colorful spinnakers of diehards who wanted to get in one last day on the water before dry-docking their boats for the winter.

Eventually, we drove back down into Wendover Crossing—the rather charming village that is centered around our MBTA train station. The train from Boston stops here in Wendover four times a day. We're on the Rockport/Newburyport line. In the Crossing, we have what Scott used to call "the Stop & Shop of the Seven Gables," the Coffee Bean, of course, the Wendover Public Library, the Hickory Stick Toy Shop, the post office, and a little pizza/ sandwich place called Big Joe's. Hillary oohed and aahed at the quaintness of it all. I knew she was hooked. You can always tell. She would live in Wendover . . . or die. I would have to talk to Cassie and Patch about their house. If they could only clean it up a little.

When we arrived back at my office, we were just starting up the front steps when Rebecca McAllister appeared from the side porch. It can be awkward sometimes, encountering my friends and clients leaving the therapist's office upstairs, but honestly, it's only really awkward the first time. There are very few people in this town whom I haven't met going in or coming out of those side doors. Mostly, it's parents bringing their kids to be "evaluated" by Katrina Frankel, who specializes in learning and developmental disorders. My office faces the side porch, and I have to admit, it boggles the mind that so many children in our town might have these disorders. My former sales associate Lucy and I used to joke that there must be something in the water, but I'm told it's everywhere. Teachers send kids off for diagnoses if they sit wrong in their chairs, I'm told.

Scott is a history buff, and he researched the old parsonage when we bought it. Apparently, the early ministers used it as an entrance for those seeking counsel from the clergy, so it's rather fitting that it serves a similar purpose these hundreds of years later.

I had seen Rebecca leaving Peter's office before, always walking slowly, always with the dark glasses. The afternoon with the Sandersons, however, she came around the corner of the porch quite abruptly and actually bumped into Hillary as I unlocked the front door to my office.

"Oh my God!" Rebecca exclaimed, breathless and then laughing good-naturedly. "I'm SO sorry."

"No, don't be. I'm fine," said Hillary.

"How are you, Hildy?" asked Rebecca. She was looking so much better. She had looked quite depressed those few times I'd seen her leaving Peter's office in the early summer. I'd never quite gotten over that thing she did with the mare and foal that morning. And then after the party and the incident at the beach with Cassie and Jake, I worried that we might be losing the McAllisters. If the wife decides she doesn't like a place, nobody stays.

"I'm great," I said. "Rebecca, meet Hillary and Rob Sanderson. They're thinking of moving to the area." I turned to Hillary. "Rebecca and her family just moved here recently themselves," I said.

"We love it," Rebecca said before they had a chance to ask. "So nice to meet you," she added, and then, I swear, she literally skipped down the porch steps. It was that kind of day; you don't get many like those in New England. I was sure the Sandersons would be back the following weekend. I gave them a folder with all the listings of the houses I had shown them.

"What about that cute place on the hill going down to the town?" asked Hillary.

"Yes," I said, "the Dwight place. It's a nice house. I promise to show it to you the next time you come up."

We made an appointment for the following Saturday.

• • •

I called Cassie Dwight on Monday morning. "I think I have the perfect buyers for your house," I said.

"Really?" Cassie said. "Hildy, that's so great. We have a deadline to sign Jake up for that school in Newton."

"I need to come over and talk to you about it," I said. "When would be a good time?"

"Could you come this morning? Jake has school."

When I pulled into her driveway half an hour later, Cassie was planting yellow chrysanthemums around her front steps.

"Lovely, Cassie," I said. She was beaming.

"Let's go inside and talk about what needs to be done before the showing," I said. "They'd like to come this Saturday. And even if these people aren't interested, we could do an open house the following Wednesday."

The house was in the same state as usual, only this time there was oatmeal smeared all over the kitchen table. Cassie grabbed a roll of paper towels and started wiping it up, all the while describing the great program at the Newton school.

"He would be there all day, with one-on-one therapy for most of the time. It's a program specifically developed for kids with his types of delays. Where we have him now, he's thrown in with kids with every disability under the sun. I mean, how is that going to help him?"

"Okay, Cassie, look. We've got to do some work on your house by the weekend."

"I know. Patch and I'll clean—"

"No, I mean real work. I've been thinking about this. I think we should hire one of Frank Getchell's crews to come in here, starting tomorrow, and do some real work. Did Patch ever find out what's under that living room carpet?"

"Yes, it's nice hardwood, he was right. But we can pull the carpet up ourselves."

"It's really a big job, Cassie. There's the carpet, the padding beneath, the tacking strips. Frankie could have three guys do it in a couple hours. It would take you and Patch days . . . and what would you do with Jake while you were doing this? He could step on the tacks."

"We can't afford to pay Frankie Getchell's overpriced crew," snapped Cassie. "Do you know how much Jake's different therapies cost? And our insurance doesn't pay the half of it. Both our parents are retired. We can't ask them for any more money."

"I know. Here's what I think we should do. I'll pay Frankie myself. Then, once the house sells, you can pay me back. I don't think it'll be much. They'll come in, rip out the carpet, patch up some of the walls. And they'll need to paint—I think . . . everything. Frankie will get three or four guys in here and they'll do in a few days what would take you and Patch weeks. The extra money you'll make on the sale will more than pay for Frank's guys."

Cassie looked down at her hands, which were resting on the grimy table. "Really, Hildy? You could do that?"

"Of course," I said. "I want to sell this house as much as you do. You have no idea how slow business is now. You're giving me something to do," I said. "A project."

I hadn't admitted to anyone else that particular truth—that my business was slow. Most people thought I was still the top-selling agency in the area, but since the corporate real-estate firms, like Sotheby's and Coldwell Banker, had moved into the area, it had become difficult for me to compete. I still managed to get some of the best listings, because I'd known the owners in this area all my life, but when buyers came to town from New York or Boston, they usually went to Sotheby's, because they imagined a certain prestige, I suppose. When these new out-of-town owners decided to resell, which they often did within a few short years, having not fully explored the reality of our quiet community, our short summers and long winters, the sometimes prolonged commute and unreliable train service to Boston, they usually listed with the broker who had sold them the place. In recent years, this broker had often been Wendy Heatherton, who'd gotten her start in real estate working for me.

Wendy had just moved here from New Jersey when her husband divorced her. I hired her, first as a receptionist, then later, after she was licensed, as an associate broker. I taught her everything I knew about the business. She paid me back by stealing my best listings and taking them with her to Sotheby's while I was at Hazelden. She'd had a banner year, while I'd had one of my slowest since I opened my own company.

I tried calling Frank Getchell when I returned to my office, but he wasn't there. He has no answering machine. He just figures if you need him that badly, you'll go out and find him. Which I did, quite by happenstance, that afternoon, when I was filling up my car at the Mobil station just outside the Crossing. Frankie pulled up to the diesel tank behind me with his bright orange pickup, and when he got out and saw me, he shouted, "Hildy. How ah ya?"

Frankie is one of the last descendants of the oldest family in Wendover. It's said that Wendover's first resident was Amos Getchell, who had some kind of falling-out with the settlement down in Salem and had paddled or sailed up here and lived for several years among the local Anawam Indians. He spent his first winter living in a massive English ale barrel down in what is now known as Getchell's Cove. He hooked up with an Anawam girl, and now all the Getchells have some Native American blood in them, because it was several generations before the family finally started integrating with the colonists who had begun settling along the waterways that led inland from the coast.

I've known Frankie Getchell all my life. He's three years older than I am. He still lives in the house he grew up in—the dark old saltbox up on the rise. It's an eyesore and many have complained about the condition in which he keeps his place. There have even been zoning meetings devoted entirely to Frankie, much to his pleasure.

Frankie's house is falling apart, paint is peeling from the decaying clapboards, and the roof sags. Strewn about his lawn are old pieces of plumbing (including about half a dozen toilets), railroad ties, pieces of architecture—lintels, fireplace mantels, stone slabs, wooden beams, balusters—and even a few monstrous oil tanks that he's salvaged over the years. Apart from his salvage/construction business, Frankie is also the chief of our town's volunteer fire crew, and he rescues some old fixtures if a house burns and nobody wants them. If you ask him, as I have on occasion, why he has a charred wooden beam lying, still smoldering, on his front lawn, he's genuinely perplexed.

"It's perfectly good" is his reply. "Why would you wanna throw away a perfectly good thing like that?"

It's all "perfectly good," and it's all for sale, all except for the house and property. His weedy front lawn hosts this perennial yard sale, while off to the side, he keeps his fleet of five of the oldest, ricketiest pickup trucks you'll find within a hundred-mile radius. We have no municipal garbage service here in Wendover, so you can either haul your own garbage to the dump or hire Frankie Getchell to come get it. I'd say 80 percent of Wendover's 2,800 residents have contracted with Frankie to have his crew haul their garbage for fifty dollars a month, which adds up quite nicely—you do the math. In the winter, during snowstorms, his guys stay up all night drinking and plowing out Frankie's customers—again, most of the people in Wendover. Frank also offers property management and caretaking, as he had done for the Leightons' pony farm, as well as landscaping and carpentry services. Everyone in Wendover refers to him as the "fix-it man." You can call on him and his crew to do just about anything that needs to be done in and around a house. His business thrives, but he appears to put not a penny of his earnings back into his own home or vehicles. His trucks regularly break down on the side of the road.

When I drive clients by Frankie's property,

some ask about the "character" who lives in "that place." I'm sure they imagine some poor, old, uneducated hermit. No, Frankie Getchell is whip-smart and easily one of the richest men in Wendover, or he was, until the wonderful McAllisters moved to town.

Frankie's property extends far behind his house; actually, it goes all the way down the rise to the estuary. He has 120 prime acres there, plus another twelve priceless acres that border my property along the river. The property has always belonged to his family. On the far side of his riverfront property are about fifty acres of wet-land that can never be developed and that have been deeded over to the Wendover Land Trust. Sharon Rice and the Land Trust officials have been trying for years to get him to at least deed them the rights to his higher (thus buildable) riverfront land after his death.

"That way, nobody will ever develop it," Sharon has said, pleading with him. "It'll be protected in perpetuity, just as it is today."

"Now, why would I care what people decide to do with that land after I'm dead?" he always shoots back.

Frankie pays very little tax on the property because he has most of it registered as farmland. The acreage behind his house has been a Christmas tree farm for as long as I can remember. Plus, apparently he has some kind of tax protection due to his Native American ancestry. But it was mostly the clutter on his lawn that caused some of his neighbors to bring a complaint about him before the zoning board a few years ago. Wendover Rise is residentially zoned.

Frank Getchell clearly operates a business—in the summer months, a very ugly, noisy, and smelly business. Often the crews finish garbage collection too late to go to the dump, so sometimes they leave the stinking garbage in the trucks for entire weekends. In the winter, there are actual traffic jams up there during the weeks before Christmas, because Frankie's farm is a "cut your own tree" place, and people come from far and wide to traipse through the snow and choose a tree and cut it down themselves.

Some neighbors wanted him to "cease and desist."

It's funny in a town like this, the way some newcomers want to believe they're tight with the locals—the real townies. Alan Harrison, a big-time Boston litigation lawyer who has a weekend place up here, is one of those, and he offered his services pro bono to Frankie, believing, as many do, that Frankie just barely manages to scrape by. And most of the town showed up at the zoning meeting to offer their support to good old Frankie Getchell, poor old persecuted Frank. They didn't really need to. Frankie was within his rights. He was grandfathered in, having run his business long before the zoning laws were written up.

Normally, I would have just waved back to Frankie but this time I needed to talk with him about Cassie's place, so after I finished pumping my gas, I walked over to where he was leaning against his rusty old truck. The old Ford was idling and music was blaring from his radio. Frankie grinned at me as I approached. I didn't care for the way he continued grinning at me as he filled his tank. We have a complicated little history, Frankie and me, a history that he finds amusing and I find, in parts, humiliating, which amuses him even more.

"Kinks, Hil," he said.

"What?"

"On the radio." He nodded at the cab of his truck. "The Kinks. Ya ever listen to this station, Hildy? They play all the oldies. All the good ones."

"Not really. Hey, I called you this morning, Frank."

"Yeah? What's up?"

"I'm trying to sell Patch and Cassie Dwight's house—Ralph Dwight's kid, Patch?"

"Yeah, I know Patch."

"Well, the place needs some work. And they have a boy with . . . problems . . . you know."

"Yeah, I know. He's retarded. See him all the time down the market with Patch."

"Yes, little Jake has very serious problems and

they need to move to Newton so he can go to a special school. Anyway, I might have a buyer, but they want to see the place this weekend. It's a wreck. It's a small house, but it needs some touch-up work on the drywall. The whole interior needs to be painted. . . ."

"Well, I got all my guys workin' on a job down Manchester this week, Hil. We're clearin' some land for a new house. It's a big job, got all my guys on it."

"*All* your guys?"

Frank Getchell's "crews" are a combination of local barflys, a smattering of undocumented Mexicans, the occasional ex-con, and, each summer, a sizable infantry of high-school and college boys who consider it a manly rite of passage to be on one of Getchell's crews. They drive, tanned and shirtless, around town in trucks, hauling trailers that rattle with lawn mowers, weed whackers, and other landscaping equipment. Or they stand, again, shirtless, gleaming with sweat, on a ladder, painting the exterior of a house and shouting out whenever a girl they know walks or drives past. At lunchtime, all the beat-up Getchell trucks can be found at the North Beach parking lot, where the guys eat their lunch on the boulders. My daughters and their friends always tried to be in bikinis at noon on North Beach when they weren't working on weekdays. But now it was fall and these boys had gone back to school.

Frankie shrugged and replaced the gas nozzle. When he looked at the price on the tank, he whistled. "Look at that, Hildy. Almost ninety bucks to fill that sonuvabitch."

"Hey, that reminds me. Somebody asked me a while back if you'd be interested in selling your riverfront lot. The one next to me. I've tried to call you a few times about this over the summer, but . . . no message machine."

Frankie squinted up at the sun and then looked at me. "Who wants it? A developer?"

"No. He's a businessman. From Boston."

"What does he want it for? Listen, the Who. Now, that's a wicked good song, Hil." Frank reached inside and turned up the volume on his radio.

"What do you think he wants it for, Frank?" I shouted over the music. "He wants to put a house on it. That acreage is really valuable. I could come up with a sale price for you that would—"

"Nah. I need it. I like to fish there." Music was blaring from the cab of his truck and Frankie started crooning along with the tune while screwing his gas cap in place.

"Oh, Frank, I never liked this song, and you're just making it worse with your awful caterwauling," I said, covering my ears and wincing. The man had no sense at all. His property was worth several million dollars and he wanted to keep it so he could fish. My commission on a sale like that would sort out my mortgage situation quite nicely.

Frank laughed and bellowed over the noisy radio, "You don't like my singin', Hil?"

"You've got some rusty-sounding chimes there, Frank; only your friends will tell you the truth. You never could carry a tune, now that I think of it." This made Frank laugh even more. He had his hands in the pockets of his jeans and was gazing off across the road, his shoulders shaking merrily.

"C'mon, Frank, don't you even want me to ask him how much he'd be willing to pay?"

Frank leaned into his window and lowered the volume of the music, saying, "Well, sure, ask him. I wouldn't mind knowin' what he'd be willin' to pay."

"Oh, forget it. I'm not gonna waste his time. You're sure you don't know anybody who wants to make a few extra bucks this week?"

"How soon do they need it done?"

"I'm planning to show it on Saturday."

"Did I see you out swimmin' last night, Hildy?" Frank asked. He glanced at me quickly, then down at the ground, but he had that insipid grin going again.

"What? Swimming last night? No. I mean . . . I suppose . . . you might have. Sometimes I go for a little dip. If it's a nice night. Yes, now that I think of it, I did wander down for a little swim. . . ."

"Yeah, I thought I saw you. I was out there, too. In my waydahs. Night fishin'. I thought I saw you. Kind of chilly last night for swimmin'."

"The water's warmest this time of year. You know that," I said.

Out in his waders? At night?

The previous evening was a little foggy in my mind, but now, unfortunately, I recalled the way I had floated out to the boathouse for a second bottle and then, later on, down to the waterfront. Naked as a jaybird, humming and cackling aloud as my girls yipped and yiked and cavorted at my feet.

I glared at Frank. *Out in his waders.*

"It's the gettin' out that kills ya, though." Frank chuckled, and I remembered squealing in joyous astonishment after my icy plunge and then the way I had staggered, cackling and cursing, out of the frosty surf, the girls underfoot, tripping me and snapping at each other.

Frank was leaning against the door of his truck and croaking along with the idiotic tune like an old toad while I was forced to wonder if he had observed my flight back to my house from the river, laughing madly, my pendulous breasts flapping, my fat ass swaying this way and that, and my hair wrapped around my face like seaweed. I had woken up that morning with leaves between my toes and sand in my hair and had wondered . . .

Well, now I knew.

I turned to my car and snapped, "I'll have to

get on the phone, figure out who else I can get."

"Nah, Hildy, wait. I'll drive up there now. See what needs to be done."

"Really, you'd do that, Frank?" I asked, softening a little. I turned to face him, even though I knew my cheeks were scarlet. "The Dwights really need the help."

"I gotta guy down in Beverly I can get to do jobs like this sometimes. Maybe him an' another guy . . ."

"That would be so great, Frank. Thanks."

"No problem, Hil."

I turned and heard him singing the last words of the song. Frankie was in rare form indeed. I had no idea what had gotten him so worked up.

Six

I would later learn, from Rebecca herself, that the McAllisters hadn't been living up on Wendover Rise a month before Rebecca realized that she had made, possibly, the worst mistake of her life. She had thought that the move to the country would lessen all the anxiety she had experienced while living in Boston. She had always felt intensely competitive, yet not quite up to par, with the other wives at Brian's firm, many of whom had interesting careers of their own. And the private-school admissions scene in Boston had almost done her in, she later told me. She thought that if she and the kids could live in the country, the way she had lived as a child, they would all be more content. She understood that she would see less of Brian, but wouldn't it be better for him to see her more relaxed and happy when he came home after a few days in the city, rather than returning every night to a fretful wife? Well, that had been her reasoning behind the move, but once she found herself up on the rise, alone with the kids and the unsmiling Polish nanny, Magda, she felt abandoned. That's the word she used when she described the situation to me. Brian had "abandoned" her in Wendover.

They had chosen to move to town in March, while school was still in session, so that the boys could make friends in their new schools. By May, she was talking to Brian about reenrolling the boys in their former schools in Boston for the fall. And by the time she had the run-in with Cassie on the beach, she was ready to start packing. Brian was exasperated with this change of plans. He was growing weary of Rebecca's impulsive disposition and was now worried about the effect that her chronic dissatisfaction might have on their boys. Brian insisted that she make an appointment to see Peter Newbold—which she did. I remember seeing her leaving his office a few times in the early summer. My office has a window out to the side porch, where Peter's patients come and go, and I had seen Rebecca wander out, wearing big dark sunglasses, looking very thin. Brian made a deal with Rebecca that they stay for the summer and not make any plans for the fall. After all, the boys loved their new school and their big rambling country house. Brian urged Rebecca to sign them up for sailing lessons and the YMCA camp, which she did.

Then he bought her Hat Trick.

Hat Trick was a young, solid black Hanoverian gelding, imported from Germany by Trevor Brown, an Olympic silver medalist and also Rebecca's former trainer. Rebecca wasn't the type to tell you this about herself, but my understanding is that in her late teens she had been short-listed for the U.S. Equestrian Team. Rebecca and Trevor had stayed in touch after she married Brian, and he often sent her photographs of promising young horses, with Brian's deep pockets in his mind.

Brian had bought his parents a house in Palm Beach years before, and he and Rebecca and the kids often visited them there during the winter months. Sometimes, Rebecca and Brian attended horse shows while in Palm Beach, and the winter before moving to Wendover, they saw Trevor show Hat Trick at the Winter Equestrian Festival —an annual show-jumping event that draws competitors from all over North America to vie for the large cash prizes. Hat Trick was only five years old and was being shown in a low-jumper class, due to his immaturity and lack of experience, but he soared over the fences like a gazelle.

Rebecca knew that the horse had the makings of a great jumper. Indeed, his price tag—in the hundreds of thousands, according to Linda Barlow—indicated that the young horse had Olympic potential. He was far more horse than Rebecca needed, but she swooned over him, and hockey-obsessed Brian was pleased with his name, so he had Trevor ship the horse up to Wendover to surprise Rebecca on her birthday, in April. Later, Rebecca would tell me it was Hat Trick who helped her the most with her transition to Wendover. She had a project.

Mamie Lang is a longtime member of the Westfield Hunt Club, and she told me that it was assumed by most of the area's riders that Rebecca would join the club so that she could use the facilities there. Westfield has two indoor arenas, several full-time grooms, and some very good trainers, but Rebecca chose to keep young "Tricky" at home with Betty and her older jumper, Serpico. She improved the riding ring that was already on the property and had a series of jumps built. She schooled the horse herself, every day. During the summer months, Westfield Hunt Club has a weekly series of nonrated "schooling shows."

Westfield has a handful of C-rated shows in the early summer and then a well-known AA show in August, which, like the Winter Equestrian Festival show in Palm Beach, brings top riders from around the country to compete in the Grand Prix jump-off, which offers a cash prize of $100,000 to the winner. But the schooling shows are meant for local riders to gain show experience. Sometimes, the trainers at Westfield and nearby barns will bring talented young show prospects to the schooling shows, just to give them exposure to the environment at horse shows, which can often be quite overwhelming to young horses. This is what Rebecca did with Hat Trick many times over the summer.

Mamie called me the first time she saw Rebecca show Hat Trick at Westfield.

"That horse is absolutely stunning, Hildy," she said. "All the trainers' jaws dropped when she unloaded him from her trailer. And even though it was a nonrated show, she and Linda Barlow had his mane and tail braided and he was perfectly groomed. Her tack and boots were polished to a shine. I overheard one of the trainers telling some of his students that that's the way a horse should look whenever he's shown, whether the show is rated or not."

Linda Barlow would later tell me that Rebecca was very particular about horse keeping. The barn was immaculate at all times, the saddles and bridles polished after each and every ride. And Rebecca showed Linda how to braid a horse's mane, not in the loose, sloppy braids held together with rubber bands that we had all made when braiding our ponies' manes as kids, but into tiny, tight, perfectly symmetrical plaits that followed the beautiful crest of her horse's neck like a scalloped piece of decorative trim on a sculpture carved out of onyx. Rebecca taught Linda to use an old-fashioned needle and yarn when braiding, rather than the rubber bands. I could imagine that they made quite an impression at that first schooling show.

Mamie reported to me the degree to which the spirited horse had acted up before entering the show ring.

"He stood straight up, Hildy. He reared up and then he sort of launched himself into the air like those Lipizzaners that you see in the circus. And Rebecca rode him like a pro. She was laughing at his antics and just kept urging him forward. Then she cantered him into the ring and they did a clear round. In the high jumpers. The horse isn't even six yet. And she's got such style, that Rebecca. She jumped clear, but she deliberately jumped the last jump from the wrong direction so that she would be scratched for going off-course."

"Why?" I asked.

"It was the right thing to do. Her horse so far outclassed the others in the show. And some people who go to these shows have never earned a blue ribbon in their class. It really means a lot to them. Rebecca scratched and a seventeen-year-old got the blue ribbon. Then Rebecca loaded that black vision into her trailer and hauled him home herself."

As the summer passed, and Rebecca attended more shows, the local horse people grew accustomed to her. According to Mamie, other people started braiding their horses' manes and tails for the shows, and arrived wearing formal show attire, like Rebecca.

"She's wonderfully old-fashioned when it comes to horses," Mamie told me. "She's really setting an example for the younger people about how horses should be turned out all the time. She's reminding everybody what horsemanship is really about."

Mamie was entranced with Rebecca and told me that she wanted me to arrange a dinner for the three of us. I promised I would, but I also gave her Rebecca's number. I figured they might have a better time, just the two of them, over a bottle of wine, without me slurping my Diet Coke between them. But they never did hook up, Mamie and Rebecca. Mamie called her twice to invite her to dinner and twice Rebecca declined politely. Mamie felt snubbed, and that was the end of that.

I did get to see Rebecca show Hat Trick once. It was at Westfield's big August AA show. Rebecca had entered Hat Trick in the Grand Prix—the most difficult and challenging course, which had the $100,000 purse. Mamie usually hosts a luncheon under a tent at the show, right next to the Grand Prix ring. It's a benefit luncheon. The proceeds go to a shelter for battered women in Salem. I always buy a table and invite clients. It's a great place to take people who are looking to buy a home in the area. The hunt club grounds are meticulously groomed and there are beautiful horses and beautiful people everywhere. One of my clients, who was seated at my table, kept exclaiming with delight that she felt like she was in a Ralph Lauren ad. This made me smile. The house she and her husband were interested in looked like it could be in a Ralph Lauren ad, too, and it could be theirs for just $1.5 million.

Brian McAllister had bought a table, and a bunch of their friends from Boston had come out to watch Rebecca ride. They were a boisterous group—clearly they had started with the champagne quite early—and Brian had introduced me around when I first arrived. Most of their "friends" turned out to be Brian's business associates. There were a few men whom he introduced as his partners, each with what appeared to me to be silly, pretty wives who had slightly overdressed for the event. Two were wearing hats, as if they were at Royal Ascot or something. This is New England. Most people wear simple summer dresses to the Westfield Benefit Luncheon. My ex-husband, Scott, told me once that I'm prejudiced against younger, prettier women. I always think they're "silly" or "ridiculous," he used to say.

He was wrong. That's not how I view all younger pretty women.

I always took Rebecca seriously, for example.

Mamie arranged for me to have a table right next to the ring, and my clients and I dined on poached salmon and fresh green beans, spring potatoes, and fresh strawberries and cream. There was a full bar. Champagne was being poured all around me. I kept my eyes on the show arena. When the Grand Prix began, Mamie came and pulled up two chairs beside me. She was with Allen Mansfield, the head trainer at Westfield. It was great having them next to me, as they told me who each rider was, which one had qualified for the Olympics, and which horses were seasoned pros and which were exciting young prospects.

Most of the riders in the Grand Prix were professionals who ran lucrative show barns nearby or in other areas of the country. Some of their horses were famous in the show world. So when Mamie saw Rebecca waiting in the warm-up area, she became excited (I had seen her consume the better part of a bottle of champagne just since sitting down) and she said loudly, "THERE SHE IS HERSELF, AL."

Allen just grunted and shook his head in disgust.

"ALLEN THINKS HER HORSE IS TOO GREEN FOR THIS EVENT," Mamie shouted at me, though I was sitting right beside her.

"Shhhhh," I hissed. "Brian and all their friends are right at the next table."

"Oops." Mamie giggled.

"I know he's too green," Allen grumbled. "There's no reason to overface a young horse like this."

"They look stunning," I said.

Mamie was laughing at Allen. "Allen's just bitter that he's not her trainer," she whispered. "I think her horse is ready for the Grand Prix. I've been watching them show all summer. And Rebecca promised she'd give the prize money to the shelter if she wins."

"You haven't seen her in a jump-off with this caliber of competition," Allen said. "This can be way too much for such a young horse."

The Grand Prix has two stages. All the entrants ride a course of challenging jumps, several of which are over five feet high. Many are "oxers"— spread jumps that are high and wide. There are jumps over large shrubs, "in and outs," where the horse has to take one or two short strides between two difficult fences, and "triples," a line of three fences with just a few strides in between. If a horse has a clear round, without knocking down a pole or refusing a jump, the horse and rider proceed to the jump-off.

The jump-off is a different course set over the same series of jumps. In this round, however, the fastest horse with a clear round wins. This is the exciting part of the Grand Prix. Riders must sometimes cut corners to shave seconds off their time. This can throw the horse's stride off and presents far more of a challenge. The horse must trust the rider completely in a jump-off. The horse will take a jump, land, and then be steered into a quick rollback and faced, suddenly, with a jump it didn't expect. The best horse and rider team is one in which the horse, after many tough courses with the rider, firmly believes *If she thinks I can do it, I can do it.* It can sometimes take years to build this kind of confidence in a naturally tentative or more timid horse. Braver and highly athletic animals can face such a round at a younger age. Rebecca clearly believed that Hat Trick was up to the task.

Allen, who had watched her show him all summer, was firmly convinced that he wasn't.

As the class began, Mamie and Allen were watching Rosemary Hines, an internationally famous American rider, on her horse, Tango. I was watching Rebecca on Hat Trick, near the entrance gate. Hat Trick was excited. He was popping his legs up in front, doing little half rears, but Rebecca just leaned forward each time he went up, then turned him in little circles. I saw Rebecca pat the horse's neck once he had settled a bit, and then I saw her look up and wave to somebody on the far side of the arena. I had to squint to see who it was. It was a man. He was making his way closer to the entrance gate and I saw that Rebecca was calling something out to him. I thought that it might be a trainer she had worked with in the past, but then, when he got closer to the gate, I saw that it was Peter Newbold.

What was Peter Newbold doing at the Westfield Horse Show?

I looked over at Brian's table and saw that they were all intent on watching Rebecca's competitor. When Tango knocked down a rail, many of them cheered, and Mamie hushed them indignantly. Rosemary Hines cleared the last jump, and the crowd in the bleachers and the spectators under the tent cheered. It had been a good round, from what I had seen, except for the knocked rail.

Now it was Rebecca's turn, and when she trotted Hat Trick into the ring, Brian's table let loose with whoops and cheers, and Mamie again asked them to lower their voices.

"You could spook Rebecca's horse," she hissed at them. "Jesus," she whispered to me, "where do these people come from?"

I watched Rebecca canter Hat Trick in a large circle in the far end of the arena. She was waiting for the starting horn.

"Look," Mamie said, "she's making him circle next to that scary jump with the Union Savings Bank sign on it, so he can get a good look at it. Rosemary's horse spooked at that jump."

Allen just grumbled something that neither of us could understand, which made Mamie and me chuckle. Then the starting horn blew. Rebecca tipped her head politely at the judges and then cantered Hat Trick toward the first jump.

I won't bore you with the jump-by-jump details, I'll just sum up her ride by saying that Rebecca and Hat Trick made it look easy. They approached each jump with the correct stride and the horse soared over every obstacle with grace and style. Hat Trick appeared to prefer a slower pace than the course called for, and each time Rebecca spurred him on, he gave a little buck—kicking his hind legs out to the side—and then charged forward. When they cleared the last jump, the group at Brian's table leaped to their feet and cheered. Mamie was cheering, too, and she elbowed Allen playfully. Hat Trick, startled by the sound of the cheering crowd, performed a short series of bucks as Rebecca cantered him in a large circle. Rebecca was laughing at the horse's high spirits and patting his neck. Then she rode him out of the ring.

"It looks like he has plenty of energy left for the jump-off," I said to Allen.

"He doesn't like speed, but she's a great rider. We'll see," Allen said quietly.

Linda Barlow was waiting for Rebecca and Hat Trick outside the gate. I looked over to where Peter Newbold had been standing, but he was gone. Maybe he had just stopped by the show with Elise and they were seated in the stands someplace. Maybe he'd come to watch Rebecca ride. Perhaps part of her therapy involved getting back into the competition world and he'd come to check on her. I looked over at Brian's table and everybody was high-fiving him and swilling champagne.

Four horses, including Hat Trick, had qualified for the jump-off. The first horse, Dante, ridden by Michael Wallace, got a clear round and a very fast time—forty-nine seconds over the seven jumps. The next rider, Canadian Linda Randolph, knocked a rail and came in with a time of 54.3. Linda was followed by Leslie Carter on her famous stallion Romulus, who got a clear round but came in at 51.5 seconds. So the horse to beat, for Rebecca, was Dante.

"What do you think, Allen?" I asked as Hat Trick trotted into the arena.

"I think if she's smart, she'll try to get a clear round, even if it means coming in too slow. Why destroy the horse's confidence by taking risks with him?"

The starting horn sounded and Rebecca cantered toward the first jump. The time doesn't start until the horse has cleared the first jump, so she took her approach nice and slow. After landing, however, she spurred him into a fast gallop around a turn to the second jump. The next jump—a high vertical one—preceded a very sharp turn back to another vertical. It was this second vertical that had caused problems for the horse that had knocked down a rail. It had looked quite difficult for all the horses. The turn threw the horses off balance and then their stride was off and they launched themselves too close to the second jump. That's why Linda Randolph's horse had knocked the rail with his hind feet. Allen had told me that the riders had all taken the turn too quickly. When Rebecca approached the first vertical, Allen was shaking his head and mumbling, "Too fast. Too fast." Hat Trick tucked his knees in front of his chest, and when he was in the middle of the jump, his body forming an elegant bascule many inches above the top rail, Rebecca shifted her weight and turned the horse in midair. The other horses hadn't been able to start their turn until a couple of strides after the fence. When Hat Trick landed, he didn't need to recover his balance by swapping his lead; he was already on the right lead, perfectly balanced and heading toward the second jump, which he cleared with ease. To approach the next jump, the previous riders had galloped around a large hedge fence and then had a straight approach to the "in and out." Rebecca decided to cut in front of the hedge. She whipped Hat Trick's head around right after the previous fence, and there was the first of the two "in and out" obstacles, only three strides away.

"OH MY GOD," cried Mamie.

"Crazy bitch," said Allen.

I could hardly stand to watch, but I did. Hat Trick looked like he was going to refuse. His body shortened, his head started to turn, and Rebecca raised her riding crop and gave him a smart whack on his flank, just behind her leg, while at the same time making an almost animal-sounding roar. Hat Trick abandoned any ideas of not jumping then, and though he chipped in a little close to the first jump, he cleared it, but then landed awkwardly for the second. Rebecca sat deep in the saddle, spurred him on two strides, and then it appeared that tiny Rebecca lifted the massive horse over the second jump, her hands almost touching his ears, her body arched over the curve of his neck. They landed and the jump was untouched. The crowd exploded in cheers. She rode the last fences with ease and ended with a final time of 47.3 seconds. Rebecca had won the Grand Prix.

The people at Brian's table were all on their feet, again with the high-fiving and pumping their fists in the air. Brian was wiping a tear from his eye. It had been an amazing performance. I smiled at Mamie and Allen, who both had rather grim expressions.

"That woman's going to get herself, or somebody else, killed someday," said Allen.

"I'm afraid you may be right," said Mamie.

"What? You should be thrilled, Mamie," I said. "All that money for the shelter."

"I am," she said. "I just feel a little sick watching somebody take a risk like that with a horse."

"But he's fine," I said. I really don't know as much about show jumping as they do. To me, and, it appeared, the rest of the crowd, it had been a stunning display of courage and athleticism shown by both horse and rider.

Allen and Mamie just shook their heads and I heard Allen cursing again. Then Mamie went over to congratulate Brian.

At the end, the top three horses galloped a victory lap around the arena, after they were handed their medals. That's when I saw Peter Newbold again. He was standing at the bottom of the bleachers, not too far from our tent. Rebecca was grinning at him as she galloped past. I saw her stand in her stirrups and wave in his direction, and I saw him gaze up at her. He was shielding his eyes with his hands. It was hard to see her, looking up the way he was—up into the blinding sunlight of that August afternoon.

Seven

I had my first little suspicion about Rebecca and Peter not long after the Westfield show, actually the same week that Frank's guys were working on the Dwight house. It was a Wednesday night and I had a closing the next morning. A big closing. A new-construction home in Gloucester with water views that sold for just under a million. This time the purchasers were mine and it was Wendy's listing. It was a rainy evening and I was going through all the paperwork for the next morning. I was also finishing off a nice bottle of Pinot Noir that I had grabbed from the MG when I arrived home. I try to make it a point to not drink the whole bottle, but if I don't finish it, I have to go back and lock the partially drunk bottle in the trunk of the MG. What if one of my daughters stopped in unannounced and saw a half-consumed bottle of wine in my cupboard? If I finish it, I can always hide it under some garbage in the kitchen. So that night, because it was pouring rain, I decided to finish off the bottle. It was just the thing. So warming. Plus, I was celebrating. I was going to be handed a big fat check the next morning.

As I put the papers into a folder, I realized that the buyer's home insurance document was missing. The buyers were not planning to attend the closing and so they'd had the document Fed-Exed to me. It was on my desk. *I need a new assistant,* I thought as I dripped the last drops of wine onto my tongue. My friend Alice's daughter Kendall was working for me while she took a gap year from college. I'd just been too busy to interview and hire somebody with more (any) skills. Now I was stuck. There would be no time to stop at the office in the morning; the bank was in Beverly, in the opposite direction of the green, and there would be traffic all the way.

When I began having my occasional glass of wine, a few months after my return from Hazelden, I swore to myself that I would never call anyone, e-mail anyone, or drive after having as little as one drop of alcohol in my system. And I had stuck to my guns on this. But that night before the closing, I realized that I was a little buzzed, yes, but far from intoxicated. It would take me ten minutes to drive to the office—fifteen minutes tops, because of the rain. I would just drive extra slow.

I pulled my raincoat over my head and ran out to the car. Soon I was driving up winding Pig Rock Lane. Honestly, I could drive the route to my office with my eyes closed. And I was far from drunk. There had been times—many times, actually—when I had driven home with one eye closed so that I could see one road instead of two. That was before rehab, of course. But now, I was driving slowly and actually quite enjoying the spooky autumn evening—the leaves whirling about in my headlights like crazed bats, the windshield wipers whipping back and forth, back and forth. There was nobody out on that rainy night but me. How lovely it was to have the whole road to oneself, to cruise along on that road, that wet black ribbon of a road that wound its way through my sleepy town.

When I pulled into the parking lot behind my office, I was surprised to see Peter's lights on upstairs. He wasn't usually up there on Wednesdays. His Volvo was parked there in the lot, and next to it was another car. It was a silver Land Cruiser. I parked next to Peter's car, stepped carefully out of my car, and jogged around the house to the front steps of the porch. I walked along the porch to the side entrance, which is closer to my office. There, I fumbled with my keys a little. I have too many keys; it's always a problem. So I fumbled with them and then I dropped them, right into the azalea bushes that are planted around the porch.

I cursed, of course, and then I decided to hop from the porch down onto the lawn. I was afraid that if I went back to the steps and walked around, I wouldn't remember which bush the keys had fallen behind. So I sort of leaped from the porch, but the grass was soaked and I slipped and landed on my ass. Murphy's Law—at that exact moment, Peter Newbold opened the side door and stepped out onto the porch.

"Hello?" he called anxiously.

I sprang to my feet. For some reason, I thought that an athletic move of some sort would be an indicator of sobriety. I was only a few feet away from Peter, and I thought he was going to have a heart attack when he saw me shoot up into the air from the ground below him.

"What the hell?" he cried, staggering backward. The man was actually clutching his chest. Then he said, "Hildy? Is that you?"

"Of course it's me, Peter," I said. It had been a while since I'd had to talk my way around a thick tongue. "I just dropped my keys. . . . Then . . . I . . . slipped when I was . . . looking for them."

I bent over and knocked the bush around a little. I tried to make all my motions fluid and natural, but it was rainy and slippery. At one point, I almost went over again and I had to catch myself by grabbing the side of the porch.

"Here," Peter said, "let me help you."

I couldn't tell if I was imagining it, but he seemed amused. I get so paranoid when I drink; that's what AA and rehab will do to you. I worry now that everybody can tell if I've so much as looked at a drink. In reality, who would be able to tell if a person was a little tipsy on a night like

117

that? It was pouring, so you can imagine how slippery the ground was.

Peter stepped off the porch, and after a few seconds, he pulled the keys out from under the bush and handed them to me.

"Thanks, Peter," I said. I started back to my car and he stepped back up onto the porch, still watching me.

"Wait a minute," I said, laughing and turning back to the office. "I never got . . . what I came for."

I stepped purposefully over to where Peter stood, back up on the porch, and said, "Will ya give me a hand up, Peter?"

Peter looked at me carefully. "Maybe you should walk around to the steps."

"Nah, this is quicker," I said, and I started to climb up. Peter reached out and grabbed my arm and hauled me onto the porch. This time, instead of groping with my keys again, I just went in through the side door with Peter. The door to my office is at the bottom of the stairs leading up to Peter's office. Next to my office door is a table that holds a potted fern. If you pull the table away from the wall, you can open a drawer in the back, which I did as Peter watched.

"I'll use these keys. I always keep a key here," I explained. "An extra set of car keys, too . . . that fucking car." My hand flew to my mouth. Sometimes I swear, but usually only when I drink. "That . . . stupid . . . newfangled Range Rover has the automatic locks and it locks me out all the time."

"But . . . you have your keys. I just gave them to you," said Peter.

"I KNOW. I know," I said, closing the drawer. I had, actually, somehow forgotten he'd found my keys. I was just so befuddled with all the worry about what he might think; about whether he might think I'd been drinking.

"So you're sure you're okay, Hildy?" Peter asked once I had opened my office door.

"OF COURSE," I announced. "Thanks for your help, I'm sure you need to go back to your patient."

Peter seemed flustered for a moment, and then he said, "I'm here alone. I'm just doing some paperwork. . . ."

"Oh, I thought I saw another car."

"Really? I think people park here sometimes. Overnight . . ."

"Okay, well, thanks," I said.

"You sure you're all right? I mean, if you hurt yourself when you slipped, I'd be happy to drive you home."

"What?" I snapped. "I'm totally fine."

Of course, the next morning I had my moments of panic. Was it possible Peter knew that I had been drinking? Did he know I had been to rehab? There was a young woman I used to see at the AA meetings in Newburyport (I went, as instructed, for a few weeks after rehab) who was one of Peter's patients, and sometimes I would pass her on the porch. I had often wondered if she'd told Peter that she had seen me at AA meetings. The meetings are supposed to be anonymous.

"Who you see here, what we say here, when you leave here, let it stay here" is a little chant everybody would say together at the end of the meetings, all standing and holding hands in a circle like a coven of smiling simpletons. Then they would bow their heads and say the Serenity Prayer, and at the end, they would say, again, together, *still with joined hands,* "Keep coming back. It works if you work it, so work it. You're worth it." And then the people on both sides of me would *finally* let go of my hands, after a gentle squeeze, and I'd be allowed to leave.

Gimme a friggin' break, I always thought on my way out. But in truth, I felt sorry for the people at the meetings. Really, you would, too. The stories I heard. There was a guy who'd let his beloved poodle out on a cold winter night, then he'd passed out, drunk, and in the morning he'd found her frozen to death on his front porch. There was a woman who'd dropped her son when he was a toddler, she was so drunk, and he'd fractured his skull. I mean, these people had problems. What if the woman from the Newbury-port meeting had told Peter that she had seen me at meetings and he thought I was like all those people? I fretted about this all the way to Beverly the next morning. After the closing, it didn't seem like such a big thing. I had just accepted a commission check for thirty thousand dollars. This would help with my mortgage situation. I was one of the most successful businesswomen on the North Shore. How could anyone, besides my ridiculous, ungrateful, spoiled daughters, imagine that I had a problem with booze?

When I arrived back in Wendover, I pulled up to the bank to make my deposit, and as I was parking, I saw Rebecca McAllister opening the back door of her silver Land Cruiser so that her boys could climb inside. Sure, a lot of people drive Land Cruisers around here. Silver's a popular color, but I paused and watched her for a moment, and I had a foggy recollection of having seen a similar car parked behind my office the night before. Rebecca had been talking to the boys as they climbed into the car, but as she closed the door and turned, she saw me and waved.

"Hi, Hildy," she said, smiling. I smiled and waved back, and then she strode over to where I stood.

"I've been meaning to call you," she said.

"Oh? What's up?"

Rebecca looked down at her hands for a minute. "It's a little awkward. Well, you were there when I had that little run-in with Cassie Dwight on the beach last summer. Her husband Patch's company did all our plumbing, and now I need to have some more plumbing done. I've had a little studio built behind the house. I've started painting again. . . ."

"Oh, that's wonderful, Rebecca. I don't know if I told you that my daughter is a sculptor. She painted for a while, too."

"No, I didn't know that!" Rebecca exclaimed. She was so cheerful. She was like she was the day we saw the foal, when I first showed her the house. She had been exuberant then, not the anxious, fraught Rebecca I had seen and heard so much about in the subsequent months.

"Anyway," she continued with a shy smile, "I know that you've known the Dwights for a long time. I really don't know what to do. She clearly hates me, and I think I should just hire somebody else, just so I don't have to deal with them. But then, I wouldn't want them to think I'm hiring somebody else out of spite. . . ."

"Rebecca," I said, "I doubt Cassie even remembers your 'run-in.' She's overwhelmed, as you can imagine. Seriously, I doubt she's given it a second thought. I'd call Patch's office number and ask him if he'd come up and give you an estimate. If they have hard feelings, which I doubt, they'll tell you they're too busy. But I know they could use the business. It'll probably help clear the air, having him working on the property again."

Rebecca smiled then. "That's what I was thinking." Then she said, "Hildy, I'd love to have you up to see what we've done to the house. Would you come over for lunch or drinks sometime? I'm alone up here with the kids most weekdays and would love the company."

I had been quite curious to see what the McAllisters had done to the old Barlow place, so I told her I'd love to, and we settled on the following Tuesday. I said I'd stop over after work. I told her not to go to any fuss, that I'd just have a quick tour and be on my way.

"No," she insisted. "Stay for dinner."

"Okay," I said after a moment, thinking forlornly about my MG. It would be good to get out. I was getting a little too solitary.

After the bank, I stopped at the office to check in and then decided to go up and see how Frank's guys were getting on at the Dwight house. He had told me he might be able to find one guy to work on the house. Two guys, tops. When I arrived, I was amazed to see several pickups parked out front, including Frankie's own orange monster. There was a small Dumpster in the driveway, filled with debris. I went inside, and there I counted five men—the bulk of Frank's off-season crew—hard at work. In the living room, the carpet had been removed, revealing polished hardwood floors. A man was applying a second coat of paint to the walls. I entered the kitchen and found another man painting the ceiling there, and, amazingly, two men were easing what looked like a brand-new stainless-steel refrigerator into the slot where the old dingy white one had stood. Frank's denim-clad legs and worn work boots were jutting out from a cabinet beneath a shiny new stainless sink. There was no mistaking those boots.

"Frank?" I said.

Frank inched his way out from under the sink and smiled up at me.

"Whatta ya think, Hildy?"

"I'm . . . blown away. Where did you get all this stuff?"

"Well, I've always got plenty of sinks lyin' around. This one, somebody ordered and it had a little scratch on the back there"—he was pointing at the bottom of the sink—"and they didn't want it anymore. Decided they wanted a different type of sink altogether. They waited too long to return this one, and they were stuck with it. So they gave it to me. Fits perfect. And Patch can plumb it when he gets home. The one they had here was all dinged up."

Frank stood up, wiping his hands on his jeans and squinting up at the paint being applied to the ceiling.

"What about the fridge?"

"Brand-new."

"Where did you get it?"

"Just got it. I know everybody wants one of these stainless-steel jobs now. It really makes the kitchen look new, huh, Hil?"

It was amazing what a new fridge and sink and clean white paint could do to a kitchen. Frank was leaning back against the counter, resting on his elbows and smiling at me.

"I thought you had all your guys on another job."

"Well, I pulled 'em off it for a few days. The owner of that place in Manchester . . . what's he gonna do, find somebody else to clear his lot in the next two days? It's fine. It's nice to be inside for a change. Patch was always a good kid. Ya know, he worked for me a coupla summers?"

Like I said, I'm not the most touchy-feely type, but I walked over to Frank and did a sort of Wendy Heatherton clasp of his hand between both of mine.

"Thanks, Frank . . . really."

"Anytime, Hildy," he said, staring down at the floor. I don't think it was my imagination. His face was a little red. I know mine was flaming.

A long time ago, when I was just out of high school, I was quite in love with Frankie Getchell. I'll never forgive Mamie Lang for sharing that with my daughters one night, years ago, after we'd had a few.

"WHAT?" the girls had screamed. Then they

125

fell over each other, contorting with laughter.

"EWWWW, gross, MOM." They were shrieking. They were laughing so hard, they could barely breathe.

"Okay, okay." I chuckled. I was a little tipsy and could see the comedy in it. They knew Frank only the way he looked now. And, of course, they were comparing him to their father, who was always so good-looking and kept himself in such great shape. "He looked better . . . then," I said.

"You mean he looked like a young gnome instead of an old one?" Tess sputtered.

"EWW," screamed Emily. "Just EWWWWW."

It's true, Frank's on the short side. And squat. But when we were in high school, I wasn't the only one who thought he was cool. Not great-looking, no, but he was rugged and sexy, and I spent a summer making love with him on strangers' boats. It was the summer after my senior year in high school. Mamie and I were both waitresses at the Wendover Yacht Club, and Frankie used to work down at the boatyard, which was right next door, refinishing and repairing boats. After work, when all the club members had left, the WYC manager—a great guy named Jim Randall—would let the staff have a few drinks. As the summer wore on, we all started inviting our friends in after work—sneaking them in through a side door to drink up the booze that had been paid for with the club members' exorbitant dues.

It was a blast. It was the summer of '69. We all liked to think of ourselves as hippies, but Frankie Getchell was the only one in town who really was. He had longer hair and smoked grass all the time—or everybody said he did. I used to cut through the boatyard on the way to work in the afternoons, wearing my little WYC waitress uniform—a navy knee-length skirt and a white short-sleeved blouse—and he'd be sanding the great wooden hull of somebody's yacht, shirtless and sweaty. I wasn't a beautiful teenager, but I wasn't ugly, either. Actually, I was told, on occasion, that I resembled Grace Slick, and I cultivated that look, with my long, thick brown hair and bangs and heavy eyeliner. Frank had been in my cousin Eddie's class and had played at our house as a child, and even though I'd pretend to not notice him, he'd always call something out to me. My name appeared to amuse him. He'd croon the words to the tune of a popular song at the time. "And then along comes Hildy. Along comes Hildy. Hildy Goo-oo-d."

You wouldn't be able to see how good-looking he once was if you met him now, but he was handsome, in a rough sort of way. He worked hard, his body was dense with muscle, and he had that brown skin in the summer from those Anawam ancestors. I used to thrill at the sound of his voice, though I tried to ignore him. Then, one night, he showed up at one of our after-hours parties at the club. We had really turned the WYC into our own little speakeasy by midsummer. We played music from somebody's transistor radio —the Beatles, Bob Dylan, Jefferson Airplane, Hendrix—and we'd all drink and smoke and dance on the bar. Twice that summer, the cops came, but we always had a few people on alert up in the "Commodore's Room," which was on the top floor of the club, and they'd see the cops coming and call down to us, and we'd all pile into the liquor storage room while Jim assured the cops that he was the only one there.

I was already a little tipsy the first night Frank came to the club, and the sight of him pleased me, to say the least. Most of the Wendover boys were wearing their hair a little longer at that point, but Frank's was really long, and it used to hang over his eyes like a thick forelock. He was always having to tilt his head a little when he looked at you, and because he was a little shy, he'd let his bangs fall right back over his eyes when he looked back down at the floor.

That night after a few beers, he and I got to talking. He asked if I was planning to go to college, asked about my dad. Both Frank's parents had died by then—they died within six months of each other, of cancer, when Frankie was still in high school. His only brother, Dave, was in Vietnam. Frank lived alone in the saltbox up on the rise, where he still lives today. After a while, we walked out on the dock, and Frankie recognized one of the Boston Whalers that was tied up there. The owner had a yacht that Frankie had just helped slip into the water a few days before. Frankie was proud of the work he had done on the boat. He wanted to show me. In those days, everybody left their keys in their boats on the WYC pier. Who would take them? Well, Frankie and I did, all summer long. That first night, we started up the Whaler, and though the water was a little choppy, we sped through Wendover Harbor, Frankie weaving in and out of the moored boats as if it were a slalom course he had designed himself. We pulled up to a long wooden sailboat—the yacht I'd seen him working on those past weeks. We tied up the Whaler to the stern of the boat and Frankie climbed aboard. Then he reached out his hand, and when I grabbed it, he lifted me up on deck.

I was a skinny little thing then.

He had a key to the wine chest. We sat on the broad bow and drank wine from a bottle. We didn't really talk. We would glance at each other, then stare up at the stars, smiling shyly. I smoked my first joint. I kissed Frankie Getchell. Later that week, we returned to the same boat, but after the kissing, we went below. He was my first. Anytime I catch a whiff of lemon oil, I'm brought right back to that dark hold and the scent of the rich, citrusy oil that Frankie had rubbed into every inch of the old salt-dried surfaces. There we crawled onto the owners' berth. There, Frankie pressed his hard body against mine. Water sloshed against the hull and I could smell salt and lemons and the new, primitive odors of man and sex. The boat rose and sank and rolled—it was a rough sea that night—and, well, I'll never forget how thrilling and dangerous it all was. And the exquisite pain of that first time that lasted for days and made my heart pound whenever I thought of it.

For the longest time, I blamed all my problems with Scott—especially all our sex problems—on the fact that Frankie was my first lover. Frank liked to get a little rough—not too rough, but just the right amount of rough. He was confident and take-charge in a good-humored way. Yes, he had a lovely and potent intensity about him that he only revealed during lovemaking, and, well, a girl likes to be handled. At least this girl does. I admit, at the end of the summer, when I went off to UMass, I cried the whole way up to school. My dad didn't have a clue as to what was the matter with me. He would have died if he had known I was involved with Frankie Getchell.

Frankie received his draft notice that fall, and he was in Vietnam by Christmas. After the war, he moved back to Wendover. I had graduated and moved back, too. With my husband, Scott Aldrich. I rarely thought about the old times with Frank.

He really had aged in a sort of ragged way. There was the night, years ago, when things were so bad with Scott, and I had that unfortunate incident with Frankie that still seems to amuse him. I was drunk. Nobody's perfect. Now I'm in recovery. I'm sure he knows that—everybody else does— so you'd think he'd stop looking so amused every time he sees me.

Frankie's crew finished the work on the Dwights' house Friday morning. I dropped off a bottle of scotch as a token of thanks, along with a note asking him to bill the job to me.

Friday afternoon, the Sandersons called. They weren't going to be able to make it up to Wendover that weekend after all. Maybe the next, they said. I called every broker in Essex County in a desperate attempt to get some people in while the house was still in good shape. I had two showings. Neither party was the least bit interested. I knew Cassie and Patch would be exhausted with the many extra outings they had planned for Jake that weekend.

"Well," Cassie said when they came home on Sunday. "Any offers?"

"No," I replied. "But I still feel hopeful about those Sandersons. Maybe next weekend. In the meantime, let's set up an open house."

Jake was in the living room, screaming and spinning.

"He's not adjusting well to the changes," Cassie said softly. "He misses the carpet."

We sat at the table for a while and listened to the boy. Then I got up to leave and Cassie locked the door behind me.

Eight

The following Tuesday, I left my office at six and drove through town on my way up to Rebecca's house. Normally, I would just have taken Wendover Rise from Atlantic Avenue, but Rebecca had said that I should come around six-thirty, and I needed to kill some time. So I turned onto my old street, Hat Shop Hill Road, which is a back road leading to the rise. Some of my clients get a great kick out of the names of the streets in our town. Gingerbread Hill, Old Burial Hill, Pig Rock Lane, and Hat Shop Hill Road are just a few. They all have honest origins. There was once a bakery on Gingerbread Hill, Old Burial Hill is the site of a historic graveyard, and Pig Rock Lane once, apparently, had a large rock shaped like a pig on the corner, when it was still a carriage road, but when they widened the road for automobiles, it was removed. Scott, my ex, loved all this stuff, but he was from the Midwest —Michigan—from a town with a history that began with the invention of the assembly line, so he got a lot more out of the local history than I did. I never knew there was once a pig rock on Pig Rock Lane until he told me.

Hat Shop Hill Road, the steep road where I grew up, once had a hat shop. It wasn't a real shop, just a business that a local woman with a flair for headwear ran out of her home sometime in the 1800s. We were 20 Hat Shop Hill. There's still a 20 Hat Shop Hill Road, but it's not the house I grew up in. When Dad died, I sold it and split the income with my sister, Lisa, and my brother, Judd. This was about ten years ago now, and the buyers tore it down and built what some would call a McMansion. There was a lot of commentary around town about the Good house being torn down. Many told me how upset they thought I must be, but I told them the truth. It hadn't been my home for a long time. It was never a particularly attractive home—just a crooked old farmhouse. My dad always felt that people had the right to do whatever they wanted with property they owned.

"But the memories . . ." people would say. Not everybody said this, but most did. I was only twelve when my mother died. That was a long time ago, so not a lot of people around here know about all that.

I rarely drive up Hat Shop Hill Road, but I did that night, on the way to Rebecca's, and I stopped in front of the new number 20. It was a sort of

McMansion, in the sense that it was massive and cheap-looking. It had stone veneer in the front and what looked like vinyl siding around the rest of the house. It had that fake multiple roofline. The "footprint" of my childhood house would have fit in that house's living room alone. But unlike many new-construction homes, this one appeared to fit on the property. I had thought that whenever I drove past, but it wasn't until that night on the way to Rebecca's that I realized why. It was because the builder hadn't clear-cut the trees on the property the way most new builders so often do now—it's always cheaper to clear-cut than to build around existing trees. This builder had left most of the mature trees, only removing the few that were too close to the house. I'd like to be able to report that I got misty-eyed when I recognized the old maple we used to use as our base when we played hide-and-seek. I recognized the tree all right; I just don't get sentimental about stuff like that, the way some people do. It was a tree. We played under it. Now it's in front of a house with central air and granite countertops. There's nothing left of our family here in Wendover except me and the ghost of a house's old worn-out footprint under six thousand square feet of hardwood, granite, and Sheetrock.

When I pulled up to the old Barlow place, I have to admit, I was a little blown away. I had heard that the McAllisters had done a beautiful job, but I had no idea that the Barlow place could ever look so . . . lovely. And I've called it the McAllister place ever since, by the way.

I got out of the car and was greeted by a large German shepherd who bounded toward me, broadcasting big blustery woofs, his hackles slightly raised. The sight of the dog would probably have alarmed some people—he was coming right at me—but I recognized a playful uncertainty in his bounce and saw that despite his size, he was a juvenile—an awkward teenager. When I squatted down and patted my knee, he came sidling over, all wagging body and lolling tongue.

"Yes, you scared me. Nicely done, beasty," I crooned. He had flopped over onto his side and I began rubbing his exposed belly. Rebecca's kids were playing on a rope swing that hung from a tree in the side yard. There was a young woman playing with them, and Rebecca came out to greet me.

"I see you've met Harry," she said, leaning over and pounding the dog on his massive chest. He closed his jaws on her wrist, playfully, and she gave him a clipped "uh-uh-uh," and he dropped her wrist instantly and tapped the ground apologetically with his tail.

Rebecca reintroduced me to Liam and Ben and their nanny, Magda. The boys had grown since I'd last seen them. I wouldn't have recognized them in a group, but I find that the older I get, the more kids just look like kids. I don't really notice them as much as I used to. On the other hand, I could have instantly picked Harry out of a lineup of similarly marked German shepherds, were there ever a need to do so. Harry was a wonderful character. The boys were just boys.

It was late in the day. The last rays of sun hit the tips of the trees, the way they do on autumn afternoons, illuminating the red, yellow, and orange treetops in the distant woods so that they shone like torches against the darkening slate blue sky.

"What a gorgeous night," I said. "Just look at that sky."

Rebecca smiled. "It's the golden hour."

" 'Golden hour'?"

"Oh, it's a term they use in filmmaking and, you know, photography. I was in a couple of films, years ago, nothing you would have heard of, but in one of them, the script called for a scene to be shot on a beach during the so-called golden hour. We spent three days freezing our asses off on a beach, just so that the lead actors could kiss during the golden hour in that stupid film."

"So it's like a sunset, the golden hour?"

"No, it's before the sun sets. Or right after it rises. Just that first or last hour of light, just like this. The atmosphere is very . . . rare and unusual. It all has to do with the purity of the light, the

136

angle of the sun and the way it hits the horizon. The light is sort of filtered. I'm much more aware of light now as a painter, of course, than I was standing shivering on that beach for that movie. All I think about is light some days."

Rebecca's words made me suddenly aware of the light shifting against the distant hills in undulating patterns, and I saw Rebecca tilt her head and gaze at her children. How pleased she looked at the sight of them frolicking in what she had called, so delightfully, this "rare" atmosphere, this "golden hour."

"See what happens to the boys' shadows? All the shadows are long but not as dark; the light is less harsh. There's just less contrast and everything takes on this special hue. There's a blueness. Well, look at the color of the roses. . . . Oh, why am I carrying on like this, let's go inside." Rebecca laughed.

"No, I'm fascinated," I said. "The golden hour."

The cocktail hour is how I had always thought of it. A golden hour indeed.

We walked toward the house, and though Halloween was still a couple of weeks away, four carved pumpkins grinned maniacally up at us from the front steps, all dentally misaligned, with moldy triangular eyes and faces that were collapsing from the ravages of the early autumn sun.

From the front yard, the house looked more or

less like the original Barlow farmhouse. It was a white antique Colonial with black shutters on all the windows. It wasn't until you entered the house that you discovered that the little old house had become an open, loftlike foyer, a beautiful front room with exposed beams and burnished wide-plank floors. All the walls had been taken down, and the massive fireplace was now in the center of a great room surrounded by oversized sofas upholstered in rich velvety fabrics of deep burgundies and gold. Cushions were strewn everywhere—cushions and throw pillows covered in brilliant silks and woven materials that looked like tapestries from India. We walked through the room and entered a passageway that was a sort of solarium, with beautiful glass-paneled walls and ceilings. The floors in this glass room were made of polished bluestone. Along the walls were shelves lined with white ceramic pots holding fragrant herbs and flowering plants. In the corner stood a lemon tree.

Beyond the glass passageway was the new part of the house. It wasn't huge, nor was it tiny. Everything, everywhere you looked, appeared to have been there always, and each thing comple-mented the next. We walked through a hall, passing a small library and a dining room, and then we were in the spacious kitchen, which was white and cool and lovely. There was a large center island with a marble countertop and on it was an open bottle of red wine with two glasses next to it. One was half-full.

"I'm having red, but I can open a bottle of white, if you prefer," said Rebecca.

It had been a while since I had been in the presence of somebody who didn't know my "history." Usually, when people have me over, they say, "Well, Hildy, we have all sorts of things to drink: Coke, Diet Coke, seltzer, water. . . ."

Rebecca's offer to pour me a glass of wine was so casual and innocent that I almost asked her to go ahead and pour me a glass of that nice Pinot Noir that she was drinking. But I didn't. Instead, I said, "You know, I think I'll just have a glass of water for now," and I mumbled something about some medication I was taking, letting her think that I was only not imbibing alcohol that night; that normally, I drink socially, just like her. Just like all the good people of the world.

"I have a stew on the stove," Rebecca said. "I hope you eat beef."

"Of course," I said.

"I'm going to have Magda feed the boys now. I want to show you my studio; then we'll come down and eat afterward," Rebecca said, handing me my water with a smile. She took a nice sip of her wine. Then she smiled at me again, in that way she has, with her eyes.

We chatted for a few moments, and when we stepped outside to see the studio, it was dark.

"We should probably look for a flashlight, but it's almost a full moon," she said as we left through the kitchen door. "You don't mind walking in the dark, I hope, Hildy," Rebecca said. "Brian keeps pestering me to get some floodlights put out here, but I hate floodlights."

"I loathe them," I said. I really do. For some reason, when people move out here, especially from cities like Boston and New York, the dark worries them, and they decide to illuminate their properties, as if they are trying to be seen from space. I love the dark, and I was pleased to learn that Rebecca did, too.

Indeed, the moon was almost full, and it was the harvest moon that month and the land around us was wild with shadows and light. Harry bounded alongside Rebecca, thrilled with the night excursion. We followed a path through a little stand of hemlock trees and then we came upon a small house with one wall made entirely of glass panes. Rebecca opened the door and, after fumbling for a moment along the wall, flipped on a light switch. Her studio had three whitewashed walls and, like I said, the one glass wall, which, I imagined, during daylight hours would have that beautiful view down to the marshland. Her paintings were huge and appeared to be rather abstract, impressionistic seascapes. I'm not an art expert, but my daughter went to the Rhode Island School of Design and did some painting before deciding on the more lucrative field of sculpting. (She shares a loft with no plumbing in Brooklyn. I pay the rent.)

Rebecca's paintings were filled with sand and sea colors, and I asked her if she had done the paintings from photographs or if she actually painted outdoors. She explained that the bigger canvases she had painted here in the studio, but some of the smaller ones she had done down at the end of Wind Point Road.

"Oh," I said. "That's a beautiful road. Did you know that's Peter Newbold's house there at the end—near the beach?" I said it before thinking and worried for a moment that Rebecca might be embarrassed that I knew that Peter was her psychiatrist, but she brightened when I mentioned his name and said, "I know." She pulled a huge canvas from the back of the studio and said, "This is a painting from a photograph taken from his lawn."

"Lovely, Rebecca," I said. Then: "So you've been to Peter and Elise's house?" I'd never been in therapy and had no idea, therefore, whether it was usual or unusual for patients to socialize with their doctors. But it made sense to me that the McAllisters and the Newbolds would get along, as couples, and it seemed altogether likely that they were all friends.

"Yes . . . well, actually, I've never been inside, but I was taking photographs down there and

Peter came wandering down the beach. I was standing almost in front of his house. I had no idea."

I was facing Rebecca when she said this, so I was able to see that she was telling me a lie. I thought she was going to continue, but she stopped talking and was biting her lip. Then she smiled and said, "Well, long story short, it turns out Peter's very into photography, too, and he said I could take photographs from his lawn if I wanted to."

"Oh, I do really love that one," I said, taking a step closer to the huge canvas she was holding up. I didn't care to pursue her little untruth. We all lie on occasion; there's usually nothing behind it. But I wouldn't lie about somebody's artwork. I don't tell people I like things if I don't. I usually just say nothing. I really did love Rebecca's painting. It made me almost smell the sea. It was beautiful.

"Actually, Peter took the photograph," Rebecca said. "He gave it to me when I admired it, and then I painted it."

"I adore Peter," I said. "He's such a nice man. I'm sure he's quite a good therapist. . . ."

I was watching for Rebecca's reaction, but when she answered, her back was to me. She was placing the paintings back against the wall.

"Yes . . . well, he's not really a therapist to me. He prescribed some medication that I needed, that's all. It . . . well, it changed my life. I've seen different shrinks over the years, and have been prescribed various antidepressants. . . . God, I barely know you and I'm telling you all this," Rebecca said. She turned and smiled at me. Rebecca had carried her wineglass down from the house, and now she lifted it from a paint-speckled table and took a sip. It pleased me to see that Rebecca enjoyed her wine. I always notice the way people drink. I like it when I spot what I think is a fellow lover of spirits. I suspected that Rebecca was my kind.

"Don't worry," I said. "People tell me everything. But I don't gossip."

And I don't, really. Not about real stuff.

"Well, there's not much to tell. Peter prescribed a medication that finally worked for me. Now I'm not depressed."

"So, I've always been curious about these antidepressants," I said. Both my daughters take them. I won't take pills. "Do you feel sedated on them? High?"

"No, most of them make you feel like shit, actually. Like a dullard swimming through some thick muck all the time. But the stuff Peter has me on . . . well, I started feeling better, little by little. One day, I suddenly noticed how good food tastes. I was eating something silly, an English muffin, I think it was, and suddenly I thought, *This is the most delicious thing I've ever eaten in my life*. That's why I've put on a few pounds. Food tastes good again."

It was true, Rebecca had gained a few, but she needed to.

"I'd be petting the dog and thinking, *How did I never notice how soft his coat is before?* I had never felt anything so soft."

"Wow, you should be on one of those commercials for the company that makes whatever you're on," I said, and Rebecca laughed. She really did make it sound appealing. It sounded like being permanently on your second drink. Not drunk, but not desperately sober. That would be a nice way to be all the time, I supposed. We looked at a few more paintings and then we decided to head down to the house for dinner.

"Your wine," I said. She almost left it behind.

"Oh, right," Rebecca said, and grabbed the glass. She sipped the rest of the wine in that glass as she served up the stew and then she drank water with me as we ate. I can't help it, I notice the way people drink. I'm always surprised by the kind of person who can have just a glass of wine or two and then switch to water. Rebecca hadn't struck me as one of those, but now it appeared that she was.

When I left Rebecca's that night, I drove down Wendover Rise, but instead of turning toward the river and my house, I decided to drive past

Getchell's Cove, just to get a look at the harvest moon on the water. There were still a few boats moored there. I recognized Oatie Clarke's old Chris-Craft and the Steins' sailboat and the Westons', and I watched them bob up and down beneath the golden light of the moon, the gentle water sparkling all around. I thought about the little sailboat I used to keep moored there in the cove. Frankie Getchell gave it to me that summer before college. It was an old Widgeon that he had found at the dump, salvaged, and repaired. He patched up the hull, painted it bright red, and told me I could have it. He taught me to sail. I don't think they make Widgeons anymore. You never see them, but they're a great little sailboat. They have a jib and a mainsail and there's room for two people, but it's still small enough to sail alone. We named her *Sarah Good*, after my ancestress, and we spent many afternoons sailing out of Wendover Harbor; me in the striped bikini I wore that whole summer, Frank, shirtless, in a pair of baggy painter's pants. We scrambled over each other's limbs, cursing and laughing, when I was learning to tack and jibe, and more than once, I managed to capsize us. A Widgeon isn't the easiest boat to right, but Frank taught me how to stand on the centerboard and use my body to rock her back upright. He taught me to do it myself, in case I was ever out alone. I became a sailor. We got so that we sailed with such ease,

Frank and me. We really didn't talk much; there wasn't the need. We'd rig her silently; then Frank would sit back against the stern with the tiller tucked under his arm and a cigarette dangling from his easy smile. I would lean into the beefy crook of his thighs, the jib sheet tucked between my fingers and my face angled up at the sun. It was just that one summer. Then I went off to college. But I kept *Sarah Good.* I had a friend with a trailer who would help me pull her out at the end of the summer, and I stored her in my dad's backyard all winter, her hull breaching up through the snow like the broad back of a red whale surrounded by a swelling white sea.

The first time Scott visited me in Wendover was the summer after our junior year. I used to borrow Butchie Haskell's skiff to row out to my mooring, and as we pulled up alongside my little dented sailboat, Scott, who was always great at impres-sions, let loose with a great cry of "My, but she's yar." We both cracked up and spent the afternoon sailing around Wendover Harbor, talking like Katharine Hepburn and Cary Grant. Of course, we both wanted to be Katharine Hepburn. I know this is hard to believe, but until Scott told me he was gay, almost sixteen years into our marriage, I'd had absolutely no clue.

Nine

"Hi, Mom, it's me, Tess. Grady's sick today. He's all right, just a bad cold. We're going to stay home with him tonight, so we won't be needing you. But thanks anyway. Oh, but call me when you get a chance. I want to talk to you about Thanksgiving."

The message had been left on my home phone. It was Friday evening.

Shortly after I returned from rehab, Tess and Michael had started asking me to baby-sit on occasional evenings. Then it had turned into an every Friday kind of thing—a date night for them, and a date night for me and little Grady. I really did look forward to my time with Grady. I won't bore you with all the doting grandmother stories, but allow me this one: I had been there the past Friday, the Friday before the night they canceled because he was sick, and Grady was sitting in his high chair. He had just finished his "supper."

When my girls were babies, their meals were rather simple affairs. I vaguely remember a plastic plate separated into two or three compartments, and I used to fill these compartments with food —meat, vegetables, maybe a little fruit. They had a sippy cup of milk. Before that, I nursed them.

Grady's meals are complicated and serious

147

affairs, each and every one of them. They have been since the day he was born. Tess had sought out "lactation specialists" shortly after she arrived home from the hospital, because she was afraid the baby wasn't getting enough milk. Once they sorted out the breast-feeding, he was colicky, so they consulted all sorts of doctors and nutritionists. A lactose intolerance was discovered, and Grady was allowed only soy milk once his mother weaned him. No milk, no cheese, no butter. And though Grady had never been near a peanut in his short life, there was a cousin on Michael's side who had a peanut allergy, so nothing with peanuts or peanut oil was allowed in the house. They were in the process of trying to "rule out" a gluten allergy.

"What's left?" I asked Tess. "What will he live on?"

Tess and Michael hated when I asked questions about Grady's diet, and Michael actually said to me one day, "We worry, when you make little offhand comments about his food issues, that you're not taking them seriously and that you might . . . forget and give Grady the wrong thing to eat."

I assured him that I knew the "food issues" were serious, and of course I would never feed Grady anything he wasn't supposed to have, though I have often entertained wicked fantasies of sneaking him a little cup of ice cream or a sliver of cake. The baby didn't eat. And who could blame him? But anyway, that Friday night, Grady had finished pushing around his meal of pureed organic peas, gluten-free pasta, and some kind of soy burger, and while I was wiping off the high chair's tray, he was just beaming up at me.

He calls me "Gammy." It makes my heart soar.

This is another reason I'm grateful to the girls for my intervention. Tess and Michael would never have left Grady with me when I drank so much. I really did drink too much; I see that now. After those months of abstinence—the month at Hazelden and the two that followed—I knew that I could go without alcohol as long as I wanted, so I never drank before going to see Grady. It was good for me to abstain for a night or two each week. Often, I didn't even have a glass of wine when I got home from baby-sitting; I was so tired that I just went to bed.

Anyway, that night, after supper, Grady grinned up at me, and I was at a little bit of a loss as to what to do with him. He was saying only a few words then, but he looked quite happy in his high chair, so I said, "Do you want Gammy to sing for you?"

"Mmmmmmmmmnnnnnnnn," he grunted, which meant yes.

So I sang "Good Morning Starshine," just like Scott and I used to sing for the girls. I just sang the first verse. That's all I could remember. I hadn't sung anything in years. When I was finished, I smiled at Grady and he grinned at me again and then clapped his hands. Then he said, "MORE," which was one of his few words, and I sang it again.

I lifted him out of his chair and changed his diaper and put him into his jammies. Then I sat on the sofa, bounced him on my knee, and sang him a few songs. I sang some Joni Mitchell songs and I sang Billie Holiday's "God Bless the Child," but I could never do a Billie Holiday song justice; Scott did a great Billie Holiday. I sang, "Wild Horses . . . couldn't drag me awa-a-ay . . ." and I sang him some of the songs Scott had written when we were in college. I even remembered most of the words.

Scott and I met after we joined an a cappella group at UMass, and then we started up our own little folk group with another couple. We called ourselves the Knobs. (Don't ask—we thought it was cool.) We used to play at these coffeehouses in and around Amherst and Holyoke. The girls teased us mercilessly about this, about how much they hated that music, but when they were little, Scott and I used to be able to get them to sing along with us in the car. We taught them to harmonize a little. Emily, especially, has a very beautiful voice, and she and Scott would sing all sorts of songs together. And I think little Grady has an ear for music. He has a natural sense of rhythm. He was bobbing his head along with the music, and every time I finished a song, he cried out, "MORE. MORE."

God, I love that child. Tess told me that was his very first word. *More.*

Of course it was. He's my grandson. He's like me more than Tess or Michael will ever see. I suspect that my first word was *more* (though whether it would have penetrated my mother's clogged mind is impossible to know). But the point is, when it comes to joy, I never have my fill. I've always wanted more, just like my little Grady.

So that Friday, after playing my messages, I was sad to be missing Grady, but I was slightly relieved that I didn't have to make the drive to Marblehead. It was cold and rainy. I decided it was a nice night to throw a few logs in the fireplace and watch a movie with my dogs. We went out to the boathouse first, of course. I realized that I would need to be moving the wine indoors soon. It would be freezing before long and I had been trying to come up with another storage spot that the girls would never discover. There was a crawl space in the cellar that I thought would be perfect. I just hadn't gotten around to moving the wine yet. It was almost eight and it was very dark, so I walked back to the house slowly, carrying the bottle by its neck, when suddenly a car pulled into my driveway. I froze, like a fugitive, the bottle hanging at my side like a spent weapon.

"Hildy?" called a woman's voice.

I was squinting into the headlights but couldn't see who was calling. Who would just show up on a night like that? I walked around to the side of the car and saw that it was a silver Land Cruiser. Rebecca was behind the wheel. She was shaking and crying, covering her eyes with her hand.

"Rebecca? What's wrong?" I asked. "What is it?"

She was sobbing. I was conscious of the fact that I was standing way too close to the road with an unconcealed bottle of wine, so I said, "Rebecca dear, come in the house. Turn off your car and come in the house."

I hadn't had company in a while. I guess in the year since rehab, I had only had a couple of close friends stop by, and Tess and Emily on the rare occasion, of course. So, when we walked into the house, I was a little self-conscious. I looked at my home, suddenly, through Rebecca's eyes— being a broker, it's second nature for me to do this—and I saw the solitary pair of rain boots next to the front door, the dogs' leashes dangling above them. We passed through the living room and I wondered if it was obvious that nobody had sat in that room in over a year. In the kitchen, in a drying rack next to the sink, were a single coffee mug and a single wineglass. I just washed them out by hand each day. I rarely cooked, grabbing take-out

Japanese on my way home, and I ate that on a paper plate in front of the TV in the den. Did the house look as desperately quiet and solitary as it had become? I fluttered about and turned on some lights, but when I glanced at Rebecca, I could see that she wasn't paying any attention to my house. She was too upset. The dogs were beside themselves with delight at having a visitor. When Rebecca knelt down to pet them, even cranky Babs licked at her teary face.

"Can I get you anything?" I asked her. Then, looking at the bottle that I was clutching, I said, "A glass of wine?"

"A glass of wine would be great, Hildy. Thanks so much. I feel awful just showing up. I was just driving by when I saw you. . . ." She was sort of laughing through her tears, the way she had done that first day I met her, when she was all bent out of shape about the stolen foal.

So I took two glasses from my cupboard. *Two wineglasses.* A warm sense of joyful relief washed over me as I poured the wine into the two glasses. I was a person of the world again. A social drinker. Rebecca clearly had no idea that she was about to engage in something dark and forbidden with me. I handed her one of the wineglasses. I watched her put it to her lovely lips. Then we both had a long sip of our wine and Rebecca smiled at me. I smiled back and, grabbing the bottle, said, "Come into the other room. I was about to make a fire."

Rebecca and I finished that bottle of wine and then we finished the better part of another. She kept saying, "No, really, I should go," but holding her glass up for me to fill it at the same time. I knew Rebecca was a kindred spirit. I can often tell when I first meet a person if they have the same relationship with alcohol that I have. They can be so fragile when sober, and I saw that in Rebecca that first day up at the farm. I don't care what alchemy the Peter Newbolds of the world are peddling these days, there's only one cure that suits us, really.

It was when we finished the first bottle and I headed out for the second that I confessed my little Hazelden history to Rebecca. She was completely unfazed. Many of her friends from prep school and college had been to rehab. They all drank now. I blinked at her in disbelief. There were tears in my eyes. It was as if somebody had revealed to me that there was a whole race of people who were exactly like me. I wasn't a freak. We were everywhere.

My confession, my little secret, must have given her the courage to explain what had her so upset that night. She had had a fight with Brian. They were supposed to go to Palm Beach for the weekend to visit his parents, but they'd had a doozy of a fight and it was determined that Brian would go with the boys and she'd stay home. Now he was gone. She had set out in her car to seek the solace of a friend, but the friend wasn't home. Then, driving past my place, she had seen me in the driveway.

"What's wrong?" I asked, filling her glass. "What's the problem with Brian?"

Rebecca took a deep breath. Then she said, "Well, the fight was about something trivial. I criticized him about something and he lost it."

"Oh," I said. "Well, it sounds like it's something you'll work out. . . ."

"I guess," she replied. Then she said, just a tad too soon, "Oh, by the way, I wanted to clear up something I said the other night. The night you were at my house."

"Yes?"

"I made it sound like Peter Newbold was my psychiatrist or something. Really, I just consulted with him once or twice. He's not my doctor. . . ."

Rebecca's very bright, and if she hadn't had so much wine, I doubt she would have let that pronouncement pop up in the middle of our discussion of her marital woes. She fed me a thought then. I recalled her delight when she'd shown me her paintings, especially the one that was of the view from Peter's house, and also her little fib about never having been in his house. Her newfound appetite, her sudden burst of creativity—it wasn't the medication. Rebecca was in love.

"Oh," I said. Then, just to test the waters, I

added, "I'm sure Peter's a wonderful doctor. He's such a nice man. I feel for him sometimes. I get the sense that he's lonely."

It was like feeding candy to a baby.

"Really?" Rebecca leaned forward in her chair. "In what way?"

We were seated across from each other, in front of the crackling fire in the two red leather club chairs that Scott had found in Brimfield one year. Just the way her whole body shifted toward me when I spoke his name, the way she studied my face; her eyes, now deep green in the reflected glow of the fire, searched mine with such intense longing. I suddenly had a sense of what it must have felt like to be Peter Newbold in those sessions that she was trying to deny they had shared. I could see her eyes quite clearly, it was a perfect setup for a reading, and wine always floods my spirit with mischief, so I decided to have a little go at it.

"Rebecca," I said, "I know you're involved with Peter. I know you're romantically involved."

She was completely silent, but, like I said, the fire was illuminating her face, so I saw that I was correct.

"You don't have to say anything. I know these things."

Rebecca smiled then and said, "I remember your ESP show at Wendy's party. I don't believe in any of that."

"I don't, either," I said. "But, if you'll let me, I'm going to see if I can tell you exactly what's happened between you and Peter."

"Well, nothing has happened, so this should be interesting," she laughed. "What should I do? Go into some kind of trance or something?"

"No, just look at me. Don't nod or do anything with your eyes that might give anything away. You don't have to tell me if I'm right or wrong. You don't ever have to tell me, if you don't want. It's just an experiment."

"Sounds like fun," Rebecca said, and then she leaned in closer and stared into my eyes. A glimmer of amusement twinkled in hers.

"I know from what you told me that you saw him a few times when you were depressed and that he gave you medication and that you improved."

"That's right."

"And then you went back for a session—no, maybe a few more sessions, and you talked about your childhood. Your mother . . . you never felt your mother's love. And your father was unfaithful to her and that made you feel that he was unfaithful to you, as well. They separated when you were in early adolescence."

"Not bad. But anybody could know that from Googling my father. There's been plenty written about him."

"Yes," I said. "Maybe that's how I know that

stuff. So you were working this all out with Peter. You had some grief. Did your father die around the time that you were going through the adoption process with one of the boys? Ben maybe? No, it was Liam."

Rebecca said nothing but maintained eye contact. You'd think people would be harder to read when they're tipsy, but they're easier because they've loosened their natural defenses a little. Of course, I'm not as sharp sometimes when I try to read after a few too many, but that night I found myself rather on fire with Rebecca.

"You started thinking that Peter was attractive during these sessions."

"Well, that's not difficult to guess. Peter is extremely attractive."

I nodded and tried not to smile. Most people wouldn't think that Peter Newbold was the most attractive guy around. Especially compared to Rebecca's own Brian, who had, just the year prior, been voted one of the sexiest men in Boston by *Boston* magazine. Well, he did own the magazine. But still.

"This was late in the summer, now, and you started running into him all over town, and each time it was a bit of a shock," I said, "like seeing a teacher outside of a classroom. It seemed like . . . fate. Almost like magic, the way you kept bumping into each other. There were some very strange coincidences."

Rebecca was now intrigued. This felt to her like I was indeed seeing into her past. How did I know this very specific thing about her and Peter? This is the key. This is how my aunt made her living, how astrologers can do readings that appear to be so accurate. We're all so alike, yet we all think we're so unique. Most new lovers think that they're surrounded by magical coincidences, that they keep being brought together by fate. This is new crush magical thinking. Most women do it.

"Did you start playing tennis together?" I continued.

This was an outright cheat. I had been told by my friend Lindsey Wright that Peter and Rebecca had been partners in a mixed-doubles tournament at the Anawam Beach Club, but I felt that I needed to turn up the volume a little, and it worked.

"Okay, this is just WILD," said Rebecca. Her cheeks were flaming and she was smiling brightly. "It WAS weird how I kept running into him. There were some strange coincidences, and the strangest was when Nancy Cheever called me because they needed a fourth for a mixed-doubles game, and when I arrived, guess who my partner was?"

"I know who it was," I said. "It was Peter."

"Go on, go on," Rebecca said.

"You encountered him one time that felt . . . electrifying. Yes. You were inside—no, wait, you were outside and you were close to your house, you were up on the rise. Were you gardening? . . .

No, it wasn't right at your house. You were riding Betty. Yes, you were riding Betty and you ran into Peter. He was running. He likes to run up Wendover Rise, but you didn't know that and it felt again like fate when you encountered him."

"Oh my God, yes. I was at the top of the hill and I could barely make out who this guy was, but as he got closer, I could see that it was Peter. When he got to the top of the hill," Rebecca continued, "he was all out of breath, but he was completely amazed to see me. He reached out his hand to pat Betty on the neck, and I said, 'Watch it— she'll bite you,' and I had to whip her head around with the rein to keep her from taking a chunk out of him. Then Betty just stood there stomping her foot and twitching her tail. You know she hates men. I really think Frank Getchell mistreated her."

"Frank didn't mistreat her," I said, angrily. "Betty's a witch."

This made Rebecca laugh with delight.

I chuckled, too, about Betty's wretchedness, but it did worry me that she'd said such a thing about Frank. It's not as horsey around here as it was when I was a kid. But everybody has dogs, at least, and many people, including myself, think that animal abuse is as heinous as child abuse. You really wouldn't want people saying that about you. Frank wouldn't abuse any living thing.

"Go on. What else?" asked Rebecca.

"The next time you encountered each other

was on the beach, in front of Peter's house."

"It was the following week," she said. "I had no idea where the Newbolds' house was, but I had driven down Wind Point Road before and knew it was a place where I could park close to a beach. So I took Harry down there and some water-colors and paper. Sometimes I use watercolors and then later make the thing an oil painting if I like it, when I get back to the studio. So I'm sitting on a piece of driftwood and painting, and I suddenly hear Peter Newbold saying, 'Rebecca?' We were both astounded. I was right in front of his house."

That's actually a private beach down there at the end of Wind Point Road. There's a big sign that says so. Signs like this don't register with people like Rebecca—people who come from money—and I'm sure she saw it, then strode right past.

"After that you started meeting on the beach regularly. Not every day . . . not every day, no, but a few times a week. You both made it seem like a coincidence the first few times, but then it got to the point that if one of you was late or missed this chance meeting, you would apologize."

Rebecca was transfixed.

"Peter was very interested in your painting. He would ask you, if he had missed seeing you for a few days, 'What did you paint?' He was so interested in your art, in your desire to paint his beach, his view of the sea. He was interested in your art in a way that Brian never was."

"Hildy, it's true, but that's because Peter is really an artist himself. He's always been interested in photography, and one day he brought out some prints of photos he had taken in the evening, his favorite time on the beach, because of the light. They were so beautiful. He really loves light and color in the way that an artist does," she said. "Did you know that about him, that he always wanted to be an artist?"

"No," I said. "I really don't know Peter that well." Which wasn't altogether true. I'd always thought I knew Peter pretty well, but now I was getting to know him a little better.

"Tell me what else," said Rebecca. "Tell me everything else you know."

"He wants to retire," I announced. "He's dying to. He's burned-out. And his marriage has been dead for years. He wants to finish writing his book, and then travel the world. . . ."

Now there were tears in Rebecca's eyes. "This is unbelievable. I know Peter's never told anybody this but me. It's all true."

God. People and their romantic idiocy. Of course it was true. True for Peter and for most men having midlife affairs. Here's the key again: Nobody wants to believe the obvious and visible reality that we are all quite the same. Most would rather believe in the invisible and the improbable—that fate is determined by the alignment of stars, that there is a spiritual entity rooting for them, for unique and wonderful them, that humans can read minds, that their destiny can be foretold and possibly altered. The simple truth is this: Most humans are very much alike. The simple and obvious truth is that there are very few variables to what a person might do, think, fear, or desire in any given situation.

"One day," Rebecca continued, "I needed to call Magda to check on the kids. It was a Friday. Peter had stopped seeing patients on Fridays because he was trying to work on his book when he was up here, and he was writing, but he always took breaks and came down to see what I was working on. So he told me to come into his house to make the call. And I did. When I hung up, he was standing in the doorway leading out to the porch. I had to walk past him to leave, and as I did, I don't know what inspired me, but I took my finger and touched his arm, just on the inside of his elbow, then I sort of traced this invisible line down to his hand. He grabbed my hand then . . . and held it. That's when it began."

That was interesting. Peter made the first move. He had drawn her into the house and then it was he who held her. I had imagined it otherwise, but now it all was spelled out for me.

"You like a man who takes charge in bed, and for all Brian's bravado and tough Southie exterior, he's a bit of a nice guy in the sack."

Rebecca nearly choked on her wine with astounded laughter.

"I can't believe you just said that. Yeah, Brian's a vanilla kind of guy, it's true."

Peter, according to Rebecca, was a very take-command type in bed. He would grab both of her thin wrists in one large hand and pin them above her head while managing to kiss her and work her clothes off with the other hand.

"It's the kissing," Rebecca said. "The man knows how to kiss."

I sighed then, and poured myself another glass of wine.

Yes, the kissing. Yes.

"You used to meet him at his office at night," I said, recalling the night I'd stopped in for the closing papers. It really was shameful how easy this all was, but I was enjoying myself.

"Yes, Peter started getting flipped out about meeting at his house. He worried that somebody might notice my car, or that we might leave behind some . . . evidence, I guess. So we met up in his office a few times, but it wasn't for therapy. It was, you know . . . they were romantic meetings. Now we meet in the office over his garage. Where he writes. Elise never goes in there. It's pretty cozy. It was set up as a little guest apartment, so there's a bed and everything. I usually park in town and Peter picks me up so nobody will see my car. Now he's all worried about you, since you have the office downstairs. Worried that you might think I was his patient or something and now you might be suspicious."

"But you *were* his patient."

"Not really, Hildy. When people are in therapy, they're in therapy for months and sometimes years. I saw him twice and then realized I didn't need it at all. It's completely different."

"Are you going to tell him you told me about the two of you?"

"Told you? I didn't tell you. You just read my mind. You pulled it out of my brain. No. Hildy, he would totally freak out if he knew we'd had this conversation. I'm trusting you. But I'm glad you know. I don't have anyone else to talk to about this. You're like a . . . sister to me."

I know she almost said "mother." She was wise to think twice. I can be a little sensitive about my age. Who isn't?

"I can trust you, right?" she asked.

"Yes," I said. "Of course."

Normally, I would have felt pleased with myself after such a successful reading. You really know you've hit pay dirt when the person believes you so much that she starts filling in the gaps for you. And it's not something I would ever tell anybody. I believed then that everybody would know in time, that things would come undone, as these things usually do. One of the spouses would become suspicious. Or, like Scott, one of them would become tired of "living the lie." I thought it likely that Rebecca and Peter would leave their marriages and end up together. Normally, I get a little twinge of the huntress, a taste of the kill when I learn news like this. I admit, I salivate a little, because there will probably be at least one property sacrificed before the whole thing is over, and of course I want the listing.

But that night in front of the fire with Rebecca, I was so enchanted with her sweet company, so happy not to be drinking alone, I didn't think about real estate at all; instead, I calmly tantalized her with little juicy tidbits about Peter Newbold. I told her about how his father, Dr. David Newbold, was a family practitioner who used to make house calls when I was little. How Peter was an only child, born late in his father's life, to a second wife. How my friend Allie Dyer used to baby-sit him during the summers and on week-ends.

"He was such a cute kid," I mused, moving the embers about the fireplace with the poker in a distracted manner.

"He was?" Rebecca asked.

"We used to play hide-and-seek—it was his favorite thing. We would hide and he would tiptoe around the house, wanting to find us, but also slightly terrified, because sometimes, when he got close to our hiding spots, we'd leap out and scare the crap out of him." I laughed, remembering now how much Peter had loved and hated this, how he would sometimes laugh and cry at once, then beg us to play one more time.

I could feel Rebecca's gaze on me as I fussed with the fire. You can't imagine what it's like to be bathing in the attention of another after so long in nightly exile. I put down the poker and saw that our glasses were empty.

"I was always surprised that he married Elise. She just never really seemed his type. . . . More wine?" I asked Rebecca.

"Oh God, no, I really should get home," she replied, but she lifted her glass up toward the bottle I was holding.

I loved her like my own child then. More. More. She wanted more.

Ten

I had a friend. I hadn't realized until that night with Rebecca that I needed a friend. In fact, I had always considered myself a woman with many friends. Most people in Wendover would tell you that they consider me a friend. But since my return from rehab, I had sort of straddled two worlds. By day I was a businesswoman, a contributor to local charities, a "friend" to my neighbors, clients, and fellow brokers. But my nights had become a little bit lonely. I rarely socialized with anyone. No more late nights with Mamie. No more wet lunches and celebratory dinners after deals were closed. I usually declined dinner parties, especially once I started drinking again.

It was odd, but during those first months after Hazelden, I didn't really have the desire to drink, and attending parties where people were drinking wasn't so intolerable. I had, somehow, lost the obsession with alcohol, and any urges I had to drink were fleeting and momentary. The consequences of ordering a drink and possibly ending up back at Hazelden were always on my mind.

Then, one day, I was in my cellar, trying to find some old photos that Tess wanted, and I came across a case of wine. Scott and I were never wine drinkers. It must have been left over from a party. I opened the box and took out a bottle. It was a Merlot. I cradled it in my hands for a moment, studying the label. I moved the bottle around in little circles and watched the dark red liquid swirl up the neck of the bottle and lap at the bottom of the cork. I turned it upside down and saw that there was some sediment at the bottom. It was dusty, so I took my sleeve and wiped the glass clear and blew the dust from the label. Then I carefully tucked it back into the box. Presumably, I'd have the occasion to serve wine to guests someday. It was nice to know it was there.

From that moment on, every second that I was in the house, I knew it was there. I thought about it when I woke up in the morning, and I thought about it when I walked into the house after work. Tess and Michael had removed (stolen) every bottle containing alcohol in my liquor cabinet while I was away. It was for my own good, they had explained. They didn't want me to be tempted after doing so well in rehab. I guess they never thought to check the cellar. It was a little thrilling and satisfying to know that they had missed something—an entire case of wine. I left it alone for a good couple of weeks. Then one Friday night, after returning home from baby-sitting Grady, I was lonely and a little sad. I had read Grady one of the girls' favorite books from their childhood—Dr. Seuss's *Horton Hears a Who*. I don't know why, but the part where the little microscopic Whos call out from the speck of dust, "We are here! We are here! We are here!" always gets me a little choked up, and I'm not the most emotional person. I don't know why that always gets me, but it does.

When the story was over, I had placed little Grady in his crib in his soft jammies. He closed his eyes, clutching his "bewkey" (a tattered old beloved blanket) to his pink cheek, and I suddenly envied him his comfort. It felt like ages before Tess and Michael arrived home, and when they did, Michael was a little tipsy. They wanted to chat, but I told them how exhausted I was, and I left.

When I finally got back to my house, I went straight down to the cellar, with Babs and Molly charging ahead of me. Babs raced comically down the steps on her front legs, only touching every other step with a hind toe and Molly, in order to hit the earthen floor first, soared over the bottom four steps in one leap, then they both sniffed maniacally for cellar mice. I marched straight to the dusty box. I removed one of the bottles. I cradled it in the crook of my arm. I carried it upstairs. In the kitchen, after some rummaging around, I found a corkscrew, uncorked the bottle, and poured some of the rich Merlot out into a wineglass, a beautiful crystal wineglass, part of a Waterford set that Scott had bought at an auction years ago. Then I took a sip. Then I took another sip—a nice long one—and I felt the familiar warmth, first on the back of my tongue and in my throat, and then down deep in my belly. I took another sip and it was everywhere. All the warmth and comfort I had missed, it all came back, just after those first few sips. It bolstered me and soothed me, the way it always had.

The goodness—that inner goodness that had been lost for so many months—revealed itself to me again. It was a cold night in late February and I sat on the couch in the living room with my dear, dear dogs beside me, and I drank that glass of wine and I refilled it. I didn't drink the entire bottle, not the whole bottle, no. All I needed was a couple of glasses of that divine red wine, and I felt as if I had surfaced from some murky underground place and that I was drawing oxygen, once again, into my stagnant blood.

But it wasn't until I finally got to share my wine with Rebecca that I realized how much I had tired of drinking alone.

It's not normal to drink alone all the time. I learned that at Hazelden.

I knew Rebecca had also been a little lonely until that night. Her kids had started at the Montessori school, and I was aware that she had become friendly with a few of the moms, but I also knew that she didn't have a real friend, a confidante.

We had a short Indian summer in early November and Rebecca brought her boys over to fish in the river a few times. I grew rather fond of young Ben and Liam. I admit that I have a slight prejudice against the often outrageously precocious products of our local Montessori school. They don't get grades and they don't keep score in games, you see, because it might deflate their industrial-size self-esteems. The adults aren't "teachers"; they're "learning partners." And I'm told that even the four-year-olds call their teachers by their first names. This, I believe, helps explain why I recently had a young Montessorieducated girl say to me in the grocery store, "Hey, Hildy, you shouldn't buy ice cream; it'll just make you fatter."

I knew the family. I had recently rented them a house, so I crossed my arms and waited for her mother to reprimand the seven-year-old. Instead, the mom smiled at her little cherub and said nothing. The child said, "Why are you buying it if it makes you fat?"

Again, I glared at her.

"Well, Ashley, that's Hildy's prerogative," her mother said.

"What does *prerogative* mean?" asked the brat.

I reached into the freezer and grabbed another pint of ice cream. "If you don't teach manners now," I said to the mother, "you're really doing her a disservice. She'll have a hard time as an adult."

As I started to walk off, the mother said, "Well, I don't think you were setting a very good example by ignoring my daughter."

So I walked back to the child and said, "I'm an adult, so it would have been more respectful for you to call me Mrs. Good. And it's rude to tell people they're fat."

"OH, puhLEEZE!" exclaimed the mother, and she stormed down the aisle, dragging her daughter along by the hand. Her daughter looked over her shoulder at me and I gave her a menacing stare. It was my prerogative.

But Rebecca's boys always called me Mrs. Good, and they looked me in the eye when they spoke to me. Rebecca had a great sense of humor with her boys, but she corrected them anytime they wavered even slightly toward disrespectful behavior, and she didn't have much tolerance for whining and complaining. One day, for example, we were seated on a couple of chairs by the river, watching the boys fishing. Liam, the seven-year-old, hadn't caught a thing.

"Mom, how come Ben has caught three and I haven't caught any?"

"Oh, Liam," Rebecca said, laughing, "don't bellyache about it. Go fish closer to where Ben is fishing."

"It's true, Liam, see how Ben's in the shade?" I said. "That's where the trout like to hide on warm days."

"Really?"

"Yes," I said. "Drop your hook close to shore; they hang out there under the stony ledges."

A few minutes later, when he'd hooked his first fish of the day, Liam said, "Hey, thanks for the tip, Mrs. Good." Then he carried the bowed pole with the trout gyrating at the end of the line to his mother. The boys always asked Rebecca or me to remove the fish from the hooks.

"Stop being so squeamish," Rebecca had chided him. Then she helped him work the trout off the hook. "Now you take it and toss it back. Go ahead."

Liam gingerly took the fish from her. He ran to the riverbank and flung it back into the water. Then he wiped his hands on his jeans, saying, "GROSS, it was all slimy, like a snake."

Rebecca laughed. "He's going to have another snake dream again tonight. He keeps dreaming about snakes, which is so adorable."

"Oh?" I said, slightly puzzled.

"It's . . . you know, he's obsessed with his penis. Peter told me it's normal for boys to have dreams like that. I love telling Peter about our dreams, mine and the kids. He's so good at analyzing them."

"Really? You tell him your dreams? Like when you're . . . *together?*" I whispered.

"Of course. Dreams are so fascinating. They're full of information about us."

"Mine aren't. I tend to dream about houses all the time. It's because I'm in real estate, I guess."

"No!" Rebecca exclaimed. "The other day I was reading a book Peter gave me about dreams, and it said that houses in dreams always represent the self. If you dream about being up in an attic or on top of a house, it represents your intellect or a search for something spiritual. The basement represents your subconscious impulses, primitive longings, sexuality. Where are you in the dreams about your house?" she asked.

"I think I'm always in the kitchen."

"That means you have an appetite for

something. You want to fill some kind of void."

I laughed good-naturedly. Rebecca acted as if she were an expert in analysis, solely based on her romance with Peter. I looked at my watch.

"Five o'clock, how about a glass of wine?"

"Okay, just one, though."

At night, at least once or twice a week, when Brian was staying in town, Rebecca would leave the boys with the nanny, after they went to bed, and she'd come sit by the fire with me and we'd have a little wine. It was usually a Tuesday or Wednesday. Thursday was her night with Peter. Fridays, Brian would be home for the weekend.

Rebecca was such pleasant company that I literally rejoiced in our friendship. She was very funny. Being an outsider, she had hysterically comic takes on a lot of the people I had known my whole life, people whose eccentricities were so much a part of the fabric of my hometown that I didn't see their irregularities until she pointed them out. For example, the Winston boys—Ed and Phil Winston. Identical twins who still, now in their late eighties, dressed in matching outfits for their afternoon walk through the Crossing. Anorexic old Diana Merchant, who, despite her advanced age, wore halter tops and heels at the grocery store. And crazy Nell Hamlyn, whose goats got loose all the time and terrorized Rebecca's horses. Rebecca did a great impersonation of Linda Barlow, who helped her out with the gardening and barn chores. I had known Linda all her life, so I had never noticed how manly she was until Rebecca strode across my living room, barking at me in Linda's gutteral, gruff manner.

We would laugh until we cried some nights, Rebecca and I. She was clearly dissatisfied with her husband and told stories of his outrageously egomaniacal behavior, which would sometimes make us choke on our wine. She also told me of the real source of her dissatisfaction with him: He was a womanizer and a cheat. He had had an affair with a young model the year before they moved up here. There had been a photograph in the *Boston Herald* showing the two, seated together, right on the floor of the Garden at a Celtics game. He had told Rebecca that the affair was over. But she didn't believe him. And, oddly, she didn't appear to care. She told me that she had cared very much at first. It was one of the causes of her depression when they had first moved here—his infidelity and her years-long grief over her own infertility. She was terrified of being abandoned by Brian, and feared that everything she did was driving him further and further away. She'd immediately regretted moving up here because she couldn't keep as close an eye on him. Laughing about it now, she recalled the way she used to phone him at all hours of the night at their place in Boston and accuse him of being with his girlfriend, then tell him she wanted to sell the Barlow place and move back.

"Imagine," she said now. "I was out of my mind. Moving up here was the best thing that ever happened to me."

I got the sense that she had come to consider her marriage with Brian McAllister a failed attempt at love. A botched effort. Now, of course, she had found the real thing in Peter Newbold.

I told her about Scott's leaving me for Richard. She'd had no idea. Everybody in town knows that Scott left me for a man, but Rebecca hadn't a clue, nor did she know about Linda Barlow's son, who was killed, as an infant, in a car accident, in which Linda, the driver, only received a few scrapes. I chose not to tell Rebecca; she would have felt awful for making fun of Linda. Rebecca meant no harm with her witty commentaries. She seemed to sail about the town on a different course than us townies, unaware of the steady undercurrents we had known and understood our whole lives. She knew only what she could observe —the surface of things—and I learned, through Rebecca, how funny things can be, sometimes, if you just look at them on a surface level.

During this time, I became aware of a change in Peter Newbold's behavior toward me whenever we crossed paths at work. I don't think I was imagining it. Peter has always been a thoughtful and considerate neighbor and tenant, but he became particularly solicitous during those weeks after Rebecca's first visit to my house. One Friday morning, we both arrived at the office at the same time and he held the door open for me, but then, instead of jogging up the steps, as he usually did, he stopped to ask me how I was doing.

"I'm great, Peter. How about you?" I was actually quite hungover.

"Good, good, Hildy."

"Are Elise and Sam coming up this weekend?"

"They're gonna try to come up tomorrow night, I hope. Elise teaches a workshop on Saturday mornings now, and Sam likes to hang in Cambridge with his friends. . . ."

"Of course," I said. I suspected Peter had been with Rebecca the night before. I wondered if he could smell last night's wine on me. I had been lonely the night before and had drunk a little more than usual. My head was splitting. I realized I was feeling a bit angry at Peter as I stood there fumbling about with my keys. I blamed him for my hangover—he had hijacked my drinking buddy, and that's why I kept drinking long after I should have gone to bed the night before.

Who the fuck do you think you're kidding? I thought, glancing up at his tousled hair and his slightly exhausted expression. At the same time, I was aware of a strange excitement I felt in the knowledge that he had been with Rebecca the night before. He had been with my Rebecca.

Nobody knew this but Peter and Rebecca and me. And I knew it without having been told. I finally found my keys and was about to turn to unlock my office door, when I said to Peter, "I'm sure you're aware that I've been seeing a lot of Rebecca lately." My head was throbbing. I think I must have still been a little tipsy from the night before and that's what made me say it.

"Rebecca . . ." Peter said.

"Yes, I gather you've been nice enough to allow her to do some painting on your beach."

"Oh. Yes. Rebecca McAllister. Yes," he said. "Yes."

"I'm so glad they moved to town. Though I don't know him at all. Brian McAllister. It seems like he's not up here much," I said.

"No?" Peter replied. I was trying to get a reading on him. He was cool, when he should have been sweating. He must have been taught this in shrink school, taught to be blank, not to reveal thoughts.

"Well, have a nice weekend," I said, finally finding the right key and unlocking my door.

"You, too, Hildy," Peter said, and I felt him watch me as I entered my office.

My friend Allie Dyer baby-sat for Peter Newbold from the time he was a toddler until he was about eight years old. Peter's father, David Newbold, was almost fifty when Peter was born, and Dr. Newbold had a busy local practice. His mother, Colette, was in her twenties, and Mrs. Newbold had a very busy social life. It seemed that she was never at home, especially during the summer months. So she hired Allie Dyer as a full-time sitter. Colette Newbold played tennis daily. She also played bridge and golf and kept a horse at Westfield Hunt Club. She was on numerous town committees and was an active member of the Anawam Beach Club and the Wendover Yacht Club, in addition to the hunt club. She was the one who started the charity luncheon at Westfield's big August horse show.

When Peter was little, Allie would baby-sit him at the Newbolds' house on Wind Point Road. Every morning, after Colette breezed out in her tennis togs or riding britches, Mamie and Lindsey and I would ride our bikes over, and we'd sun ourselves on the beach in front of the Newbolds' house, then devour whatever they had in their refrigerator. Colette never complained. She didn't seem to mind who was watching Peter, as long as it wasn't her.

When Allie was old enough to drive, we took Peter everywhere with us. He was probably five or six years old when we started taking him to North Beach, where we'd meet up with boys and flirt and swill Cokes and smoke cigarettes and run around in the surf in our bikinis. Allie was making a dollar an hour, as long as we had Peter with us, so we always had him along. Peter picked up all our slang, which amused us. We taught him to wolf-whistle at pretty girls we didn't know, and when the girls would turn and look, we'd convulse with laughter, little Peter giggling loudest of all. We taught him to give the peace sign out of Allie's car window. We taught him to give the finger, the four of us shrieking with laughter at the astonished faces of the little old ladies he flipped off. Mamie still has a photo of Peter with sunglasses and a cigarette dangling from his lips when he couldn't have been more than seven. Another time, we took his picture as he posed on Mamie's boyfriend's motorcycle. We put a ban-danna on his head and made him look like Peter Fonda in *Easy Rider.* He loved hanging out with us, and we usually forgot about the facts of his tender age and his gender when it was just Peter and us girls. We'd be splayed across the sand in our bikinis, talking about boys and who was making it with whom, and Peter would just sit there and listen. We'd complain about our periods and about our parents and school, and Peter would just be drawing in the sand, taking it all in. We often had plans for the evening that we would discuss throughout the day, and Peter would sometimes beg to be included, which made us laugh. But there were times when Colette needed a nighttime sitter, so we took him to parties on the beach, or to the movies or to one of our homes. We got the sense he was lonely at home with his parents. He didn't have many friends his own age, but when we asked him about this, he said they were all immature. No wonder. He spent most of his early years with a bunch of teenagers. Sometimes when he assumed he would be included in what we were doing, we had to remind him that he wasn't really our friend.

"You can come, as long as Allie's getting paid," Mamie would say, and Allie would shoot her a disapproving glance. Peter had a little crush on Allie. We all knew it, and Mamie's comments were bound to have hurt his feelings.

"Well, it's the truth," Mamie would mutter. "No point in letting him think there's any other reason he's hanging out with us. He's friggin' eight. We're his paid friends."

"MAMIE," Allie would say, giving Peter a little hug. But it was true. And Peter knew it.

Here's a very sweet story about Peter Newbold: Once, on his birthday, he received a ten-dollar bill from his grandparents. His mother asked him what he was going to spend it on. He told her that he wanted to spend it on ten hours with Allie. Mrs. Newbold told this story to Allie when Peter wasn't in earshot, and they both laughed and agreed that it was adorable, but later Allie told me that it made her feel uncomfortable. Soon after that, Allie's family moved to New Hampshire and the rest of us got our jobs at the Wendover

Yacht Club, so we didn't see Peter much anymore. Still, I've often thought that those summers spent listening to us girls and all our crazy talk prepared him for his vocation as a shrink. He was always a good listener.

When Peter started up his private practice in Wendover, he worked first from an office above his garage and then, about ten years ago, he started renting the office upstairs from me. One February evening, several years ago, we were snowed in, and as we waited for one of Frankie's crew to come with a plow, we sat in my reception area and split a bottle of champagne that a client had sent me. Peter told me about his work at McLean Hospital. He had gone there, years ago, to complete his residency and had stayed on as staff psychiatrist when he was finished. He had become quite interested in schizophrenia during those early years—in fact, that was considered his specialty. He had published numerous papers on the subject—clinical papers that were meant to be read by other professionals. He also had always had his private practice in Cambridge, as well as up here, with what he called the "worried well."

His work with the severely ill had inspired him to write a book about "attachment." It was called *Of Human Bonding.* This was a book written for the general public, more or less a pop-psychology book, I guess. He signed a copy and gave it to me, but I confess, I never read it until after the whole situation with Rebecca, and then I scoured it, desperate to find out everything I possibly could about Peter Newbold. Normally, I read only novels. But that night, waiting for the plow, I asked him about the book. It had just come out a few months earlier. He talked a little bit about the parent/infant bond. About how important it was. Stuff everybody knows, really. He talked about childhood traumas. Then, in the middle of our little chat, he suddenly said, "For example, when your mother committed suicide, you were how old . . . ten? Eleven?"

I was completely floored by this. I wasn't surprised Peter knew about my mother. Most people in town knew about her, so he would have heard about it, even though he was very young at the time. But I don't think anybody, in all those many years since her death, had actually stated the fact of her death so plainly to me until Peter did so that afternoon. People referred to my mother's "tragic" or "untimely" death, but never, ever, her "suicide." Not even my father. It was actually several years into our marriage before I told Scott, one drunken evening, about the way my mother died. Then I instantly regretted it, because he, the lover of history, wanted to know every detail. He was surprised that I had never had any kind of grief counseling or therapy when it happened.

"I don't think they had that kind of thing up here then," I had told him.

Of course, when Scott and I split up, we had the girls see therapists, to "process their grief." Their school counselor had recommended it. Tess was fourteen, Emily twelve at the time. And they've both been in therapy, on and off, ever since. I still pay their therapy bills, though I'm less and less able to afford them. I've told the girls I think it's a bit of an indulgence. I've never been in therapy and I manage quite well. If anything, in my opinion, therapy has made the girls, especially Tess, more brooding and self-absorbed. She went through a stage where she was completely obsessed with finding out every detail about my mother.

"What was *really* wrong with her?" she would ask me, and sometimes, if I'd had a couple of drinks, I'd offer up what I knew. "She had manic-depression. The doctors told Dad it was manic-depression."

"Bipolar," Tess would proclaim excitedly. "It's called 'bipolar' now."

"Okay. Fine," I'd reply.

"Well, it must have been hard for you, having a mother with such unpredictable moods," Tess would say.

"Honestly, I didn't really notice. I don't think I paid a lot of attention. We were at school all day. In the summers, we spent our time outdoors, mostly. . . ."

"Because your mom found it so hard to cope?"

"No, because that's what all kids did in those days."

I would usually try to change the subject, but Tess would steer me back. "It's important for me to know," she'd say. "My therapist wants to know my history. I mean, if your mother was mentally ill, and such an alcoholic, and we know that there was insanity on your father's side, going back to Sarah Good—"

"Oh, please, don't start up with the witch business again," I'd cry out. "The poor old hag was hanged. Let her rest in peace."

Scott and our younger daughter, Emily, had a theory about my witch ancestress, Sarah Good. Emily even wrote an essay about Sarah Good in high school, called "Goodwife Good." Here's what she and Scott learned: Sarah Good's father killed himself when she was a young child and when her mother remarried, her new husband took her inheritance. Sarah married once, at age sixteen, was widowed, and married again, this time to a man named Good. I guess she had a screw loose, because she somehow caused their ensuing bankruptcy and debt, and the Goods—including their four-year-old daughter, Dorcas—were soon homeless beggars. Sarah Good was not a sweet, humble beggar. She was antisocial and belligerent. She would knock on the doors in Salem Village and, if she was refused charity, would issue a series of incoherent curses under her breath. She and her daughter were unwashed and wore others' cast-off rags for clothes.

Sarah Good was one of the first three women in Salem accused of witchcraft, when the mass hysteria began, and her own little daughter, Dorcas, and her husband both testified against her. Here's something I find so, so sad about the case of Sarah Good: Four-year-old Dorcas was also accused of witchcraft, and because of her youth and ignorance, she confessed. She was chained in a dungeon, like the others, and when she was interviewed by magistrates several days after her arrest, she told them that her mother had given her a snake, and that the snake bit her thumb and sucked her blood. The officials assumed that the snake was a "familiar," and this pretty much sealed Sarah Good's fate. She had been pregnant when arrested, and after giving birth to her baby (which subsequently died), she was hanged. Dorcas Good was eventually released. So deranged was she by her time spent chained in a dungeon that she was deemed "never good for anything" by her father, who received some restitution for his damaged progeny. She must have been good for something, to some man, as I am her descendant, as are my daughters.

Emily's paper asserted that had Sarah Good lived today, she would have been diagnosed with a severe form of mental illness—bipolar disorder or schizophrenia. She cited the witnesses' descriptions of Sarah Good's odd behavior—her inclination to mutter things to herself and others, her sometimes hostile and antisocial nature. There is a genetic component to these mental illnesses, Emily wrote, and she made reference to Sarah Good's suicidal father. Scott helped Emily research her paper and she received an A. The essay was actually entered in some kind of statewide essay contest. She didn't win, but she did receive an honorable mention.

Scott was always fascinated by this theory, about this double line of madness in my family. He never met my mother, of course, but he was quite preoccupied with what he called the "ironies" of her situation. For example, the fact that my mother spent a good part of my childhood in Danvers State Hospital, an institution for the insane. Many don't know that the Salem witch trials actually took place in Salem Village, which is now Danvers, in very close proximity to the hospital where my mother was confined more than once. Scott got a big kick out of the fact that Danvers State Hospital, built in the late 1800s, was originally called the "State Lunatic Hospital at Danvers," and that the hospital stood on Hathorne Hill, which was named after John Hathorne, one of the judges in the Salem witch trials.

"They actually called it a lunatic hospital," he would call out to me as he read from one of his stacks of library books. "Did they still call it that when your mother was there?"

"No, of course not," I would reply impatiently.

Scott knew I hated talking about the place. Most everything he knew about my mother, he had learned when we were half in the bag, both of us. Drinking always loosened my lips. Apparently, it had had the same effect on my mother. When she was "up," according to my dad—I actually don't recall her periods of mania very well; I don't think they happened often—she would drink to slow herself down a bit, to get a little sleep, but she would overdo it, I guess. I've been told that she ended up at Danvers once, when I was very small, because she drove over to the home of Reverend Howell, who was then the minister of the Congregational church. (Another favorite irony of Scott's: Reverend Howell's former dining room is my current office.) She marched into his dining room and, as Reverend Howell sat at the dinner table with his wife and three young children, asked why he kept raping her and sodomizing the children of the parish. I didn't know about that until my aunt Peg told me, in hushed, faltering words, a few days before I left for college. We went to the Congregational church every Sunday of my youth. Mrs. Howell had taught my Sunday school class and led us in the church children's choir. She was always so kind to me. I had no idea.

The first time I remember my mother going to the hospital in Danvers was after my brother, Judd, was born. I was six; my sister Lisa was about four. I guess my mom had postpartum depression after each of us was born—they just didn't know as much about it then. She became very depressed. She slept all the time. Aunt Peg came over and stayed after Judd was born. My cousin Jane is just a year younger than I am, and Eddie is three years older, so it was fun having them at the house with us all the time. One day, Peg was doing something in the kitchen and she tried to get my mother to hold Judd. My mother kept refusing tearfully. Finally, she whispered into Peg's ear that she was afraid to hold him because she might take him into the bathroom and drown him in the tub. She had repeated visions of doing it. My mother hadn't bathed in weeks. It turned out, she was afraid to go near the bathtub because of the visions of drowning the baby.

So back she went to Danvers State. I do remember her hospitalization this time, because we went to visit her there. After a few drinks, Scott could usually persuade me to tell him about it. Mostly, I remember the smell. It just filled the air at Danvers State—the smell of urine, feces, ammonia, and some strange amalgamation of chemically tinged body odors. You walked into the stench the minute the attendants opened the doors to the wards. You never stopped smelling it, because you were just completely immersed in it. You had to go home and soak in the tub for an hour and shampoo your hair over and over again to get the smell out. My mother was very confused and mostly silent during our visits. She must have been heavily sedated. But some of the other women on the ward, they cackled and swore, and one told me she could see the devil above my head. He was always there, in a vapor, she told me. She kept staring at the space above my head and shaking her head with wild eyes, then looking at me with pity. We never went back to visit after that. Eventually, Mom came home.

My mother was depressed. What else can I say? Scott and the girls were always curious about her, but I haven't a lot of details. She loved animals. Our cat, Calico, was one of the few things that was guaranteed to always make my mother smile. She taught me to knit. She liked to read. She needed quiet. She was rather pretty. When I was twelve, she killed herself.

It was on one of the first days of summer. I remember my brother and sister and I were just giddy with the excitement of no school that morning. My mother stayed in bed, which wasn't unusual. We rode our bikes down to the market and our dad gave us doughnuts for breakfast. Then we went to my aunt Peg's—she lived down the road from us—and played with our cousins, Janie and Eddie. Eventually, Peg took us home. It was suppertime and Peg said she had a feeling, a premonition. She wanted to make sure my mom was feeling okay.

Mom was still in bed. The bedroom door was locked. Peg knocked and knocked. Then she called my dad, who came home and propped a ladder against the house, and I climbed up and into the small upstairs window. My dad was too big to squeeze through the window frame; my aunt Peg, weeping and wringing her hands, was too anxious. So I climbed through the window and ran to the bedroom door and unlocked it. I remember that I held my breath as I ran through the room, for some reason, as if I were swimming underwater from one side of a pool to the other. I just caught a glimpse of my mother out of the corner of my eye. She was curled up, facing the wall. I unlocked the door and ran past my father. I don't know how I knew she was dead. I just did. She had swallowed every pill in the house (and we had a houseful of pills).

Afterward, for years, I felt a strange guilt about running through the room like that. I should have gone to her. In fact, people who knew the story assumed that I had actually done just that —walked over and tried to wake her somehow. But I didn't. I'm not sure why I feel that guilt. I still feel it at times. Somewhere, deep inside, I think that maybe if I could have held my hand in front of her nose to see if she was breathing, like my father had done when he ran into the room, she might have been revived. By my need. Like that mare Rebecca had saved that first morning, revived by the presence, the simple and undeniable need of her baby.

But my mother knew we needed her when she took all those pills. There was no denying our presence. We weren't babies anymore. We were wild, my brother, sister, and I. Always tearing through the house. Telling on one another, having raging fights that spilled into her room. Jumping on her bed, screaming accusations about one another. Judd was always in trouble in school; he's a cop now, in Swampscott. My sister, Lisa (now a makeup artist in L.A.), and I had howling, slapping brawls and we'd shriek and curse at each other in front of my mother, trying to get her to take sides. Sometimes she would. Usually, though, she'd tell us that she needed quiet. She was too tired. She wanted us out of her room.

"You're all driving your poor mother out of her mind," Aunt Peg used to shout at us when she stopped in to "check on things," which she did regularly. We were, too. We knew it. We seemed to drive her into herself, make her distant and sad. But once she got that way, during what I now realize were her very depressed times, our mother didn't even seem to know we were there. We could be jumping around her bed, screaming and cursing and kicking one another, and she'd just turn and face the wall.

We are here, we are here, we are here was our constant chaotic, cacophonous cry.

Who gives a fuck, I guess, was her answer.

Eleven

I had been invited to Tess and Michael's for Thanksgiving dinner. It was going to be Tess, Michael, and Michael's parents, Nancy and Bill Watson. Emily was coming from New York, without Adam, who had decided to spend Thanksgiving with his own family, for some reason, this year. And Scott was coming. It was the first time since our divorce that we would be spending a holiday together with the kids. When Tess first presented the idea to me, several weeks earlier, I had balked.

"Just have Scott. I'll have dinner with Aunt Jane," I had said. My cousin Jane lived in Wendover, and in the past I had spent holidays with her and her family when Scott was with mine.

"Mom, why?" Tess had demanded. "Dad's all alone and you're all alone. I know you two get along fine. Dad said he just spoke to you last week."

It was true. Scott had called from his home in Lenox to ask my advice about whether he should put his house on the market now, or wait until the spring. Now that he and Richard had split up, he wanted to move closer to Marblehead, so he could see more of Grady. I had told him to wait. The Berkshires are beautiful in the spring, but the fall and winters are a little desolate, in my opinion. Scott knows that my opinion on the Berkshires is based on one visit to Lenox in midsummer twenty years ago and multiple readings of *Ethan Frome.* But he took my advice. He was going to wait until spring, and in the meantime, he made frequent trips to Brooklyn to see Emily and to Marblehead to see Tess. He always was a dedicated father.

Thanksgiving week marks the beginning of a slow-down time for me. It's a time I usually look forward to, but this year was different because the preceding months had been very slow. Plus, it was right before the holidays, two years earlier, that I had been shipped off to Hazelden. This year, holiday invitations had already started to arrive, but I didn't feel inclined to attend any of the parties. People get so drunk at holiday parties. I used to love that; it made me feel like a normal drinker. Now, prim and sober at parties, I often find myself cornered by somebody's shit-faced husband who's determined to have me hear his incoherent monologue about Barack Obama or how much he's always loved the sea. And, of course, there are always those people who ask me how much their property is worth. People have always asked me this, and it can be a little irritating. It's like asking a doctor about your niggling cough while at a social occasion. Sometimes I'd actually sold the house to the person doing this. When I was drinking, I'd usually tell them it was worth at least 10 percent more than what they'd paid, just to make them happy. Now I'm tempted to admit, "Not even close to what you paid for it," just to see the look on their faces. In general, I had been refusing invites for holiday parties, but I did finally agree to go to Tess's and be with the rest of the family.

The day before Thanksgiving, I was doing some paperwork in the office when Rebecca blew in. She was wearing riding britches and boots and a navy windbreaker. She looked windburned and radiant. It was an unseasonably mild day and she and Linda Barlow had trailered her two horses Serpico and Hat Trick down to Hart's Beach for a ride. The horses were fresh, unaccustomed to the sound of the surf, and they had had a long gallop. They had ridden all the way past Wind Point Road, Rebecca mentioned, in an offhand manner. All the way past Wind Point Road and back.

"We've been so lucky with this weather," I said. "What a great day for a ride on the beach."

Rebecca had seated herself on one of the armchairs that faced my desk. She rested the ankle of one boot on her knee and leaned back.

She looked my office over as if for the first time, taking everything in.

"This is a great office," she said. "Did your ex do the decorating?"

"Of course," I said. "I'm hopeless at that kind of thing."

Rebecca grinned. "Did he used to like to shop with you? For clothes, I mean . . . your clothes?"

"Yes," I groaned, and we both started to laugh. Rebecca thought it was hysterical that I'd had all these clues, all those years, and never knew Scott was gay. And it *was* funny when Rebecca made little jokes about it.

"He was constantly bringing me things home from Boston and New York, things that I would never have bought myself but that were actually great. . . ."

I could see that I had lost Rebecca's attention. Somebody was unlocking the side door—the entrance to the upstairs offices—then there were footsteps on the stairs. Rebecca's face was flushed, and it wasn't just the windburn.

"That must have been Peter," she said, picking up a paperweight that was sitting on my desk and pretending she was examining it.

"I don't think so," I said. "Peter rarely comes in on Wednesdays. The Newbolds usually do Thanksgiving at Elise's sister's house. In Concord, I think. That was probably just Patch Dwight. There's a leaky faucet up there."

"Oh," said Rebecca. The paperweight—a simple crystal dome with a digital clock set into its center—had suddenly become a source of great fascination to Rebecca. She was examining it very carefully, holding it up to the light and looking at the ceiling through its curved perspective.

"Hey, by the way, did you ever call Patch about getting a water hookup in your studio?"

"Yes," Rebecca said. "Well, actually, I had Brian call. You were right. He was happy to do it and was really nice when they were doing the work. Now I can wash out my paintbrushes in the studio."

"Have you been doing a lot of painting?"

Rebecca brightened. "Tons. I'm doing a whole series of these giant oil paintings of the moon over the water. They're from photos Peter took, mostly. One of them, though, I actually painted at Peter's one night. It was a night when the moon was full and you just couldn't capture the size of it with a camera. But as soon as Peter saw it, he called me and told me to bring my paints."

We heard Patch running down the stairs again, and Rebecca jerked her head around to watch him walk past my window. Then she turned and smiled at me. "You're right. It was Patch."

I had glanced down at some papers on my desk when Rebecca said, "Hildy, Peter's a little upset with me. With both of us, really."

"Oh? Why?"

She was picking at one of her fingernails.

"Wait, let me guess. He knows that you told me about what's going on between you two."

"Yes, I told him how you . . . came to know about it . . . and he was really upset. He said that you took advantage of me."

"Advantage?" I was trying not to laugh. I had taken advantage of Rebecca. That was rich, coming from Peter Newbold.

"Don't get upset, Hildy. It's all fine. He just thinks that you made me tell you stuff that I wouldn't ordinarily tell anybody. He thinks your whole psychic thing is an act."

"Rebecca, it *is* an act. I told you that. I don't read people's minds, not in the way you think I do anyway. But I didn't make you say anything. I'm shocked that Peter thinks you are so malleable that I could . . . Well, now that I think about it, I guess I'm not surprised; he seems to have had great success manipulating you."

"HILDY. How could you say that? That's one of the cruelest things anybody has ever said to me. We're very serious about each other, Hildy. You know we are. You know all about it."

"Well, tell Peter I won't tell anybody. Who would I tell? Nobody up here even knows his wife. I'm sure people think he carries on with all his patients. . . ."

This was below the belt. "I'm sorry," I said. "I didn't mean that."

"It's okay," Rebecca said. "Peter told me that you'd react very angrily if I talked to you about this, but I had to. You're my closest friend up here. The thing is, Peter's not just worried about Elise finding out. He could lose his license to practice if this came out. Psychiatrists can't have intimate relationships with their clients. It's against the law. In some states, he could go to jail for what has happened between us. Even though he was my doctor for only a short time."

"Against the law for two adults to have a relationship? Two consenting adults? I don't think that's true, Rebecca. Maybe in Puritan times, but now you're allowed to have sex with whoever you want, as long as you're both adults. I hate to say it, but I think Peter's feeding you a line of bullshit here. . . ."

"What on earth? It's not a line. . . ."

"I'm paying alimony to a man who was carrying on with another man for two years while we were married. The law saw nothing wrong with that. In fact, somehow, I am responsible for supporting him financially, him and, at one time, his partner, because I earn more money. So I don't see how it could be against the law for you and Peter to be carrying on as you are. Perhaps Peter wants you to think this so—oh, never mind, I'm sorry."

"Hildy, it's okay, but you're wrong. I've looked it up. It's against the law. Because some unethical doctors in the past have taken advantage of their patients. Some patients develop transference and they think they're in love with their shrink, but it's not real love. It's not like what Peter and I have. But I was never really Peter's patient. Not really. Not for long anyway. We're in love."

Rebecca looked so fragile then, so vulnerable, I felt bad about what I had said.

"I know you are. I know."

Rebecca sat forward in her seat then and looked into my eyes. She wanted a reading.

"You do? You know how he feels? You can tell me, Hildy. Don't spare me. I really need to know. I know that you know."

"I don't." I sighed.

This is why I stopped doing this kind of thing years ago. People want you to tell them that they're special; that there's some kind of cosmic meaning to their life's journey and a foreseeable fate that is just for them. A bright, happy fate just for special old them.

"Hildy. Hildy, just look at me, just for a minute."

I did. It made me shiver. Poor Rebecca.

"Yes. Yes, of course he loves you. Now stop worrying. Why don't you come over tonight? After you put the kids to bed. Come over for a quick glass of wine."

"I'd love to, Hildy, but I can't. Brian's on his way out here. My in-laws are coming for Thanksgiving. I guess I'd better get home and get changed."

"Have a happy Thanksgiving, Rebecca," I said, and she wished me the same.

I watched her walk out the side door and heard her pause for a moment at the bottom of Peter's stairs. Then she stomped along the porch in her riding boots, and in a few moments I heard her car speed off down Church Street.

I worked late that day. I was getting all my accounts organized for the end of the year, and when I left my office, it was dark. The darkness took me by surprise because the clock on my desk had said three-thirty. In fact, the little clock in the crystal paperweight on my desk has said three-thirty ever since then, though I've replaced the batteries numerous times. I'm not saying it had to do with Rebecca—still, I did recall what Brian had said that night at Wendy's party about Rebecca's strange magnetic field and its destructive effect on electronics. But that paperweight clock is cheap, made in China. It probably stopped days before Rebecca even touched it. I just didn't notice.

I walked along the driveway between my building and the Congregational church and I turned up the collar on my coat. There's always a wicked east wind that whips in between the two buildings when the weather turns cold. I blew into my hands and looked up at the church's tall windows, which were brightly lit from within. It was Wednesday night—the night the church choir usually holds its rehearsal for the coming

Sunday's services. I often see them from my office window, through the church's fogged panes: Sharon Rice, Brenda Dobbs from the Crossing library, Frizzy Wentworth, old Henry Mallard, and some I don't know. On nights that I worked late, I enjoyed watching them from my desk. I usually couldn't help but smile at those earnest townsfolk, their hymnals held aloft, their mouths moving in keen, pious syllables, their eager, submissive eyes fixed on a choir leader who stood just out of sight. That night before Thanksgiving, they were working a handbell recital, and I slowed my steps as I passed. The church's walls are thick and solid and no music could be heard from where I stood, but I watched the congregants as they held their bells, one bright brass, oak-stemmed clanger in each hand. They moved the bells up and down in what appeared, from where I stood, to be a random sequence. I thought about how these Wendover Protestants looked no different from the folks who peopled the choir when I was a kid. Those Massachusetts women, hair bobbed, no makeup, as sexless as children or Pilgrims. And the men, those paunchy family men, all chiming in with their bells; all together and each alone. Up. Down. Now . . . now . . . now . . . in a sequence set by somebody I just couldn't see from my driveway.

I have no idea who runs the music program at the church now, but when I was a child, it was Mrs.

Howell, the minister's wife. I was very fond of Mrs. Howell; she was the one who first got me interested in music. She made me love music, really. Mrs. Howell conducted both the adult and the children's choir. Sometimes the children's choir joined the adult choir for hymns; on other occasions, we children sang our own hymns during church services. Mrs. Howell said that the sound of children singing made her feel God's presence most clearly, and she taught us not to be afraid to sing; not to worry about hitting false notes, but to sing out with our hearts. She said that none of our notes would appear off, or false, if we sang like that.

Yes, I was very, very fond of Mrs. Howell.

One year, when I was in second or third grade, she chose me to sing a solo—the opening verse of "O Holy Night" for the Christmas Eve candlelight service.

"O Holy Night!" I began, all alone at the altar, my thin, wavering voice venturing out into the aisles and pews of the old church. It was so dark and so cold in the church that Christmas Eve. Once-familiar faces were distorted beyond recognition by the flickering light and the snaking tendrils of black smoke that arose from the hand-held candles. The only person I could see clearly was Mrs. Howell, who stood right before me, smiling calmly, her cupped hand cradling the air in smooth upward motions, her lips mouthing the words along with me.

"The stars are brightly shining," I warbled on in a semi-whisper. "It is the night of our dear Saviour's birth."

The church was full. Most everybody I knew sat in the pews, but I couldn't see them. My hands shook and I clutched the sides of my red plaid Christmas skirt to steady them. Then I drew a deep breath and continued, my eyes fixed on Mrs. Howell.

"Long lay the world in sin and error pi . . . i . . . ning. . . . [gulp]. Till He appeared . . . and the soul felt its worth."

Then (oh how joyous) the choir, young and old, and the entire congregation joined me.

"A thrill of hope, the weary world rejoices, for yonder breaks a new and glorious morn. FALL ON YOUR KNEES!" (This was where you could hear our old Mr. Hamilton's baritone, and Mrs. Riley's sweet, shrill soprano hovering above us all.) "O, HEAR the angel voices! O NI-I-IGHT DIVINE . . . Oh night when Christ was born. . . ."

Words can't describe the sense of comfort and community you feel, singing alone and then, suddenly, being buoyed up by the rest of the choir. I sang the rest of the carol, grinning broadly and searching the pews for the faces of my friends, my father and my mother, and now I could see them in the warm candlelight. There they were. There they all were, singing along with us. I remember my mother that night, how she sang, and how she smiled up at me, tears streaming down her face.

When Mrs. Howell taught us that carol, during Sunday school, she had us all draw pictures to go with each line. I was assigned the line "till He appeared and the soul felt its worth." I drew a baby in a manger with a little halo over his head and rays of sunshine emanating from him. Mrs. Howell said, "I like the yellow rays of sun you used to express the soul and all its worth." I grinned proudly, though I had just drawn the baby Jesus the way I had seen him illustrated many times—always with a little halo and the rays of golden light. The soul. Divine in all its worth? Can you imagine an adult feeding this nonsense to children?

The next day was Thanksgiving, and I walked my dogs after breakfast, then put on a wool skirt and sweater. The weather had changed; it was going to be a cold Thanksgiving Day after all.

I left my house around noon. Tess wanted everybody to arrive by one, as she planned to serve dinner at three. Emily and Scott had arrived at Tess's the night before, and Michael's parents lived just down the road. They were all there by the time I arrived.

Like I've mentioned, it's hard now to be around people who are enjoying their drinks. Tess and Emily usually are careful to not drink much around me. I knew they'd have a little wine, but they'd act as if they weren't enjoying it. The Watsons barely drink at all. So I had toyed with the idea of arriving a little later. I had even considered having a small glass of wine before I left the house. Many people have wine with lunch when they're not working. But I feared they would smell it on me. Plus, really, that's the kind of thing women at Hazelden talked about doing, during their shameful active-alcoholic days— having a drink to brace themselves for an occasion. I wasn't like them. I didn't need it. So I arrived on time, at one, and found old Bonnie on the front porch.

It was cold, so I let her come inside with me, and immediately Tess, who was just walking past the door with a large cheese platter, said, "Mom, I just put her out. I want to put these on the coffee table, and she's going to eat them."

"Oh, Tess, it's freezing out. Can't you put her in your room or something?"

"No. She'll just whine and scratch on the door. Grady's napping and she'll wake him up. Put her out. Please."

"Okay, okay," I said, grabbing Bonnie by the collar and steering her back outside. I promised her that I would sneak her some turkey later and she sank down heavily on the porch with a groan.

I went back inside and everyone greeted me, even Nancy and Bill Watson, with stiff hugs. Why must everybody hug all the time? Scott was holding a Bloody Mary in his hand. I happen to love Bloody Marys. In fact, when Tess asked me what I'd like to drink, I started to ask her for a Diet Coke but then changed my mind and said, "I'll have a Bloody Mary . . . just without the vodka."

"A Virgin Mary, huh?" Scott laughed. Then he said, "I'll make it, Hildy," and I followed him into the kitchen. It was good to see Scott, I have to admit that. I like him, I always will. When I married Scott, I married my best friend. Our worst years were those in which he knew that he was gay but neglected to share that with me. Once we separated, after the initial pain of rejection and the financial squabbling, I was able to recognize my old friend in Scott, and I know he did with me.

Tess was hustling around the kitchen with Nancy Watson, and when we came in, she looked a little exasperated.

"Um, Mom, Dad, we've got everything sorted out in here. Why don't you go out and join the others in the living room?"

"I'm just making your mother a drink," said Scott.

"Oh, okay," said Tess, and I saw her watching Scott's drink ingredients out of the corner of her eye as she basted the bird.

"When do you think Grady'll be getting up?" I asked Tess.

"He usually gets up around two, now that he's down to just one nap a day," reported Nancy.

I smiled at her and thought, *Yes, I know, sweet cheeks. You take care of him every day.*

Scott squeezed a lemon into my drink and tapped a few extra drops of Tabasco in, just the way I've always liked it. We went back into the living room, but Michael and Bill were watching football. Scott and I have never really followed sports, but we stood there for a few minutes. Michael and Bill were on the edge of their seats. "No, no, NOOOO," Michael suddenly called out, pounding the couch with his fist. Scott and I were looking at the TV, trying to figure out what all the commotion was about. I watch television sports in much the same way that a cat watches television. I like all the action, and I'm able to follow the movement of the figures on the screen, but I have no idea what's going on.

"Well, that's it," said Bill.

"ARRRGGGG," said Michael.

Scott and I smiled at each other. "Come look at the dining room table," he said. "I set it up this morning."

We went into the dining room, and there it was. A Thanksgiving dinner table fit for *Martha Stewart Living*. Scott collected French china and beautiful antique tablecloths and napkins, and he always shared his bounty with the girls. He had left me with a treasure trove of collectibles, myself, but I could never put a table together like Scott. He had arranged cut flowers in vases. He'd used pinecones and bunches of beautifully colored leaves for a centerpiece. He had made little votive candleholders out of tiny gourds. We pulled a couple of chairs back from the table and, after sitting down, tapped our drinks together.

"Cheers," I said.

"Cheers, Hildy," said Scott. We sipped our drinks.

"How long are you staying in Marblehead?" I asked.

"I'm going back tomorrow, really early. I can't find anybody I trust to run the store when I'm away. I'm only open on weekends in the wintertime."

"Oh, right, tomorrow's the big shopping day, isn't it?"

"Maybe at the Gap. Not so much in the antiques business. But we—I usually have a pretty good day."

Scott's former boyfriend, Richard, used to be his partner at the shop, but he moved back to New York when they broke up. Scott and I sipped our drinks again and smiled at each other. Scott looked . . . puffy. Well, let's face it. He looked old. I'm sure he was thinking the same thing about me.

"So, you're still on the wagon, huh?" Scott asked.

"Not on the wagon," I chided jokingly. "I'm in recovery."

"Right, I beg your pardon," he said. Then he said quietly, "Do you go to AA meetings?"

"Are you out of your fucking mind?" I whispered, and he roared with laughter.

"The girls are always reporting to me how well you're doing in the 'program.' I finally had to ask them, 'What program?' I thought you'd gotten yourself a TV show or something. They said, 'AA, Dad,' like I was a moron. I think they're trying to get me to cut back, too."

"Well, if they invite you over for dinner, and it's not a major holiday, my advice is, run for your life."

Scott laughed and then said, "But really, Hildy, I think it's amazing what you've done. Staying sober and all that. It's really amazing. I know you did it for the girls, but it's done you so much good. I can see the change in you. Really."

Maybe that's not his first Bloody, I thought. *Change.* People see what they want to see.

Grady awoke, as scheduled, at two. Nancy bustled up the stairs to get him, and when she brought him down, he was wearing a pair of miniature gray trousers and a little white oxford shirt.

"Good God," Scott muttered to me, "look at the little Republican."

"Okay," I whispered. "It's official. You've had too much to drink."

Scott laughed a little too loudly and Tess and

211

Emily shot us annoyed looks before scuffling off into the kitchen together.

We all played with Grady. He was at such a fun age. A walker and a talker and a charmer.

Nancy was having him recite all the letters in the alphabet, which she had taught him. She asked, "Who's that?" pointing to Michael.

"Dada," Grady gushed.

"And who's that?" (She was pointing to Bill.)

"Papa."

"That's right. Papa, did you hear what Grady said?"

"Mmmm-hmmm," said Bill, turning and winking at Grady before fixating on the TV screen again.

"Who's that?" Nancy asked, pointing at me.

Grady had become distracted by the pile of crackers on the cheese platter that rested on the coffee table in front of him.

"Grady, who's that?" Nancy repeated, trying to get Grady to look at me. She tried to turn him around, but he shook free of her hands and stuck a cracker in his mouth. Then he reached for the Brie.

"No, Grady," Nancy cried, swooping him up and away from the tempting platter full of deadly dairy products. "Let's go see if your mommy has a snack for you. But first, give kissy to Grandma Hildy."

Grady was crying for the cheese platter, and

when she brought him to me, he was shaking his head and saying, "No, no, no, no, no."

"He's always a little fussy when he first wakes up." Nancy smiled apologetically.

"I know he is," I said through gritted teeth. Honestly, if she hadn't had my grandchild in her arms, I would have clocked her on the head. Could she have been more obnoxious about Grady? I've never liked Nancy Watson. She's a nitwit. When not watching Grady, she's busy "scrapbooking," which is her hobby, and Tess is always showing me the sickly-sweet scrapbooks featuring Grady that Nancy puts together, seemingly, every week. I always smile as Tess flips the pages for me, and I say things like "Imagine having all that time to devote to something like this." Or "I think I might like it better if it just had the photos and not the hearts and cartoon teddy bears and everything." Nancy's latest scrapbooking gimmick was to have "thought balloons" coming from Grady's head. These were meant to be humorous. Grady would be wrapped up in a towel after his bath and the thought balloon would say, "Ahhhh, another day at the spa." I always stared at these completely stone-faced whenever Nancy or Tess showed them to me. Of course, they would be convulsed with laughter and pointing and shaking their heads at each turn of the page.

The dinner was taking forever. My head was

pounding. I had come to the conclusion, over the past weeks, that I really did need to switch from red to white wine. The red was giving me such headaches. I had read it has something to do with the tannins. It just affects some people that way—with the headaches.

After an eternity of awkward small talk with Scott, it was time to sit down to dinner. Emily was opening the wine in the kitchen.

"Mom? What would you like?" she asked.

I was tempted to ask for one of Grady's juice boxes. It just always felt so infantilizing (this is a word you learn in rehab) when people asked me what I'd like to drink. I noticed that Bill and Nancy were smiling at me in the most patronizing way.

"Scott, just mix me up another one of these Virgin Marys," I said.

He mixed up my little virgin drink.

My little drink for naughty girls who have given up the privilege of drinking grown-up drinks.

He handed it to me and then we were all helping carry in the turkey and the stuffing, the mashed potatoes and Brussels sprouts and peas, the squash and the special gluten-free pasta with soy butter, which was the only food from his restrictive diet that Grady could be enticed to eat. We did the usual running around, looking for the gravy boat and trying to find a salt shaker that actually worked, and trying to figure out what that burning smell was, and finally I found myself all alone in the kitchen with my Virgin Mary. Everybody had sat down, but Tess had forgotten to put the pies in the oven.

"I'll do it," I had said, turning on my heel. I was the only one who hadn't sat down yet. I put the apple pie and the cherry pie in the oven. Then I poured a little vodka into my Bloody. Not too much. But not too little, either. Really, Thanksgiving is a lot to ask of a sober person. I just needed something to take the edge off.

I sat down and Bill Watson said grace and we all raised our glasses and toasted one another. I sipped my drink. I hadn't had anything but wine since I'd started drinking again. In my mind, wine, somehow, wasn't really drinking. Vodka, I thought as I took my second sip, definitely was.

So what?

We tried to get Grady to eat a little bit of turkey. Scott and I had persuaded Tess to place his high chair between us. I went to give Grady a little bite of my mashed potatoes, but Michael cried out, "Hildy. No. There's butter and milk in the potatoes." I caught Scott's eye above Grady's little head then, and we both tried not to laugh. Scott's nostrils flare when he tries to control his laughter, and I couldn't help it. I turned and coughed into my napkin, my eyes blinking back tears of mirth. The way Michael had said it—as if I were trying to slip the baby a spoonful of arsenic.

Emily entertained us with a story about one of her roommate's efforts to find a date on eHarmony. It was hysterical, actually. Emily is very, very funny. She gets it from Scott. I went in to get another glass of "tomato juice." I made another grown-up Bloody. When I sat back down, Grady began clapping his hands and humming, and I said, "You know, I think Grady has a natural gift for music."

"Mom, I can't believe you just said that," gushed Tess. "He does. I was just telling somebody that the other day."

"Of course he does," said Scott. "What songs do you know, Grady?"

Michael and Tess tried to entice him with songs from his baby videos. Everybody was well into their second glass of wine at this point, and we all teased them about the stupidity of that music.

"I've been teaching him some real songs," I said. "Songs that Daddy and I used to sing to you girls. . . ."

"Oh great. Grady's learning Grateful Dead songs," Emily said with a smirk.

"WHAT?" Scott and I protested together, and then it was like the old days, when it was just Scott and Tess and Emily and me.

"I have always HATED the Grateful Dead," I said, swilling my "juice" and laughing at the notion.

"Me, too. The Dead. PLEASE," said Scott.

"Grady, here's a song by the great Nina Simone—"

"DAD. NO!" The girls shrieked in unison, laughing hysterically. I almost choked on my drink, it was so funny, the idea that Scott might start singing Nina Simone songs in front of the Watsons.

"No," I said finally, "Grady likes Simon and Garfunkel. I taught him 'Scarborough Fair.' "

"You did, Hildy?" Scott asked, smiling at me lovingly. "Sing it," he said. "Sing it to him now."

"No," I giggled. I was blushing.

"C'mon, Mom," Emily said.

"Well, I can't sing it alone. It needs the harmony," I said.

"DAD . . ." the girls pleaded.

"I can't believe this. You girls used to hate it when we sang together." I laughed.

"No we didn't," said Tess.

"Well, we only hated it when you did it in the car," Emily said.

"Oh, that's right. That sucked. Actually, don't sing, guys," said Tess. So of course we did sing. We did an okay job of it. We sang, smiling at each other over Grady's head, which swiveled so he could look first at Scott, then at me, then at Scott again. We hit a few off notes. Scott kept flubbing the words, but when we hit the chorus, we hit it just right. It was so nice. It felt like the nicest thing. At the end, Grady slapped his palms on the tray of his high chair.

"More," he said. "More."

Everybody laughed when he said that, and I saw that Emily was smiling and shaking her head and wiping away tears with her napkin. She's always been the most emotional of us, Emily, but it was such a sweet moment.

"Don't get us started, Grady. You'll be very sorry," said Scott.

"Well, I had no idea you both had such lovely singing voices," said Nancy Watson.

"The girls sing beautifully, too. Do you still have your guitar, Tess?" I asked. She was pouring herself another glass of wine.

"I do someplace. Up in the attic, I think. I can check. But I am NOT singing with you guys."

After we had finished dessert and the bulk of the dishes was done, everybody sat around the fireplace while Tess tuned her guitar. I was finally allowed to let Bonnie inside, and when I took her into the kitchen to feed her, I just topped up my drink a little. That was it. I wasn't going to have another drop. I had to drive home. Scott wandered in just as I was squeezing in a little lemon.

"Good old Bonnie," he said. "And how are your little familiars?"

Scott had always called our family's dogs my "familiars." It was part of his running joke about my witchiness—this allusion to my pets as my familiar spirits. We had a dog when the girls were little, a handsome husky mix named Luca, who used to urinate on Scott's most cherished belongings and chew up only Scott's shoes and belts. Scott often angrily alleged that the dog was doing my bidding, which delighted me.

"Babs and Molly aren't familiars. They're nothing like Luca. He looked like me; he even acted like me."

"Now you're being too hard on yourself," Scott said.

"What do you mean? Luca was a great dog. Loyal, stoic, smart . . ."

"Mean, vindictive, and untrained is how I recall him," Scott laughed.

"See? Just like me. The pair I have now are no familiars of mine. Well, maybe Babs is. A little bit."

"Babs is that nasty little biter, right? I think you're really more like the other. The sweet, smiling one. You just don't like people to know it."

"NO. I'm nothing like that Molly with her desperate neediness." I laughed.

Scott asked me to do the trick with Bonnie that I used to do at parties. I can get dogs to obey simple commands without using my voice or obvious hand gestures. I don't have to know the dog to do this; I just get the dog's attention with a piece of food and then they listen to me. I grabbed a piece of turkey from the sink and called Bonnie over to me and then I moved the hand with the turkey up a few inches. The dog sat. I waited until she moved her eyes from the turkey to my face and then I stared back at her and exhaled slowly, leaning in toward the dog ever so slightly. There was a pause and then Bonnie lowered herself into a "down" position. I tossed her the turkey.

"MOM? DAD?" Emily called from the living room. "What are you doing?'

"Nothing, honey. Mommy's just bewitching the dog," Scott replied, laughing, and I shoved him as I followed him into the living room.

A few minutes later, I was bouncing Grady up and down on my knees and singing:

> Trot, trot to Boston
> Trot, trot to Lynn
> Watch out, little boy,
> That you don't . . . fall . . . in.

At the beginning of the last line, Grady always gets worked up and starts to squeal with excitement because after the words *fall in,* I always open my knees and his little bottom swoops down between them for a moment, and he feels as if I might drop him onto the floor. But then I bounce him back onto my lap with my hands. Grady has always loved this; he always laughs and cries out for more. The girls had always loved this game, too.

Scott finally got the guitar tuned. The Watsons were sipping their coffee and finishing off their pie. Scott was a great impersonator and he sounded best when he sang a song exactly like the original singer. For example, that night he started with "Sweet Lorraine," and he sang it just like Nat King Cole. Imagine "Sweet Lorraine" with a guitar. You'd be surprised how nice that can sound, the way Scott plays it. Then he cajoled me into singing one song with him.

"Just one," I said, relenting. We sang a very slow version of "Sea of Love," which we used to sing in our coffeehouse days. We had developed a sort of haunting, mournful version of the song. We hadn't sung it in years. This time when we were finished, there were tears in my eyes, and Scott leaned over and kissed me on the cheek. Then it was time for Grady to go to bed.

"I'll take him up," said Nancy.

Grady was sitting on my lap, so I stood up, holding him, and said, "Don't be silly, Nancy. You've been doing everything tonight. Just relax. Let me take him."

It seemed that everybody was a little taken aback by what I had just said, and it occurred to me that I might have said it a little too loudly.

"It's just that I know his whole routine and everything," said Nancy.

"Well," I replied, laughing indignantly, "I put him to bed every Friday night."

"I'M PUTTING GRADY TO BED!" Michael said.

Nancy and I both laughed then. We all did. Really, we were acting like a couple of old nanny goats, so I handed Grady over. First I snuggled with him a little. I buried my face in the fleshy curve of his neck and tickled him with kisses. He giggled hysterically and I did it again. Then I did it again.

"Okay, Mom," Tess said, looking at me carefully. "I don't want to get him all worked up before bedtime."

"Al-righty," I said, handing him off to Michael. Michael is a great, great father. I often forgot that, so I reached my arms around Michael and Grady and said, "I have to leave, so if you're not back downstairs before I go, good night, my dear boys, and thank you, Michael, for a wonderful, wonderful Thanksgiving." I hugged them both again.

"You're very welcome, Hildy," Michael said.

"You're a wonderful, wonderful father! I hope you know that." I couldn't resist, I gave them both another little hug.

"Wow, thanks, Hildy. Say 'nighty-night' to Gammy," he said to Grady.

"Ny-ny," said Grady.

Michael took Grady upstairs and Bill and Nancy and I got our coats. I hugged the girls, my sweet, sweet girls, and told them how much I loved them. They stammered their loving responses. Then I hugged Nancy and Bill. Honestly, despite their dullness and their tendency to claim Grady as their own personal grandchild, you have to love Nancy and Bill Watson. They really are the salt of the earth. You really can't find a more easygoing guy than Bill Watson. And Nancy always means well. Tess is lucky to have such wonderful in-laws. I told them so.

Scott walked me out to my car and opened the door for me. "That was so great," he said, "being together. Being a family again."

"It was," I gushed, hugging him. We kissed. It was a real kiss, on the lips, and afterward I said, "Why did you have to end up being so fucking gay?"

This made Scott laugh, and I climbed into my car and backed out of the driveway very slowly —I knew I had had a tiny bit to drink; you can never be too careful—and headed for home.

It took me a good forty-five minutes to drive home. I drove slowly. But I was in such a cheerful mood. Tonight had confirmed for me something that I had thought for some time. I was better company when I drank. The girls thought my drinking was harmful. Well, tonight I had proven that it was the opposite. It was helpful. Everybody had a better time when I drank. The girls and Scott and I hadn't laughed like that in ages. If my drinking was so mortifying to the girls, I would just do what I had done tonight. Just

223

quietly have a little bit. Just to take the edge off.

When you drive into Wendover, you can head into the Crossing and then take Pig Rock Lane down to River Road, where I live, or you can drive up over the rise and take the long way around. I decided I would drive up over the rise. I was a little curious to see what kind of a crowd Rebecca had for Thanksgiving. When I drove past her house, I saw five or six cars in the driveway. I drove on past. Coming down the rise, I passed Frankie's place. He had a fire going; I could see smoke spiraling up out of his chimney in the moonlight. There was a light on in one of the downstairs rooms. There was just his truck in the driveway. I wondered whom, if anybody, he might have had Thanksgiving dinner with. I admit it—I had the urge to pull in, to knock on his door. But I drove on past. This is something I learned in rehab: Avoid jackpots.

At Hazelden, people talked a lot about all the "jackpots" they'd had during their drinking careers. They'd tell their drinking story, their "drunk-a-log," and say something like "I was doing well, had a great job, great kids. I'd go two or three months, just drinking socially. And then I'd hit another jackpot."

A jackpot was a DUI arrest, or a drunken public scene. Getting fired for being drunk on the job. For a woman, it was often waking up in a strange place with a strange person. One woman I met at

Hazelden went to a bar to drown her sorrows over a lost relationship, and when she came out of her blackout, she was in a resort in the Bahamas with a very nice man, who was, nonetheless, married. These were funny stories, now. Everybody laughed, even the people telling the stories, because they saw that they weren't the bad/crazy person they thought they were. They had a disease. It was called alcoholism. There was a solution. It was called Alcoholics Anonymous, and it usually included a "higher power."

God.

Everybody was supposed to tell their stories, starting from their earliest drinking experiences to how they ended up at Hazelden. When it was my turn, one evening in "group," about a week into my stay, I started my story as many of the others had. I told about how, from the time I had that very first beer, up on North Beach with a bunch of high school kids, I liked the way alcohol made me feel. I talked about how it helped me with my shyness when I got to college. How I believed I was prettier, funnier, smarter, and really much nicer when I drank. Everybody was nodding as I shared this. They were "identifying." Alcohol had had the same effect on them in the beginning. Then they all sat back and waited for me to begin telling about how it all went wrong. They wanted to hear about my jackpots. I continued to talk about all the good times. The coffeehouses we played in, Scott and me, and how alcohol soothed my stage jitters and made me sing better. I explained that my pregnancies were good for me. I cut way back. Quit cigarettes and marijuana and never started again. Then, over the years, how I just loved my drink or two at the end of the day. Loved the way drinks loosened me up at parties, especially after Scott had left and I felt so lost at sea.

"Most of all," I summed up, "I miss having drinks with people I love. It makes me love them all the more."

Then I was finished. Usually people gave a rousing round of applause after one of these "drunk-a-logs," but when I was finished, there was a pause, then a polite clapping of the hands belonging to my roommate and a new woman who was in her very first group meeting.

Celia, the counselor and leader of the group, cleared her throat. Then she said, "I get the feeling you left something out of your story, Hildy."

"Oh," I said, and I thought hard. "Well, I've been drinking for years, you can't expect me to remember everything that happened." This made people laugh, which pleased me.

"Didn't you get arrested for driving under the influence of alcohol?"

"Well, yes. But the truth is, I never would have been arrested if I hadn't accidentally rear-ended a state trooper."

Now the group roared with laughter. It *was* funny. I laughed, too.

Celia said, "I think you should read chapter five in the Big Book, Hildy. It's about being honest. The first step in being honest, in overcoming our disease of alcoholism, is to admit that we are powerless over alcohol, that our lives have become unmanageable."

"I grossed seven million dollars in real-estate sales last year alone. I have raised two wonderful daughters. My life didn't become unmanageable until I came here. . . ."

Why didn't anybody get this?

A guy I liked in the group, a very funny black guy named Raymond, said, "I don't get why you *did* come here, Hildy."

I had to admit then that my daughters had accused me of being an alcoholic. That they'd had an intervention. I always stumbled over that word, always almost said *inquisition* instead of *intervention.* After that, everybody in the group tried to help me work on my denial. If you want to get out at the end of the twenty-eight days, it's best to stop the denial talk and share some war stories. I'd had a few jackpots. I woke up in the wrong place once or twice in college. There was the DUI, as well as some blurry business lunches, various drunken monologues that I had delivered at dinner parties. And then there was the thing with Frankie Getchell. But I kept that to myself.

It was years before I went to Hazelden when I had my Frankie Getchell jackpot. First, I must explain that this was when my marriage to Scott was at its most desolate. We hadn't had sex in six years. He claimed that he had a "low libido." Amazingly, I believed him. Well, I partially believed him and partially felt that I had become so unappealing that he just wasn't interested in having sex with me anymore. I believed there was something wrong with *me*. So I was at Mamie and Boatie's annual Christmas party. They usually have at least a hundred people there and it's always a great party. One year, Mamie put a pair of antlers on her daughter Lexie's Shetland pony and brought him into the party. Mamie ended up getting kicked in the thigh, the pony was so startled by the crowd, and then it broke loose and galloped into the kitchen, smashing plates and scaring the catering staff half out of their minds.

Anyway, that year there was a big snowstorm the night of the party. I *had* had an awful lot to drink. Scott wasn't with me. He was in New York, "antiquing." I was to find out later what "antiquing" can do for the libido of certain people. So the party was winding down, and when I got in my car, it was stuck on a patch of ice in their long driveway. Everybody else had left and my car was blocking the garage in such a way that neither Mamie nor Boatie could get a car out. Boatie called Frankie, knowing he'd have guys out plowing, to see if one of them could give me a ride home. They had begged me to stay, but I still had the girls living at home and didn't want them to wake up in the morning and not find me there.

So the plow arrived and I hugged Mamie and Boatie good-bye, then slid out across the ice to the truck. The driver had jumped down to help me climb into the passenger side, and I saw it was Frankie. Frankie Getchell. I was wearing a clingy black dress and high heels—I was in far better shape then—and he really had to help me negotiate the climb into the big filthy cab of his truck. Then he climbed back into the driver's seat.

"Hey, Hildy," he said, putting the truck in reverse.

"Hey, Frankie. I didn't think you'd be coming. . . . I thought it'd be one of your . . . guys."

"Nope. Me."

We drove through the blizzard. You couldn't see the road. The wind blew the snow in great swirls at our windshield and it felt like we were flying through space, being pulled silently into a swirling vortex of stars. I told Frank that if he squinted, like I was doing, it would seem like we were in a rocket ship, with stars and tiny planets spinning past us. Frankie chuckled, and I looked at him to see if he was squinting, as I had suggested. I saw then not the Frankie who had grown paunchy and bald, who had an unexplained limp and a thinning ponytail, whose car smelled of garbage. I saw the Frankie who'd held me so tight those hot, slippery, salty nights on all those other people's yachts years ago.

"More," I'd sometimes whisper to him. "More." Frankie always made me feel like there would always be enough for me. But now I was in a marriage that was a sexual wasteland. My husband was a good friend and good father, but now I wanted a good fuck. I told all this to Frankie, in more or less those words. He was looking at me and smiling and shaking his head. It's all a blur, a shameful blur (where are black-outs when you need them?), but I do remember him turning a little red in the face.

"Let's just stop at your house, Frankie, just for, you know . . . just for a few minutes." I was wearing sheer Donna Karan black hose and I had kicked off my shoes and was rubbing my toe up his leg.

Frankie actually did stop in front of his driveway, and he said, "Really, Hildy?"

"Yes," I said, and then I burst into tears.

"Okay, that does it. I'm taking you home."

"You think I'm disgusting, don't you?" I sobbed.

"Nah, Hildy, you're just hammered. Go to bed and sleep it off. You'll feel different tomorrow."

Of course, I woke up the next day feeling COMPLETELY different and wildly humiliated. It was one of those mornings when I woke up gripped with the paralyzing terror, the agonizing realization that my drinking was out of control.

It wasn't the first time I woke up feeling that way. I often awoke that way before Hazelden.

I never wake up that way now, because, as I said, I've learned not to set myself up for jackpots. I've sorted it all out. I drink moderately enough that I can see a jackpot and avoid it.

So I drove right past Frankie Getchell's that night and climbed into bed with Molly and Babs, my sweet girls, my sweet, sweet bitches, and fell right to sleep, just full of Thanksgiving.

Twelve

"Rebecca McAllister called three times already this morning," said my receptionist, Kendall, when I walked into my office on Monday morning.

"It's nine-fifteen," I said. "She's already called three times?"

"Yeah, she left two messages on the machine. And then she just called a few minutes ago."

I went into my office and dialed Rebecca's number. She picked up after the first ring.

"Hildy?" Rebecca said. She was giddy and out of breath.

"Hi, Rebecca. What's up?"

"Oh. Nothing. How're you feeling?"

"Fine . . ."

Rebecca laughed. "I was a little worried about you last night."

Last night?

"Oh?" I said.

"I was really into the idea of you coming over when you called, but I was glad that you decided not to. We waited up, you know, Brian and I."

"Oh yeah, well, I ended up going to bed."

This is what you do. This is what blackout drinkers do.

Until Hazelden, I thought everyone who drank had blackouts. I had had them ever since I started drinking in high school. I would have no recollection of even attending a party, which, I would learn the next day, I had been the life of. "I didn't even know you were drunk," my friends would often say when I told them I had no memory of seeing them. I came to think of myself, during those times, as operating under the control of some kind of charming, devil-may-care automatic pilot. I would be at a party, or a bar, or a restaurant, having a few drinks and a pleasant conversation, and then it would be the next day. Only later would I learn that I had driven a group to the beach for a skinny-dip, or convinced everyone to dance on the bar, or even seduced somebody I barely knew.

As the years went by, however, after I became a wife and a mother, it was no longer very funny to forget hours at a time. It was seen, by some, as an indication of some sort of a problem. So I became quite adept at blustering my way around the last night's recollections. I'd offer vague answers to queries about how I had gotten myself home and fumble my way through forgotten conversations with others. I made real-estate deals in blackouts, invited people over, told secrets, expressed loving sentiments to casual acquaintances, and all this stuff had to be undone while sober—usually under the bludgeoning sledgehammer of a hang-over. So you can see how drinking alone, in my own house, after my trip to Hazelden, had offered a nice solution for me. What a relief not to have to wake up with all that bullshit to undo. I thought I had given up drunk-dialing, but apparently, according to what Rebecca was telling me, I had taken it up again. Or rather, my scheming autopilot had. At Hazelden, during an "alcohol education" session, a counselor discussed blackouts: "When you're in a blackout, your conscious mind is not at work. You are operating, mainly, on very primitive instincts. You're like a beast." My beast had called Rebecca and now I had to cover its tracks.

"I realized that it would be better just to go to bed," I said again.

Rebecca laughed. "Well, I worried about you driving. From the sound of your voice. But when I called back and you didn't answer, I figured you had turned in. It sounds like you had a great Thanksgiving, though."

"It was actually quite wonderful," I replied tersely. *Ugh. What had I said?*

"I just love the way you and Scott have such a great friendship. I don't think things will be so jolly with Brian and me, once we split up," Rebecca said. Then, before I had a chance to say anything, she asked, "Have you noticed if Peter is up at his office today?"

"I just got here, Rebecca, but it's Monday. Why would he be here?"

"I don't know. But he's not at the hospital. I've been trying all morning."

I looked at my desk clock, which still read three-thirty. Then I looked at my watch.

"It's nine-forty," I said. "I'm sure he's just not there yet. What's so urgent anyway?"

"Urgent? Why does it have to be urgent? I haven't seen him in over a week. I need to talk to him. He's usually at the hospital by eight. Now I'm thinking something bad happened over the weekend."

"Rebecca," I said, "I'm sure everything's fine. It was probably a very hectic weekend, with a lot of partying. Who knows, maybe he's a little hungover from the weekend and overslept. . . ."

"What? Do you think he enjoys his time with Elise? That he parties with her? You told me yourself the other day. He's in love with me! His life with Elise is hell! I'm just afraid something's wrong."

I said nothing then. Rebecca was being rude. I had a headache.

"Hello?" she said finally.

"Yes, I'm here," I said, leafing through a pile of mail on my desk.

"Hildy, will you tell me if he comes in?" Rebecca asked, her voice softer now. She was pleading, like a little girl.

"Yes, dear, of course I will," I said soothingly. After I hung up the phone, I worried about her a little. I worried about her and Peter.

Business continued to be slow, but during the last week of November, I received an offer on Cassie and Patch's house. I had shown a New Jersey family, the Goodwins, the house twice, so I knew they were interested, but they had grumbled about the "state" of the place, so I didn't hold out much hope. Frank's home-improvement efforts had not been long-lived. But the Goodwins wanted to live in Wendover, it was just the right price for them, and they loved the location. The offer was slightly low. Cassie and Patch countered, and a deal was reached. I was thrilled. That night, I admit, I had myself a nice little celebration toast with Babs and Molly. Cassie and Patch had been thrilled when I told them the sellers had agreed to their terms, and Jake, well, he didn't know it, but he was going to be going to a school that had the possibility of really helping him. It made me feel good that I was a part of that. I finished off the bottle of red that I had been drinking, but it had been nearly empty when I began, so I opened another.

The next morning was gray and there was a wet, rainy snow coming down—what the weatherman calls a "wintry mix." I was a little late arriving at the office, and as soon as I entered the reception area, Kendall jumped up from her desk, visibly flustered.

"Rebecca McAllister is in your office. She was waiting here when I arrived."

"Ah fuck!" I said. Kendall actually flinched.

I walked into my office and saw Rebecca peering out the window at the falling slush.

"Hi, Rebecca, what's going on?"

Rebecca turned, and when she saw me, she heaved a very dramatic sigh of relief.

"Oh, Hildy, I'm so glad you're okay."

"Well, I'm fine, of course."

"Do you remember anything about last night? About after you left my house, I mean?"

What? My heart was pounding. "Last night?" I said.

Rebecca walked over and closed the office door. I sat down at my desk.

"Hildy, I haven't wanted to say anything, because I know you're very sensitive about your drinking, but I think you really need to go back into treatment or something. You don't even remember coming over last night, do you?"

Breathe. I had to remember to breathe in and then to breathe out.

"No, I didn't go anywhere. I went to bed. I have a lot of work to do this morning, so maybe we can catch up another time. . . ."

"I know. The Dwight deal. You told me last night."

Now I had a foggy recollection of a phone conversation—of speaking on the phone, in my bed.

"That's right, I remember now. You called," I said. "I was half-asleep; that's why I couldn't remember at first." I began busily moving papers around my desk. It was to hide my shaking hands. I was nervous, and when I get nervous, my hands shake.

"No, Hildy," Rebecca said sadly. Why did she have to sound so full of pity? "I didn't call you. You drove over to my house. You were . . . just, well, out of your mind. I wanted to drive you home, but it was Magda's night off and you wouldn't let me anyway. You woke up Ben with all your shouting."

It's like a suctioning of the soul, being told the things your body does when your mind is in that dead zone. It's like having your very skin peeled off, like being publicly stripped down to some gruesome inner membrane that nobody should see, and revealing it to all.

I never tell a person what they did when they were drunk. I would never do this.

"You drive around this town at night drunk out of your mind. Am I the only one who knows this? I hope so. I haven't said anything to you or anyone else about my concerns, because this town shuts down so early, I didn't really think there was any danger. Every house in Wendover is dark by eleven, so I never thought it was that big a deal that you like to haunt the roads at night after a few too many drinks. But, well, now I'm nervous. If you're calling and visiting me, I can't help but wonder who else you might be calling. Who you might have told about me and Peter."

I had gone to bed. I remembered putting on my nightgown. I had been awakened by the phone. Or had that been a dream?

"And now Peter's worried about it, too. He told me."

I looked up from my papers and said, my voice quivering with rage, "I am SO sick and tired of being brought into this mess between you and Peter. I have no interest in what you two do. I have told nobody. . . ."

"You mean you don't *remember* telling anybody."

"Just get out, Rebecca. I have work to do. I have to work for a living. My father wasn't rich like yours. I do very well, in case you hadn't noticed, and I don't think I would be considered such a success if your ideas about my drunkenly talking about trivial gossip like the stupidity between you and Peter—"

"Hildy, I came to you as a friend. Peter told me this would happen. That you would react angrily. . . ."

"Rebecca, get out of my office. Please!"

Thirteen

The Goodwins signed their contract, a deposit was placed in escrow, and a building inspection for the Dwight house had been set up. The buyers needed to close by February 1. I had been shaken up a little by Rebecca's crazy accusations, but within a few days I had let it go. Rebecca was unstable. I had always suspected this about her. Her boyfriend had been her shrink. That pretty much summed it up. I decided that I should keep her at arm's length for a while, not only because of her nastiness to me during her visit to my office but also because, in recent weeks, I had run into Brian McAllister a few times. They'd been mostly brief encounters at the gas station or the market, but once it was in front of a shop in the Crossing. He was with the boys. They were shopping for a Christmas present for Rebecca. Brian had given me a warm hug and told me how much they loved Wendover; how thrilled they were that I had sold them their dream home. I couldn't even look at the boys. I felt complicit in Rebecca's transgressions, somehow. Like a silent accessory to a very serious domestic crime. Rebecca's affair no longer entertained or amused me. I decided to keep my distance for a while.

I was heading into the post office a few days after the Dwight contract was signed and I bumped into Frank Getchell, who was on his way out.

"Hey, Hildy," he muttered as he walked past.

"Hey, Frank, wait," I said. He turned around to face me.

"I've got some good news. I've sold the Dwights' house."

"No way," Frank said. He was grinning at me. He seemed to be trying to think of the right thing to say, but he ended up just saying, "Cool."

"Yeah, so thanks for doing all that work. I still haven't gotten a bill."

"Oh. Guess I haven't gotten around to sendin' it."

"Okay, well, thanks again."

"How's the real-estate business?" Frank asked.

"Slow. It'll pick up in another month or so. When the weather gets a little nicer. I never got an offer on your property. Why don't you put a price on it?"

Frankie just laughed. "Okay, fifty million dollars."

"C'mon, Frankie. You should think about it . . ."

"Hey, I was out with Manny Briggs the other day. Sometimes I go out with him this time of year; he never has a crew in the winter. . . ."

"Yeah, I bet," I said.

Manny was probably the sixth or seventh generation of Briggs men who were commercial lobstermen in Wendover. Manny and his dad had once had a fleet of lobster boats, but now he just had one or two. It was always easy to get high school and college kids to crew in the summer, but in the winter, the kids were back in school. It was hard, cold work. Manny is exactly my age. My friend Lindsey dated him in high school and I dated a friend of his, and we used to go out with them before dawn and spend the mornings sunning ourselves on the bow. The boats stank of fish and fuel and the sweat of the boys. Lindsey and I ate lobsters that whole summer. I always brought a couple home for my dad and Lisa. Judd never liked lobster. I haven't been able to eat one since, actually. You go off them if you eat too many. I bet Manny Briggs hasn't eaten a lobster since he was a child.

"Yeah, so I saw that house that Santorelli guy is buildin' out on Grey's Point."

This caught my attention.

"You did?"

"Yup." Frankie was turning to leave and I grabbed his sleeve, making him laugh. He was toying with me. He knew I was dying to hear about the Santorelli house out on Grey's Point.

"So? Is it huge? Is it ugly?"

Vince and Nick Santorelli were local builders who had made a fortune in the eighties and nineties building "spec" houses on the North Shore. Their houses were considered to be very high-quality, well-constructed homes. They worked with a Boston architect and had built some notably vast and attractive houses in Ipswich, Manchester, and Beverly Farms. Houses that sold for millions. The previous year, they had bought a property at the end of Grey's Point that had been owned by the Dean family for many generations. Now the youngest Dean kids were grown and no longer spent their summers in Wendover. They had, easily, the most coveted parcel of land in the whole town. It was eight acres—the entire point. If you sited a house properly, you could have an ocean view from every window. The Deans had listed the property at five million dollars. Just for the land. And Vince Santorelli had bought it. There had been all sorts of talk among the local brokers about it. The Deans had listed the house with a Coldwell broker named Simon Andrews. He sold it to the Santorelli brothers, who planned to build a house that Simon would sell for them. Very shortly after the deal closed, maybe six months later, Simon Andrews had a heart attack at the gym, running on the treadmill. So nobody knew who the Santorellis would list it with, once the house was finished, and for how much.

I had driven past the property many times. There was a long driveway lined with centuries-old hemlock trees leading out to the point. The Santorellis had put a chain across the drive, so it was impossible to drive up and have a look. Well, not impossible, but it would have been trespassing. Trucks had been going up and down that driveway for almost a year now. You could see the construction from the water and I had heard reports all summer about the progress.

I really wanted that listing. It was becoming hard for a private broker like me to deal with the Sotheby's and Coldwell Banker corporate brokers. I needed a few prime properties to reestablish myself as the area's top broker, not only some of the older homes of longtime residents but also a few of the newer, grander estates. Soon there would be no more townies left with any loyalty to me and everybody would just want to list with whichever broker had the highest sales. I needed the Santorelli property and wanted to approach the brothers with a real understanding of the property. This was going to be the biggest sale in Wendover history.

"Well, it's big, Hildy. Wicked big. I wouldn't say it's ugly. I wouldn't mind livin' in it. Big wraparound porch. It's lookin' good, for a house.

I liked the place better when it was covered with trees, though."

"I really want to see it, Frank. Do you think Manny would let me go out with him some morning?"

"Only if you help him pull some traps." Frank laughed.

"I can band 'em up," I said. Lindsey and I had become experts at banding lobster claws that summer in high school, though one sliced my finger good and I ended up with a pretty bad infection from it.

"Nah, you wouldn't have to. Manny'd be happy to have you along. You'd have to come tomorrow. Boat comes out the end of the week for the winter."

"All right. I will."

That night, Rebecca came over. It was a Thursday, the night she usually spent with Peter, and she had stopped at my office that afternoon, distraught that he had canceled on her. He had called her that morning to say that he wouldn't be coming up that weekend. Rebecca didn't know it, but I had heard her walk up the stairs to his office and jiggle the handle of his door before she tiptoed down and knocked on my door. *Did she not believe he wasn't there,* I wondered, *or did she want to go in and have a little snoop?* When she came into my office and told me how upset she was that she wouldn't be seeing him that night, I felt sorry for her. I invited her over to my house, and she had accepted, tearfully.

She brought Japanese and a bottle of white wine. When she opened it, I said that I wasn't really in the mood for wine, and poured myself a glass of seltzer. Rebecca needed to understand that I don't *need* to drink.

Rebecca was moody and distracted. Liam was having trouble with math. Rebecca didn't like the teacher and she wanted Brian to go with her for a conference, but he wouldn't be able to do it until after the holiday break. She had been asking him for weeks to make time for this, and he hadn't. He was in New York on business. He had urged her to hire a tutor, which, for some reason, enraged Rebecca.

"My mom and dad outsourced their parenting to others. I'm not doing it. Brian is a financial whiz, but I don't know anything about math. He could really be helping Liam. But he won't take the time."

"Well, maybe you could hire a tutor just temporarily," I said.

"Peter is so involved with Sam. Did you know that?" she asked.

"No. Actually, I've often thought that it's a shame Peter spends so much time up here without Sam. I'm sure Sam misses his dad."

"I'm sure Sam does, too. Too bad Elise is such a shrew about keeping him in town on weekends.

Peter has to come here. For his work. Now he just told me that he's going to be spending more weekends in Cambridge. And he's going to be coming up here on Fridays instead of Thursdays."

"Oh, so that's why he didn't come up today?"

"Actually, he's not coming up this weekend at all," Rebecca said, refilling her wineglass. "He said he won't be up much until after the New Year."

"Oh. Sorry."

"I have to make some changes."

"What kind of changes?"

"The situation with Brian has become intolerable. I can't stand being in the same room with him."

"Oh," I said. Then I asked, "Are you and Peter making any kind of plans?"

"Well, no specific plans, no. He actually has been talking about us maybe taking some time apart. He doesn't mean it. He's been miserable with Elise for years. We're meant to be together. I think he just wants to keep things between us quiet for now, but I want to start making some plans by the summer. In the meantime, I might not wait that long before I change the locks on Brian."

"Well, be careful. Don't do anything rash. I have a great lawyer, if you want. He's the best guy in Boston. Maybe you should talk to him before you do anything else."

"Is it Dave Myerson?"

"Yes," I said. "How did you know?"

"You said the best guy in Boston."

Rebecca, somehow, is able to obtain the services of the best guy at anything, anywhere. It's another thing I've noticed about people who come from her type of money. Somehow they're just plugged into this "best of" network, wherever they go.

"Peter'll be up soon," Rebecca said. "He needs me."

"I'm sure he'll be up. You know, I think I will have a glass of that wine now, if you don't mind."

Rebecca poured the wine into my glass in such an absentminded fashion, I almost wondered if she even remembered her recent wild accusations. See, this is what I mean about Rebecca's mood swings. She's just not very stable. I had a long sip of my wine, then another, and then I felt a warm rush of compassion for Rebecca. Sometimes, when I haven't seen her in a while, I'm taken aback by her beauty. Her beauty and her fragility.

"You know," she said, "we're collaborating on a project with his moon photographs. We've been enlarging them, cutting out the moons and pasting them onto canvas, and then I paint over them with these beautiful colors of the sea, and I've even integrated some collage into some of them. Covering them with bits of kelp and shards of sea glass."

"They sound so lovely, Rebecca," I said. "I'd

love to see them. I imagine they're quite beautiful." I finished the wine in my glass.

"That's the thing," said Rebecca. She was leaning in close to me, the way she always did when she was feeling her wine. "They are beautiful, beautiful pieces. And neither of us could create such a thing alone. Do you see what I mean? I just . . . I never felt this way about anybody, Hildy. I know we're meant to be together. I think about him when I wake up—he's the first thing I think about, and he's the last thing I think about before I go to sleep. I've become so forgetful. Do you know the other day I forgot to pick up Liam at the bus stop? He walked home in the snow."

"Oh, Rebecca," I said. "You have to stop obsessing over him, it's really not good." The bottle of wine stood on the table between us—by my calculations, enough left for exactly one and a half more glasses. I wouldn't move for it. I wouldn't give Rebecca the satisfaction.

"It's not just me, Hildy. Peter's constantly thinking about me, about us. You have no idea how lonely he is. You don't know how lonely we both are when we're apart."

I poured all the remaining wine into my glass then, annoyed with Rebecca again. Rebecca had children at home. She had a husband and a lover. Peter had the same setup. I lived alone. My children were grown and I hadn't had a lover in too many years to count, but they were the lonely ones and I was expected to feel pity for them.

"You have no idea what that kind of loneliness is like," Rebecca sighed.

"No?" I asked.

The next morning, I awoke at four-thirty to my blaring alarm. I made a large pot of coffee and pulled on my thermals and then some heavy sweatpants and a turtleneck and a thick wool sweater. I poured the coffee into a big thermos. I grabbed a box of blueberry muffins I had bought the day before, at Sue Doliber's bakery. I was rummaging through my closet, looking for some warm gloves, when I heard Frank honking outside. He had told me he'd pick me up at five. I found the gloves and pulled an old pair of Bean boots over my thermal socks and then out I went into the pitch-black morning.

Frank leaned over and opened the passenger door and I handed him my thermos and muffins, then climbed up into the truck.

"Where's yer hat, Hildy?" Frank asked. "It's freezin' out there."

"I don't need one," I replied. I really look awful in hats. I have a rather long nose. For some reason, hats tend to make it longer.

"Manny has a boxful of hats and gloves and stuff on the boat. Plus some foul-weather gear. It's wet out there."

"Jesus Christ, Frankie," I said, trying to find a place on the floor to put my feet. The floor of his truck's cab was filled with debris—empty soda cans, wrappers, old newspapers, door handles, a bicycle seat, a couple of lobster buoys, a tackle box, and what looked like a petrified, half-eaten bagel. I lifted a rusty old horseshoe from where it lay next to my boot. "What is all this crap?"

Frankie just chuckled and shook his head. "Yeah, she needs a good cleanin', that's for sure."

"But how does an old horseshoe find its way into your truck?"

"It's good luck. Found it on a job site. Thought I'd keep it for luck."

"I think you're supposed to hang them up like this," I said, holding the horseshoe with the arc in my palm, the two ends pointing up. "Otherwise, all the luck pours out of the ends."

"Yeah, well, I just haven't had a chance to hang it, I guess." Frankie smiled.

I propped it up on the windshield.

"I don't know how lucky yer gonna feel if I have to slam on the brakes and that sucka comes flyin' back and breaks all yer teeth, Hildy."

I laughed and tossed the horseshoe back on the floor.

"I brought coffee and muffins."

"Didja? Great. We usually have breakfast at the Driftwood when we come back in, but we're always starving by then."

We drove through the dark, slumbering town of Wendover, and there was not another car on the road. When we arrived at Wendover landing, there were a few local lobstermen parking their trucks and calling out gruff greetings in white gusts of breath to one another. They were the diehards. Most lobstermen pulled their boats from the water in November. We parked right next to Manny's rusty old blue pickup. The night was dissolving into a cold silvery dawn, and the old shops around the wharf began to take shape all around us. We climbed out of the warm truck and I pulled my turtleneck up over my chin. Frankie grabbed some gear out of the back of his truck and we headed over to the landing.

The tide was low and the ramp from the parking lot down to the dock was steep, and although Frank easily strode down carrying coils of heavy rope and my bag of coffee and muffins, I had to hold the rope railings and walk down carefully. There was a time when Lindsey and I used to skip down this ramp barefoot.

It was that moment of dawn on the waterfront when the sky and sea both take on the exact same shade of gray and the horizon is lost. There was just a boat, seemingly floating in air, with Manny in bright cautionary yellow. Manny was wearing the yellow foul-weather overalls that are the lobsterman's uniform even on the hottest summer days.

Manny's big. He's about six-five and rather stout and he still has tufts of curly reddish gray hair sticking out beneath the hats he always wears. I suspect he's balding, as I haven't seen him without a hat in a good twenty years. In the summer, he wears grimy trucker's caps; in the winter, knit fisherman's hats.

"Got somethin' for Hildy to wear? She didn't bring any gear," Frank said, stepping aboard and then reaching out a hand to me. I took his hand and tried to leap nimbly aboard, so that it would feel to him that I was just as light a little thing as I once had been. I sort of staggered into him. Frank laughed and steadied me. I pretended that nothing unusual had happened. I just walked back to the stern, examining Manny's boat. She was called *Mercy*.

Commercial lobster boats all have more or less the same design. The bow, directly in front of the cabin, is short and usually swales up in the center, so in rough seas, water can easily fall off to both sides. It was on these sloping planks that Lindsey and I used to sprawl in our bikinis like a couple of young, wet, sunburned figureheads that summer so many years ago. Every time I have a mole removed, I think of Manny's old lobster boat.

The cabin of Manny's current boat, like most lobster boats, was designed for the captain and crew to stand, but there were a couple of tall, swiveling captain's chairs. A roof and a windshield offered some protection from bad weather, but the back of the cabin was open to the aft section of the boat, which was designed to hold dozens of lobster traps. Most of Manny's traps were already set, so there were only a few tied to the sides of the vast aft deck, to replace any damaged traps we might find.

Manny's boat was certainly not as high-tech as some of the newer lobster boats you see in and around Wendover harbor nowadays. But it did have all sorts of gadgets he'd never had on his old boats, and Manny proudly pointed them out to me. There was a GPS system, satellite radio, ship-to-shore phone, which you'd think would be obsolete now that we all have cell phones, but Manny said that the cell service gets sketchy once you leave the harbor.

Manny started up the engine, and the still morning was suddenly filled with the engine's thick, earnest chugging. The smell of dead fish and gasoline and salt was all around. Manny and Frank poured buckets of dead fish into the massive, reeking bait tanks and started scooping them into tiny mesh bait bags. Frank jumped out onto the dock, untied the lines, then jumped back on board, and we were off.

It occurred to me as we cruised through the near-empty harbor that I had never been out on the water in the winter. Well, there was the winter in the early sixties when the harbor froze over and we all skated from the landing to Lighthouse Point, but I had not been out on a boat after October, ever. It was freezing. Frank had been right. Manny offered me one of the chairs in the cabin, but even there, the wind burned the tops of my ears and I was sprayed with surf from the side of the boat.

"Manny, where do ya keep all ya extra gear?" Frank hollered when he saw me covering my ears with my gloved hands.

"There's a big old plastic bin down below. Go have a look, Hildy. Otherwise, you're gonna get soaked," shouted Manny.

Shouting and hollering are the only ways to communicate on a commercial lobster boat; the engine is so loud. The men tend to say little to one another while out on the water, which may help explain why they say so much, so noisily, while seated at Barney's, a local bar, in the afternoons.

I opened the hatch to the little cabin beneath the bow and found the bin, and soon I was wearing my own pair of fish gut–stained coveralls, though mine were dark gray, and a matching gray rain-coat, about five sizes too large. The hat selection was grim. There were two knit hats, both of which were filthy and encrusted with who knew what. I sort of shook out the least offensive and pulled it over my head, and then I slunk to the stern of the boat and pretended I was admiring the view of the disappearing harbor. I didn't have to pretend for long. I looked at the long jetty leading out to Lighthouse Point and recalled leaping across those rocks with my brother and sister when we were kids. We used to fish off the jetty. My brother caught a sand shark there once.

At the mouth of the harbor is old Peg Sweeney's Rock, which is said to be haunted by the ghost of a young Wendover woman who was raped and murdered by a band of pirates there two hundred years ago. Supposedly, at night, you can still hear poor Peg Sweeney's screams as you pass that rock. Generations of kids have motored, paddled, and sailed past the rocky ledge on summer nights and have scared one another half out of their minds with their own gasping and screaming. We motored out toward Singer's Island. When I heard the engine lull, I turned to watch Frank take a long hook and snag up one of Manny's black-and-gold buoys from the water. He pulled the buoy up, and Manny grabbed it and threw it over a cinch. Then he pushed a button and the cinch reeled in the line itself. When we were kids, Manny and his crew'd had to work the cinch by hand.

Manny saw me grinning at the impressive mechanics of the thing and he hollered, "Hydraulic cinch. Nice, huh, Hildy?"

"Wicked nice, Manny," I said, and then I scrambled over to see what he had pulled in. Three keepers, a couple of crabs, and a cull. Frankie reached his hand into the wooden trap and tossed the crabs back into the water. He held a measuring gauge to the cull—it did look like it might be on the short side—but it was good, so he threw it into a holding tank with the others. Then he threw a bait bag into the trap, and I instinctively stepped back. Frankie hitched the lobster pot back to the casting line, which, as we drove off, would yank the trap back along the deck and into the water from the boat's open stern. One of the reasons Lindsey and I used to perch on the bow is because of the danger of standing on the aft deck of a boat. Your foot can get caught up by the rope and you'd be pulled over in an instant, when the traps are being set. Manny always worried about us unless we were up on the bow.

Manny was driving on to the next buoy and Frank was busy banding the claws of the captured lobsters to prevent them from culling each other.

"Give me some gloves, Frankie," I said. "I'll band 'em."

Frank managed to find me a pair of the thick neoprene gloves and I started snapping bands around the flailing, clacking claws of the lobsters. I'd forgotten how beautiful fresh-caught lobsters are in all their dappled hardness, before their mottled scalloped armor of semiprecious hues—sapphire, topaz, and emerald—fades into a general muddy green. The lobster loses its luster in a tank. You should really see one when it's first pulled from the sea, when it still defiantly grips a piece of sea-weed in its claw and tries to flip you off with its tail.

Frank snagged the next buoy and we settled into a little routine of catching pots, banding, then baiting and setting the pots back in the sea. The sun was well up above the horizon now and we had all removed a layer or two. The work warmed us up. Finally, we were approaching Grey's Point.

"Drive 'er on a little closer to the point, Manny," Frankie called when he saw me squinting off at it.

Manny steered the boat toward shore and then I saw it: a big, beautiful Nantucket-style home with a sprawling porch. It faced the end of the point, and yes, it had views from all sides. It was going to be stunning. I noted the cedar shingles on the roof, counted the chimneys, got a glimpse of a three-bay detached carriage house.

"Whatta ya think it'll go for, Hildy?" Manny asked.

"They'll ask ten and they'll get eight," I said.

I was already designing the brochure in my head. I'd have an aerial photo taken, and one from the water, too. I'd put an ad in *Boston* magazine and *The New York Times Magazine*. The Santorelli brothers would be crazy not to list it with me.

Manny and Frank hooted. It was an outrageous sum. I knew I could get it, if only I could get them to list it with me.

"Okay, I've seen enough," I said. Then I remembered the coffee.

"Anybody want coffee or a muffin?"

"Hell YEAH," said Manny. I passed out the muffins and, lacking cups, we all took turns sipping the coffee from the thermos. It was still good and hot. We chugged out to the next lobster pot.

It was late morning when we had set the last trap, and Frankie and I leaned against the side of the boat on the way back to the harbor. I was smiling. I hadn't had so much fun in years. Out on the water with two old friends. An exciting real-estate prospect. We were heading into the wind on the way back and we all put our layers back on. It had been a good haul. Thirty-eight keepers.

"Any of that coffee left, Hildy?" Manny called back.

"Yeah, here," I said, passing him the thermos.

"Hey, Frankie, go in the hold. There's a bottle of Jameson in there. We'll make us some Irish coffee."

Now that just made me smile. An Irish coffee sounded like just the thing.

Frankie looked at me uncertainly.

"What?" I asked. "Go ahead."

"Okay." He smiled. "I thought I heard that you quit drinkin' or somethin'."

"Well, I quit drinking too much is all," I said, which seemed to please him, and he clambered off into the hold and returned with the bottle of Irish whiskey. He poured a healthy amount into the thermos, and then he poured in a little more. He handed it to me first. I took a sip and smiled at its delightful wallop and passed it on to Manny and Frankie.

It was a half hour's ride back to the landing, but we took our time. I felt the sun on my face, and when I closed my eyes, it was no longer winter, but many long-gone summers all at once, beaming down on me with such a golden brilliance that I couldn't see for a moment when I opened my eyes and I had to blink until the blurred shapes of Manny and Frank took their familiar forms against the horizon again. We cruised past the seemingly endless stretch of beach in front of the Hart estate and then we passed the strip of private beach in front of the Newbolds' house. We all gazed silently at a small woman in a parka with a fur-lined hood who stood on that narrow strip of sand. A German shepherd was leaping in front of her. She threw a large piece of driftwood for the dog and he streaked across the beach after it, then carried it triumphantly back to her. How lonely she looked, from where I stood then, shoulder-to-shoulder with a couple of Wendover's own; three old townies with carefully preserved memories of one another, memories of the way we looked and felt in the best of our youth. I imagined that Rebecca would be horrified to learn that I had spent the morning out on a lobster boat with Frankie Getchell and Manny Briggs. She knew them only as they were now, a couple of stinky old bachelors, long past their sell-by dates. I had been madly enamored of both of them when I was a girl, and now I was once again as we moved through the harbor, the hot whiskey thawing my memory. I looked at Manny, whose whiskers were gray but whose teeth, when he grinned, were still strong and white. Frankie, standing a few feet away, had the angular profile of an Anawam chief, from where I stood watching him, and when he turned and caught me looking at him, I blushed like a schoolgirl and looked back at the shore. Rebecca was wrestling the driftwood from the jaws of the dog, then she flung it once again across the beach. I pitied her then. Pitied Rebecca all alone on the beach—all alone on the private beach where she didn't belong.

We passed Singer's Island and Lighthouse Point and old Peg Sweeney's Rock. We drank the Irish coffee until the morning took on a lovely semilucid calm, and when we got back to the dock, I hosed down the deck while Manny and Frankie unloaded the tanks and traps. Then Frankie took me home. He dropped me off in front of my house. He had to check on his crew. I had to take a nap.

"Why don't you come over for dinner tomorrow night?" I said.

"Dinner? Well, I dunno, what's tomorrow?"

"Saturday. I'll make a stew. Something simple."

Frank seemed to have to think about this a little too long, so I shrugged and started to climb out of the truck, and then he said, "Okay, Hildy. What time?"

"Come around seven."

I did take a little nap, and when I woke up, reeking of whiskey and bait, I took a shower and walked my dogs. Then I drove up to the office to check in with Kendall before she left for the day.

"Cassie Dwight called and said it was kind of urgent," Kendall said when I walked in. She handed me my mail and the rest of my messages and I went into my office to call Cassie.

"Can we push back the closing date, Hildy?" asked Cassie.

The buyers had originally wanted to close by February 1, and I had pushed them back until the end of the month. They had to be out of their house by March 1.

"I don't think so, Cassie," I said. "What's the problem?"

"We still haven't found a place in Newton or anywhere near there. It'll be really hard to get a rental with Jake. . . ."

"Well, it's against the law for anyone to discriminate against you because of Jake, first of all, and second, it's just impossible. The buyers need to be out of their house by the first of the month."

There was a long silence. Then Cassie said,

"They were holding a spot for us at the Newton school for the spring term, but the spot is gone. Now they can't take us until the fall. If we move now, we'll have to find an interim program. Patch will be commuting all this way for nothing. I'm just wondering what'll happen if we . . . back out. Of the sale, I mean."

I was floored. Finding a buyer for the Dwights' house had seemed like a minor miracle. Now Cassie was hoping another miracle would happen in four months, when it suited her.

"You'll have lost a huge opportunity, Cassie. I can't guarantee we'll be able to find you another buyer by next summer."

"I know, but isn't the summer a better time to sell? Aren't more people looking?"

"Yes, and more houses will be listed in your price range," I said.

And they won't have holes in the walls and stains on the floors is what I didn't say.

"Patch thinks we should pull out of the sale," Cassie said quietly.

"Okay, listen, Cassie. It's Friday afternoon. I want you guys to think about this over the weekend. Maybe I can find something for you to rent around here. But I really think you should sell now."

"But if we spend all that money on a Wendover rental, we'll be spending down our income from the house."

"Just think about it," I said.

Fourteen

"Hi, Mom. I want to come home. I have a friend who's driving to Boston Sunday morning and then I thought I'd take the train out and stay until Christmas. I had a fight with Adam and this whole roommate situation sucks. I need to get out of the city for a while."

This was Emily's message on my voice mail Saturday morning. Christmas was a week from the coming Tuesday. I had spent the morning out shopping because I had invited Frankie for dinner. Now I was regretting the invitation. It had seemed like a grand idea when we were all chummy in the back of Manny's boat, but really, what did Frankie and I have in common? What would we talk about? Frankie didn't like to talk at all.

I wasn't surprised at Emily's message. I knew that she had had a falling-out with one of her roommates and now the other was siding against her. They were three artists in their mid-twenties. They needed to grow up. Emily worked as a temp and was free to come and go as she pleased. She spent months at artists' colonies. Last year, she had spent the whole summer on the Vineyard, teaching art. Now she wanted to come home, and I'm ashamed to admit that I was less than thrilled. I had gotten into a little routine with my nightly wine. But now I wouldn't be able to, with Emily there.

Well, it was probably for the best. I was getting a little complacent with the whole "moderation" thing. I woke up more mornings than not with wine headaches, and the drunken phantom calls to Rebecca had unnerved me. I would have my dinner with Frankie, have a little wine with him, and then leave the stuff alone for a while. It was all stashed in the cellar now. And it would make tonight more of an occasion. Frankie wouldn't tell anyone that I wasn't going to AA meetings, that I wasn't in "recovery." He and Rebecca had become my only true friends, in this regard.

I made up the stew and left it on the stove to simmer. I had bought fresh bread at the bakery and was planning to make a salad just before Frankie arrived. I walked my dogs and then took a shower. I shaved my legs. I shaved under my arms and around my—well, around my bikini area, if you must know—we're all adults here. I dried off and began slathering myself with a fragrant body lotion that one of the girls gave me every year for Christmas.

Then I came to my senses.

What the hell was I doing? My skin was loose, except around my girth, where it was stretched taut. My hair was brittle, my face was covered with fine lines, and my entire body sagged. Even my fucking knees had started to sag. How did I not know to expect saggy knees? It suddenly struck me as profoundly pathetic that I was preparing for a date, a date with Frankie Getchell, and that I was fretting about *my* appearance. My girls had said it—the man looked like a gnome. And it was highly unlikely he was primping and pruning anything in his pubic region in preparation for our date.

I had had a few dates since Scott and I split up. Disastrous encounters with portly older men whom clients had tried to fix me up with. Nothing ever came of them. We had dinner and called it a night. But the idea of a date with Frankie had never crossed my mind since my divorce. Frankie, well, let's just say that people would be a little shocked to imagine me and Frank Getchell on a date. I was a businesswoman—the town's most successful business owner, really. He was the town garbageman. He was the fix-it man.

So what? Who would know? I'd loved him once. Who would guess it now?

Frank arrived at seven. He was all clean-shaven, with a crisp shirt and what looked like a brand-new pair of jeans. I had, in recent years, acquired a body that looked best in skirts, and I rarely wore pants. So that night I wore my usual black tights and skirt and a black sweater. I hadn't expected Frankie to get dressed up, but his jeans and ponytail made me feel ludicrous for even coming up with the dinner plan in the first place. Molly and Babs made a huge racket over Frank's arrival. He leaned down to pat them, and when Babs snapped at his hand, he laughed and pulled it away just in time.

"Watch her," I said.

"They don't call 'em bitches for nothin'." Frankie laughed.

Don't insult my bitch, I thought, trying to figure out what on earth had inspired me to invite Frank Getchell over.

He had brought me flowers. They were the kind you get at Stop & Shop, a bunch of oddly bright mums and a couple of droopy yellow roses with some baby's breath and a fern thrown in. He handed them to me and I took them and thanked him. I was stirring the stew, so I just dropped them on the counter.

The wine! I had brought it up from the cellar just as Frankie arrived and now I passed it to him with a corkscrew and he opened it while I stirred the stew. I turned the heat down and took two wineglasses down from the cabinet and handed them to Frankie, who did the pouring.

"Cheers," I said in an almost exasperated tone —I couldn't help myself. We clinked glasses and took a sip.

"Nice haul yesterday out on Manny's boat," said Frankie.

"Yes," I said. I took another sip. "What would be his usual haul on a winter day like yesterday?"

"I dunno, sometimes we get over thirty, sometimes just a dozen or so. . . ."

The wine was so nice.

"That stew smells good," Frankie said.

"Oh, I know, and you must be starving, Frankie. I just want to make a salad. Grab a chair and make yourself comfortable."

Frankie had been in my house before, on a number of occasions. He had cleaned a bat's nest out of my chimney once, and he supervised his crews when they did their big fall and spring cleanup of my property. They removed leaves, cleared gutters, and replaced storm windows and screens. He knew his way around my house, but now that he was my guest, he seemed to be looking at it for the first time.

"You sure lucked out with this house, Hildy." He leaned against the counter, watching me chop vegetables.

" 'Lucked out'? What do you think, I won it in the lottery or something?" I was laughing now and sipping my wine.

"You've done real good for yourself. I guess that's what I meant to say."

"Well, you haven't done so bad yourself, Frankie. You know, if you sold that lot next door, you could buy a house twice this size."

"Right, and let some lawyer build a mansion next door for you to wake up and look at every day?"

I smiled at him then, even though it was a joke. It was a sweet idea, that Frankie was keeping the land there for me. I smiled and finished off my glass of wine. Frankie poured me another.

The salad was ready and so was the stew. I turned and saw the bunch of cellophane-wrapped flowers that I had plopped onto the counter and my heart soared with loving sentiment over Frankie's sweet gesture. The idea that Frankie had walked into Stop & Shop and chosen these flowers to bring to me! I had married a man who would be appalled at the thought of grocery store–bought flower arrangements, and look where his exquisite sense of style had gotten me. I carefully unwrapped the flowers and placed them in a favorite vase of mine—a green fluted vase, the color of sea glass. I plumped and arranged the flowers and then I carried them into the den and placed them on the coffee table.

"Look how they brighten the room," I said, and Frankie grinned and nodded.

My kitchen table is quite large, which seemed awkward. Instead, I decided we'd eat in the den, in front of the fireplace. It was the right thing. It's nice and dark in that little room and so cozy with the fire. There didn't seem such an urgency to converse with a crackling fire to admire. The stew was good, the meat just the right tenderness. I make a nice beef stew. I rarely cook anymore, but it's one thing I do well, my stew. We sipped our wine and settled into an easy conversation about some of our old friends. We laughed about the old Wendover Yacht Club parties. He asked if I knew what had ever happened to *Sarah Good*, the sailboat he had given me. I had to think about it for a while. I really had no idea. My dad must have hauled her off to the dump at some point.

Frankie in the firelight. The rich Pinot Noir. I was beginning to soften. My heart, my mind, even my skin and bones seemed to shake off their brittle edginess. I was softening. It's what wine does for me, and what's wrong with shedding one's armor once a day, especially in the warm company of an old friend? We had been sitting in the club chairs in front of the fire while we ate, but now the flames threw off too much heat and we moved back to the sofa and even had to crack a window for a few moments to let out some of the heat. The night air was crisp with the aroma of pine and the river and there was a damp vapor that smelled like snow. We both agreed that it smelled like snow. We looked out at the moon with its smudged halo and agreed—snow was coming.

We finished off the wine and I asked Frankie if I should open another bottle. He said, "I don't know, should you?"

"Well, I really don't drink much anymore," I said.

"Mmmm-hmmm." He smiled.

"Listen, Frankie, I'm still so embarrassed about

that night you picked me up from Mamie's. I never get like that anymore."

"Aw, never mind. Go get another bottle before you make me embarrassed, too."

I ran downstairs and grabbed another bottle. When I came up, I smelled . . . was it . . . pot?

Yes, Frankie had lit up a joint. I hadn't smoked pot since I was in college. Scott had always liked it better than I did anyway, but now the smell of it made me feel like a teenager again. Well, the first time I ever got high was with Frankie.

"D'ya mind, Hildy?" Frank asked, holding up the joint. "I realized after I lit it that I shoulda asked first."

"No." I laughed. "Not at all. It's just that the last time I smelled that stuff was when I came home too early on a night when my girls decided to throw a party."

I uncorked the wine and sat down next to Frankie. I nestled up against him, just a little. He handed me the joint and I took a hit. I inhaled, then coughed it back up, laughing at myself, and then put it to my lips and inhaled again before handing it back to Frankie.

"No more," I said when he tried to pass it back to me a moment later. I was a little drunk. But not too drunk. Another glass of wine wouldn't hurt.

Frankie finished the joint. I turned on the stereo. I put in a CD, and then I started to dance around the room to a Van Morrison song, which made Frankie chuckle.

"Remember how we all used to dance at the Wendover?" I laughed. "Come on, dance with me, Frankie."

Frankie just smiled. His eyelids drooped slightly from the fire and the pot, but his eyes twinkled with amusement. "I never did any of the dancin'. You go ahead, though, Hil. I always liked watchin' you dance."

I took my full wineglass from the table and sipped from it, then moved it in graceful arcs in front of me, gazing at it adoringly, as if into the face of a lover. I glanced at Frankie and then I guzzled the remainder as if it were whiskey before tossing the glass into the air. I meant to catch it, but my toss was off, and Frankie lunged and grabbed it just before it hit the coffee table, and then I really started to dance. The CD was one that Scott had made for me—a collection of songs from our college days—and now Janis Joplin was belting out "Piece of My Heart." I was gyrating my hips and swinging my hair around in front of my face like Janis, and you know, I can sing to Janis like no other. I've always loved her. I placed my hands on Frank's knees and sang those opening words, sweet and soft, asking him if I didn't make him feel like he was the only man. Frank wrapped his hands around my wrists, but I wriggled free, belting out, "Honey, you know I did!"

I moved my hips in slow circles, singing along, and soon Frank and I were both laughing and shouting the words aloud. Then Frankie had me by the hand and pulled me on top of him on the couch and then I was kissing Frankie Getchell. Then I was really being kissed good and hard by Frankie Getchell. I hadn't been really kissed by a man in so long. I was straddling his lap, his hands were buried in my hair and my palms were placed on each of his rough cheeks, and we seemed to want to hold each other's mouths in this kiss, to not let it end, until finally we did, and then we were kissing again, all over, and groping each other like a couple of teenagers. I pulled back for a minute, smiling a bit shyly as I started to move off his lap, and then Frankie seized our wine bottle by its neck and said, "Ya better get runnin', girlie" (it was an old game), and I let out a squeal of delight and he chased me upstairs and along the hall to my room, the dogs yapping and growling and snapping at his heels like a couple of crazed spirits.

We were just drunk enough not to care how fat and old we looked, just drunk enough for me to do an elaborate striptease and for Frankie to hoot it up as if I were twenty. Then he grabbed my hand and we were in the bed, and it was just like those nights in the holds of strangers' yachts. Just like those sweaty, salty nights with the waves slapping against the outside of the hull, except for one thing. The tentative knocking on my bedroom door and the sound of a grown woman's voice calling, "MOM? MOM?"

Frankie and I froze.

"Did you hear something?" I whispered.

"MOM?"

It was Emily. She was home.

"Hi, honey," I said, trying to sound as crisp and bright and sober as a nun. Frankie lay completely still at my side.

"Um . . . Mom? Are you . . . with somebody?"

"Well, yes, dear, as a matter of fact, I am. Did you want something?" I asked, still trying to chirp soberly. Frankie was trying not to laugh and was making little choking, snorting noises. I scowled at him.

"No. . . . Good night," Emily said, and I heard her scamper down the hall to her room.

"Oh my GOD," I said. I kept saying it.

"What's the big deal?" Frankie whispered.

"Did we leave an empty wine bottle down there?"

"Uh, probably."

"I'm supposed to be in recovery."

"Huh?"

"My daughters sent me to a . . . a . . . rehab place."

Now Frankie was cracking up. "A rehab place?"

"Yes," I hissed. "They think I don't drink. They

273

think I go to . . . AA. Stop laughing. It's not funny." I burst into tears.

"Awwww, Hildy, stop. Whatsa matter? You're the mom, right? Why are you actin' like a kid? You're supposed to be the one in charge, you can do whatever you want."

I just shook my head and said, "Frankie, can you leave?"

"Yeah."

"Will you take this bottle with you and take the one downstairs?" I was frantic now, and Frankie jumped out of bed and started dressing.

"What's she gonna do, call the vice squad on us?" he whispered, and I couldn't help it, I had to smile. I was still a little drunk, but now I felt shy about climbing out of bed all naked, so I said, "Come over here and give me a kiss before you go, Frankie."

He did. Then he glanced out the window and said, "It's snowin', I gotta get my guys out with their plows anyways. See you around, Hildy."

And then he was gone.

The next morning, I was up at dawn and carried the wineglasses down to the kitchen, washed them, and put them away. I dumped out the stew that I had left out on the stove all night. I tidied up the den, looking for any evidence of the joint we had smoked, but I found nothing. Then I took the dogs for a walk. It had been snowing since Frankie left and now there was a good four inches on the ground. It was Sunday, so nobody had plowed River Road yet. There was no sound but the gentle crunch of my footsteps in the clean snow and the excited huffing and whining of the dogs as they sniffed out rodents beneath snow-mounded bushes. It was a gentle, earnest snowstorm. The snow fell vertically, instead of blowing sideways as it can in a nor'easter, and it fell in great puffy flakes, like multitudes of cotton balls. It gathered on the dogs' fur and on my shoulders and mittens and made it hard to see very far down the road. All the world was covered with the whiteness of the storm and it was hard to imagine anything dirty or ugly lay beneath this fluffy bounty of white.

Years ago, when I was a girl, we had a blizzard that lasted for five days. It snowed day and night. The town didn't have all the road-plowing equipment that it has now, and when the snow stopped, Hat Shop Hill Road was nowhere to be seen.

We had an old toboggan. Somebody—one of my dad's customers—had given it to him the year before, because they were moving down south and wouldn't need it. All the kids on our road and all the surrounding roads, all the kids who lived up on Wendover Rise made their way over to Hat Shop Hill Road that day and we turned the road into a half-mile-long toboggan run. It's the steepest road in town, and the straightest. Kids brought their Flexible Flyers and their flying saucers and their inflatable tire inner tubes, but our toboggan was the best ride down, and suddenly we Goods were the most popular kids in Wendover. Everybody begged to be next on the toboggan ride. We could pile five kids on at a time, six including Judd, who was the smallest but insisted on taking each ride down and then being pulled the long way back up the road.

School was closed for an entire week. On the second day after the snow stopped, a truck made it down Hat Shop Hill Road with a plow, flattening the snow, tamping it a bit, but not clearing it down to the pavement. This made for even faster going, and that's when my cousin Eddie and Frank Getchell had their brilliant idea. They would run a hose from our house, which stood almost at the top of the hill, and pour water down the road to make an ice run, just like the bobsled run in the Olympics.

My dad was at work, my mother—who knows, maybe she was in the hospital then, but she wasn't around. So Eddie and Frankie attached a hose to the outside spigot, but when they tried to turn it on, no water came out. Frankie's dad was in construction and Frankie, though he was only thirteen or fourteen at the time, knew how to go into the cellar and turn on the outside water line. Soon there was a steady stream of water pouring down Hat Shop Hill Road. We waited in our cellar while the water was running. There was a bulkhead hatch to our cellar that we could climb in and out of and it was nice and warm down there. It smelled of laundry and damp cellar and sometimes of our cat Calico's kittens, which she produced there once or twice a year. We weren't allowed to take our friends in the house when nobody was home, but the cellar was allowed, and that day there were at least a dozen of us down there.

Whenever we went inside, Judd would start crying because his little toes and fingers had become so cold in his wet mittens and socks that they were numb, and as they thawed, they hurt him. Lisa or my cousin Jane or I would hold them under warm water in the cellar sink and we'd tell Eddie to stop calling him a baby and a faggot, since he was only five. Eventually the boys turned off the hose and we had to wait again for the water to freeze, but it didn't take long.

It was late afternoon and the sun had moved down below the trees, and the road, in the dimming light of day, was a steep white slope with a silver racing stripe that gleamed down its center. It looked like a ribbon of glass. There was a lot of shouting about who should be the first to ride down. Frankie and Eddie had engineered the thing, so it was a given that they would be first. Judd would cry unless he was allowed, so it was decided that those three would go first—Judd sandwiched between the two older boys. In order not to demolish the little walls of the run, the boys had to lay their legs alongside the legs of the person in front of them. They needed a push, and Frankie, who sat in the back, asked me to do it. "Good n' hard, Hildy," he said, so I gave it my all. I got a running start. I grabbed Frankie by the shoulders and ran along behind, pushing, pushing with all my might, and as they hit the iced slope, I couldn't resist—I hopped on behind Frankie. There was plenty of room. My legs were sticking out to the sides and he grabbed them and wrapped them around his waist, shouting at me about not wrecking the run. And then we were off.

The toboggan had been fast before, but nothing like this. We flew down Hat Shop Hill Road, the ice singing beneath us. Little swales in the road shot the toboggan into the air again and again, and each time we hit the ground, we seemed to gain momentum. We all screamed, Eddie, Judd, Frankie, and me. We screamed ·in unison—a thrilled, terrified, joyous, electrified cry to the heavens, to anyone who might hear us. The wind whipped my eyes full of tears and I buried my face in Frankie's back. Faster we went, faster and faster. The road levels off near the bottom, and before the run was iced, the toboggan always came to a gradual stop well before the stop sign, well before the intersection with Atlantic Avenue,

Wendover Crossing's main street. But the water from our hose had run down to the end of the road, and now so did we.

"Eddie," I screamed, "stop us." We all put our legs out, but they just slid along the frozen surface. The road leveled off, but we flew along as if propelled by jet engines. Ahead of us, cars and trucks moved along Atlantic Avenue.

We all had the idea at the exact same time. Eddie went one way, Frankie and I the other, with little Judd tucked safely inside Frankie's arms and legs. We all bailed, rolling off the sides of the toboggan as it sailed at lightning speed across Atlantic Avenue, where it ran afoul of Bucky Garritty's dad's station wagon. The toboggan slid under the front tire and the car skidded across the street and across the sidewalk and through the picture window that graced the front of Allen's Pharmacy.

Today, I suppose there would have been a lawsuit of some kind. Nobody was hurt in the collision, thank God, but Dad found out about it in no time (the market was two doors down from where Allen's used to be—it's a CVS now), and he let us have it. Eddie caught the worst of it, being the oldest. My dad let him have it in the face and whacked him around his head, and the rest of us got whacked on our backsides, but we were so padded with snowsuits, we just howled to let him think he was finished with us. I think Dad threw Frankie in the snow a few times and told him he was going to call his dad.

"You coulda all been killed, do you understand that?" Dad kept hollering. We thought he might just kill us for coming so close to getting killed.

Our bobsled run became legendary. When school started up again, the story had been stretched to involve us sliding under a truck before the collision, and Eddie invented all sorts of heroics for himself—one version involved him plucking Judd from the toboggan just a nano-second before it was run over. He left out the part about how he and Frankie forgot to shut off the water valve, causing our pipes to freeze and burst and causing Dad to make more outraged phone calls to the Getchell household. Many years later, Dad laughed until he wept, recalling the story, but he didn't see much humor in it at the time.

When the dogs and I returned to the house, Emily was in the kitchen, in bare feet, sweatpants, and a tank top.

"Good morning, Emily," I said cheerfully. I gave her a little hug.

"Mom, it's FREEZING in here. Can you turn up the heat?"

I walked over to the thermostat, but it was set at sixty-eight, where I like it.

"It's winter," I said. "Put on a sweater and some socks like a normal person."

" 'A normal person.' Do you know how

damaging it is to hear from you how abnormal you think I am?"

"Oh, Em," I said, laughing a little, trying to lighten the mood, "it's just an expression. I know you're normal."

Emily sighed, and then she smiled and said, "I know."

"Did you find the coffee and everything okay?" I asked.

"Yeah," Emily said, holding aloft the mug from which she had been sipping.

"Great, great," I said. "I thought you said you were coming home today. I didn't expect you last night."

"No, I guess you didn't," Emily said.

I poured myself a cup of coffee. My head was throbbing. No more red wine.

"Mom, was that Frank Getchell's truck outside last night?"

"Yes," I said, opening the fridge, looking for the milk.

"And were you . . . in bed . . . with Frank Getchell?"

"Well, that's really none of your business."

"Mom, I just can't believe, of all the guys your age . . ."

"What?" I demanded, spinning around and glaring at her. "What guys my age? Where are all these guys my age? And what's wrong with Frank? You don't even know him."

"He's the . . . garbageman."

"He owns a maintenance company that handles garbage removal, among many, many other things."

"Were you drinking? I saw a bottle of wine on the table . . . and it smelled like somebody had been smoking weed when I came in."

"Frank drinks. And he smokes. All my friends drink."

"But you weren't . . ."

"No. Of course not."

The relief on Emily's face. You'd think she and Tess had spent their childhoods carrying me out of bars. I know how awful it seems to just so blatantly lie to one's own daughter, but it was for Emily's good. For her peace of mind. She was upset about Adam. She had enough to worry about.

"So what's going on, Em?" I asked, and Emily filled me in. She wanted to move out of the loft and into an apartment with Adam. It infuriated Emily that Adam wasn't ready to move to that next step. "We've been together for two years," she said.

"I don't know, Emily, maybe it's for the best. Maybe you should be seeing somebody with better . . . prospects . . . for the future."

"What do you mean, 'prospects'?" demanded Emily.

"I mean a job," I said. "It would be nice, I think,

for you to be with somebody who earns a steady income." I couldn't believe these words were coming out of my mouth. I was a child of the sixties—a feminist who had forged her own way, never relying on my husband for support. But now I thought how nice it would be for Emily to wind up with somebody who would take care of her. I didn't need that, no, I had always taken care of myself. But it would be nice not to have to. It would be nice for Emily not to have to, I mean.

"I knew you were going to say something like that. You've never had any faith in Adam as a musician. His band is about to get signed. The other night he did a gig at Irving Plaza and there was a rep from Sony. . . . Oh, forget it. I knew you wouldn't understand this. I'm calling Hailey. I'm going to see if she'll go have lunch with me. Maybe we'll go down to Marblehead and see Tess."

"Emily, I'm not trying to be unsupportive. I just want you to be realistic, that's all."

"Whatever," she replied, stomping upstairs to her room.

It stopped snowing and Emily did go down to Marblehead with her friend Hailey. I spent the afternoon reading the Sunday paper, and when it started to get dark, I thought I'd have just a hair of the dog—just a little glass of wine—while Emily was out. She made me so nervous with all her prying, and truthfully, I had a little hangover.

Hangovers always fray my nerves. So I went downstairs and uncorked a bottle and poured myself a little mug of wine. I used a mug, just in case Emily arrived home early, and I left the bottle downstairs behind an antique framed botanical print that Scott had left there.

I used to hate my cellar. It's an old house, near the water, and the cellar has such a low ceiling that I must crouch when walking through it. Still, I get cobwebs across my face. The cellar has a hard dirt floor that is often damp and somewhat slimy, even though I run a dehumidifier all year around. There are mice down there and spiders, and once, not long after I bought the house, I ran down there for something and almost stepped on a long, dark, slithering snake. The thing was at least three feet long. It sidled across the earthen floor and then disappeared into a crack in the stone foundation, sending me shrieking back up the stairs. But now I had become accustomed to the cellar. I quite loved the feeling of being underground. It was toasty in the winter and cool in the summer. The furnace hummed, the water heater hissed. All the vital organs of the house were healthy and hard at work.

And, of course, my wine was there now. I went downstairs each evening with my flashlight and ducked around cobwebs, and when I saw the occasional mouse, I knew that its days were numbered, due to the resident snake. I no longer set traps, preferring, instead, to let nature take its course. Mice must have a warm place to spend the cold months, snakes must eat, spiders must weave intricate webs to capture their tender prey. I must have a drop of wine at the end of the day. This is how I experienced the cellar of my house now. It harbored a wonderfully symbiotic ecosystem, of which I was an integral part. Often, when I drifted downstairs for a second bottle of wine, I imagined, with some degree of delight, that when I died, I would haunt the place still, and that the spiders and mice and the snake would know me, even then.

Fifteen

Molly woke me, licking my face and whining. It was pitch-black, I couldn't see a thing, and I only knew it was Molly because of the feel of her rough coat beneath my fingers. I wanted to go back to sleep, but when I reached around for my pillow, I found nothing but a hard-packed dirt surface. I lay there for a moment. Something crawled across my hand and I sat bolt upright and realized, by the feel of the ground beneath me, and the damp smell, and the sound of the furnace, that I was lying on the floor of the cellar.

A thin stream of light came from the slightly open cellar door at the top of the stairs. I stood and staggered toward it. Clever Molly must have opened the cellar door with her paws. Now the dogs were licking my hands as I walked, wobbly-legged and dizzy, to the bottom of the illuminated stairs.

If I wake up early, after some heavy drinking, as I did that morning, I often enjoy a wonderful, tipsy hilarity, which I have learned to relish while it lasts, because it's always followed by the sharp dagger plunge of a hangover, which will rip away at my gut and saw at my brain and fray my nerves to within a hairsbreadth of the snapping point. I was still in that loose-limbed half-life—not quite drunk, not quite sober—while climbing the stairs, and I recalled, with some astonished amusement, the events of the night before.

I had poured myself a mug of wine and turned on the TV, to discover that one of my all-time-favorite movies was on. It was Alfred Hitchcock's *Notorious*, with Ingrid Bergman and Cary Grant. I really couldn't have been terribly drunk, because I remembered the movie ending. I think I had gone down only once, or maybe twice, to refill my mug, but that was all. The movie ended and I realized that Emily would be home soon and that I might appear a little tipsy, so I decided to go to bed. But that was a particularly delicious wine that I had opened and it seemed a shame not to finish the bottle. It's never as good when it's been uncorked overnight. So I made my way downstairs and was about to refill my mug with the remains of the bottle, when I heard footsteps above me.

"Mom?"

Emily was home. She had Hailey with her, and I decided that the best thing was to let them think I was in bed. Hailey lived up in Newburyport, so I assumed she was planning to stay the night.

I settled down in the blackness, next to the botanical print I couldn't see, and drank the wine from the bottle. I could hear the girls talking. Now, while dragging myself up the stairs by the handrail, I remembered that I had found it very exciting to hear their conversation without them knowing I was below their feet. It was thrilling. I'd felt like a spy or a ghost or a witch, and I recalled how I'd giggled wickedly into my hand at the things they were saying.

Of course, now I had no real recollection of what it was that they'd actually been talking about. All I remembered was that the girls wouldn't go to bed. They'd been laughing and gossiping loudly, and I'd smelled something being heated on the stove. Soup? No doubt they had been doing a little partying themselves, but by then I was stuck. It would be impossible to explain to them why I had been down in the cellar for so long. So I bided my time with my wine. When I finished the bottle, I opened another—the corkscrew was right there—I just wanted a few more sips while I waited out the girls.

Then it was the next morning and Molly was licking my face.

When I got to the top of the stairs, I peered out the door just to make sure that the coast was clear. I could see through the living room windows that it was early dawn. There was no chance the girls would be awake. I walked to the front door and let the dogs out, then went to the kitchen and drank a very tall glass of cranberry juice. I took four Advil and drank another glass of juice. I teetered back to the door—I really was still half-crocked, though I had no idea how I could have gotten that drunk from just a little wine—and I let the dogs back inside. I called the office to inform Kendall that I would be arriving later that morning. Then the dogs and I climbed the stairs to my bedroom and went back to sleep.

Later in the morning, after I had showered, I went downstairs. The late-morning sun was streaming in through the windows and the kitchen was warm and bright. So fucking bright. The girls were eating their breakfasts, and they exchanged giggles and knowing glances when I appeared in the kitchen.

Could they have known? Did I go upstairs last night and not remember it?

"Good morning, Hailey, Emily," I said.

"Hi, Mrs. Aldrich," said Hailey. The girls' friends still forget and call me by my married name sometimes. I don't mind it.

"Morning, Mom," said Emily, staring at her plate.

"What's so funny?" I asked, hoping they wouldn't tell me; imagining myself dancing drunkenly around the kitchen before them the night before, singing, drinking straight from the bottle—all the things that were half memories from some time or another. Perhaps last night, perhaps nights from years past. Who knew. I never remembered everything, but sometimes I recalled the looks of embarrassment from my girls, even when they tried to laugh along with me and their friends, when I'd had a few. I'd always offered their friends a drink, even before they were of age, which had made our house a very popular place during high school. The girls hadn't complained about my drinking then.

Emily replied, "Nothing, we just were wondering where you were last night. Out until after two in the morning?"

"Well, I was at . . . a friend's."

"Mom, you don't have to be so secretive. Just say it. You spent the night at your boyfriend's."

"Okay, I was at my boyfriend's," I said. Because I would rather have them think I had stayed at Frankie's, that I had spent the night anywhere but passed out on the cellar floor. The whole night, which had seemed so amusing only a couple of short hours ago, now seemed like a dark, dark tragedy. A jackpot. I had passed out in the cellar, with spiders and who knew what else crawling all over me. I thought of the spongy feet and greasy fur and beady black eyes of mice. I thought of the way snakes sidle about with their lashing tongues and quickening tails, the way they like to heat their cold scales in warm, dark places.

"So you and Frankie are a . . . couple?" Emily giggled.

"Emily," I said.

"What?"

"Mind your own damn business," I said, and turned on my heel and went back up to my room. I pulled my boots from my closet, an action that sent the dogs (always so annoyingly underfoot) into leaping and ecstatic displays of joy. Down-stairs, I grabbed my coat and the dogs' leashes and out we went into the bright midday sun. There was still snow on the ground, but the sun had melted the top layer and warmed the air. Every-thing around me shone with the reflected sun's intense glare. I shielded my eyes with my hands and decided not to leash the dogs for a walk on the road, but, instead, to take the short wooded path to the river.

Each step was torture. The hard cellar floor had made my back tighten up, and I was trying to discern whether it was my back muscles or my kidneys that were screaming spasmodically with every breath I took. My doctor had recently told me he wanted to check my bone density, but now I realized there was no point. I could feel every bone and vertebra in my back and legs disintegrating like chalk with every step. A few more steps and I could very well be just a fully clothed but deflated pelt of human flesh lying there on the path, blinking up at the sky. And my head. My fucking head. Well, it served me right. The cellar's dirt floor was where I belonged. It was fitting. Had Emily discovered me there, she would have reported back to Tess and I would never be allowed to baby-sit, or even hold, little Grady again. Babs, the terrier, is a yapper, and every time she let loose with one of her shrill yips and yikes, it took every ounce of will I could summon not to plant my boot in her ass and send her flying into a snowdrift.

When we finally arrived at the riverbank, the coolness, the washing, rushing sound, the smell of salt water and fish and something else—perhaps the wet marsh grass peeking out through the snow? Or maybe the sand? Did sand have a smell? Well, it all made my head light, and my muscles, even my aching, dissolving bones seemed to take hold, to get a grip. Everything evil, all the self-doubt and self-loathing, seemed to wash down into the sand below my feet. Ahead, standing as vertical and still and proud as a statue was a great blue heron, perched on a rock. I caught my breath at this vision, which put the dogs on high alert, and in an instant they saw it, too.

"No. Molly, Babs," I cried out, but they raced off, causing the giant bird to lower its head, shrug its great winged shoulders once and again, and then launch itself into a slow, flapping ascent across the semifrozen water. The great bird soared over us and we all stared at it, Molly, Babs and me, blinking, blinking into the dazzling sun, and then the sky was made blurry by my tears, and I won't say I was suddenly aware of God's presence or that I had one of those "spiritual awakenings" they carry on about in AA. It wasn't anything like that, no. But I think that for a moment then, like the line in the carol, my soul felt a sort of . . . worth. A sense of being worth something. I guess it was because the bird seemed so hulking and prehistoric, yet it somehow flew. And I had behaved dismally and primitively last night, yet, amazingly, nobody knew. I had my sweet dogs, and the river, and my beloved daughter in the house. I had everything. I still had everything. Like Ebenezer Scrooge, I was awake and alive and I still had everything—I had more than enough for me.

I resolved, then and there, to stop drinking again. I would go back in the house. I would make my daughter's favorite meal. I would call Grady just to hear him babble over the phone. I would not drink today. I would not drink tomorrow. I would not drink the next day, or the next.

When I returned to the house, I found a big

beautiful spruce tree propped up next to the front door. Onto one of the branches had been speared a piece of yellow lined notepaper with the hastily scrawled words "Merry Christmas, Hildy. Call if you want help putting it up. Frank."

Frankie had given us a tree every year, for as long as I could remember. Even when I was married to Scott, Frankie always gave us our tree. I considered it a nice way of thanking me for all the business I sent his way through my clients—mostly newcomers to town with lots of need for Frankie's services. But this morning, I was so moved by his gesture that my hand shook when I lifted the note from the tree. True, my hands always shake when I'm hungover, but this was different. I was all soppy with love for the man who had cut down this tree, just for me. Dear Frankie.

I entered the house and Emily said excitedly, "Frank Getchell dropped off the tree. Let's decorate it today."

"Okay, but I have to go into the office for a little while. Let's do it tonight. Call Tess and see if she wants to bring Grady up to help. Michael's away on business this week."

"Okay," said Emily. Then she said, "You should call Frank and see if he'll help, too."

"I will," I said after a short pause. "I'll see if he wants to stay for dinner."

When I got to the office I did call Frank, but

of course, there was no answer. No machine. I did some paperwork and checked out the MLS listings, but there was nothing new on the market. I told Kendall that I was going to close the office the following week and then reopen the Wednesday after New Year's Day. This week, I told her, she could just come in mornings to open mail and check messages and call me if there was anything important. I wanted to spend some time at home with my family.

I left the office around three and headed up to the rise. I passed the McAllisters', but the house was dark and still. They had gone to their house in Aspen for the holidays, as they did every year. Linda was taking care of the dog and horses and she had told me how bitterly Rebecca had complained about going, the day they left.

"I don't even ski," she had hissed at Linda as they packed the car. "I spent my winters in Florida, riding, when I was a kid. I hate Aspen. . . ."

"It must be rough," Linda had said, laughing as she told me this. I had laughed with her, but now, passing Rebecca's house, I felt sorry for her. I had ever since I saw her on Peter's beach all alone that day. All alone in the cold.

I drove past the McAllisters' and on up the rise to Frankie's tree farm. There were cars and trucks parked up and down his driveway. With all the fresh snow covering the antique toilet garden in front of his house, the whole place looked very quaint and picturesque. College boys, home for the holidays, were making a little extra cash with the tips they were handed after dragging the trees down the hill to the parking area and loading them onto the cars that were parked there. I walked around the back of the house and up the path a short distance to where it opened up into a field of spruce trees. There I found Frankie standing next to a bonfire, collecting payment for a tree from a family I recognized but couldn't quite name. I thought the husband had gone to school with Tess, but I wasn't sure. They all greeted me as if they knew me and I greeted them warmly, and when they left, Frankie and I just stood there, looking up the hill at the trees and the families, watching our breath leave our mouths in modest little puffs.

"Thanks for the tree," I finally said.

"Sure, Hil," he replied.

"Well, when you finish here, do you think you might be able to come and help us set it up? It's pretty big."

"Yup," Frankie said. "If you want it set up before dark, I can send one of the boys—"

"No," I said. "You come. Whenever you're done here. Stay for dinner . . . if you want. Tess might bring Grady, my grandson, up."

Frank said nothing. This was something I remembered about Frankie. He was one of those rare individuals who said nothing when he didn't know what to say. Not only that but when you spoke to him, he would look in your eyes for only a second, if that, and then he'd look away. That's why I always had such a hard time reading him. Now we both just stood gazing up at the hill. After my invitation had dangled awkwardly unanswered for several minutes, I turned to leave and said, "Or just send one of the boys."

"No, Hildy," Frank said. "I'll come. Maybe around six."

"Okay." I smiled. "See you then."

When Frank arrived, Tess and Grady were there and, of course, so was Emily. I ignored the amused glances I caught between the girls. I had made a lasagna that afternoon, and after Frank placed the tree in the stand, he and I went into the kitchen while Emily strung lights on the tree and Tess tried to keep Grady from pulling them off.

In the kitchen, I asked Frankie whether he'd prefer wine or beer.

"What're you gonna have?" he asked.

"Sparkling water," I said cheerily.

"Oh," said Frank, glancing toward the living room, where the girls were. Emily was having a glass of wine. There was an open bottle on the counter, so he said, "I'll just have a glass of that wine, if you don't mind, Hil."

"No, not at all. I hate it when people don't drink

because of me." I poured him a glass and then began preparing a salad.

Frankie watched me, then whispered quietly, "So you never drink when the girls are around, huh?"

I laughed and said, also in a whisper, "No, and now I've given it up completely again."

I watched Frankie working this over in his mind. His face took on a rather grim expression, and I laughed again and said, "It's not because of the other night. I had fun that night. I just . . . need to give it a rest is all."

Frank nodded and little Grady came tottering into the room. "Gammy!" he exclaimed.

"Hi, Grady, my love. Frank, have you ever seen a more gorgeous child?"

Frank smiled and looked Grady up and down. Grady was looking Frank over, too, which made Frank chuckle and say, "Yup, he's a keeper." Then he asked Grady to give him five and they slapped palms. He asked Grady how old he was and Grady sort of stood and drooled.

"He's two," I said, answering for Grady.

"Where do you live?" Frank asked Grady.

"Frank, he's two!" I exclaimed, laughing. "Haven't you ever met a baby before?"

"Well, I thought by the time they can walk, they're pretty good talkers."

"Only the geniuses, and thank God Grady's not one of those," I said, pulling the child from the dog's water bowl, which he had begun to drink from. I lifted Grady up and started nuzzling his neck with kisses, which made him shriek with laughter.

"Who's your favorite in the world?" I asked.

"GAMMY."

"Who do you love more than that Nancy person?" I laughed. I winked at Frank and mouthed the words *the other grandma.*

"GAMMY," Grady squealed.

"Here, Frank, hold him while I finish this salad."

Frank set down his glass and reached out his strong arms for little Grady. Grady enjoyed being held by Frank, enjoyed studying this new face. I finished making the salad and we had dinner and then we all decorated the tree. When we were finished and the wine was gone, Tess and Grady left and Emily went up to bed. Frank got ready to go, too, but I said, sort of abruptly, "You can stay if you want."

Frank said nothing. He was thinking.

Then I said in a nicer tone, "I want you to stay," and Frank smiled and grabbed me tight and kissed me with great urgency, hard and strong, the way I like it.

Sixteen

I sold one house in February, just outside the Crossing—a split-level ranch that went for well under the asking price—and I was in negotiations for somebody to buy some commercial office space in Manchester, but other than that, business continued to be slow. The Dwights had pulled their listing and were planning to list the house again in the spring. I told Cassie that I thought they were making a huge mistake. She had stopped in the office one day in February to talk about it while Jake was at school.

"We just couldn't move now. The school here isn't great, but at least it's a familiar place for him to go each day. If we moved to Newton, he would have been home all day and he would have regressed. And he would have driven us out of our minds. . . ."

"But you should have let me help you find a rental here."

"Hildy, we need to just move once. Jake really does best when things stay the same."

"Okay, so when do you want to list it again?"

"We were thinking June. That way, if it sells right away, we can plan to close right before school starts in Newton."

"But, Cassie, houses don't usually sell right away. Not in this market."

"We're going to have to try our luck," Cassie said. "Not that we're the luckiest people in the world."

"Okay, we'll plan to list it June first. And I'll call the buyers."

By the beginning of April, I had a few clients who were looking in Wendover. One family—two Boston lawyers and their six-year-old daughter—was looking for a house that could be converted to a "green," ecofriendly house. This was a first for me, believe it or not. These people wanted to live "off the grid" in a house that would be powered by wind and solar energy. They wanted to gut it and replace all the old materials with ones that didn't "off-gas" toxins into the air they would breathe. The wife had suffered miscarriages before they had removed some toxic carpeting and mold from their apartment in Boston. Only then were they able to conceive. Now, for the health of their child, they wanted a house that would be "clean and green." The wife was very enthusiastic about this. Honestly, she seemed a bit obsessed. It was easy to show them homes, though, because they didn't really care how a house looked on the inside. They were more interested in its "orientation"—whether it faced north or south and what kind of light it would receive. I talked to them about looking at some land. It can be much cheaper to build a place like this than to try to convert an older home.

"Oh, but we've always loved the charm of the old New England homes."

"Well," I said, "the really old ones are pretty well insulated, which should help with energy conservation. The colonists who built them needed to conserve heat, so they're usually built with small windows so that heat can't escape."

"Yes, but now that we have thermal-pane windows, we would like to install those and add extra windows to allow the sun in to heat the place. And solar panels in the roof . . ."

You see what I have to deal with. They want it old, but they want it new.

I was seeing Frank, very quietly. We never went out. Neither of us liked to, really. Frank always came to my house, always at my bidding. We'd see each other by chance. I'd drive past him and he'd honk and slow down. If we were on quiet back roads and there were no cars behind us, he'd back up and smile at me, ask me how I was doing. I would say something like "Stop over for some chili tonight, if you feel like it." He always felt like it. Sometimes we'd watch movies and sometimes we'd watch the fire and chat. I know I have said that I know everything that goes on in this town, but Frank really knows everything. He has the fire department scanner, for one, which I believe he keeps at the snoop setting, where you can hear every dispatch in this and the five surrounding towns. He knew that the O'Briens were divorcing, that the Halsteads were expecting a baby, and that poor Ethel Quinn had inoperable brain cancer. He had kept me apprised of the Santorelli property out on Grey's Point. As soon as the siding went up, I planned to approach them with a proposal.

And, amazingly, Frank knew all about Rebecca and Peter. I found this out late one warm afternoon in early May when we were walking the dogs through Frank's riverfront lot, the one next to my house. Frank reminded me that he had seen me skinny-dipping one night the summer before, and I started laughing. "I was a little drunk," I said.

Now that I didn't drink anymore, it was easy to laugh about my former ways. I was like those people I used to listen to in meetings. That lady who drank alone, who disgraced herself on occasion, was gone. She would not return, as long as I didn't drink. Instead of feeling diminished by this knowledge, it empowered me. I wasn't that person anymore. And I felt better. I was losing some of that extra weight around my middle. I had Frankie around a lot and I felt less lonely.

We wandered down to the beach. The sky had taken on a sort of dusky hue, and the sea, still ice-cold from the winter, glittered with multitudes of tiny whitecaps that disappeared, one after another, with a great *whoosh* as they were churned onto the sand.

"It's the golden hour, Frank," I said.

"The golden hour. Haven't heard that since the war."

"Really, you guys knew about the golden hour in Vietnam?"

"Yeah . . . it's a medical term."

"No it's not. It's a filmmaking term. Rebecca told me about it. It has to do with the fading light at the end of the day."

"Well, in Vietnam it had to do with gettin' medical care to a patient in the first hour after he was hurt. There's this critical hour, well, more or less, after a major injury when, if you don't get medical help then, your chances of survivin' go way down. I used to drive the field medic truck."

"I didn't know that's what you did in the war, Frankie. I guess I've never heard you talk about the war at all."

"Yeah, well, who wants to talk about that? You know," he said suddenly, "I used to see yer crazy friend Rebecca with Peter Newbold, out on his beach at night. All last summer, they'd be cavortin' around half-naked in the dark. I guess they thought nobody could see them. But when the bluefish are runnin', I like to fish at night. I just row my dory off Hart's Beach, and you'd never know I was there. I was surprised he'd start

303

somethin' up with her—him being a shrink and all."

"Why?" I asked.

"Because she's wicked crazy, Hil. I know you're friends with her, but she's a serious nut job. I thought she seemed okay that first time I met her, when you showed her the house, but she's got a screw loose."

"She's not that bad," I laughed. "I know one of your guys pissed her off once. What happened?"

"Skully White drove up there to pick up garbage—not long after they moved in—and his truck broke down, and you know, there's no cell service up there on the rise. . . ."

"Frank, your trucks are a disgrace. Why don't you get a couple new ones so they're not breaking down all over town?"

"What're you talkin' about? They're fine. Why would I get new ones when the old ones still run?"

This made me chuckle. It wasn't just that Frank was a miser (which he was). He also just hated new things. He was averse to any kind of change. "So what happened, up at Rebecca's?" I asked.

"Skully knocks on the door of the house and the baby-sitter tells him she can't let him in to use the phone 'cause the mom's not there—she's up ridin', in the ring behind the barn. Skully walks up to the barn, but nobody's ridin'. So he goes in the barn and there's yer witch friend in the wash stall. She had stripped herself down to her underwear to hose herself and the horse off. When she saw Skully, she flipped out. Started screamin' at him. . . ."

"I don't blame her. Do you know how hot and sweaty you get riding in the summer? She must have felt very embarrassed having crusty old Skully White standing there gaping at her in her underwear."

"Yeah? Well, Skully had to walk all the way down Wendover Rise to the Browns' house to use a phone to call me. When I drove up to jump-start the truck, Rebecca came out of the house screamin' at me about trespassin' and about how she was gonna call the cops. I said, 'How am I trespassin'? You hired us to remove your garbage.' She said, 'Now you're fired, so you're trespassing.' Then she said, 'If that truck's not out of here in ten minutes, I'm calling the cops.' "

Frank laughed, relaying this. "Like I was gonna get arrested for havin' a garbage truck break down on a job."

It was amusing, I was chuckling, too, at the idea of Rebecca's reaction to Frank and Skully. The idea that she was somehow threatened by these two guys. Two gentle men I'd known all my life. Old Skully White used to work in the market for my dad. He took over the butcher counter when Dad bought the store. He and Dad always restickered roasts and turkeys during the holidays for certain families who were having a bad year. I doubt Stop & Shop carries on that tradition. Skully helped out my brother, Judd, when he drunkenly drove his pickup into a ditch one night. Skully towed him out with one of Frank's old pickups and a winch before the cops could come. He never told my dad. Just warned Judd to shape up—which he did, eventually. But my point is, Skully White is a good guy. He received his nickname, "Skully," after he fell from a tree when he was in grade school, cracking his head open and fracturing his skull. Nobody remembers his real name; at least nobody I know does.

"Rebecca's a little tightly wound, it's true. She might be a little crazy," I said, "but so are a lot of people in this town. And who cares about her and Peter? They're hardly the first married couple to be having an affair in this town."

"There's somethin' really wrong with her, that's all I'm sayin'."

"But in what way?"

"She's huntin' him . . . stalkin' him. Whatever you call it."

"How do you know?"

"Well, he hasn't been up here much. We do his maintenance. I plowed snow off his driveway one Friday and she must've drove by five times. She's always wandering around on his beach when he's not there—we used to see her from Manny's boat."

"I know she's a little obsessed," I said. "I guess she's in love with him."

"Her husband owns a hockey team. He flies around in a private jet. I wonder what she wants from Pete Newbold is all."

"Frank, she's in love with him. Are you too cynical to believe in love? Maybe she doesn't want anything from him. She might just be in love with him."

"That kind of huntin' of him, it doesn't seem like love. There's somethin' abnormal about it, if you ask me."

"Stalking," I laughed. "Not hunting. Stalking."

"Whatever," Frank said, pulling me close. "I'm gonna start stalkin' you if you don't quit laughin' at me."

"Promise?" I said, pulling away and starting to run toward the house.

"Promise," Frank bellowed, and he chased me home, me screaming with delight, the dogs snarling and snapping at his heels.

The call came at three-thirty in the morning. I was curled against Frankie and had to pull myself from the thick curve of his body. He grumbled and tried to pull me back against him, but I brushed his arm away and fumbled for the phone.

"Hello?" I gasped. You always think some-body's died when you get a call like that, in the middle of the night. My heart was pounding.

"Hildy?" said the quavering, unrecognizable voice.

"Yes, who is this?" I asked.

"It's me . . . Rebecca." She was sobbing.

"Rebecca? What is it? Are you okay?"

Frankie was now sitting up in bed, gazing at me.

"Peter told me he wants to end our . . . relationship. He's done with me."

"Rebecca, I'm sorry, but it's three-thirty in the morning. Why are you calling me now? Call me in the morning. We can talk then."

"I've been trying to call Peter all night, but he must have unplugged his phone. It keeps ringing. I've tried him in Cambridge and up here."

"Okay." I sighed. "I don't think you should call him in Cambridge."

"HE WON'T RETURN MY CALLS."

"Rebecca," I said softly, "think carefully about what you're doing. If Elise finds out about you and Peter, she could tell Brian. It could be really, really bad. Think about Liam and Ben, Rebecca."

"I HAVE been thinking about them. They're the first thing I think of, always. I thought Peter was going to leave Elise and help me raise my boys."

I said nothing. What could you say? I shook my head at Frankie, rolling my eyes.

"Hang up," he mouthed.

"Now, now, for some reason, he . . . he doesn't even want to speak to me. I want to come over,

Hildy. I want you to do a reading. Tell me what's really going on."

"I don't do that, Rebecca. I don't know what's going on in anybody's mind but my own, and even that's sort of foggy most of the time."

"I've seen you do it, you've done it to me."

"I can't tell you what people are thinking, especially if I can't see them. And even then, it's not really their thoughts. . . ."

"I think he's planning on coming up. In the next few days. I think he's been coming up without telling me. If he does, try to talk to him, Hildy. Try to read what he's saying and get the truth."

"You know," I said, "the thing that bothers me the most about this whole situation is that it sounds like what you need is a good shrink, and the best one around is now your ex-boyfriend."

"WHAT? I can NOT believe you just said that."

"Said what?"

"EX-boyfriend."

"You just told me he doesn't want to see you anymore."

Now Frankie had clasped my wrist. "Hang up," he said, aloud this time. I shook my head and moved the phone over so that we could both listen to Rebecca's ranting.

"That's how he says he feels right now. It's not how he really feels. That's why I need you to talk to him. Please, Hildy. I think . . . I think he's trying to get away from Elise and can't. She has this almost satanic power over him. It's sick. . . ."

"Okay, Rebecca, I have to go back to sleep. I have to go to work tomorrow."

"Hildy"—Rebecca sniffled—"will you please try to talk to him? I had a bad crash on Tricky the other day. I trailer him over to the hunt club sometimes to use the ring. I set up an 'in and out.' I guess our stride was off. We crashed trying to jump the second jump. Tricky fell. He almost landed on me. It's because I was so distracted. All I can think about is Peter. If you talk to him, I know you can get him to see the right thing to do. . . ."

I felt a slow rage coming over me. Mamie had told me about Rebecca's bad fall. She had also told me that Rebecca was banned from riding at the hunt club unless she started working with one of the trainers there. Mamie said she had heard from Linda Barlow that Rebecca was planning to send Hat Trick back down to Trevor Brown in Florida.

"She's ruining that horse," Mamie had said bitterly. "What a waste."

Now Rebecca wanted to use poor Hat Trick, and me, to manipulate Peter Newbold. A man I had known since he was a toddler. A man whose father gave us lollipops when we were vaccinated, who stopped by the house, frequently, after my mom died, just to check on my dad.

"I'm not planning on seeing Peter, Rebecca," I

said finally. "Imagine how upset he'd be if he knew we'd had this conversation. I'm not getting involved in this. I have nothing against Peter."

"Ha, that's very kind of you, considering the things he's said to me about you. He told me that you're a drunk and a manipulative scammer with your psychic act and that I was crazy to have ever let you suck all that information out of me. He called you a vampire. 'Like an emotional vampire' were his exact words when he described your tricks. . . ."

"Good-bye, Rebecca," I said. I was shaking, but I tried not to let it show in my voice.

"Wait, no, Hildy . . ."

Frank pulled the phone from my grip and slammed it down on the table, and I burst into tears.

"What are you doin'? Aw, Hildy. Don't cry, I told you she's a crazy bitch."

"Why would Peter say such mean things about me?" I sobbed. "I've never done anything to Peter."

"Hildy, baby, don't listen to that crazy bitch. She made that all up. Listen to me, now. Stay away from her."

When I arrived at my office the next morning, Kendall gave me my messages. One was from Ron Bates, the real-estate lawyer. The other two were from Rebecca. I called Ron and he told me he had a client who wanted to buy the

Dwight house. They were offering the asking price, $475,000. Cash.

"Who's the buyer?" I asked. I was thrilled, of course. I had shown the Dwights' house several times since we had put it back on the market, but the place was always in such disarray, it just seemed like a waste of time.

"The buyer wants to remain anonymous. Wendover Crossing LLC is the name on the offering sheet."

"It must be the Clarksons, the couple who own the lot next door. That's a smart move, to combine the properties. When do they want to close?"

"They said they're not in any rush, but they could close right away if necessary."

I hung up and immediately called Cassie with the news. She was ecstatic. The school in Newton had a summer program. If the buyer could do an early closing, they could move as soon as they found a new place.

When the Dwight agreement arrived, I drove it over to Cassie's. Jake was home from school, sick, so she couldn't get to my office. She greeted me at the door enthusiastically. Jake was standing behind her, swaying and singing incoherently.

"He knows I'm excited." Cassie smiled. "He heard me telling Patch over the phone and he knows something exciting is going on," Cassie said, beaming at Jake. The boy had grown, just in the months since I had seen him last.

"Hi, Jake," I said, but he just kept singing and swaying. Cassie and I sat at the table and she signed all the papers.

"I called the school in Newton. They have a summer program that starts in June and they're holding a spot for Jake. Patch and I are going to look at some houses tomorrow, when Jake's in school."

"I'm so happy for you all," I said, and I truly was. The Dwights deserved a break and now they were getting one.

"Let me know when you find a place and we'll set up a closing date," I said as I left, and even though we're not the touchy-feely type, either of us, Cassie hugged me tight before she locked the door behind me.

Seventeen

I found out about Peter Newbold's plan to sell his house from, of all people, Henry Barlow. Henry, the self-appointed AA spokesmodel, who used the Coffee Bean as his little personal sobriety salon.

I had planned to go into the office that Sunday, just a week before Memorial Day, because I wanted to start working on the Santorelli proposal without Kendall and the phones to distract me. I decided I would grab a coffee at the coffee shop, imagining that I would be the only one there at seven o'clock on a Sunday morning. I had imagined wrong. Henry was arriving just as I was, and he greeted me with a warm hug and a big "Mornin', Hildy."

We ordered our coffees and Henry asked me how I was doing. It was such a loaded question. He didn't want to know about my health, or my business, or my grandchild—all the things that mattered to me. He wanted to know if I was "sober." Well, yes, I was sober, so I said, "I'm doing great, Henry. Really great. Business is a little slow this time of year, but the weather is starting to warm up and people are beginning to look. I have a few exciting listings coming up."

"Yeah, I hear the Newbolds are sellin'. Whatta they askin' for that place? Right there on the beach and everythin'. Gotta be worth a wicked lot, that place."

"The Newbolds?" I said. "Peter and Elise Newbold?"

"Yeah, Doc Newbold's kid."

"I don't know anything about that," I said.

"What? I thought you'd be the broker. Doesn't he have his office in your building?"

"I think you're mistaken, Henry. They're not selling, as far as I know," I said.

"Yeah, well, I'm pretty sure they are. Hannah Mason told me. She does their cleanin'. They've been cleanin' out their attic, the cellar, the garage. Newbold's wife was up all last week, driving her crazy. They're trying to get the house ready to be shown. That's what Hannah told me anyway."

I just stood there staring at him. It was a little bit much to take in.

"See, if you came to more meetin's, Hildy, you'd know all the stuff that goes on in this town."

I had forgotten that Hannah was in AA. It was true, what Henry had said. People never talked about local gossip during the meetings, but afterward, when people stood around sipping coffee or smoking cigarettes outside of the churches, that was when you could really get an earful. The kid with the pierced eyebrow who ran the Coffee Bean handed me my coffee.

"You're sure about this, Henry?" I asked.

"Yup," he replied.

"Thanks." I went out, got in my car, and drove to Wind Point Road. The Newbolds' house stood there, as it always had, a Federal-era beauty at the end of a private road, right on a private beach. It had been in the Newbold family for generations. It was worth millions. There was no broker's sign on the lawn. Yet. But if what Henry had told me was true, if the Newbolds had been talking to a broker, the only alternative to me, really, at this end of the market, would be Wendy Heatherton at Sotheby's.

Peter's father had been my family's doctor for years. I was Peter's landlord. I had known him since he was a baby.

It was the business with Rebecca, of course. The

thing that didn't make sense was the fact that Rebecca had stopped by my office a few days after her middle-of-the-night phone call and had told me cheerfully that she and Peter had patched things up. They were back together again.

It had been the week before, early Wednesday morning, after she dropped the boys at school. She walked in, greeted Kendall cheerfully, and then stuck her head into my office.

"Hey, Hildy? Do you have a second?"

"Um, sure . . ."

Rebecca sat on the chair across from my desk and smiled at me somewhat sheepishly.

"I'm so sorry about that call the other night," she said.

"Not at all, Rebecca. Don't give it another thought."

"Well, I just wanted you to know that everything has been sorted out between me and Peter. We're back together. We had a long talk the next day. He was so sorry, so apologetic." Rebecca was staring down at her fingernails as she said this.

"What? Rebecca, that's wonderful," I said, though I was completely fed up with both of them. A *vampire,* he had called me. I wouldn't let either of them know how much this hurt me, so I asked, "How are the boys?"

Just then, the UPS man walked up the side porch with a package, and Rebecca's head swiveled around.

"Rebecca," I said, "Peter is never here on Wednesday. You know that."

"I wouldn't be so sure of that," she said, smiling. "I think I talked him into coming up today."

"Isn't he at the hospital on Wednesdays?"

"Usually. He told me he might take the day off, though. He missed me during our . . . misunderstanding. I miss him terribly. I called him last night. He was a little annoyed, I think."

"You called him at home? Again? After you and he patched things up?"

"Well, yeah. He gets so busy at the hospital that he forgets to return my calls. I need to talk to him sometimes. I was frantic last night. I had this feeling . . . it was like a premonition that something had happened to him. That's happened to me before, Hildy. When I was away at school as a kid, I woke up in the middle of the night, hysterical. I knew that my dog, Freshy, had died. I'd had that dog since I was five. I loved her. That morning, right after breakfast, my mother called. Freshy had died. So you can see why I had to reach out to Peter. I thought either something had happened or something was going to happen to him. I had to warn him. You're not the only one with psychic gifts. I've had premonitions before."

"Did Elise answer the phone?"

"No. Peter did. He wasn't happy. I told him how worried I was. Told him to be careful because of this sense that I had . . . that something might happen to him."

"It's just not the best idea to call him at home," I said.

"You think I don't know that?" Rebecca sniped.

"Sorry," I said, turning my attention to some papers on my desk.

"No, Hildy, I'm sorry. The whole thing has me a little stressed. It'll all be better when we sort everything out. How we're going to tell Brian and Elise. And the kids. But once it's sorted out, everything will be better."

"I know," I said reassuringly. "This is just a tough time. Things'll get better. What are you doing for the holiday weekend?" Memorial Day was coming up.

"We have to go to Nantucket. Brian's business partner has a house there."

"That sounds nice," I said.

"I hate islands," she said.

We chatted about the boys and the horses, and then Rebecca was off. But that night, on my way home, I swung by the Newbolds', and sure enough, a light was on. Peter had come up midweek, just like Rebecca had said he would.

I drove to my office building, but instead of going to my own office, I walked up the stairs to the second floor. I own the building, so of course I have keys to Peter's and Katrina's offices. I tried several of the many keys on my key ring before I was able to find the right one to unlock Peter's door. I pushed the door open, half-expecting to find the office all packed up in boxes, but it looked as it always had. I had been in there on various occasions. Peter's ceiling used to leak. He had asked me to have it painted a few years back. I had hired a couple of Frank's guys to do the job and I had gone in when they were finished, just to check on things.

It was a cozy space, with two armchairs facing each other and a leather sofa off to the side. An antique Persian rug covered the beige commercial-grade carpeting that I had installed, at his request, for soundproofing. Along one wall was a book-shelf filled with books about psychotherapy, psychoanalysis, neuroses, personality disorders, depression, addiction, psychosis, schizophrenia. There was Peter's own book about bonding. There were also framed photographs of the moon above the sea—photos that Peter had clearly taken from his beach. Photos like the ones that Rebecca had told me she was using for her paintings.

I wandered over to his desk. I knew I shouldn't be poking around his office, but I felt the entitlement of the betrayed. On his desk was a photo of him, Elise, and Sam, right there on the beach in front of their house; in front of the house that I had determined was probably a safe bet at a list price of five million. Next to the desk was a filing cabinet, and, yes, I opened it. He should have kept it locked. It had all his patients' records in it. There were the names of my manicurist, my daughter's best friend from high school, the mortgage officer at the Union Bank in Beverly, that nice Brenda from the library, Manny Briggs. What fun I could have had, had I been in a more mischievous frame of mind. But I was looking for one file and it wasn't there.

I slammed the drawer shut and left the office, locking the door behind me. Down I stomped to my office and logged on to the MLS site. Nothing. Fifty-three Wind Point Road wasn't on the MLS yet, so there was a good chance that a contract hadn't been signed. It wasn't even nine a.m. on a Sunday, but I flipped through my Rolodex—that's right, I still use a Rolodex—and I found Peter's contact numbers. I dialed his cell phone first. He picked up on the second ring.

"Hello?" he gasped. He was breathing heavily.

"Peter? Hi, it's Hildy."

There was a pause, then more panting. "Hey, Hildy. What's up?"

"It sounds like I caught you in the middle of something," I said. *Sex* is what I was thinking.

"I'm running," Peter said.

"Are you up here?"

"No, I'm down in Cambridge, running along the Charles. What's going on?"

"That's what I was going to ask you, Peter. What's going on?"

There was only the sound of his breathing now. It was slowing down a bit.

"I thought I saw some lights on in your house the other night. And your car."

"I drove up for a few hours on Wednesday. I had to get some things."

"I hear you might be selling your house."

A long pause, then: "Yeah, well, I was going to talk to you about that."

"Oh," I said, and I let out a little laugh. "That's what I figured. Well, I'll be happy to sell it for you. When are you coming up? I'll prepare a contract. I already have a buyer in mind. . . ."

"Um, listen, I was planning to drive up there this afternoon to pick up a few more things. Do you mind if I stop over?"

"Sure, what time?"

"I could be up there by three."

"Okay, come to the office. I'll be here."

"Great," said Peter. Then he said, "Hildy, I haven't told anybody about our plans. I'd appreciate it if you wouldn't discuss this with . . . anybody until we've had a chance to talk."

"I'm not planning to talk to *anybody* in the next few hours, Peter."

I tried to work on the Santorelli proposal while I waited for Peter, but I couldn't focus. If Peter was selling, I needed that listing to convince the Santorellis to list with me. If Wendy had one of the most expensive listings in Essex County, they'd want to list with her. Why shouldn't they? I had to have the Newbold house. I needed it. But even more to the point, I deserved it. Wendy had moved to the area less than ten years ago. Sotheby's was an international real-estate chain. Peter's dad believed in our town, believed in supporting local businesses. I had always been good to Peter, as a neighbor, as a landlord. I'd known him since he was just a little boy.

Perhaps he was planning to list with me.

Then why didn't I know about it yet?

These thoughts ran through my mind, then they ran through my mind again, and then again. By the time Peter arrived, I had whipped myself into a bit of an indignant rage. "Come in," I hollered when he knocked gently on my door. "It's open."

Peter stuck his head inside. "Hey, Hildy," he said.

"Hey."

"Do you mind if we go upstairs? I don't want anybody wandering in while we're talking."

"Sure," I said.

As I followed him to the stairs, I glanced out the window and noticed that my car was the only one in the lot.

"What'd you do, run all the way up here from Cambridge?" I asked.

"What?"

"Where's your car?"

"Oh, I parked it behind the church."

Oh Jesus, I thought. Frankie had been right. Peter Newbold was acting like a jittery rabbit. Like somebody's prey.

When I entered Peter's office, I looked around as if I hadn't been in there in some time. As if I hadn't been in there just a few hours earlier. Peter closed the door behind us and I walked across the room and sat in one of the two armchairs. He opened a small refrigerator in the corner of his office.

"Are you thirsty, Hildy?" he asked.

"No, I'm fine, thanks."

"I'm dying of thirst. I guess from all the running," Peter said, and he put a bottle of water to his lips and drank it in great audible gulps. When he turned to face me, he seemed a little taken aback.

"What's wrong?" I asked, looking around.

"Nothing," Peter said, chuckling a little. "It's just that when I'm doing therapy, that's the chair I usually sit in."

"Oh. This is your chair? You want me to switch to the other?"

"No, no, not at all," said Peter, and he sat in the chair facing me. I looked at him. Yes, it was true, he was planning to list with Wendy. I saw it clear as day.

"So," I said, rubbing the leather arms of the chair with my palms, "this is where all the magic happens, huh?"

Peter forced a smile. "Well, I wouldn't call it magic. . . ."

"Right, I guess it's a science," I said.

Peter shrugged.

"Or is it an art?" I asked. "I heard on a radio show the other day that medicine is more art than science. I wonder if that's true for psychiatry."

Peter said nothing.

"Do you think it is? Do you think what you do is a form of art?" I asked.

Peter looked at me. "No," he said finally.

I looked around his office and then out the window to my right. From where I sat, it was possible to see down into the inside of the church next door. The choir was rehearsing, as they often did on Sunday afternoons. From Peter's office, I could finally see who led the choir. It was Lucy Louden, a music teacher at Wendover Academy. I watched her right hand carving time into the air and her mouth moving in exaggerated syllables. The members of the choir gazed up at her and then down at their hymnals as they sang along. I thought of dear Mrs. Howell, of how she'd taught me to hold notes. How she'd helped me, once, by sewing up the loose hem of my Sunday skirt with a needle and thread she kept in her desk. How she'd gently squeeze my shoulder sometimes when she walked behind my chair during Sunday school.

"So you'll be selling the house that's been

in your family for . . . four generations, is it?"

"Three."

"Oh, only three?"

"Yes."

I turned and faced him again. I nodded. Peter looked so ill at ease. I liked the distance between the chairs. It was a good distance for readings. My aunt Peg always had her customers (her "clients," she called them) sit not too close, but not too far away, either. Ten or twelve feet was the optimal distance. Farther away, she couldn't really read them. Closer, they could get carried away. "They want to crawl into your lap sometimes," my aunt had told me. "People get pretty emotional and it helps if there's some kind of space between you."

"Is there a standard to the way you set up chairs in an office like this? A shrink's office?" I asked Peter.

"What?"

"I know people used to lie on couches, facing away. But now I understand that it's typical to face the patient. I was just wondering if there's some kind of recommended distance between the patient and the shrink."

"There is, actually. I can't recall the exact number of feet, but this is roughly the correct space. You need to have a—oh, why are we even talking about this?"

"No, I'm interested, really."

"Well, there's a whole science behind the therapeutic office environment. You want the patient to feel safe, of course. You don't want too many distractions. People often don't notice anything about the office until they've been here many times. Then they're so aware of it that they notice the slightest change. Like a plant that's been moved from one side of my desk to the other. It's important for a patient to feel that this is a safe place in order for the therapy to be effective."

"Hmmm," I said. "Did you ever know my aunt Peg?"

"Of course," said Peter, "the fortune-teller. Everybody knew her. I think my mom went to see her a few times, although she didn't usually believe in that stuff. My dad told her she was wasting her money. He thought your aunt was a bit of a charlatan. I hope you don't mind my saying that."

"Of course not. Many people thought that, but in fact, she wasn't a charlatan at all. She wasn't deliberately trying to perpetuate some kind of hoax or fraud. She really believed she had psychic powers, though she was just really good at doing what you described that night at Wendy's dinner party. Cold readings. Guessing. It was all trickery, but even she didn't know that. I think that's the difference. I think a charlatan is a deliberate fraud."

"I suppose," said Peter.

"I know you're no charlatan. You truly believe there's some kind of science that takes place here, that your vast training enables you to analyze and offer insight, but it's just another kind of cold reading. I bet you could say the same thing to a dozen randomly selected people, offer the same insight, and it would apply to them. Like a horoscope."

"You're simplifying things, Hildy. Actually, you're being a bit ridiculous. My years of practice and my training allow me to offer a *little* bit more than a horoscope."

I nodded. He believed himself.

"You know," I said, "I've never claimed to have any gifts, any kind of powers. I always tell people that it's like a magician's act. I've never claimed to be a psychic or profited from it. It's always been just for fun."

"But sometimes you *do* profit. You're able to access information from people, so you profit from what you learn. Even if the profit is just a little enjoyment. A little self-satisfaction."

"Oh, well, I guess you would know something about that. About what feeds a . . . what did you tell Rebecca I was? Oh yes, an emotional vampire."

"I'm sorry Rebecca told you that. It's not what I think, Hildy. I was just furious at her for telling you about us."

"Never mind. Let's talk about the house," I said. "You're going to give me the listing, right?"

"No, we're giving Wendy the listing, Hildy. But you already knew that."

"Why, Peter? Why Wendy and not me?"

"You know why."

"Yes, it's because of Rebecca."

Peter kept his gaze on me and I could see that I was correct.

"Why are you pulling me into this thing with you and Rebecca? I couldn't care less about what you guys are up to. No offense, but I find your whole affair rather dull. I could really use the listing, though, Peter."

"I'm sorry, Hildy, it just seemed . . . cleaner to keep you out of it. You've become such good friends with Rebecca."

"I've known Rebecca for less than a year, but I've known you all your life. How is that fair? And are you forgetting that I'm the only private real-estate business left in Wendover? Your dad used to care about local people, about small businesses. I thought you did, too."

"Sure, Hildy, it's just that—"

"You're not being sensible here, Peter. Everybody knows you and I go way back. Don't you think it'll raise a few eyebrows if you don't list with me?"

"I'm really sorry, but it's less complicated this way."

" 'Less complicated'?" I was becoming exasperated. "Peter, what I don't understand is why you would compromise yourself by being with Rebecca? Why would you risk it? Oh, wait, I see now. You really were in love with her."

Peter said, "Of course I loved her. I guess, maybe, I love her still."

"Yes," I said softly. I almost felt sorry for him. "Then why can't you go away with her? Just move off someplace exotic?"

"There are laws, Hildy. There are laws that ban therapists from seeing their patients, and I'd lose my medical license if it was discovered that I was having an affair with Rebecca. Besides, she doesn't love me. I know that now, even if she can't see it yet. It was all an illusion for her. She saw me as a powerful figure in her life—a sort of father figure. Plus, she has the boys, and I have Sam and Elise. I've discussed all this with Rebecca. She knows it's over, but she's having a hard time coping. I thought I'd wait to tell her about the move. Make it a clean break."

"Wait until when?"

"Until she's . . . adjusted."

He looked down and then, after rubbing his forehead, he gazed up at the ceiling and back at me.

"There's something more," I said. I saw that he was holding something back. He was so exhausted that he just gazed at me and let me go to work.

"There's something you're looking forward to. You've been offered a position someplace? Is it something like that?"

He was so easy to read.

"It's a better position. It's abroad." (This was a guess; his glance down and to the left showed me I was off.) "No, no, I see it's not. It's pretty far though." (Yes, I caught the affirmation in his glance.) "It's on the West Coast." (Right again.) "Yes, it's in California. You've been meeting with administrators. You went to California twice—wait, no, more, three or four times over the last few months. It's in . . . L.A." (Ugh, no.) "Not L.A. San Francisco . . ."

Peter was trying to keep his breathing regular, but I saw him catch his breath for a nanosecond when I said "San Francisco." *Bingo*.

"Well?" I demanded.

"Hildy, it's the kind of appointment you work toward your whole career. I'll be the director of one of the most prestigious psychiatric hospitals in the country. I start in three months. So, you're right, that's why we're selling. Elise is very excited. Her family is from the West Coast, and, well, we're heading out to San Francisco next week to look at houses."

"Have you told Wendy that she has the listing?"

"Yes."

I turned and looked out the window at the church. The choir was finished practicing. You could just barely see them now through the fogged panes. They were gathering their coats from the pews, bidding each other good-bye. Soon they would be home with their families. You had to envy them, from where Peter and I sat in his darkening office. You had to envy them, heading home now to their families and their honest Sunday suppers.

The daylight was almost gone, but Peter hadn't turned his office light on. I was certain he was afraid Rebecca might drive by and see it, so we just sat there in the cold, dim room. I gazed around and noticed that the floor slanted to such a degree that Peter had needed to wedge a small paperback book under one of the desk's legs to make it stand even. It was an old building. Over the years, it had settled at a slant. I thought about the people—maybe even some of my own ancestors—who might have sought counsel from one of the ministers who lived and worked there in the parsonage, many years ago. I wondered if any of those ministers had fallen, like Peter, from grace. It was always from love, this kind of undoing. I pitied Peter; really, you had to feel sorry for him. I tried a different tack.

"I can't imagine Wendover without a Dr. Newbold. You and your father always took such good care of us all. Won't it make you sad to leave here? Just a little sad? Leaving this town and the people you've known all your life?"

"I've always wanted to leave this town, Hildy. I live in my father's house. I went to my father's prep school. I went to the same fucking medical school as my old man. I think that was part of what I found so attractive about Rebecca, her . . . otherness. She lived in Africa; she speaks five languages. Did you know that? She's so worldly, so energetic. I really thought that maybe we could be together. I don't know what I was thinking. She was my patient. I'd never be able to practice again."

"Peter, I'm sorry about your situation. Really. But I still don't see why you wouldn't list your house with me. That's all I care about in this situation. I just really could use the listing. And, well, I think your father would have wanted you to list it with me, rather than with Sotheby's, for Christ's sake. Have you signed a contract with Wendy yet?"

"No. I think she was sending some papers over to the house. They're probably there now. I was planning to go over them and sign them tonight."

"Listen to me now, Peter. I'm Rebecca's friend. I think I can help you. Don't sign Wendy's papers."

"Hildy." Peter's voice was so strained. "I'm in a pretty desperate place right now. I was foolish to let things with Rebecca get so out of hand. I've never intentionally hurt anybody in my life. Rebecca and I are both adults. People have affairs all the time. Why is mine a crime?"

"I don't know, I guess shrinks are not considered to be mortal creatures. Apparently, you have magic powers. I have no idea. I don't make the laws, and I don't judge what happened between you and Rebecca. But I can help you, I think. I can help you sort things out. I just really need you to list with me."

"No, Hildy, I'm terribly sorry. Elise and I already promised it to Wendy. She's already taken photos for the brochure."

My pity evaporated. *An emotional vampire,* he had called me.

"Wendy Heatherton is a fool. She should have waited until you signed the contract before she started designing a brochure. I can help you, Peter, but you have to list the house with me."

"You're a real piece of work, Hildy Good," Peter said. "I've never been able to speak truthfully to any person in this office, since I've only ever had patients in here, but now I can say what I really think. You're a real nasty piece of work, trying to blackmail me this way. Now, when I'm at the end of my fucking rope."

"Peter. I'm just doing business. Small-town business with an old friend. This is getting all twisted up. I have a relationship with Rebecca. I have a relationship with you. You have a relationship with Rebecca. So what? This is about business, Peter. My livelihood. I don't care about your affair and I'm not going to tell anybody. I don't know how you think I could. But I must say, I think you handled this wrong. You're not much of a judge of character. I wonder what you were doing all those years in psychiatry school."

"What do you mean?"

"Frankie Getchell is a high school dropout, but he told me he knew Rebecca was crazy the minute he met her. You believed she wouldn't tell anyone about your affair, yet I've known for months. Peter, don't you know women at all? I would have thought you'd have learned something about the female brain during those summers hanging around Allie and Mamie and Lindsey and me. Didn't we teach you anything about women?"

Peter let out a deep breath and his face relaxed. "I think about Allie Dyer sometimes. I always recall the way her hair smelled like apricots. And a yellow bikini she liked to wear. But, truthfully, if I saw her on the street today, I probably wouldn't even know her. I wouldn't be able to pick her out of a crowd."

"No, that's true, you wouldn't. She died of breast cancer five years ago."

"Oh," Peter said. Then, looking out his window, he mused, "The way her hair always smelled. I guess it was her shampoo. Sometimes I'll smell it on a person. . . . It always brings me back."

I thought about how little Peter had wanted to buy ten dollars' worth of Allie's time. Ten dollars' worth of her attention and affection and what he perceived as love. Now people paid him for much of the same. All except Rebecca. With her, he had tried to bury the business end of the thing and make it all about love. And now that it was blowing up in his face, he was thinking about dead old Allie Dyer's shampoo.

"Peter, listen, I'm giving you my word: I haven't told anybody about Rebecca and you, and I won't. But I want you to list with me. We'll do a quiet listing. I won't put it on the MLS and I won't advertise. I'll just put the word out with the other brokers. All you have to do is call Wendy and tell her you've changed your mind. That you're listing with me. I can help you," I said.

"Do you know your daughters wanted me to help them with your intervention? They called me and asked me to help."

I felt my cheeks burn.

"And?" I said. "SO?"

"I told them I don't believe in interventions. I don't think they work. You can't make a person stop wanting to drink. I told them that, but they didn't listen. You can't remove a person's denial for them. Denial is like a blanket surrounding a person who's, well, almost naked underneath. You can't just pull it off of them. You can't just expose them to the cold and all that shame. A person can only remove it for herself when she's ready. And I guess I was right, they should have listened to me."

"What do you mean? I haven't had a drink in months."

"I know, Rebecca told me. I'm glad you finally sorted it out for yourself. I'm glad for you, Hildy, I really am. And now . . . it also . . ."

"What?"

"Well, it gives me more confidence. In listing with you. In trusting you."

The rage inspired by his insinuations about my character, about my alleged alcoholism was not in the least bit soothed by his sudden announcement that he would list with me. But I didn't let him see. *He's a shrink,* I thought. *He knows the right buttons to push.* I wouldn't grant him the satisfaction of letting him think he had gotten to me. What a scam, psychiatry. This was a low blow, but I took it with grace. A real alcoholic would have become flustered and angry.

I smiled. "So you'll list with me?"

"Yes."

He signed the contracts before I left his office.

The next morning, Wendy called me in a rage, threatening to sue. She carried on about something to do with "egregious interference with a contract."

"What contract?" I asked.

She hung up on me.

Eighteen

I met with Vince and Nick Santorelli the following Friday. We were at the Barnacle, a restaurant next to the landing at Wendover Harbor. It was a busy night, the start of Memorial Day weekend. I presented my proposal. I had all my plans about the aerial photos and the *New York Times Magazine* ads. And I had the Newbold property in my portfolio—one of the nicest properties in Essex County, asking 5.5 million. A record for Wendover. I told them to take their time and consider my proposal. Vince said that they didn't need to take any time. They wanted me to have the listing.

"Let's drink on it," said Vince. "What'll you have, Hildy?"

"I'll have a vodka," I said. I didn't give it a thought, really. It had been five months since my last drink, but I didn't hesitate for a moment when Vince asked what I'd like.

"Vodka? Vodka and what?" asked Nick.

"More vodka," I said, and the brothers laughed and ordered three Stolis on the rocks. We clinked our glasses and toasted Grey's Point.

I only had a few drinks with the brothers and then I headed for home. I was flying high. I really was having a hard time coping with all my fabulousness. I stood to make a fortune this year. A FORTUNE. I drove toward the Crossing, but instead of turning home, I headed up Wendover Rise. I drove past Rebecca's dark house and on up to Frankie's. His light was on and smoke was coming out of his chimney. I thought about knocking on his door, but instead, I called him from my cell phone.

"Yup?"

"Hey, Frank."

"Hey, Hildy."

"What're you up to?"

Silence. Then: "Not much. Where ya at, Hildy?"

"I'm outside your house, in my car. I wanted to see if you felt like coming over."

"Ya been drinkin', Hil?"

"What? Why?"

"I just thought you told me you quit is all."

"Well, I just got the Santorelli brothers to list their property with me. WE'RE LISTING IT AT TEN MILLION DOLLARS." I was laughing and bellowing the news at the same time.

Frank laughed. "Come in if you want. I'm not sure if I feel like goin' out."

I thought this over. I had never been inside Frankie's house. I'd seen enough of the outside to make me satisfied with never setting foot inside. There was nothing in this world that Frankie didn't think was worth salvaging, and I imagined his house piled to the rafters with his recovered "treasures."

"Whatta ya have to drink?" I asked.

A pause, then: "Beer's all."

"Come on over to my house, Frankie. I have some wine in my cellar."

"Nah, I'm tired, Hildy. Go home. Go to bed. Don't go openin' any of that wine, now. Just go to bed."

"What're you trying to say? You think I shouldn't drink? Because of what my daughters think? I'm the most successful Realtor . . . the most successful businesswoman in this whole town. In this whole fucking county. Who are you to tell me what to do? I'm not a child. I'll do whatever I want. I'm going home to celebrate, you son of a bitch."

"G'night, Hildy," Frank said. "Drive careful."

"Fuck you."

I did go home and open that bottle of wine. Frankie Getchell, the fix-it man, the *garbageman,* thought he knew best about what I should do? It was laughable. It made me laugh. I stormed down the cellar stairs, grabbed a bottle, and marched back up to the kitchen with it hanging from my clenched fist like a club. I would drink the wine in my den, not the cellar. I would drink as much of the wine as I pleased. Frank Getchell and that fucker Peter Newbold thought they knew me better than I knew myself? The way Peter had praised me for stopping drinking, like I was a child. What a laugh. He knew whether I was an alcoholic or not? I'd never been drunk in his company, ever. Some doctor. Well, I was not a child. I was a very successful businesswoman. I would celebrate with a little wine. I wouldn't drink the whole bottle, no. I just wanted a glass or two. Just to celebrate. In the den, not the cellar. In the den, like any civilized person, with my dogs beside me, and a nice CD playing.

I poured the wine into one of my favorite wineglasses and took a sip. I was amazingly sober, considering I had already had three drinks with the Santorellis, but the wine tasted off. I guess it was the fact that I had started off with the vodka. It just didn't taste as delicious as I had remembered it. I turned up the music and sat on the sofa. Babs and Molly snuggled up beside me. I sipped my wine and tried to summon up the joy that should have been mine—that *had* been mine only a short while ago. Who was Frankie Getchell to tell me what to do? If only my dad could have lived to see the day when I would stand to make hundreds of thousands of dollars in one day alone.

I considered calling my sister, Lisa. It was much earlier in Los Angeles; still early enough to call. But I had vowed never to drink and dial, even if I didn't feel particularly drunk. It caused jackpots, and who needed those? Not me.

I finished my glass of wine. Was it possible that

I had grown immune to the effects of alcohol? I just wasn't getting buzzed off the stuff. I must have been so wound up about the deal that I couldn't get drunk. I poured myself another glass, then I sat back against the sofa, and just as I was taking a sip, Molly pawed my arm, as she often does when she wants to be petted. Wine spilled all over the front of my new blouse.

"Get OFF," I hollered, and swiped at both the dogs until they jumped from the couch. *Fucking* dogs, I thought. Molly was *so* annoying, so needy, with her constant pawing. And Babs was going to get me sued someday, the bitch, if she didn't stop snapping at people. I finished the wine in my glass and glowered at Molly, who was now squirming and grinning horribly.

There was just a little left in the bottle. It would be a shame not to finish it. I wasn't even tipsy.

"MOVE," I hollered at the dogs. I couldn't stand the way they were staring at me and the way Molly still grimaced so. "GET," I shouted, and I watched with some satisfaction as they slunk off to the kitchen.

There was still a little wine left in the bottle. It seemed a waste not to finish it off. I wasn't even tipsy.

Frankie was there when I woke the next morning. I had fallen asleep in my den, slouched over on one of the leather club chairs, half-undressed.

When Frankie shook me awake, I was wearing only my bra and skirt.

"This . . . isn't . . . the way it looks," I said after I'd had a few moments to take myself in, but he was already in the kitchen, rattling around with the coffeemaker.

In the bathroom, I saw yesterday's makeup smeared all over my face. I took a shower, put on some clean clothes, and when I went back downstairs, Frank had a pot of hot coffee waiting.

We drank our coffee in silence. Then I told him I was sorry about yelling at him the night before. He didn't say anything. I was a little shaky, even with the coffee in me. I hadn't really felt the alcohol the previous night, but I felt it now. Soon, I knew, I would be sick with remorse and shame. I walked over to where Frankie sat. I knelt down next to him and placed my head in his lap, wrapping my arms around his legs. I felt Frankie's hands in my hair—he was stroking it gently, which made me smile and sniffle a little—and then, without warning, he grabbed a chunk of my hair in his hands and pulled my head back so that I was looking up at him.

"What the FUCK is wrong with you?" he demanded. He was actually growling when he said it. Growling through his teeth like an animal. His eyes were swollen, as if he had been crying, and I saw now that his face was filthy.

"What?" I whispered.

"Do you have any idea what you did last night?"

"Well, yes . . ."

"No, you don't, you fuckin' lush. Do you know I spent the entire night coverin' your tracks? That if you get caught, I'm gonna get nailed, too? I TOLD YOU TO GO HOME LAST NIGHT."

"I did."

"I meant STAY home."

"What are you talking about? I did stay home." I was trying to rummage through my thick, throbbing brain; trying to find the missing pieces, the tiny bits of fractured images that lingered from the night before. I had come home. I had opened the bottle. I had spilled the wine. . . .

"I came home, Frankie. I did. I remember everything. I just fell asleep."

"Get up. Sit in the chair," said Frank. He couldn't look at me. I sort of staggered to my feet. I had to grab the chair to steady myself and then I sat at the table, facing Frank.

"Your windshield's all smashed in," said Frank.

"My windshield?"

"Yeah, hood's dented and the windshield's all cracked—on the passenger side. Looks like somethin' bounced off the front of your car, then hit the windshield."

"Wait . . . no," I said. "I was home all night."

"I was out last night late because of an emergency. The Dwight kid's missing. Patch's kid."

"Oh my God," I said. "Oh how awful . . ."

"I heard it on my scanner. Drove right over there. Sleepy Haskell was the cop on duty and he told me that the kid let himself out somehow. I guess there was all kinds of confusion with the family packin' up to move. First the kid's cat disappeared and then the kid must've gone out lookin' for it. The mom is out of her mind. So I helped them look for a while, then I drove by here. Saw your car parked half on the lawn, still runnin', Hildy. Headlights blazin', and then I saw the windshield."

I made my way to the foyer window. I made my way to the foyer window by sort of propelling myself off the wall of the kitchen, then off the door frame, then the wall of the living room until I was finally in the foyer. My balance was off, it was true. I was in shock. I was in a state of complete shock.

"Where's my car?" I whispered.

Time seemed to slow down. I had the thought that I was in a dream. I'd had these dreams a lot when I first stopped drinking. After I had a few months of sobriety together, I would still sometimes dream that I had gotten drunk and embarrassed myself or hurt somebody. But then I would wake up and the relief . . . well, it was really something. I was fine. I hadn't gotten drunk, not the night before, not the night before that. Not in months. Maybe this had all been a dream. Maybe I'd never started drinking again at all. Maybe I would wake up again and have one of my Hazelden daily meditation books next to me, and a coin announcing a year of sobriety.

As my father used to say, "And yah, maybe the moon'll fall outta the friggin' sky."

I walked back to the kitchen, and when I saw Frankie turn so that he didn't have to look at me, I began to cry. I bent over the kitchen counter and buried my face in my hands.

I said it again: "Where's my car?"

"I ran it down to a guy I know in Lynn. A guy I can trust. He's gonna fix the dents on the hood and replace the windshield. He's not gonna tell anybody."

"Frankie, really, I would remember if I had gone out. And I didn't hit anything on the way home, after I spoke to you. I wasn't even drunk. But . . . where's Jake? Have they found him? Is he okay?"

"No, the whole town's out lookin'."

"Frankie . . . you can't be thinking that I . . . Are you crazy?"

"Whatta you think I thought when I saw your car? WHAT THE HELL AM I SUPPOSED TO THINK? You hit somethin'. And you must've gotten out of the car, because there was blood all over your friggin' blouse."

It was hard to breathe.

"Frankie, that was wine. Where's the blouse? You can smell it. I spilled wine all over it. . . ."

"Smell it? I burned it."

I really did feel like I might faint, and I'm not the fainting type. I just couldn't get the air into my lungs.

"Hildy, sit down," Frankie said now in a slightly gentler tone. Somehow I managed to take the few steps to the table and sit back down on a chair next to Frank.

"Maybe we should call the police," I whispered. "Maybe you should call Sleepy and let me talk to him. I know it's best in this type of situation if you come forward."

"Yeah, right, report that you smashed into somethin' but don't remember what it was, the same night that a handicapped kid goes missin'."

Now I was really crying. Frankie rested his forehead in his hands.

"Hildy, maybe you hit a deer," he said finally. "Maybe that's what happened. Deer run off when they're hit, usually. A deer or a dog. The boy would've been found by now . . . if you hit him. He wouldn't have been able to go far."

"Stop saying that," I begged, grabbing his hand and clutching it.

"The thing is, Hil, we both know that even if you didn't hit anybody last night, there could always be a next time. When this is all over, when they find the kid, the thing you gotta do is, you gotta stop drinkin'."

What Frankie said made sense. If I *had* hit

Jake—oh, how my pulse raced when I even thought about it—but if I had hit him with my car, he would have been found by now.

"I didn't go out last night. I didn't hit anybody. How could you even have thought that, Frank? I mean, *really.*"

"You can stop drinkin' again, Hildy. For good this time. I really liked the way you were when you weren't drinkin'. I really liked you better that way."

I dropped Frank's hand. "Well, that must have been nice for you. Did it ever occur to you that I might like you better when I AM drinking? That I really don't like you much at all when I'm sober? Does anybody ever consider the way *I* feel?"

Frank just sat staring at me. I couldn't help but notice that his old shirt was stained with grease. His hands were rough and chapped and looked dirty, as they so often did, especially after work.

"You're just like my girls. You only think of yourselves. I have to change *my* behavior, so *you* all will like me better."

"I'm not thinkin' about myself, I'm thinkin' about you, Hildy. It's what I've been doin' all night long."

"So that YOU'LL like ME better. Well, what about what I like and don't like? I like myself the way I am."

Frankie was walking toward the front door, which enraged me.

"I like myself fine just the way I am, except for one thing . . . this stupid arrangement I've got going with you. Did you see me listed with the top fifty most successful business owners in Massachusetts two years ago?" I was shouting now. Shouting and crying. I guess you'd say I was a little hysterical. "And you, the fucking fix-it man, *the garbageman,* think you know better than me how I should live my life? That's really outrageous."

Frankie stopped, and without turning to face me, he said quietly, "Listen, Hildy, you're a drunk. You can't go there now, but when this thing has some time behind it, you better go back to that place your daughters sent you and stay a good long time."

"GET OUT OF MY HOUSE. I had nothing to do with Jake's disappearance. I was home last night. Just mind your own business. And get me my car back as soon as possible. I want to go see Cassie."

But I was saying it to nobody. Frankie had left.

I admit, I was a bit of a mess. How could Frankie have said such awful things? And where was Jake? I searched for my phone with the intention of calling Cassie, but when I finally found it on the floor next to the fireplace, I had a fuzzy recollection of calling somebody the night before. Yes, now I remembered. It was Frankie. I had tried to call Frankie, but he wouldn't pick up his phone.

I had wanted to convince him to come over. I often get all mushy with sentimental ideas when I drink, and I recalled now that I'd felt this crazy urgency to be with Frank, to tell him how much I loved him. I must have been hammered. Was it a dream, or had I put on lipstick and fussed with my hair and wandered out to my car in the middle of the night? I had a recollection of doing so, of floating out to my car so that I could go see Frank.

What have I done?

Scott used to keep a pack of Marlboros in the cabinet above the fridge, and though I hadn't smoked in years, I dragged a chair over and climbed up, head pounding, hands shaking. I found a twisted old pack with three cigarettes left in it. I lit one and coughed. It tasted horrible. It was old and stale. I took another drag. I felt the little nicotine buzz. I needed it to clear my head. The dogs were barking incessantly and I shouted at them to shut the hell up. I would need another drink soon, but I waited. Frankie was coming back with my car. It wouldn't do for him to think I had been drinking after all his wild accusations that morning, so I sat at the table, puffing on my butt, crying like a baby.

I saw a movement in my living room. There was somebody in my house.

"Rebecca?" I cried.

Why Rebecca? I don't know. I sensed Rebecca there. Instead, Peter Newbold stepped into my kitchen and made me scream. My nerves were shot.

"Peter, what? Why didn't you knock?"

"I did knock, Hildy. Didn't you hear me?"

I took another drag of my cigarette and shook my head. *Why did Peter have to show up now*? I supposed he suspected me as well in this whole Jake business, and when I looked up into his eyes and saw how red they were, I knew that he did.

"Peter, what's going on?"

"Are you alone, Hildy? Is anyone else here?" He was looking around my kitchen. I supposed he was looking for Rebecca.

"No, nobody's here but me, Peter. Rebecca's in Nantucket for the weekend. What's going on? Have you heard the awful news? About Jake?"

He slumped down into a chair across from me and said, "Yes, I was on my way over here and saw all the police cars in town. I stopped for a while."

"So they haven't found him?" I whispered.

"No, not yet. I came to talk to you about Rebecca, Hildy. But now, with this sad business about the missing child, it all seems so much less important. Seeing those poor parents downtown, now . . ."

Now what? Why was he looking at me like that? Did he think I was somehow responsible for Jake's disappearance, too?

"I have no idea where Jake is. I was home all

night. I can't imagine what happened to him," I said, looking at my cigarette. I took one more puff, then I dropped the butt into my remaining coffee.

"I know. Nobody knows where he is." Then he said, "Hildy, I need to make sure that Elise and Sam are going to be okay. I came over to ask you if I can count on your discretion. Can I trust you?"

"Of course."

"I mean, no matter what happens, can I rely upon you to not tell anybody about what happened between me and Rebecca?"

"Peter, why are you asking me this again? I have more important things to think about. Patch and Cassie are certainly out of their minds with worry. I'd really like to go to them."

I stood up to make a fresh pot of coffee, but I had to steady myself for a second by gripping the back of my chair.

"I spoke to Rebecca last night. She knows about our plans to move, and she's . . . threatened to reveal our affair if we proceed. My career will be over, my family destroyed. I'll be unemployable, unable to send my son to school. . . ."

"I didn't tell her, if that's what you're thinking, Peter."

"I know that, Hildy. It seems almost impossible to keep a secret in this town, but I think you can keep secrets. I think you *do* keep them, when you need to."

"Of course I keep secrets," I snapped.

Oh my head.

"I just want your promise. It's not for me, not just for Elise and Sam, either. It's also for Rebecca's own good. Why should her husband and children get dragged into this mess? Once I'm gone, I know she won't say anything. That's why the sooner I leave, the better. I'm leaving today, Hildy. I just wanted to stop to say good-bye, and to make sure that I can count on you."

"Peter, I think Rebecca is used to getting what she wants; in fact, I'm quite sure of it. I don't see how your leaving town today will in any way satisfy her."

God, the man has to get a clue, I thought. How could he call himself a psychiatrist and have so little insight? Well, Peter was always a little weird. They say all shrinks are. That's what draws them to the profession, I guess, a need to come up with answers, to fill in the missing pieces of their own jigsaw psyches.

I had to hold the coffeepot with both hands in order to keep the water from sloshing over the sides when I filled the coffeemaker. "Anyway. You can count on me, Peter."

"Why are you so shaky, Hildy?"

"I'm not." I turned on the coffee and then walked back to the table and sat opposite Peter. I looked at him and what I saw made me brace myself against the back of my chair. I know I've said it's all a gimmick, but the truth is, I can read intentions and certain types of thoughts people are having. Anyone can, if they're taught, the way my aunt taught me. I learned by watching her. I saw the way she was able to clear a path through the air with her gaze, and if the room were to have burst into flames around her, she wouldn't have noticed. That's how locked in she became with the subconscious of another. It was the submerged memories, urges, longings that she saw in the flicker of an eye in response to a question; secrets and fantasies that she saw in the fluttering of eyelids or the pulsing vein of a temple. Mild thoughts are like whispers, but intense feelings of love, hate, joy, fear—well, it's almost hard to hang on when you're trying to read them, they can be so fast and furious. When a person has evil on his mind, he shouts it with his thoughts, and they almost drown out his words.

"I just don't like the way you're looking, Hildy." I heard him, finally, over all the noise of his rage and despair. "You look like you might do something . . . well, something crazy, for lack of a better word."

But I read the following, loud and clear: *Hopelessness and something else. Hate? No. It's death. He has death on his mind.* I had to look away. He was a reader himself. I didn't want him to see my fear.

"Maybe you should take something, Hildy. I

have something. It's just Xanax. A mild sedative. Let me get you some water."

Peter walked over to the counter and started opening cabinet doors. "Where do you keep your drinking glasses?" he asked. "Oh, here they are."

I heard him fill the glass with water, then put it on the table in front of me. Next to it he placed a small pill bottle, filled with tiny white tablets.

"No thanks," I said. "I don't like to take pills. I feel fine."

"Please, Hildy, I can smell the booze on you. You must have had some time of it last night. Just take one. It'll help you take the edge off. I've already taken a couple myself."

Peter was gazing down at me, and I quickly looked away.

"I told you, I don't like taking stuff like that."

"Well, sometimes we need to. When the doctor tells us to. Hildy? Hildy, did you hear what I said?"

I reached for the pill bottle and held it against my chest so my shaking hand wouldn't rattle its contents.

"I had such an awful night last night, Hildy."

"Why?" I asked. "What did you do?"

"I thought Rebecca might come here after I got that crazy call from her. I wanted to talk to her. To both of you. When I stopped here, your car was gone. Where were you last night, Hildy?"

"I was out with some business associates. Why do you care?" I was weeping. My eyes were filled with tears, my nose dribbling everywhere, and my tissue was a sodden piece of pulp clutched in my tight fist. One of the dogs suddenly scampered across the floor in the living room.

"KNOCK IT OFF," I hollered. "Sorry," I said to Peter. There was no response.

"Peter?" I turned and looked around. Where had he gone?

I sat back at the table. I knew I had tissues in my purse, so I lifted it from where it hung on the back of my chair and started fishing around in it. That's when I felt Peter hovering over me.

"What are you doing?" I demanded, spinning around in my chair. He was staring down at me and again I saw death in his gaze.

Die. Die. Die. The thoughts pulsed in the air all around me, becoming louder and stronger, beating in time with my heart.

Now I recalled the way he had told me he had such confidence in me, just a few days before. The way he had told me that he knew I wouldn't drink. He knew how to plant a negative suggestion as well as I did. It was like telling a child that you know they won't touch the candy that you left out for them—tell a person *not* to think about something and you plant an obsession. Did he plant the suggestion that I get drunk?

He wanted to "make sure" I wouldn't tell anyone about him and Rebecca. How was he planning to make sure of that?

"Hildy. I think you should take the medication. I'm worried about you. You seem a little unstable. Please. Take the medication now."

That's when I felt the little hairs on the back of my neck—my "hackles," as my aunt used to say—rising, and I felt my fingers and toes grow numb. Sometimes my aunt would get a very angry person in her home for a psychic reading (sometimes a complete nut job), and she said she always knew they were unbalanced because her "hackles" would go up the minute they entered a room.

"Hildy, look at me," Peter said. I had been looking down at the glass of water. I knew he could read emotions, and fear is the easiest emotion to read—easier than anger, even. I sniffled and dabbed at my eyes with the sodden tissue, then I dug around in my purse some more, avoiding his gaze. Rebecca and I were the two people who stood in his way, who threatened his future. What had he been planning for us?

"Excuse me, Peter," I said. I tried to keep my voice steady. "I'm just going to get some tissues from the powder room."

Peter placed his large hand around my wrist. His hand was so cold. "No. Stay where you are," he said. Then, in a gentler tone: "Your pulse is racing. It's best to sit quietly. Have some water. I'm worried about you."

We stayed like that for a moment, his large

hand on my wrist, my eyes fixed on the table.

"You're in shock," said Peter. "You're withdrawing from alcohol—that's what a hangover is, just withdrawal—and you're in shock from the news about Jake. You need to rest now."

I really needed a drink. I wondered where Rebecca was. I wondered, again, why Peter had been out looking for us last night, two women with the knowledge and power to destroy his life. He'd been out hunting two witches last night; now he had his hand clenched around my wrist. My head was pounding. *Oh, God, for just one drink . . .*

"I know you're thinking about how much you'd like a drink now, Hildy, but it's not a good idea. Take the pill. It'll soothe your nerves."

Babs and Molly were suddenly skidding and barking across the floor in the other room again, which made Peter turn in his chair. That's when I managed to pull away from him and stagger to my feet.

"What was that?" asked Peter.

"It was just the dogs," I said. I was backing away from him now. "They bark like that all the time, Peter. They . . . they drive me insane."

"Where are you going?"

"The bathroom." I was afraid to turn my back on him, so of course he could really see my fear now.

"Hildy, you look like you're going to faint."

Peter took a step toward me.

I turned and ran.

I ran past the powder room, through the old pantry, and then I flew down the stairs into the cellar. I made sure to pull the door behind me first, though, and it slammed shut for an instant, just long enough for me to duck into the darkness at the bottom of the stairs. Then Peter opened the door, which cast a yellow shaft of dust-speckled light down the center of the old wooden steps. The bulb in the cellar's only light fixture, a dangling ceiling socket, had burned out weeks before. I'd never gotten around to replacing it. I could hear Peter trying to click the light switch at the top of the stairs on and off, to no avail. Now I was on my knees, crawling behind the hot-water heater. The heater isn't terribly far from the stairs, but it's in a dark corner and there's a little space between where it stands and the wall. I was trying to wedge myself into that space.

"Hildy"—now the tone was kind and gentle— "it's me, Peter."

My heart was racing.

"Hildy, it's just me, Peter."

I was quiet as a mouse.

"Hildy, I think you're being paranoid. This is how you get when you have a hangover, isn't it? You start imagining things. You think people are thinking unkind thoughts about you. I'm not, Hildy. I've always admired you. I remember you when you were just a teenager. Remember? You and Allie and Mamie and me? I remember once we stopped at your house to get something and your mother was sitting on the porch."

The tears had started again, but I had to be careful not to sob. He was walking tentatively down the stairs. The cellar door had partially closed behind him and he was feeling his way along each step with the toe of his shoe.

"She was so beautiful, your mother. I remember that she had a cat on her lap and she was smiling at all of us."

Oh, the tears. It was so hard to breathe.

He was at the bottom of the stairs now and had turned and was making his way slowly through the dark. I had a vivid recollection of playing hide-and-seek with him when he was a little child and Allie was baby-sitting him—when I was really still a child myself—and I recalled the way Peter had loved it when we would jump from our hiding places and scare him silly. The hunter turned into the hunted, that was his favorite part. Now I was the prey and I thought my heart would pound right out of my chest. I wondered how close he was, when I heard the crashing of bottles a few feet away from me. He had stumbled into my empties. They had been there all winter. I was keeping them there until the spring, when I planned to take them to the dump. In the early morning, when nobody would be there.

"Oh, Hildy, please let me help you. You can get better. Your denial, your delusional paranoia right now, it's all part of the disease. Why are you hiding? It's just me. It's me. Your friend Peter."

Then the strangest thing happened. I saw myself from a different perspective. I saw myself as Peter must have seen me. As, perhaps, everyone saw me. I saw myself as a drunk. A pathetic old alcoholic. Maybe I was not really the dynamic businesswoman, successful mother, and various other titles that I liked to attach to my name. Maybe I was like those people in those sad meetings. Maybe I was just Hildy. Nobody special—just an old alcoholic. Hildy Good, alcoholic. A regular old garden-variety alcoholic.

"Hildy, let people help you. You can get through this. You have so many people who love you. Your daughters, your grandson."

Why had I run into the cellar? What a crazy thing to do. Why was I trembling behind the hot-water heater? I really had a vision of myself, then, a frantic, strung-out old lady, hiding in the cellar from a doctor—a friend—who was trying to help. A man I had known since he was a toddler, whose father was so kind to us, *so kind,* after Mom's death. Not an unhinged murderer who was stalking me. What a delusional idea. It was Peter Newbold.

"It's just me, Hildy. It's just Peter."

"Peter," I whispered. Then I managed to stand up. "I'm over here."

I felt his arm around my shoulder.

"It's okay," he said. Then he led me back to the stairs. He had to help me walk up. I felt so weak. His arm was around my waist.

"Take some deep breaths, Hildy. We're almost there. Just a few more steps."

"Okay," I sobbed. "Okay."

When at last we arrived at the top of the steps, Peter reached over my shoulder to push the door open, but before he actually touched it, it had flung open wide, and there stood Frank.

I fell into Frankie's arms. "I'm sorry," I sobbed. "I'm so sorry. I did go out in my car last night."

Frankie held me for a moment and then he tilted up my chin and looked at my face.

"No, you're all confused, Hil."

"I was out driving last night, Frankie. I was drunk. I don't remember. I hit something. . . ."

"She doesn't know what she's sayin'," Frank said. He pulled me close. "Shhh," he said.

"I didn't see anything." I sobbed into his chest. "All I remember is a loud crack and then wondering how such a thick cobweb got on my windshield. It was so hard to see on my way home. I had to look out the passenger window."

"Shush now, Hildy, it was a dream. I was here with you all night. What're you doin' here, Newbold?" Frank asked.

"I had something I needed to talk to Hildy about," I heard Peter say. "I'm leaving town today, and I wanted to say good-bye."

"Hildy was with me all night," Frank said. "She's all confused."

"Yeah, I know. Hildy, I'm leaving that medication for you. It'll help. Bye, now. Good-bye, Frank," Peter said.

"See ya," Frank grunted.

When Peter was gone, Frank helped me to a chair and sat next to me. He put his hands on my wet cheeks and looked into my eyes. He brushed something, a cobweb or some cellar dust, from my hair and said, "They still haven't found Jake, Hil. But Skully just brought your car back from Lynn with a brand-new windshield. They touched up the scratches on the hood. The guys down at the shop said it looked like you hit a tree. It was probably a limb that hit the windshield, based on the scratches on the hood."

"I remember going out in the car last night, Frankie. I wanted to go to your house. I wanted to be with you. I felt so alone, and I missed you so much. I could have hit him. I could have hit anything. I just wanted to be with you."

"Shhhh," Frankie said. "Go wash your face, then I'll drive you into town. You can help search for Jake. Don't tell anyone you were out in your car last night. There's no point to it. It was a tree. It had to have been a tree."

"I can't go now, Frank," I said. "I need to rest. Maybe this afternoon."

Frankie nodded. "Okay, go to bed, though. Go get some rest. Don't talk to anyone, Hildy. Don't tell anyone about yer car."

"Okay," I said. "Okay. I'm sorry. . . ."

"Shush, Hildy. Stop with that, now."

I couldn't sleep. I tried. I curled up on my bed and tried to sleep, but I kept having those wakeful dreams I so often had. Semilucid dreams. I don't usually recall my dreams when I'm fully asleep, but when I'm trying to doze or relax, I will sometimes be carried off into a stream of dreamlike thoughts—daydreams, I guess you'd call them, not quite awake, not quite asleep. That afternoon, I dreamed that it was night and I was driving my car fast over some hardscrabble roads that caused my tires to skid. Something dark smashed against my windshield, sending tiny little faults, like the spreading fissures you see in cracked ice, all across my windshield, but I didn't stop. I was speeding along, trying to see through my cracked windshield, and I caught a glimpse of the road here and there. A turn came in the road, and my foot flailing for the brake awoke me with a start just as my car started to flip over the guardrail.

I watched the shadows crawl across my ceiling. There was a fly buzzing against one of the window screens. Maybe it was a wasp. Then I was on the floor of my cellar, looking up at the ceiling there, but the cellar was filled with water and I was holding my breath. I wanted to swim to the surface, to the cellar ceiling. I wanted to shoot to the surface, to breach triumphantly, to suck in the good air above the sea in great gasps, but I didn't because Jake was there, swimming above me, dog-paddling madly, his head just above the surface. I didn't want to frighten him, so I stayed there, flattened to the floor of my underwater cellar until he lowered his face into the water. His face was gone, ravaged by crabs and minnows, and I awoke myself with my own scream.

I got out of bed. The dim afternoon sky gave me some comfort. It was almost the golden hour. Almost time for a drink. I never drink before five—only alcoholics do that—but I realized I might have to nudge it a little closer to four that day. My nerves were shot, I was shaking, my head was pounding, and I was plagued by the image of the swimming child. I wondered if I should tell Cassie about my vision, but I just couldn't face her yet. And what comfort would it give her to know that I'd had an odd daydream about her son swimming in deep water? Like I said, I always have dreams of water. Still, I thought I should call Cassie. I couldn't face her in person, but I wanted to hear her voice.

The woman who answered introduced herself as a friend, Karen somebody. I asked to speak to

Cassie and was told that she was out in one of the patrol cars.

"Can I take a message?" Karen asked.

"Just tell her that Hildy Good called, please."

"Okay."

"Also, do you know if they've started any kind of water search? Are they searching in the ocean for Jake?"

"Um, yeah. I think I heard something about that. There are some patrol boats out searching along the coastline, and people on the beaches, of course."

"Okay, well, thank you," I said.

That was that. I couldn't offer anything else, I just had the dream of him swimming and I couldn't tell where he was or even see for sure that it was him. They were already searching the water. There was no need to mention the vision to Karen or Cassie or anybody else. There was nothing I could do to help the Dwights.

I washed my face, brushed my hair, and then went down to the kitchen, and on the counter, I saw Frank's Red Sox cap. He had left it there earlier, and now I snatched it up angrily. How many times had I told him how disgusting it was to leave his hat on the counter? I tossed the cap on the floor and was just about to remove a wineglass from my cabinet, when I heard the front door opening. It was Frank; I recognized his footsteps. I knew the heavy clunk of his boots.

Why did he have to come now, when every living fiber of my being was screaming for a drink?

"Hey, Hil," Frank said when he entered the kitchen, and I said, "Hey."

Frank gave me some updates on the search effort. Everybody else was out searching. There were dogs now, and helicopters.

"Are they searching the water, Frank?"

"Yeah, Manny, Robbie Brown, a few other lobstermen, and a bunch of fishermen are out with their boats. And the police boats are out. They can't start with dive teams at this point. . . . Well, let's hope they won't never have to. You should go to Cassie's, Hil. I know she'd like to see you."

"I'll go later," I said. The truth was that I couldn't look her in the eye. Not dead sober like this, not with my nerves completely shot. Frankie had planted the nightmarish thought about hitting the child with my car and now I needed a little wine to wash it away.

Go away now, Frank, I thought.

I needed that wine, just a little, to take the edge off.

Bye-bye now, Frank.

"The good news is that the dogs found his trail goin' down into the ravine behind the house, down into the woods. It looks like he was stayin' away from the road," he said, snatching his hat up from the floor. Then, after ramming the cap down over his balding pate, he poured the cold remains of that morning's coffee into a cup.

Frank Getchell will always drink cold coffee, rather than "waste" it by pouring it out and brewing a fresh pot. I'm sorry, but there's something diseased in that kind of mentality. It's one thing to be thrifty, but Frank goes too far. I had deluded myself that he was just a little eccentric, just an old-fashioned New England Yankee with his whole "Waste not, want not" ethos, but now I had to face facts: There was something very seriously the matter with Frank Getchell.

"He would have been found by now if he was injured, Hil," Frank was saying, leaning against the counter and swilling the cold coffee.

I suppose he meant the words to be comforting, but they just reminded me of his crazy suspicion and his ugly words about my drinking that morning. How are you supposed to forgive a person for that kind of betrayal?

"I spoke to Cassie's friend. She sounded so . . . overwrought," I said calmly. I didn't want him to know that he had hurt me. I didn't want to give him the satisfaction.

"Everybody is. I'm pretty wiped myself. I thought I might crash here for a while," Frankie said. "I would've gone home, but I didn't want you to be alone."

He tried to pull me into an embrace, but I wriggled free.

"Why don't you want me to be alone?"

"What do you mean, *why?* I just was worried about you."

"Worried that I might get drunk? That I might drive around killing people again?"

"Hildy . . ."

"That was wine on my blouse last night, Frank, not blood . . . wine."

"Yup, fine. I didn't sleep last night. Let's talk about this later."

"Yes, I know you didn't get any sleep last night. *Thank you.* Satisfied? Thank you for staying up all night driving my car. Thanks for fixing everything, Mr. Fix-it. That must have been expensive, getting those guys to work on a car at night. How much do I owe you?"

"Don't worry about it now, Hil."

"Be sure to bill me for what I owe you for your time."

"For what?"

"For your *time.* For the time on the job last night, Frank, driving the car there and everything."

I meant to hurt him, and when he hesitated, closing his eyes for a moment, I took some comfort in the idea that he was reeling from my well-placed and much-deserved blow. That's what any normal person would have been doing; any normal person would have been insulted that I had so coldly turned a kind favor into a business transaction, but in fact, Frank had closed his eyes because he was *calculating the number of hours he had spent dealing with my car.* He managed to mentally tabulate the figures faster than any calculator and then he calmly produced a sum that sent *me* reeling.

"Are you out of your goddamned mind?" I said, laughing bitterly. "I wouldn't pay you that much if you spent all week working on my car."

"I haven't sent you a bill in a few years, but my hourly rate is a little higher now. Plus . . . holiday weekend, so double time, and I gotta pay Skully, too. He followed me down there and drove me back."

I had fucked this man. I had nestled in his arms, whispered tender words into his ear, and covered his body with kisses.

The garbageman.

"Well, I hope you don't mind if I send the check in the mail. Feel free to tally up all the other charges, too. I need you, Frank, I know garbage can't get to the dump on its own."

He nodded at me when I said this. I was searching for some pain in his eyes, but I couldn't read any there, so I added, "Isn't it garbage day today? Isn't it Friday? Shouldn't you be out collecting garbage?"

Frank turned to go, but on his way out the door,

he called back, "It's Saturday. Take it easy, now, Hil."

Take it easy. That was a parting shot, if ever I had heard one. Of course he would know that "Take it easy" was an AA slogan. Everybody has seen those lame-ass bumper stickers. I was shaking with rage. I needed my wine, but I wasn't going to take any risks. What if I decided to drive over to Cassie's after I'd had too much?

As soon as I heard Frank's truck roar off, I grabbed my car keys from where Frankie had left them on the table. I needed a drink, but Frankie had made me so crazy with his ideas about my driving drunk that I actually thought I should flush the keys down the toilet before I opened my wine. I couldn't see any other way. How else are you supposed to hide something like a set of keys from yourself? But I had the keys to a few of my listings on my key chain. I really needed those. That's when I had the idea of tossing them up on the roof. I would never climb up on the roof drunk. I wasn't even sure where my ladder was. I walked out the door and flung the set of keys onto the roof before I had a chance to think about it twice. I watched them roll back toward me, and I jumped sideways, so they wouldn't land on my head, but they had settled into the gutter. I was careful to note the spot where they had fallen— just to the left of the front door. I would find them tomorrow. Now I needed to stop my heart from racing and my hands from shaking. I needed to go down to the cellar; back down in my cellar, down below the ground, where it was always so warm.

Nineteen

I prefer that the girls call before they drop in at my house. It's the considerate thing to do. I'd never just show up at one of their homes—I respect *their* privacy—but my adult children have never lost their sense of entitlement when it comes to me. I heard that childish entitlement, plus a hefty dose of suspicion and blame, when Tess demanded that I tell her what I was doing up on my roof the following morning. She actually sounded slightly hysterical.

"I'm not *on* the roof, dear. I'm on a ladder," I said evenly, smiling down at her. I wouldn't let her know that her childish prying had annoyed me. She had Grady in her arms and he was waving up at me. "HI, GRADY," I called down, waving back.

I had taken one of Peter's pills an hour before. Then I had taken another. I had awakened with a doozy of a hangover, but the pills had worked great magic upon my nerves. God bless dear Dr. Newbold. I waved to Grady again and the ladder tipped slightly away from the edge of the roof.

"Hold ON," Tess said, rushing over to hold the base of the ladder. Then she cried out, "MOM. You don't have anything on under your night-gown. What if somebody was walking by?"

"Who would come walking by?" I laughed, steadying myself by clutching the gutter. "Nobody just stops in unannounced. That's considered rude."

Then I saw what I had been looking for. My car keys were resting in the gutter, just inches away from my hand. I scooped them up while casually surveying the rooftop.

"What are you doing?" Tess demanded.

"I've been having problems with a leak. In the attic. I wanted to see if the gutters were clogged. Now move away from the ladder, dear. I don't want to slip and land on you and Grady."

It was hard to climb down with my cluster of keys in my fist, but I managed it. Dr. Newbold's magic pills. There was nothing I couldn't do that morning. And I had a bottleful of the pills in the kitchen. There would be enough for days, Peter had assured me during his visit the previous night. He would give me more. There would be enough.

"Come inside," I said, smiling with this thought. I kissed Grady, he said, "Hi, Gammy," and Tess burst into tears. "I heard about Jake Dwight on the news this morning. Why didn't you call me yesterday, Mom? He's been missing for more than twenty-four hours and nobody called me. I stopped at Cassie's and there were so many cars there, but Cassie and Dwight are out searching with everybody else. . . ."

"He's been found," I said joyfully.

"HE HAS? When?" said Tess.

"Peter Newbold stopped by last night and told me the great news."

I had been half in the bag when he told me, but I was pretty sure that was what he had said.

"No, Mom, it's all over the radio. I passed all these groups of searchers this morning. He's still missing."

I braced for the wave of anxiety to hit me, but . . . nothing.

"Peter wouldn't just make something like that up," I said. *Had I just dreamed that he had come by?*

"Well, come inside now," I said. "I'll make some coffee."

Tess followed me into the kitchen, and as I started to fill the coffeemaker, she said, "What happened to your other chairs?"

I turned and was surprised to see that there were only two chairs at the kitchen table. There are usually four. Four charming little antique chairs with hand-spooled legs and wicker seats that Scott had picked up at some estate sale or other. Now there were only two. This was perplexing.

Then I had a foggy memory.

I had carried a chair down to the cellar last night—those little kitchen chairs are so light, it was easy to carry by myself. I needed a place to sit. I figured I wouldn't fall asleep on the floor if I was sitting upright on one of those stiff chairs. I placed the chair in my favorite corner down there and had just returned to the kitchen for a corkscrew when Peter arrived. The man was absolutely loaded. I don't know where he had been, but it was obvious that he had been drinking before he arrived here, and he was quite amused when I invited him to join me in the cellar for a little wine. He carried another chair down for himself.

"I needed to have the seats refinished. The wicker was getting worn, it all needed to be replaced," I explained to Tess as I measured the grinds into the coffeemaker. I was so relaxed. This was usually the time in the morning when the alcohol started to burn out of my system, when I felt those glass shards in my gut and a hammering in my forehead. But thanks to whatever Peter had given me, Zantax or Zanaz— whatever he'd called it—I was calm and felt no pain. And even the confusing news about Jake didn't affect me the way it should have. I knew that Jake was safe. I knew it. Peter had told me so.

Tess placed Grady on the floor and then followed him as he toddled from my kitchen into the dining room and then on into the living room.

I had told Peter, the night before, about the time I woke up on the floor down in the cellar and he agreed with me that this was a clever solution.

He sat on one chair and I sat on the one opposite, smiling at Peter. Dear Peter Newbold. We were so close that our feet almost touched.

Peter understood why we needed to stay in the cellar. He knew I didn't want Frank to come back and see me drinking. I didn't want anybody nosing around—the whole town was in snoop mode, unfortunately, with Jake Dwight missing. I just needed to drink off the night before. Peter understood this. I would stop drinking again, Peter assured me, taking a hefty swig from the wine bottle I passed him. We didn't bother with glasses.

"I'm so glad you came back, Peter," I had said when I was uncorking another bottle of wine. "Do you know, you're the only person who's ever come down here with me? I don't like to drink alone. That's why I liked drinking with Rebecca so much. OOOPS, maybe I shouldn'ta mentioned Rebecca to you, Peter. I'm . . . I'm so sorry."

"No, don't be, Hildy," Peter said as I passed him the bottle. "Everything's fine now."

"It is? Oh, I'm so glad, Peter," I gushed. "I can't stand the idea of you two hating each other."

"No, I never hated her," he had said, smiling at the thought and taking a healthy sip of the wine. "I love her still." What a difference in his demeanor since the day before. He looked so happy now.

"You know, I rather love her, too," I admitted, giggling shyly into my hand.

"I know," Peter said, winking at me.

"Do you think she has a lot of . . . inherited wealth? You think old J. P. Morgan had enough cabbage that it still supports the progen . . . the pro-genie . . . Wait, what's the damn word . . . the . . . her generation?"

"I would think so, but you know, she would never talk about money."

"No, people from her kind of money—old money—they never like to talk about it. They're *soooo* refined. *Sooooo* above it all. You know, it always bothered me that Rebecca married a billionaire. Why not leave the billionaires for a poor girl like me?"

"You're not poor, Hildy Good. You're worth quite a lot, but you just keep losing sight of that. You're not poor at all." He handed the bottle back to me.

"Nor will you be, Petey, once I sell your house. You're gonna be rich, rich, RICH."

Peter shrugged and smiled. "Sam and Elise will be, I suppose."

"What are you talking about?" I said. I took a swig from the bottle. "Sam and Elise won't leave you. Don't worry, I'll make sure they never find out. And I'll keep an eye on Rebecca. But why are we carrying on about this? POOR JAKE. Poor Jake Dwight. What has happened to Jake, Peter? What'll Cassie and Patch do?"

"Jake's fine," Peter had said. He seemed

surprised that I hadn't heard the news already.

"What?" I cried out. "Has he been found? Where is he? Is he home?"

"He will be soon," Peter said, smiling.

I cried tears of joy at the news. "Peter, I thought . . . I had a little accident last night and I thought maybe I accidentally bumped into him with my car. . . ."

I remembered having looked at his chair, but it was empty. He must have left, but I didn't recall him saying good-bye. I was drunk; time does strange things when I've been drinking. I forget little bits of time. I lifted the bottle to my lips, then leaned over and patted the girls, who lay at my feet. My sweet girls. My sweet familiars. And Jake was safe.

Jake was safe.

When Tess returned to the kitchen, I told her again about Dr. Newbold's news.

"When did you see him?" she asked.

"Last night. He stopped by for a little while. Maybe the people you saw hadn't heard that Jake was found," I said.

"No, Mom, I told you, it was on the news this morning. Let's go see what's going on. The search parties . . . all the organizers are on the green. Let's take the coffee with us. I want to go help."

"Okay," I said, but when she was filling her coffee cup, I hurried downstairs to the cellar. Perhaps it had all been a dream. But there were my two kitchen chairs. There were three empty wine bottles lying next to them. I tiptoed back up the stairs and closed the cellar door carefully behind me.

Twenty

If you just happened to be driving by Wendover Green that hot spring morning, you might have thought you were passing a festive country fair. People were milling about everywhere. Old people, young people, small children. And there were balloons. Everybody was carrying brightly colored balloons. The Congregational church had become the official headquarters for the Jake Dwight search effort and Trooper Sprenger was there, standing on the top of the steps to the church, hollering out instructions through a loudspeaker. He was thanking everybody for coming and asking that people enter his cell phone number into their phones so that they could contact him immediately if they found any signs of Jake. People were handing out flyers with a photo of Jake on the front. Sharon Rice handed one to me and I looked down at it in dismay. There was young Jake, gazing into the camera. In large bold type were these instructions:

IF YOU FIND JAKE, DO NOT ATTEMPT TO TOUCH HIM. JAKE IS VERY

FRIGHTENED OF BEING TOUCHED BY PEOPLE HE DOESN'T KNOW. PLEASE SPEAK HIS NAME QUIETLY AND DIAL 911 IMMEDIATELY.

It was all so confusing. I knew that it was possible that Peter had just had his information wrong, or that he was confused due to his drunken state, but he had filled me with this idea—no, *more* than that—an absolute conviction that Jake was safe.

Sharon Rice's husband, Lou, had set up a table on the lawn next to the church and was handing out water to the volunteers. John Althorp, the manager of the Hickory Stick Toy Shop, was using a helium tank to blow up dozens of colorful balloons. He was handing them out to all the volunteers with a great flourish and a smile, adding to the bizarrely festive atmosphere, which was spoiled only by the presence of Trooper Sprenger, the flyers, and the search-and-rescue dogs. Tess and I walked through this strangely merry and mournful scene in a sort of daze, when, suddenly, I felt someone grab my arm. I almost leapt out of my skin.

"Hildy?"

It was Mamie Lang. She had dozens of balloons clustered above her head and was trying to untangle some of the strings that were wrapped around her hand.

"What's with all the balloons?" Tess asked.

"Jake loves them," Mamie said, and she handed one to each of us. Grady began giggling and batting at the balloon. "If you find Jake, you're supposed to just show him the balloon and hope he approaches you."

Tess was tearing up.

"Aw, honey, do you want to leave Grady here with me and Mamie so you can go search with the others?" I asked, touching her arm tenderly.

"No," she said. "I want to keep him close. But, Mom, come with me. Let's go together. You look a little stressed. The walk will be good for you."

I hesitated. My anxiety was starting up again. My convictions about Jake's well-being were starting to fade. I needed another pill. Maybe I could sneak one from my purse while we walked.

"Okay," I said finally.

It was Tess's idea to search the bird sanctuary behind Old Burial Hill. The sanctuary was only a short walk from the Dwights', and though there wasn't a trail leading there from the woods behind the Dwight house, Tess reasoned that Jake might not be one to look for trails. He was likely to just blaze his own. I looked at the roadside as we drove to the sanctuary, staring at the gullies and weeds with dread.

We parked the car on the side of the road and I helped Tess put Grady in his backpack. Grady protested at first. He wanted to walk, but we distracted him with the balloon, and once we began walking, he enjoyed his vantage point from above Tess's shoulders and he batted her head with excitement.

"What a great idea, those backpacks for kids," I said as we headed into the cool shade of the wooded trail. "I wish we'd had those when you girls were babies."

"I think they had them," Tess said. She was leading the way, taking great strides but being careful to duck around branches so that Grady wouldn't get scratched.

"Really? I don't remember them."

Tess let out a little laugh. "I doubt you were out looking for one," she said.

This was Tess's old gripe. I didn't spend enough time with them when they were little. I was working. Somebody had to pay the bills. This fact of life never seemed to penetrate the girls' bitter reminiscences of their childhoods.

"I would have liked to have one. To take you on hikes like this when you were a baby. . . ."

"Really?" Tess replied. "Watch your step here, Mom, it's rocky and a little slippery."

We were starting down a slope toward Hodge's Pond, which was at the center of the preserved sanctuary land.

"Tess," I said, "I would have liked to have spent more time at home with you girls. I had to work. Your father never made any money in antiques.

He actually operated at a loss most years."

"Mom. I know. Why are you bringing this up?"

"You brought it up. By making the remark about the backpack."

We were being careful now. We were at the steepest part of the trail. Tess was making her way down sideways and I supported Grady's backpack from behind, in case she slipped.

After a few minutes, Tess said, "It wasn't just that you worked all day. It was at night, too. You went out so much. . . ."

"In those days, you really had to entertain clients more, Tess."

"I know, but even on nights when you were home. You would be pretty sauced. Before dinner even."

"What?" I said. "I didn't start drinking that much until after Daddy left."

"Oh, okay, think what you want," Tess said bitterly, and then she stumbled and grabbed a tree trunk while I grabbed Grady's leg until she was steady. We were almost at the bottom of the hill, but we stopped to catch our breath. Grady batted at his mother's head. "Go, Mommy, go," he cried out.

We both laughed then, Tess and I. Tess turned to face me. "I'm sorry, Mom. I can't believe I'm still holding on to those old resentments, even now, when you've given up drinking and everything. I should go to Al-Anon or something. I'm sorry."

Tess hugged me then, and I hugged her back. "I'm proud of you, Mom," she said.

We made our way through the quiet woods. The path was heavily shaded here. Blissfully dark. I knew that in a short while the trail would open onto the meadow that surrounds the pond and that the sun's bright rays would be upon us again. It would have been nice to have remained in the protective shadows of the great old oaks and hemlocks just a little longer. Just to clear my head a little. Just to give me a few minutes to stop my hands from shaking so.

Twenty-one

In the sixty years I've lived in Wendover, people have drowned. There's a fierce riptide—a strong seaward current—just above North Beach and sometimes people get caught in it. Somebody from Boston drowned at North Beach a few years ago and now there's a Coast Guard sign down there on the beach with diagrams about what to do and what not to do if you're caught in a riptide. The last thing you should do in that situation is start swimming for shore, but that's the first and only thing you want to do. There's the beach, just yards away, but the more you try to swim toward it, the harder that greedy current sucks you back out to sea.

The thing to do, if you're caught in a riptide, is to swim parallel to the shore. The thing to do is to relax and swim parallel to the coast and not panic. You can swim out of the current that way. But most people—kids especially—the minute they feel the loss of control, the fierce grip of the sea, they'll panic and paddle and kick like crazy, and it won't be long before they're gulping water, before the seawater enters their stomach and lungs, and then it's all over.

I've heard that drowning is painless, that when the lungs start to absorb more water than air, a sort of euphoria sets in, and the panic dissipates and soon the body becomes aquatic.

One day, not long ago, Tess made me watch a YouTube video of a woman who had had a near-death drowning experience. Tess's intention was to soothe me, I know, to make me feel better about what had happened. The woman on YouTube said that she was swept from a rock by a rogue wave and was unable to make it to shore in the rough water. She eventually sank, holding her breath for as long as she could. Then she had to inhale.

She described the feeling she experienced when inhaling the sea as "exquisite." There had been a beautiful blue light. A symphony. A timelessness.

Then she was rescued.

A drowned body will initially sink, but then it will rise to the surface again, once decomposition begins. It has something to do with gases formed by bacteria. And I've heard that the body will sink again, and then rise again, and it's only after the body has risen to the surface the third time that it will settle, finally, to the ocean floor. But I think that may be an old wives' tale. I think it was my cousin Eddie who told me that when I was a kid, but he may have had the story mixed up with the story of the Resurrection of Christ.

Who knows.

The body found floating outside Wendover Harbor that Sunday morning was discovered, unfortunately, by two Wendover boys—the Hastings brothers: Connor and Luke, ages thirteen and fourteen. The Hastings have always been a big sailing family. The boys' dad ran Wendover's race week every year and all four kids sailed. That morning, the boys were planning to sail out past Peg's Rock, even though their father had told them not to leave the harbor.

Peg's Rock was not completely out of the harbor, the boys reasoned, and you could always catch a strong wind there. So they rigged up their 420 racing boat and set off. They chatted above the flapping of the sails and the rising wind. It would be a good sail. They approached Peg Sweeney's Rock and listened, as all kids do, for the cry of the ghost of poor Peg. Then they sailed on a little farther, toward the mouth of the harbor. They had a strong headwind and wanted to ride it just a little longer. They leaned back mightily as the boat heeled over and they shouted to each other with bravado. They were flying. They steered around colorful buoys marking lobster traps and aimed their bow for Singer's Island. They would only sail on a little bit farther, just a little bit farther, and then they would turn back.

Suddenly, just ahead and right on their course, they saw what looked like an inflated white plastic bag floating in the water. When they sailed closer, they realized what they were seeing were the white shoulders and partially submerged torso of a human body floating facedown. They glided past, gasping and cursing, forgetting for a moment to watch the wind, and for a brief instant, the current actually pushed the body against the boat's stern, causing the boys to scream and almost capsize the boat in their frantic efforts to come about and head back for the harbor.

Luke, the younger brother, burst into tears, though later, when his older brother Connor reported this, repeatedly, he denied it. The kids didn't mention Jake Dwight to each other at the time, but they both had the boy on their minds. They sailed for the harbor, Connor manning the tiller with shaking hands. Ahead of them, a lobster boat was leaving the harbor. It was Manny Briggs's boat. The boys waved their oars frantically at Manny and he turned his boat toward them, and when he was alongside, he reached out with a gaffer's hook and pulled the boys' sailboat along-side the chugging *Mercy.*

The boys told him what they had seen. Manny had old Joe Sullivan with him, and the two men tried not to think the worst. "Lower yer sails quick and climb aboard."

"I bet it was a dead seal. People always think dead seals are bodies," Manny grumbled after fashioning a towline from *Mercy*'s stern to the bow of the little sailboat, but he was so anxious that his back seized up on him when he reached out to help the younger boy onto his boat, and he cursed and shouted at the older boy to hurry and jump on board.

"It was a body. It was a dead person," Luke cried, running to the bow and pointing.

They were at least fifty feet away, and Manny was scolding the boys for sailing out of the harbor on such a windy day, when the boys cried out, "There it is," pointing to something floating in the water ahead. Manny had a very sick feeling about what he saw drifting in the current. A fishing boat had sunk off Gloucester when Manny was a kid, and Manny was out on his dad's boat when one of the bodies rose from the bottom of the sea. He never forgot the man's face. He still had dreams about it. When they got closer to what was clearly, now, a floating body, the boys cried out, suddenly strident and confident in the company of the men.

"That's it. AWWWW, SICK," Luke cried.

Manny turned and barked at the boys. "Shut the fuck up and get astern. Don't look at it. I mean it. I don't want you kids seeing this shit, ya hear?"

"Yes, sir. Okay," the boys said, and they scurried to the back of the boat.

It was a body. Facedown, drifting toward shore. Manny grabbed an arm. The skin was spongy with bloat, yet the limb itself was stiff and ice-cold to the touch. It was clear that the body had been floating for quite some time. Manny noticed the way the legs and arms dangled like limp sausages below the body, acting like draglines or ballasts —keeping the body from turning over.

Joe wordlessly tossed Manny a coil of rope and then grabbed the ship-to-shore radio to call the Harbor Patrol. Manny used a long pole to keep the body alongside the boat. He used the rope to fashion a harness around the chest of the body, then across the shoulders. He did all this without turning the body over. "So the kids couldn't see," he'd explain later. In truth, he would eventually confide in Frank, he couldn't bring himself to turn it over and look at the dead person's face. He knew what the teeth and pinchers of the under-water scavengers did to a codfish, and he could see that already some toes and fingers were missing. So Manny leaned over, his back wrenched in agony, and he held the body by the rope harness, his hands moving back and forth like a puppeteer working a life-size marionette for an audience many fathoms below.

Rebecca McAllister wasn't involved with the search for Jake Dwight that Memorial Day weekend. It wasn't that she didn't want to help; she just had no idea that he was missing. Rebecca wasn't as anchored to the town and its citizens as some of us locals. She wasn't in regular contact with the other moms and she never watched the morning news. She had returned very early Sunday morning from Nantucket. The boys were staying with Brian, but Rebecca made an excuse to return to Wendover and drove back alone. She needed to speak to Peter.

She left the Cape before dawn and was back in Wendover by nine. She had driven up to her house on the rise on the back roads and had thought the groups of people walking along the roadside as she passed were doing some kind of annual spring cleanup—the town did organize that kind of thing every year. Rebecca had been up all night and now that she was home, she wanted to be with Betty.

When she arrived in the barn, the mare lifted her gray head from her hay and nudged Rebecca when she entered her stall; then she returned to her breakfast, munching peacefully. Rebecca leaned against the mare, one arm over her withers, the other looped under her thick neck, and she pressed her wet cheek into her mane. The wonderful musky odor of horse filled her, she told me later, not with the usual joy but, instead, with sadness and longing. Peter was planning to take away all her joy. He already had. She couldn't even find happiness in her beloved Betty.

When Betty finished the last of her hay, Rebecca quickly brushed her, bridled her, and led her out of the paddock and onto the driveway. She moved the mare over to the fence and stepped up onto it so that she could swing her leg over the mare's broad back, and then they started off down the drive.

They made their way down Wendover Rise. The road is quite steep near the top, and Rebecca leaned back to help Betty balance her weight over her hind end. The sure-footed mare plodded along happily. They were headed for the beach. The pony knew that soon she would be able to splash about in the cool water.

There's a small wooded area of marshland called Steer Swamp near the bottom of the rise, with a path that leads to Hart's Beach. Rebecca always cut through the trail surrounding the swamp to avoid the busy beach road, and that morning Betty turned onto the path on her own. She knew the way. Rebecca was thinking about Peter. She was thinking about how she wouldn't let him leave her. It wasn't the right thing—for him, or for her. For anybody. She had spoken to him briefly, several days before, and now he wasn't answering his cell phone. He had taken a rather threatening tone, now that she thought of it, which was uncharacteristic of him. He kept warning her to think about what she was doing and telling her how desperate he was.

She had yelled at him. "YOU'RE desperate? What about me? You can't just abandon me. I won't let you go, Peter. If you do, I'm going to report you to the administrators of that new hospital. I know you don't believe I'd do it, but I will."

"Rebecca, think carefully, now," he had warned her again. "Just watch your step."

"What are you going to do?" she had scoffed. "Kill me?"

Now she regretted mocking him. This wasn't the way to make him come around. She would call him when she returned. She would be more reasonable and she knew that she could convince him to be more reasonable, too. San Francisco was a terrible place to live. Did he have any idea how much it rained there?

Suddenly, the mare spooked and spun. Rebecca almost fell to the ground.

"Whoa, Betty, shit . . . whooaaaa."

Betty was snorting and spinning. Rebecca, who was riding bareback in shorts and sneakers, was only able to stay on Betty by wrapping her long legs around her sides and clutching a handful of mane.

"Whoa. Hooooa."

The mare stood then, frozen. She held her breath like a deer who has just spotted the hunter, thinking, perhaps, that if she stood perfectly still, the predator wouldn't see her. Rebecca held her breath, too. Then she heard a rustling in the bushes, which caused the mare to spin again and rear. Rebecca couldn't hold on. She slid off, managing to land on her feet, and she held the reins in her hand as the mare reared again, trying to pull herself away.

"Betty. WHO'S THERE? Betty," Rebecca cried out. Then she saw it—a dark figure moving through the thick marsh grass toward her. She called out again.

"Who's there? Who is it?" called Rebecca, terrified.

She heard a splash, followed by a strange wailing.

Rebecca stepped toward the sound, Betty stomping after her, snorting with fright, the mud making great sucking sounds with each step of her hooves.

Rebecca pushed her way through the swamp grass, and then she saw him. It was a boy. It was Cassie Dwight's son, Jake. He was filthy and staggering away from her through the boggy wetland, looking over his shoulder at her fearfully, tripping, rising, tripping again.

The child was soaked and shivering. Bloody scratches marked his face.

"Jake," Rebecca cried. The child kept moving away. "No. Jake, come back." The panic in Rebecca's voice further unnerved the pony and she snorted in fright, then whinnied loudly. Jake stopped, frozen, facing away from them.

Rebecca stood still. It was so quiet there in the marsh. Rebecca told me later that she wondered why it was so silent. You couldn't even hear birds or peepers. There was not a sound, not the slightest breeze.

Betty sniffed the air and upon sensing that Jake was a human, not a bear, but a human child, she let out a long sigh and then lowered her head and grazed on the marsh grass.

Jake turned and watched the mare. The grass was long and had wispy tufts that tickled the mare's muzzle, so she blew loud *ppppppbbbbbbb* noises through her lips as she grazed. Rebecca was tempted to call the boy's name again—he was shivering so hard, and now she saw that his lips were chapped and flaked. He looked so ravaged that she started to cry in desperation for him, but now that he was facing them, she feared frightening him, so she just stood quietly next to Betty, tears streaming.

No, Jake, no. Don't run away. Come to me, she thought, but she remained silent, and after a few long minutes, the boy started moving toward them, his head cocked slightly to the side, his gaze on the mare's face.

"Sneakahs. I want Sneakahs," he said. "Sneakahs, please."

Rebecca looked at the child's bare feet and thought that he wanted shoes, not knowing that he was calling out the name of his beloved cat. Betty lifted her head, her ears pricked toward the boy, munching away thoughtfully at a mouthful of grass; then she lowered her head again. Jake splashed through the small boggy area until he was quite close to them, his feet sinking into the cold mud. "Sneakahs," he moaned. Betty pushed her nose toward the boy to sniff him. Betty had always liked Rebecca's own boys—it was only men she hated—and Rebecca didn't worry that the mare would bite him. Betty just sniffed at the air around the boy, and then she was about to tear at another patch of grass when the boy made a loud purring sound. Betty swung her head toward Jake again, and this time she took a step toward him, very curious about the sound coming from his lips.

Jake raised his hand and touched the mare's muzzle. The purring vibrations moved through his body, and Betty must have found the sensation on the tender skin around her muzzle quite pleasing, because she just stood there, letting him rest his hand on her nose. Jake purred and smiled.

After a moment, Rebecca gently tugged on the mare's reins, pointing her head in the direction of the road. Then she turned her back to the boy and the mare and walked very slowly. Horses don't like to follow you when you're staring at them, and she reasoned that the boy might feel the same way, so she just stepped slowly back along the path and the pony followed her. When Rebecca glanced over her shoulder, she saw that the boy kept his hand on the mare's muzzle and walked at her side, making the loud purring sound. Rebecca worried that Betty might step on the child's bare feet with her iron-clad hooves, but Betty kept her head out to the side a little, toward the boy, pushing him away slightly to keep him just far enough away from her feet that she wouldn't step on his toes. She loved the vibration of his touch and the sense of a small living thing at her side, a small needy thing that followed her. And with that a vague memory of the smell of birth and milk and then joy rushed through her veins. I'm a mom; I know how she must have felt. I can imagine the tingling in her udder when she pushed her nose into the child's small hand.

The path was rough with stones and roots; they had to move slowly. Rebecca tried to guide them around the worst parts, mindful always of Jake's bruised and bloody bare feet. At last, they arrived at the road. Rebecca steered the mare and the boy to the roadside and was just trying to figure out how they would ever make it up the steep hill to her house when a pickup pulled up. It was Frank. The truck screeched to a halt and Jake immediately began flapping his hands and imitating the screeching sound, which made Betty startle and jump away from him.

"No . . . Betty," Rebecca said.

Frank jumped out of his car and started toward them, and Betty flattened her ears back against her head. She swung her haunches out toward Frank, lifting one of her hind legs menacingly.

"Frank, wait, stay back," Rebecca said.

Jake was walking back in the direction of the woods, flapping his hands and making little screeching sounds, like the truck's brakes.

Nobody moved for a moment; then Betty lowered her head and cropped away at the nice green roadside grass. Rebecca started to make the *pppppbbbbbb* sound with her lips—the mare's sound—and immediately Jake stopped and stared at the horse. Then he started with the loud purring again. He limped back to the mare's side, and Frankie called out to Rebecca, "Watch the mare." But she said, "Don't worry, she won't hurt him. Can you call his mom, Frank? Can you call Cassie and tell her we're here?" The tears were really flowing then. "He really needs his mom. Call her, Frank."

Frank doesn't carry a cell phone, but he had

his fire-dispatch radio and he radioed Sleepy Haskell, who was with the Dwights.

"We've got Jake. He's okay. We're down the bottom of the rise, just before the path to the swamp. No lights and sirens, Sleepy. And don't anybody else come down here. Just you and Cassie, Sleepy, keep it quiet," Frank said, knowing that all the first-responders in the county were listening in on their radios and scanners, and that this warning, coming from him, would be taken seriously.

When Sleepy arrived with Cassie and Patch, Jake ran into his mother's arms. Patch and Cassie showered Rebecca with tearful thanks after she gave them the quick details of how she and the mare had found him, and then they bundled the child into the squad car and sped off to have him examined by a doctor.

Frankie stayed there, alone with Rebecca. They didn't speak. He watched Rebecca try to pull herself up onto the mare's bare back. She was drenched in sweat and swatting away the pesky flies that now swarmed around her and the mare. She wept and swore, trying to lead the mare to a boulder, but the mare kept stepping away before Rebecca could mount.

Frank walked over to help, and Rebecca said, "Watch out, Frank. You know she'll kick you."

But Frank grunted at the mare, "Watch yerself, Mama, watch it now, shhhh," and he ignored her flattened ears and angry foot stomping. He stepped to Rebecca's side and gave her a leg up with his linked hands, hoisting her up onto the mare's back. Then he watched Rebecca turn the mare and start up the road to their home—back up to the old Barlow place, up at the top of the rise.

Twenty-two

Tess and I realized, before we even parked my car back at my office, that Jake had been found. Wendover Green was still swarming with people, but now they were all hugging one another and wiping away tears and smiling. When we joined the group, we heard the news. The McAllister woman had found him, we were told. Already the crowd had managed to construct, collectively and unconsciously, a legend, as communities tend to do in this type of situation. Having been given only the bare skeleton of a story about the events surrounding the rescue of the child—something about Rebecca McAllister, her horse, the boy—they had filled in the gaps and added flesh to the thing in order to make it more real. Rebecca had taken it upon herself to search for the boy on horseback. She followed his tracks into Steer Swamp. He was asleep when she found him, but she woke him up and managed to get him onto the back of the horse. Then she climbed up behind him and rode out of the swamp, where Frank and Sleepy met them. It didn't add up to me, but what did it matter? Jake had been found. He was fine.

Tess seemed content to stay and chat with some of her old friends. She had let Grady out of his backpack and he was running around, chasing another small boy and giggling. I was exhausted and, well, Peter's pill was wearing off. I needed another, or, even better, a nice glass of wine. Just a glass. I told Tess that I had to get home to take care of some business. "Why don't you have one of your friends drop you off at my place later to get your car?" I said.

"No, I need to get home and make dinner," she replied, and after saying good-bye to our friends, we loaded little Grady back into the car.

Half an hour later, I was standing in my driveway, waving Tess and Grady off, and before they were out of sight, I had already popped one of Peter's pills. Why not a pill *and* a glass of wine? It was a night to celebrate. Why not feel really good?

It was fortunate that I had taken the pill, because within the hour, Frank arrived to tell me the news about Peter. When I heard the pickup in my driveway, I assumed he was there to apologize. Peter's pill and the little bit of wine had softened me and I smiled as he approached and even hugged him. "Thank God, Jake's safe," I said.

"Let's go inside, Hil," Frank replied.

Manny had called Frank as soon as he was onshore and told him how they had plucked Peter's body from the sea. Frank wanted to tell me before I heard it on the news.

"He must've gone out for a swim and got caught in the riptide there. That's a wicked ripper up on North Beach," Frank said, though we both knew that Peter, a Wendover native, would know how to escape the strongest current by going with the flow; by ignoring the urge to struggle and panic.

"Have they been able to revive him?" I cried. "Is he okay?"

"No, Hil, the medical examiner says he'd been dead for more than a day."

"Well, that medical examiner is wrong. Peter was here last night. With me."

"When?"

"He came by, I don't know, it must have been midnight. Maybe even later. He just wanted to see how I was doing." I left out the part about the basement and the drinking.

"No, Hildy, his car's been parked down at the parkin' lot at North Beach since yesterday mornin'. Sleepy told me he would've ticketed it, even though he knew it was Newbold's, but he was too busy searchin' for Jake. He couldn't figure out why Peter had decided to park it there. He must've driven past it half a dozen times yesterday. It was still there this mornin'. Still there, you know, after they found him."

"But that's impossible. Maybe he was driving somebody else's car last night. Or . . . something."

Frank was looking at me carefully then. Neither of us knew what to say.

"He was here," I said, crying softly.

Frank pulled me close and I wrapped my arms around him.

"His clothes were in his car, Hildy. They were the same clothes he had on when he left here yesterday mornin'. People noticed his car there startin' yesterday, just a little while after he left here. He must've gone straight to the beach. He went swimmin' in his boxers. He probably just didn't know the current there as well as he did on his own beach. There's already some rumors goin' around that it was a suicide, but I've been settin' people straight. That tide's wicked fierce down there at North Beach. You could be an Olympic swimmer and not be able to pull yourself out of that mess."

"He was here last night," I said.

"You're stressed out, Hildy. I think you might've dreamed you saw him."

There had been a Dr. Will at Hazelden when I was there. Yes, that's right, we called the doctors by their first names, but we had to put the title "Dr." in front of them, you know, because of their egos, and Dr. Will was in charge of "alcohol education." He told us that blackouts weren't normal, that craving alcohol at a specific time each day indicated a person was an alcoholic, and a number of other "facts" that I found quite irksome, as they were all things that I had experienced, though I was not an alcoholic. The brainwashing that goes on at those places. He had also talked about some kind of alcoholic psychosis. Apparently, some alcoholics start hallucinating in the later stages of the "disease," and I had been rather pleased to learn about this, as I'd never had any kind of thing like that. Now, standing there with Frankie, I couldn't help but recall the doctor's words. Had I imagined that Peter had been with me downstairs? It wasn't a dream—I had carried the chairs up from the cellar as soon as Tess drove off. But had Peter been there at all?

Frank stayed with me that night. I couldn't bear to be alone. We didn't really talk about it, we just sat and drank wine—not too much, but not too little, either—and we occasionally thought aloud about what we might have done differently had we known that Peter might have been planning something drastic.

"He didn't *plan* it," I kept telling Frank, and myself, whenever our musings veered in that direction. "It was an accident."

"Well, it was painless, that's for sure," Frank had reasoned, topping off his wine. "Water's still too cold for swimmin'. He would've gotten confused quick in the freezin' water. Your mind goes first; all the blood rushes to your core, to protect all the organs, you know. . . ."

"Yes," I said as he passed me the wine. "He just went swimming and the cold confused him." Then I said, "Do you think that was his . . . ghost I saw here. Last night?"

"Nah, Hildy, c'mon. A ghost? You had a dream."

"My aunt used to tell me she was visited by . . . you know . . . spirits. Of people who had just passed."

"Yer crazy aunt Peg?" Frank said. "C'mon, Hildy, stop thinkin' about it."

Frank stayed in Emily's room that night and then he stayed away for a while. I had just enough pills left to help me sober up over the next few days—to wean me back to my more moderate drinking levels, to the way I was before I had quit drinking. It was healthier, I realized, to drink moderately than to quit altogether and then end up going on a binge the way I had. The key was moderation.

But it was hard to look at Frank in the sober light of day, and I guess he found it hard to look at me, because, like I said, he stayed away for a while. I had thanked him for all he had done with my car, but he knew I was hurt. Hurt that he had thought I could have killed Jake. Hurt that he had called me a drunk and a lush. The things he had said to me. And he didn't apologize, which he really should have, now that it was obvious how off base his accusations had been.

But we're at an age now where we have to let things slide a little. We had grown used to each other's company over the past year. So, we kept our distance, then, one afternoon in late June, I ran into him in the Crossing and asked him what he had been up to.

Same old.

I told him he could come for supper if he wanted.

He did.

It was just supper, though. It was impossible for me to imagine, now, how I had ever been intimate with Frankie Getchell. I considered not having anything to drink that first night, but that would have felt like a concession. An admission that he was correct about my drinking. I could control how much I drank. Easily. And I was going to prove it to Frank. I would continue to enjoy my daily wine, but I was going to be more careful. Moderation. Moderation was the key. Frankie never said anything about my drinking again. Sometimes I sensed that he was watching how much I drank, but that was probably my imagination. Rehab ruins your drinking forever, I swear. Even if you're not an alcoholic, you'll question your drinking habits for the rest of your life.

Elise Newbold tried to pull the Wind Point

Road listing from me soon after Peter's burial—she had always wanted to list with Wendy, but we had a contract, so she really couldn't, and I did end up selling the house only a few weeks later.

I sold it to a couple from New York. They had been coming up on weekends to look at homes in the area. The husband was a film actor. They had three young children. When I drove them out to Wind Point Road, I asked them what had brought them to Wendover. The wife said she had always wanted to live in a small New England town. She had moved frequently as a child and wanted her kids to grow up in a regular town, rather than in New York or Hollywood.

"We want the kids to grow up in a real community where they can set down roots," she said, as if you can just set down roots anywhere. She asked how long I had lived in the area.

"All my life," I said. "My parents grew up in Wendover, too, and all my ancestors are from this area. My eighth-great-grandmother was Sarah Good—one of the witches tried in Salem."

"You're kidding. That's wild!" the actor exclaimed.

"So she must have been called Goody Good," said the wife, laughing. "The poor woman. No wonder she ended up being a witch."

"Yes." I laughed with her.

When we pulled up to the house, the husband and wife marveled at its beauty. "Right on the beach. Look, kids," the actor said, and we all climbed out of the car. The kids stayed on the beach while the parents followed me to the front door.

"I love old houses," the wife said when we walked inside. "You can just feel the history of this place."

"Yes, it's really quite charming," I agreed, trying to ignore the echoes of childrens' laughter that bounced off the bare walls, the games of hide-and-seek that gamboled all around us as we moved from one cold, empty room to the next. I had hosted a little party of one the night before, and well, sometimes, just a couple of times over the past couple of weeks, I imagined that I heard and saw things when I was hungover. Sometimes, things that weren't there. It was my nerves.

"Is the house . . . haunted?" the wife asked breathlessly.

They hadn't heard about Peter's suicide and I was under no obligation to tell them. This was just a question a lot of people ask about such an old house, this business about it being haunted, and sometimes it's hard to gauge how the buyer would like you to answer. Some people won't consider living in a house that's said to be haunted. Others really hope that there will be some wonderfully annoying ghost in the house that they can tell their dinner guests about. But I was startled by the wife's question because there was so much noise in that house, the joyous calling of Allie and Peter, and just a moment before, for a split second, as I glanced out a bedroom window, I had seen another sort of ghost. She was standing on the beach, looking out at the sea with a German shepherd at her side. My heart raced at the sight of her and I spun around to see if my clients could see her as well. The actor was checking the ceiling for signs of water damage; the wife was peering inside a closet. When I looked out the window again, I realized that what I had seen was a pile of driftwood.

I saw Rebecca only once after Peter died. She stopped in at my office one afternoon for a chat. She looked different. There was a calmness. There was no pacing about, no looking out to see if Peter was walking past, no glancing up at the ceiling to see if he was there. She was quite composed. She had found a new therapist by then, a woman this time, and she had been encouraged by this woman to tell Brian about her affair with Peter. It was to help her with her grief, Rebecca had told me. To help with her healing. I don't see how this helped Rebecca in the long run, because Brian served her with divorce papers the day after she told him, and the last I heard, Rebecca had moved to her mother's house in Virginia. But she and Brian were quiet, the scandal never broke about her affair with Peter Newbold, and, of course, I never talked about it with anybody but Frank. Peter's death was determined to be an accident by the medical examiner, and Sam and Elise were able to collect Peter's life insurance, which I have heard was quite substantial.

"I just want to make sure that Elise and Sam are going to be taken care of," he had said in my kitchen that morning, just before he walked off the edge of the town, *our* town, into the sea.

First, do no harm. Isn't that it? *First, do no harm to others.* Isn't that the doctor's oath?

I've never forgiven Rebecca, I doubt I ever will. I blame her for Peter's death. Peter, who had never hurt a soul in his life; who had spent his last hours making arrangements for his family, for Rebecca, even for me, with the sedatives, and the kind words that crazy morning. Like any good doctor, closing out his cases before retiring, Peter was making sure that everyone would be taken care of after he was gone.

No, I'll never forgive Rebecca, but Frank seems to bear her no grudge. When he talks about her, which is rarely, it's as if he's referring to a sort of natural and unavoidable disaster, like a destructive storm that blew through our town and left nothing but wreckage in its wake.

"That was the winter of Rebecca," he'll say, in reference to something that happened during that time. "That was during Rebecca."

Cassie Dwight has kept in touch with Rebecca.

She tells me that she writes to her on occasion and always includes photos of Jake—at his new house in Newton, at his new school. She sent me a picture, too, recently, in a lovely little mother-of-pearl frame. I keep it on my bedside table. In the photograph, Jake is cuddling his big orange cat and he's smiling.

The other day, a young woman named Elizabeth admired the photo of Jake and asked me if he was my son. I admit I was a little flattered that Elizabeth thought I might be young enough to have a ten-year-old, although, to be honest, Elizabeth is coming off crystal meth, has only a few teeth, and doesn't always have the most accurate perspective. Still, I felt good. I told her a little bit about Jake and about my own daughters and little Grady.

Elizabeth is in the room two doors down from mine. I'm back at Hazelden. I checked myself in at the end of August. Nothing happened, really. I didn't get caught driving drunk. I didn't drop Grady or embarrass my children or anything. I didn't come back because of the things Frankie had said to me about my drinking, or after Tess made me feel so awful during our search for Jake. My memories of these little deaths, these little crucifixions, along with so many others over the course of my drinking life, were so powerful and utterly fraught with shame and misery that they sent me down to my cellar more hastily each night after Frank left my house. Where else could I have gone, honestly? What else could I have done?

But I did end up coming back to Hazelden. I sold the Grey's Point property three months after Peter died and then I made the call. The counselor who answered the phone, a recovering drunk named Fran, remembered me.

"What happened, Hildy?" she asked.

"Nothing," I said. "I'm just ready to come back, that's all."

But something had happened. It was just a little thing; just the littlest thing really, when you look at my whole story.

It was the night before the Grey's Point closing. Frankie had shown up at my house unannounced. I was having a little wine on my patio and I made some kind of snide remark about his appearance. He often shows up at my house straight from a job, covered with dirt and paint, and it annoys me.

"You could make an effort," I had said. Frankie told me he wanted me to go somewhere with him in the truck. He wanted to show me something.

"Bring the wine," he said when he saw me hesitate.

"I don't *need* to bring the wine," I said. It bothered me that he seemed to think that I *needed* it.

I stepped into an old pair of sandals. It was another hot night and I was wearing shorts and a

T-shirt instead of my usual skirt and blouse. I thought Frankie was going to show me a house he wanted to buy.

That was Frankie's new thing—real estate. By the way, it was Frankie who had been the anonymous buyer of the Dwights' house, not the Clarksons. He bought it to fix it up and resell at a profit, he told me. I found out about it not long after the Dwights moved. Now he was letting Skully White stay there. Skully was too old to haul garbage and Frank was letting him stay in the house and do some work on it to pay his rent. I figured that Frank was finally seeing the wisdom of investing some of his earnings, rather than letting it all sit in some bank (or in some mattress—who knew what Frankie did with all his cash), so I was more than happy to go look at a property with him.

He drove me down to Getchell's Cove. It was that time in the evening, in the summer, when the water is as still as glass and the sun has begun to set below the horizon, leaving just an aura of pinks and pale blues to light the sky in a sort of splendid tribute to the dying day. Frankie parked the truck, and when we got out, I saw it. It was a Widgeon, just like *Sarah Good*, my old sailboat, with a freshly painted red hull resting on the sand. The sails, new and brilliantly white against the darkening sky, had been rigged, and now they flapped lazily in the warm breeze. I wandered

411

over and looked at the old worn wooden tiller and the sun-bleached wooden seats.

It was *Sarah Good*. You could still see the spot in the hull where Frankie had patched it all those years ago.

"Where did you find her?" I had asked finally. It was hard to get the words out. It was hard to take it all in.

"It's been in my shed for years. Your dad must have gotten sick of havin' it in his backyard and he hauled it off to the dump. I found it there, one day, years ago. Brought it home. Fixed it up, eventually."

"So you salvaged her because you knew I might want her back someday?" I asked. We were pushing her along the sand toward the water now.

"No, you know I hate seein' stuff get thrown away, Hil. I didn't have any plans for it. I just couldn't see leavin' it there, a perfectly good thing."

I'm not a nostalgic person. I don't like the kind of sentiment people attach to *things*. I really don't care about history and old things the way a lot of people do, so I don't know why my legs went all rubbery on me when we slid her into the surf. It was just an old boat, but when I climbed aboard, I had to face the bow so that Frankie wouldn't see my tears, and I barked something to him about hurrying up.

"We're gonna lose the light," I had grumbled at him.

"There's plenty of light," Frank laughed. "We've got time." He pushed us off with a few running strides, then he leapt aboard, too, and I leaned back against his thighs and we set sail.

Frankie had been right to salvage the old boat. He was right; she was perfectly good. Why did tears spring to my eyes when he said those words—*perfectly good?* I guess that's when I first had the idea to come back here. But I didn't say anything to Frank about it. I just pressed my wet cheek into his thigh for a moment, and when I felt his rough palm against my forehead, I tilted my head up so that I could press my lips into his, and then I turned my face back against his thigh, still embarrassed about the crazy tears, but I was smiling too.

Frank trimmed the sails until the little old boat leaned herself into a headwind and then she really took flight. It was the golden hour. We sailed straight ahead, out of the cove, out into the quiet waters beyond. We sailed until we could see the lights coming on in the houses of Wendover, all along the waterfront and up on the rise. When Frankie finally brought her about, we found ourselves in irons in the still water, our sails luffing, but we just waited. We knew it would come. A fresh westerly breeze was all we needed, and it did come, all at once, filling our sails with a sudden exhilarating gust and pushing us back over the shadowy currents, over the black kelpy shallows, over the rows of frothy white surf until we rested our bow, finally, on the rocky familiar shore of Getchell's Cove.

Acknowledgments

I wish to thank my agent and friend Maria Massie, who read this novel in various stages and offered encouragement as well as invaluable criticism along the way.

I am also deeply grateful to my editor, the lovely and brilliant Brenda Copeland, as well as the other great people at St. Martin's Press: Laura Chasen, Sally Richardson, George Witte, Meg Drislane, Carol Edwards, Steve Snider, Stephanie Hargadon, and Laura Clark.

Many thanks to the following friends and family members—they know why: David Albert, Candace Bushnell, Jen Carolan, Marcia DeSanctis, Alice Hoffman, Judy Howe, Heather King, Julie Klam, Meg Seminara, Jane Risley, Carla and Antonio Sersale, Sherrie Westin, and Laura Zigman.

And, of course, my everlasting love and gratitude to my dear, dear family: Devin, Jack, and Denis Leary.

Center Point Large Print
600 Brooks Road / PO Box 1
Thorndike ME 04986-0001 USA

(207) 568-3717

US & Canada:
1 800 929-9108
www.centerpointlargeprint.com